COYOTE
IN THE
CORNER

Ian Burdon

GOLDSPINK

ISBN 9798486136405

Cover design & typesetting by Raspberry Creative Type

Websites: https://www.ianburdonwriter.com
https://www.cosmicsurfer.co.uk

for Dad

CONTENTS

A KINDNESS

Eleanor murdered Uncle George on her twelfth birthday. Good old George with his presents and funny faces. Baby-sitting George who did dirty things, their special secret that Mummy and Daddy wouldn't understand. Everybody's best pal George, who said he loved her, and warned that if she ever told anyone she would be taken away from Mummy and Daddy who wouldn't want her any more. Wouldn't-hurt-a-fly George who asked for a special kiss at her birthday party, when she stabbed him twice in the leg with a kitchen knife, slicing his femoral artery clean through in two places, then buried the blade hilt-deep in his guts in front of her school friends and their parents.

Oh no, they all said, not George, *such* a lovely man. They called her a vicious, hateful little bitch, and said they wished she had never come into their lives and they could understand why her real mummy got rid of her. Then the police and social work Emergency Duty Team came and took her away, just like Uncle George said they would.

The school, her refuge, where she topped the class in every subject, erased her from class photographs, as though she'd never existed at all.

The consultant paediatrician diagnosed Eleanor's gonorrhoea and said she exhibited clear signs of chronic physical and psychological trauma. The media pilloried his over-zealous diagnostic regime and said he had an agenda and wasn't to be trusted.

The judge called her a walking embodiment of the very worst kind of evil and a clear and present danger to society. She was placed in secure accommodation a long way from her family and friends.

On her fourteenth birthday, dripping from the shower, wrapped in a towel, she was grabbed by Davy, the intern with a pass key to the rooms, a judge's son. He pushed her against the wall, ran his hand under the towel, over her appalled skin. She bit his face so hard he needed reconstructive surgery to his cheek, nose, lips and ear. She told her psychologist that Davy was lucky she didn't have a knife or he'd be just as dead as Uncle George. She didn't tell them about the distant, encouraging voice in her head when she'd killed George and disfigured Davy.

She was put into solitary confinement after that, though her case notes didn't mention it. The notes said she responded positively to targeted epiphenomenological intervention methodologies, and her key performance indicators, based on structured interactions with clinical staff, demonstrated good progress towards a long-term goal of rehabilitation and independent living. No one questioned the notes because no one knew what they meant, but they sounded positive and targets were met.

On her sixteenth birthday, she was tossed onto the streets to be cared for in the indifferent community.

Her parents moved house without telling her, and no one would say where they had gone. She'd only found out she was adopted when they rejected her and had no idea who her birth parents were. So she survived on the streets, crusted and infested, until she met Ryan, who said there was room in a squat in an abandoned Edwardian brewery in the Old Town. She wasn't interested in his stash of blow and jellies, but the place in the squat sounded just the thing.

The brewery was under permanent threat of demolition. A sign outside said the site was an exciting development opportunity for iconic signature-brand shops, offices and executive accommodation, outline permission already granted. But it was dry and warm, and she could wash and have privacy.

And she could read, her escape, an addiction fed by stealing paperbacks from charity shops. She read everything she could. No one prejudiced her against it so she discovered poetry: Norman MacCaig, Douglas Dunn, Sylvia Plath, Ted Hughes, Seamus Heaney, all brought her joy. She loved the classic novels too, especially Austen, Hardy, Dostoevsky and Heller, but she also gorged on popular fiction: warrior princesses wielding flashing blades in the cause of arbitrary justice, or epic space operas set on bright new worlds beyond the grime of the streets.

Ryan suggested Anne Rice's *Interview with the Vampire* and her world changed. The brooding masculinity of Louis de Pointe du Lac and Lestat de Lioncourt gave her tingles. She luxuriated in the theatrical exuberance of stories that rose above the ridiculous to saturate her in their blood-ripe world. Immersed in the rich, sour fragrance of Rice's word cloud, Eleanor bonded with the vampire Claudia, and dreamt about the tickle of a vampire's fangs at her throat.

As Claudia she faced the daily humiliations on the streets: the pensioners who spat in the paper cup she held out for loose change, the men who flashed her, the men and women who propositioned her, a fiver a fuck, the Jesus-freaks who preached salvation with their eyes down her blouse.

She tore out all of their throats, sucking them dry of blood and marrow, bathing in their gore and terror, tossing aside their lifeless husks, while disinterested cars and buses passed by on the drab suburban high street, under the blank stare of CCTV cameras.

'Lenny? Are you OK?'

'It's fine, just old stuff.'

'Sounded like a nightmare.'

She was in bed trying to read, but kept dozing off. Each time she did, she saw Uncle George bleeding to death on the kitchen floor, his frantic eyes, the staccato jerk of his fingers, his grubby, chewed nails. Sometimes she thought she saw him hovering, bewildered, above his body.

'Do you want to talk?'

Ryan knew she'd say no, she always did. She never talked about how she'd got there, and never asked others either. People said she'd murdered someone, and taken Davy apart (they all remembered Davy).

'Can I ask you something personal? Is it true you did Davy in?'

'Aye.'

'What happened?'

'He tried it on so I ate his face.'

'Cool! You're Claudia after all.'

'They're just stories Ryan, just fantasies. There aren't any vampires really.'

A dog barked somewhere in the night, roaming the empty streets.

'Whatya reading?'

'*Siddhartha.*'

'Never heard of it.'

'It's about a guy who meets Buddha but wants to do his own thing. It's good, it makes you think.'

'What about?'

'About how things could be worse, and how to get your head sorted.'

'I'll stick with the vamps.'

'I want more than that, Ryan. More than this.'

Ryan eyed her when he thought she wasn't watching. She didn't mind, he was OK: he'd never tried it on when others did all the time, and he listened to her, with no angle. She could like a boy who listened, and he had that smile and those eyes, and the tight jeans. But that triggered memories of Uncle George, panting and grunting above her, while she lay still and quiet and waited for it to be over. Until the next time, and the next, and the next, until she stabbed his leg and rammed the blade into his lardy belly and watched him bleed to death.

Goods trains rattled the old walls and rafters, rumbling through the space between the brewery and a high wall. Some wagons bore hoppers, others shipping containers, painted with asymmetric logos of corporations of which no one had ever heard. The trains shunted unknown commodities around an unmapped network; no one seemed to know where the line went or where it started.

Eleanor enjoyed sitting at a window overlooking the waste ground, colonised long ago by rosebay and ragwort and giant thistles. It was home to songbirds, rodents and foxes, and smelled of dust and primrose and axle grease. A kestrel often hovered overhead. Bats flitted from roosts in the railway tunnel, hunting the swarming insects that shared the evening air with thistle down and parachuting rosebay seeds. She learned the names from nature books.

Sometimes at dusk a caravan of travellers on snow-white horses passed through the margins of the yard, fiddles and pipes playing for their journey from nowhere to nowhere.

Water flowed far below the building, forgotten springs feeding forgotten wells below splintered floorboards and wormy joists. She fancied it as her own holy river, her own private Ganges. It sparkled and chattered deep underground, while she sat close to the edge, water lapping her toes, waiting for a ferry to carry her across.

If she ever had a baby of her own, she would never betray it, never stop ferrying it across all of the rivers of its life. This was so true she could screw her eyes up really tight and feel love and certainty bursting out of her.

Eleanor decided to try and see the Buddha in everyone she met, even if they were mean to her.

It was hard.

For every person who dropped a coin into her cup, five more ignored her. She was told to go home, to get a job. She tried to imagine the lechers as naughty children, as people with problems of their own, to picture them naked and vulnerable and scared. She tried not to think about her life, but to focus on how to be better, despite everything.

In the twilight of a warm April, she filled the shadows of the derelict stables with the smell of leather polish and manure, heard the soft murmurings of stable-lads wiping lathered froth from the bits of the great Clydesdales that pulled the beer wagons around the streets. Sometimes the lads wore Ryan's tight jeans and had his warm brown eyes and curly hair. The last of the low sun glinted on the brasses, scattering light around the stalls.

A man came out of the alley down the side of the building, He was tall and slim with broad shoulders and a brush of dark hair, in a well-cut suit over a button-down shirt, with no tie. His arm was around the throat of a young woman, dragging her backwards towards the waste ground. He'd stuffed a rolled-up piece of cloth into her gasping mouth, like a trumpeter muting his horn. Her eyes screamed.

Out of sight of the main road, he threw her to the ground and kicked her, hard, brutal, and took out a short knife, holding it to her throat with one hand, fumbling with his belt and trousers with the other.

He never knew Eleanor was behind him, never registered the pain as a half-brick hammered the base of his skull and his own knife slid behind his ear into his brain. Eleanor looked once at the woman, who fled into the night.

Eleanor stood breathless, light-headed amongst the primroses, staring at the dead man at her feet. Her second victim. Siddhartha stood on the other side of the river, his boat floating free in the tumbling current.

She laid the body across the track in the darkness of the tunnel. Soon, a long succession of fifty-tonne wagons mangled the remains beyond recognition. The man she'd just killed watched everything. She blinked and shook her head, and he was gone.

Dragonflies in Brownian motion filled the air around her, iridescent green eyes glowing, tiny, faceted emeralds whirling in impromptu dust-devils. She could not help but laugh in delight, and heard a voice call her name, but it called her Allison, a name she'd never had.

Another shake of her head and the dragonflies vanished, leaving only the noises of the city at night.

She checked her clothes for traces of blood, wiped the knife clean, and tossed it into the stand of gently swaying foxgloves, hidden from casual eyes, while moths and bats flittered above her head and the last of his blood soaked into the indifferent earth.

She slept her first dreamless sleep for as long as she could remember. In the early hours, Ryan came back from scavenging food waste from supermarket bins and looked in to see if she was still awake. She pulled him to her, unfastened his jeans to free his surprised cock. She wrapped her legs behind his arse, pulled him deep and deeper, again and again and again, until his grateful gasps became shouts.

The ghost of Uncle George stood by the bed, leering, groping himself, trying to insinuate his spectral form into her. All the hatred and anger, the humiliation and loss she'd pushed down for so long, surged up from deep inside her, out through her mouth. Uncle George evaporated into the eternal nothing at all, and Eleanor felt the clagging suffocation of all he had done to her lifted from her soul. She came with a fierce strength.

Soon, she teased a grateful Ryan to another erection and mounted him, straddling, arching, putting his warm hands on her breasts, nipples hard in the chilly air. She lost herself in thoughts of nothing until he yelled his release and she felt the hot splash inside.

Ryan swung his legs out of the bed and reached for his knock-off Calvin Klein boxers. Eleanor grabbed his arm.

'Where do you think you're going? You wanted me for long enough, now's your chance.'

'I'm pregnant.'

She couldn't read the range of emotions that flitted across Ryan's face before he composed himself.

'Are you sure?'

'I haven't had my period for four months.' There was no understanding on his face. 'You know what a period is, right?'

'Um, is it, er, I mean—'

'Whatever. It's our baby.'

'Don't you have to see a doctor or something?'

'No! No doctors. No social workers, no case workers, no nobody poking their nose where they're not wanted. This is for us, together. Our own baby and no one to fuck with us.'

He went out shoplifting, and didn't come back.

Two men came into her room wearing hardhats and high-viz orange jackets, surprised to find a sobbing girl on a filthy mattress surrounded by paperbacks.

'You shouldn't be here, miss. This place is coming down next week. I'm afraid you have to move on.'

'Where to?'

'Your parents? No need to look at me like that, miss. Is there no one at all? You can't stay here.'

A locomotive dawdled along the tracks, naked without its train. Fox cubs rough-and-tumbled under an elder growing through a crack in the hardstanding. A mutilated body decomposed.

'No one.'

'Do you want me to call social services?'

'Fuck no!'

'Is there a problem?' A new voice. A very tall man, balding, in his seventies, she guessed, maybe older, entered the room. He wore a commanding manner like an overcoat over his very good suit. He looked around at the pile of filthy clothes and discarded food wrappers, the stacks of books.

'Yours?' He ran his finger along the spines as though checking the shelves in a second-hand book shop. 'I take it you have nowhere else to go or you wouldn't be in here. Right: pack up anything salvageable and we'll get you a shower and some clean clothes and a meal. I have a place you can stay while we sort this out.'

The man unnerved her and she couldn't say why. It was as though he wasn't a man at all, as though he were something else entirely, but she didn't know what.

'Of course. You have no reason to trust me. Wait here, I'll be back soon. Gentlemen, let's allow the young lady some privacy.'

Outside the window a large bulldozer moved onto the site, followed by workmen and other plant and machinery. They were still some way from the quiet spot where the body lay under tall flowering stems that shimmied in the gentle breeze, but it wouldn't be long until it was found. She tossed *Siddhartha* onto the pile of discarded books and packed her old rucksack with her few belongings.

The old man came back with a young woman. She was just as tall, brunette, perhaps in her mid-twenties. She and the man both had strange earlobes. Neither looked Caucasian, but they didn't look African or Asian either. Her every sense recoiled. The man put a carrier bag just inside the door, but did not enter.

'Ah! Good. All packed, I see. This is for you. And this is Margaret.'

Margaret said, 'I understand if you don't trust us, you've never seen us before, but we'd like to offer you hospitality before you're on your way. We have a bath, clean clothes, a bed, and hot food. It's your choice. I'll be outside while you think about it.'

Choice.

She'd chosen to seek the Buddha, but she'd fucked that up: Buddha was long gone and she was a wretched thing, rejected by two mothers, a killer of two men.

There isn't much enlightenment found in killing men, however gross they were. She wasn't about to trust this

Margaret either just because she was a woman – not all of the worst care assistants were men. Margaret didn't do anything threatening or possessive, though: she just stood in silence the other side of the open door.

'No!' yelled the voices in her head, but the decision was easy: free food should never be refused. In the bag were an apple and a banana, which she ate, savouring their sweetness. She took out the clean clothes and stripped down to her pants and old, frayed bra, two cup sizes too small, despite her underfed frame.

'Oh! You're expecting!'

Eleanor's covered herself with her arms, awkward, gangly.

'Have you seen anyone? A doctor or anything?

'I don't like doctors.'

'Hmmm, well, we can sort that too if you want, someone private. We can talk about it later. What's your name?'

'Eleanor,' said Eleanor, surprised she answered.

'Well, Eleanor, why don't we get you sorted then we can talk some more.'

'Is your place nearby?'

'No, it's quite a way out of the city, an old country house, quite historic really. We have ponies and everything.'

'How could you tell? I'm barely showing.'

'Let's put it down to female intuition. Shall we go?'

A long black car waited outside. She folded herself into a plush leather back seat while the older man, whose name she did not know, sat in the front with Margaret and their driver. She tried to work out where they were going, but got lost when they turned off the by-pass and took roads past abandoned industrial estates and retail parks, by farms and villages to the edge of moorland. *Never get into a car with strangers*, Mum had said, when all along the real danger was already in the house.

How could Mum not have known about George? After all she grew up with him in the same house. And all the world shrank into a clear, firm answer: her mum knew all the time, and did nothing to stop it.

The road narrowed and curved into a long valley through which a tumbling stream chortled and chuckled. They turned off, up towards the hills, and came eventually to a remote glen. There, up a long driveway, they reached a large house that straddled, and predated, the ancient county boundary. The site was in the crook of a burn that rose as a spring on the hill above and tumbled with surprising force. The property was shielded from the road below by old-growth trees.

Margaret gave an expansive sweep of her arm indicating the whole estate.

'Welcome to The Leyes.'

The house was white walled and terracotta tiled. Its gables and windows, dormered attics and glass and metal extensions were constructed around a much older core. The exterior woodwork was picked out in gloss black, fresh enough for the smell of the paint to catch in her nose. Dad used to read her stories of fantasy houses like it in eternal summer holidays. The grounds were extensive and bordered by mature trees, with well-tended lawns and flower beds. Fruit bushes masked a large Victorian greenhouse and vegetable garden, accessed through an arched pergola wrapped in Virginia creeper. Eleanor could smell stables nearby, as Margaret led her to a side door.

'This is your flat. You can be as private in here as you want to be. There are clean clothes inside but they'll probably be a bit baggy for you. We can get some more later if you let me know your sizes. I'll let you settle in and I'll come back in an hour or so with some soup and tea.'

The flat was clean, compact, and better than anything Eleanor could remember. It was better even than her Granny Arthur's big house, where she was always too frightened to touch anything in case she was told off. She dropped her rucksack on the floor and closed the door behind her. Without hesitation, she turned the thermostat until the shower was as hot as she could stand, massaging shampoo into her crusty scalp, feeling the tangles fall from her hair. She rubbed soap into every pore of her body, forcing out all the months of ingrained grime. Once she felt clean enough, she ran a hot bath and relaxed into the oversized tub, skin tingling as though she were reborn.

Her head underwater, the pulsing of blood in her ears was like the water in the deep wells below the brewery, her private Ganges. Maybe she could go down to the burn later, sit close to the edge, and lose herself in its chatter. Maybe her time with these strangers, away from the dangers and temptations of the world she knew, would let her choose again to be someone else, or at least not be a person she didn't want to be.

Maybe, maybe, maybe. Too many maybes. She didn't even know who these people were, or where she was, or why her nerves were so on edge. Something about The Leyes unsettled her as much as the old man and Margaret did.

Eleanor lay across the bed in baggy sweat pants and T-shirt, a towel round her head, examining her toenails with a critical eye. Margaret returned with the promised tray of soup and tea and fetched a sports bag.

'Try some of these for size. They're kind of bland but they'll keep you going until we can buy some more.'

Margaret had an executive smoothness, and a casual disregard for the quality of both her own clothes and those she passed over. Eleanor tried to hide her chewed fingernails and calloused feet. Her hair, which felt clean and full seconds ago, was drab by comparison, and she had yellow teeth. She stared at the floor.

'Why are you doing this for me?'

'The short version is Ephraim lost his family in the war. He was just a baby, and was somehow spirited here to Britain. Then he lost two of his own children and ever since has taken people in trouble under his wing until they can manage on their own.'

'Yes, but why me?'

'Your books, I think. He loves books. You had Hesse by your bed, and poetry. You don't see people reading poetry much anymore, or Hesse for that matter. So he saw a kindred spirit. You'll like his library – I'll show you round it later if you want. Now, do these fit? And we can see about your hair and nails when you've had something to eat.'

Later, they walked round the grounds. Margaret was careful not to ask any prying questions, and Eleanor was careful to volunteer no answers. They talked about life on the streets and how it was in the squat, but nothing personal. Eleanor didn't offer her surname, but she allowed Margaret to call her Lenny.

'Do you like music, Lenny?'

'Yes, but I don't hear much, just the buskers usually. Sometimes at Christmas on Princes Street there are brass bands and things and they're good.'

'What about church music?'

'Hymns and stuff? No. I don't know it.'

Oh God, no: not Holy Rollers.

'No, I mean choral music, the great masses and the modern music of Taverner and Maxwell-Davies?'

'Sorry.'

There were three ponies at the stables, coats sleek in the afternoon sun. The beasts ambled across the paddock to greet them. Eleanor remembered how to make a pony feel comfortable when she petted it, how to whisper meaningless syllables into its ears and gain its trust.

'You know ponies, then?'

'Not really, just holiday memories from when I was a little girl. We went pony trekking a few times.'

'Well, they've taken quite a shine to you, it's like you have a gift for it. They don't usually give their trust so quickly.'

Nor should they, thought Eleanor, *I've killed two men. And I don't trust you or your boss either.*

'They are Milly, Molly and Mandy. Not very original names but they're the ones they came with, we rescue ponies when we can. Mandy here is pregnant, by the way. Did you say you were about four months gone? So your due date will be near hers, then, in January. We don't know who that dad is either.'

'Oh, I know who he is, just not where he is. He legged it when I told him.'

'Bastard! When was that?'

'Last week.'

'The shit. He can't have gone far. We can help find him if you want.'

'No. He's just a boy, just a wee lost boy.'

She hated her tears, the vulnerability, the shame. Margaret handed her a packet of paper hankies.

'Have you thought what you'll do, Lenny? About the baby.'

'I'll love it and care for it and never let it go. Alone if I have to, though I don't know how.'

Milly, Molly and Mandy thrust their heads at her hand, butting for attention. Each wanted her ears scratched, hoped for a treat.

'Well, you can stay here until you work something out, if you want. You'll be good company for Mandy.'

An obstetrician, Sarah, a neat, unfussy woman, visited. Eleanor had not kept track of dates in the squat, and her periods were irregular anyway. Sarah estimated a due date of 21 January plus or minus a week.

'The bairn's fine,' said Sarah. 'You, on the other hand, have gone too long without proper food; you're naught but a rickle o' bones. My prescription is a proper diet and plenty of herbals from the garden here.'

Ephraim and Margaret were almost wholly vegetarian and ate well from the organic produce of The Leyes. Eleanor ate the same, supplemented with a small amount of fish or white meat.

True to her word, Margaret took Eleanor to Ephraim's library, near the oldest part of the house. The room was octagonal, with high ceilings, and lined from floor to cornice on all sides with hardwood shelves, broken only by two doors and two high windows. It smelled of leather spines and old wood and beeswax. The other door, on the opposite wall, was locked.

The books covered every possible subject, and Eleanor could tell many of them were very old indeed, although the oldest were on higher shelves, reached by a ladder contraption that rolled around the wooden floor on castors, along runnels and grooves scored into the varnished surface.

'Fiction and poetry are mainly on that wall over there,' said Margaret, pointing. 'There is a lifetime's education in here for those who are interested.'

In the centre of the room were two deep-backed leather armchairs separated by an old table. Floor-standing electric lamps curved over the back of each chair. Near the second door, a small glass cabinet was inset into the shelves. Inside there were some small glass cups, each no bigger than an upturned daffodil trumpet, sitting on a wooden platter, its patina polished by years of handling.

Eleanor barely heard what Margaret said: she had never seen a room so beautiful in all her life, and lost herself in the titles.

Eleanor spent a lot of time reading, and could often be found down by the river or sitting in the cool hollow of a massive and ancient yew tree, which stood in its own enclosed space to one side of the formal gardens, accessed through a gated gap in the stone boundary wall. She read *Siddhartha* again, in a different translation. He didn't kill anyone on his journey, but perhaps there was still hope she'd get her head sorted, a chance she would find more than the shitty life she'd had.

However good the book, however comfortable she felt in her reading spot, every day she was at the stables, where she insisted on playing her part in Mandy's care.

She didn't trust Ephraim and Margaret, but she got used to them. The veterinarian who visited from time to time to check on the Mandy's progress, reminded her of some of the medical staff in her secure accommodation. He had a possessive shadow in his eyes, like Uncle George. Another old lecher: she'd met enough to spot the signs.

Despite the pervy vet and the lingering distrust, she was happy and became companionable with Margaret, who seemed to have no life away from Ephraim, even though the old man himself was only there occasionally. He bestowed beaming smiles on her when he found her reading in his library. Tournier's *The Erl King* made a big impression on her, as did Grass's *The Tin Drum*. She forgot all about vampire stories, and sometimes, when she felt the flutterings of the baby, she managed to go a whole day without thinking about the two men she'd killed or the one whose face she ate.

Most mornings, after breakfast, she and Margaret walked around the perimeter of the grounds, chatting.

'They found a body near that warehouse yesterday, the one you were living in.'

Oh shit!

'It was over on the other side of the railway lines. The police reckon it was a suicide because it looked as though he'd had been hit by a train.'

'Do they know how long it's been there?'

'No, it's badly decomposed. Oh! You mean maybe it was there near you all the time? *Bleagh*, How creepy. Anyway, do you know what you'll do once the baby is born?'

'No. I wondered if I could stay here for a while and maybe find a way to pay my way?'

'That shouldn't be a problem. Ephraim's taken quite a shine to you, and having a baby around would give him a new lease of life. Have you thought of any names yet?'

'Loads.'

'What about your parents' names?'

Eleanor turned away.

'Touchy subject?'

'No. Yes. Sort of. I never knew their names. I thought I did but then found out I was adopted. Then they threw me out as well.'

Margaret put a tentative hand on Eleanor's shoulder and pulled her closer, holding her tight.

'I don't want that for my baby. I don't want it not to be loved.'

'Your child has so much to offer. Did you ever try to track down your birth-parents?'

'No. I wouldn't know how, but sometimes I think that if I met them I would know them straight away, that I'm just the latest in a chain stretching back in time, just like Govinda sees in Siddhartha. Does that sound weird? All those faces in my mind; all those voices calling out to me.'

'What do they say?'

'I can't make them out. Sometimes they seem to be warning me, but I don't know what about, they don't tell me.'

Eleanor allowed herself to be hugged for a long time before they fed Milly, Molly and Mandy. That day, she felt the baby give its first real kick. Later, she told Margaret her whole story.

'The body by the warehouse?'

Eleanor kept her eyes fixed on the ground.

'I killed him. But she needed me, what else could I do?'

'You saved her.'

'At a price.'

'He deserved it.'

'But I didn't. All I want is to be good, to be a good person, and all I'll ever be known as is a killer. I don't suppose I can explain that properly, what it feels like.'

Margaret looked towards the tops of the trees on the nearby hill waving on the breeze, her eyes unfocused. After a while, rain fell, washing the air between them.

'Can I stay? After the baby is born? I'll find ways to help you.'

'Yes, of course,' said Margaret, dabbing her eyes, wiping away rain, or tears, or both.

Eleanor was in the stables, wrapped up against the January winds. Mandy looked weak and distressed. The mare's pregnancy had been difficult. The pervy vet said it was touch and go. Eleanor's waters broke while she scratched Mandy's ears. The flat was prepared for the home birth she wanted, and Sarah was soon there, accompanied by a no-nonsense midwife who took charge. Eleanor was much healthier than when she first arrived, but Sarah insisted she be cannulated in case saline or other intervention was required. After several failed attempts to fit the needle into a vein inside her left elbow, then the back of her left hand, it slipped into her right arm and was taped into place.

Labour was rapid, with half a tank of Entonox to help things along. Margaret held Eleanor's hand the whole the time, and it was Margaret who, after the midwife tied off the umbilical cord, handed the squalling bundle to a radiant Eleanor.

'Congratulations Lenny,' said Margaret, 'You have a gorgeous daughter, and a lively one too.'

'Thank you. Thank you, thank you. I couldn't have done this without you.'

'Have you decided on her name?'

'Margaret,' said Eleanor, holding her daughter tight and smiling through her exhaustion.

'Here, let's wrap her and check her over. We'll get you cleaned up.'

Margaret couldn't find Ephraim, but at the paddock she found Mandy foaling. With a rueful smile for how the day was turning out, she hand-delivered the foal, calling out for help that didn't come. By the time Ephraim and the vet arrived it was all over.

The vet looked over to Mandy and her foal, which was already trying to stand on its spindly legs. Mandy was trying to stand too, but failing.

'Margaret did a fine job Ephraim, a very fine job. And the youngster is splendid.'

'I'm proud of her.' He watched the weakened Mandy with concern. 'What about the mare? Do you think she's good for another?'

The vet shook his head. 'She's played her part. We can always rescue more. It will be a kindness.'

Ephraim looked at Margaret.

'Are you comfortable with that?'

'I'll see to it,' said Margaret, watching the exhausted Mandy nuzzling and licking her foal clean. She picked up the modified Taser from the bag beside her and checked the charge as she walked round the paddock perimeter.

She discharged the device on full power into Eleanor's sternum. Sarah and the midwife drew a sample of Eleanor's blood and injected Eleanor with a measured dose of very high-grade heroin laced with strychnine. They removed the cannula and all clinical traces from her body.

The vet and the midwife drove away with the infant Margaret, umbilical cord and placenta securely stored. A plain white van took Eleanor's remains for disposal. Ephraim put an affectionate arm around Margaret's waist as they passed through the gate in the wall to the sacred yew.

'The first is always the hardest. I'm proud of you.'

'She named the baby for me, Father, she named it Margaret.'

'Yes, they often do that. Remember what I taught you: humans are not pets. Are you sure about her birth-parents?'

'Only the mother, the father is unknown. I checked Ryan's research myself.'

'Any signs?'

'Some: she sensed the voices of her ancestors calling her, but had no idea who they were, or why they called.'

'And Ryan?'

'One more job, then we're done with him.'

Crows cawed in the high branches of the trees around them.

'Did you read the latest?' he asked.

'The surveillance material? Their satellites and drones? Yes.'

'And the assessments from the Arctic. Your case is established: well done.'

'The Cascade will go ahead?'

'What choice do we have?'

Sarah joined them. Ephraim raised a daffodil flower-sized crystal cup to his lips, as did Sarah and Margaret. They closed their eyes and held silence for a few moments, until Ephraim said:

'We follow the ancient rite and honour her memory with her blood. For Eleanor: she died happy and healthy. *Mortuus est ut nos vivamus*: this we do in remembrance of her.'

THAT I MAY SWIM

Comes by now old Thomas Weir, condemned Major Weir, late of the town guard and his sister's bony flanks. Comes he now, whimpering, slavering; hauled over the snow-packed Gallow-lee on the hangman's horse-drawn sled. Caw canny cuddy: you don't want the Major's pintle up your arse; don't want to get knocked on the head and burnt with the old lecher.

And up gets Tom, chattering and shivering. He'll be hot in hell soon enough, tied to the post while the rope goes around his neck. The impatient pyre, already kindled, snatches his gaze, grips it tight. Hot tar and coals scent the cold morning air. There's the hangman in his red cap, holding his end of the rope as he stands ahent the stake, waiting for the nod to proceed. Get on with it lad! Burn the old bastard and let's get some warmth. We haven't got all day to stand here freezing.

Hard now the hangman hauls, and Tom is weeping and repenting as the garrotte bites, eyes bulging, ancient sinews straining.

It's the wirrying of old Thomas, Angelic Thomas, saintliest of Calvinists, purest of Puritans, comforter of married women and their daughters, off to his doom, as the justices commanded for this eleventh day of April sixteen hundred and seventy. May his spirit roast in the fires of damnation as earth-bound flames dance galliards about his still-twitching corpse, tossed now onto the pyre with his cursed walking-staff.

What's that? He's still alive? Can he feel the catching of the filthy cloth that shrouds him? Did he scream? Or was it just hot air rolling out over his toasting tongue?

Here! Watch where you're pushing, fat arse! We'd all like to warm our fingers while Thomas blackens and cracks. We're not all like blank-faced Aphrêm over there, watching, noting everything. Aphrêm the apothecary, some say alchemist, some say worse. Big-eared Aphrêm, dispassionate, while old Tom's fat rolls and crackles and spits, and the shimmering air smells for all the world of hog-roasts on Uphaly days of blessed memory.

This is the true story of Thomas Weir, not the one they tell to frighten bairns on winter nights when nightmares tumble heels-o'er-hurdies across the roofs of the Old Town; not the one shouted in pamphlets and broadsides around Europe. It's 1643, as good a time to start as any, and Captain Weir, his uniform smart, strides down from the West Bow, past the Tollbooth, side-stepping the filth on the pavement, flicking away litter with his long staff, his prominent nose drawing in chill Edinburgh air blawing up from the Forth.

He's home, secure in the knowledge of his Salvation, fresh from putting down papists in Ulster with hagbutt and sword, here to visit his wife, Isobel, relict of John Burdoun, mother to his deceased bairn, also Thomas, born a respectable seven months after their marriage. He's home to press for recovery of debts due by John Burdoun's creditors, to press his name and sword (and 200 merks) to the Covenanter cause, and, says the country gossip, to press his tarse wherever it finds a wet welcome, swiving for the greater glory of Kirk and Crown.

Margaret, Allisoun and Bethia, John Burdoun's surviving lassies by Isobel, keep their distance. They miss their father, a burgess and Guild-brother, more than two years dead. They miss the smells from his booth and the confits and confections he made. Their childhoods were full of sugar candy and almonds, cloves and cannel, annet and carvel, mace, saffron, nutmeg, liquorice, figs and raisins. All the foods of a merchant's booth were theirs: peppers and rice, dates and olive oil. And there were mysteries for small children in John's stock – alchemical pans and trenchers, sconces, strings for virginals, pap glasses, ventois glasses, urinal glasses, bombasine, wool, and worsted yarns.

They have no love for the tall, serious soldier. Margaret, eldest at twelve years old, is barely a woman but not too young to mistake the captain's eye resting on her a little too long. Allisoun, eleven, dreamer, seer of ghosts, detests him from the beginning, is punished for the vehemence of her warnings to Isobel not to become involved with Major Weir, which she insists on calling him though he is only a Captain-Lieutenant. Bethia, ten, keeps her opinions to herself. Isobel, mistress of her own house, well used to the ways of men, and no stranger to gossip, greets him as a good wife before they fall to discussing business. Robert Burdoun, the surviving son of John by his first wife, is trying to exert himself as heir, and there are lawyers to be paid for court actions.

Domestic duties complete, Isobel relieves Thomas of most of his coins and dismisses him to be about his own business, to polish his weapon, perhaps, or attend to his devotions, both of which are in his plans, but not immediately: he has a pressing need to commit the sins for which he will later repent. Many's the league his prick has roamed in service of the thankless mouth. He dresses as a plain indweller of the town, and decides against the charms of his mistress Elspeth. He points himself instead to Leith and all its anonymous pleasures and poxes.

Later, he visits the premises of Aphrêm the apothecary to purchase powders and unguents to ease his sores from the Irish campaign. He makes private enquiries about remedies for female maladies and conditions, aches and sickness, and also the quickening of the womb; a particular womb, he gives cause to understand, which is not a part of his wife's person. Aphrêm, as tall as the captain, though darker of hair, with bright eyes, examines the specimen before him.

'Such remedies are known to my Guild, handed down from antiquity, but I am bound by laws of men and God to refuse you. Out of respect for your rank I think, perhaps, we should forget that this conversation commenced.'

Aphrêm moves with his customary care to prepare the remainder of the items requested and present his account. His figures are as neat and precise as his movement, his letters, no rough secretary hand for him, are as graceful as his voice, which carries the echo of an origin the captain cannot place, neither England nor Flanders, Dordrecht nor Danzig. Mediterranean, perhaps, and to the east: Greece, if he is any judge, which he is not.

'Master Aphrêm, perhaps I might reframe my enquiry: in a situation such as I describe, what should you advise?'

'Why, Captain, I should advise a poor sinner to seek the solace of our Lord and the mercy of the Kirk.'

'Indeed, and you would be correct. And yet I must press you, sir, man to man, and ask if there be any remedy in nature for that which nature hath wrought?'

'Man to man?' Aphrêm pauses, distant amusement in his eyes. 'I am given to understand that women have their own lore in these matters, Captain. It is a pity you are not able to consult your wife, Isobel Mein I believe? I have heard that such remedies are used amongst the heathens and ungodly, but never in a God-fearing nation, a nation, forsooth, in which gallants such as yourself,' Aphrêm inclines his head, 'defend the faith with vigour. Your service with Colonel Home has brought you some measure of renown, has it not? Renown you might hesitate to put in risk through scandal.'

'Thank you.' Thomas returns the bow. 'I am curious, however, about those heathen practices. Perhaps there is merit in research into those abominations, for the better understanding of our Lord's grand design and the avoidance of Satan's snares. As to risk, *whom He did predestinate, then He also called, and whom He called, then He also justified.*'

Aphrêm considers the captain as an army chirurgeon contemplates a particularly curious wound.

'Indeed, it is as you say: *who shall lay any thing to the charge of God's elect*? There may be merit in the research, though the knowledge is all around in plain sight and sound. You may be familiar with the savin tree planted, by all conjecture, to destroy fruit? No? Well, I must draw your attention to the fate of those many wretches with knowledge of herbs and plants, accused of witchcraft by your fellow religionists for much lesser researches, who are wirrit and burned, their ashes scattered in the mosses and lochs of the country. Have you no fear that such a fate will also befall you?'

'No sir, for who could fail to distinguish the scholarly enquiries of honest men from the foolish devilry of cunning-women and their familiars? The two are quite distinct.'

'Then, Captain, if you insist, I will aid you, though I will not supply you with any necessary ingredients: those you must obtain by your own efforts. Also, I will not disclose any matters privative to my Guild.'

'Master Aphrêm, I am obliged, and honoured to be accepted as your pupil.'

'Perhaps: you have not yet heard my fee.'

'Rest assured, I am due substantial sums from the Estates anent my service in the cause of our Lord in Ireland.'

'Your coin does not interest me, sir. My fee is this: when you purge a quickened womb, I want the bairn.'

Isobel adjusts her embroidered coif and smooths the clean apron she wears over her tawny-brown gown with rabbit-fur trim. She has no need of a hat atop her coif, and steps out for her daily walk, avoiding the ordure on the ground. She cannot escape the flies, but barely notices the scampering rats in the pends and closes running perpendicular to the High Street. Her circumstances are more reduced than she could wish since John's death, and the claims of his son are unwelcome, but Robert does not have control yet. She has sufficient to engage a lawyer to recover the debts owed to the umquhile John, and the captain has an income.

The marriage suits both Thomas and Isobel without any tedious need for declarations of love between them.

Thomas's family have some pretention to grandeur, not wholly without historic foundation, but with little to sustain it in the present. Of his sisters, she knows only that Jean, whom he visits often, teaches vulgar school in Dalkeith. Isobel has only met Jean once and did not form a good impression: the woman sat at her loom all afternoon, smoking a clay pipe, regaling her with opinions on everything from the perfidy of Egyptian travellers, and the manifest propensity of Episcopalians to unnatural vices, to the beneficial qualities of certain mushrooms growing in nearby meadows.

Isobel walks up the slope of the street, into the glare of the sun which shifts closer to the Castle in the late afternoon. At the Tolbooth she pays her respects to the severed heads, hands and limbs rotting on spikes. She has the Sight, though she doesn't know how or why it came to her. Her mother, Marioun, died when Isobel and her sister were infants, and her father, also John, fanatic that he is, permits no discussion on the subject.

Thomas is ahead of her, walking towards the Castle. Expecting to observe her philandering husband visit a mistress or a merry house, she follows him. He turns left at the Bowhead onto the West Bow, descending the steep dog-leg to the Grassmarket. A pomander is at her nose against the stench of manure, animal and human, and of the malefactors rotting in chains on the gibbet, their air-dried faces like fleshy gargoyles come down from a cathedral spire. The street is crowded. She expects Thomas to turn onto the Cowgate but instead he enters premises she does not recognise. She walks closer to see what she can see, colliding with a woman in green and apologising profusely.

It comes on her without warning. Glancing through a window, she is struck a sharp blow inside her head by an overwhelming knowledge of wrongness. Thomas stands with his back angled towards her in conversation with something which her eyes tell her is a man but the Sight tells her is something else: something predatory. As she stumbles and walks away, she tries to recall where she has seen such a scene before. It was when she was a girl, she remembers, visiting a relative outside of the town. The memory declines to crystalise, and she slips into a kirk where she composes herself as if in silent contemplation. She looks up to where plaster saints once sat but now are empty alcoves, where occasional pigeons roost to mock the superstitious, their *prr-coos* a running counterpoint to the unadorned monotone of three-hour exegeses of the Word. There is no comfort, no instruction. Isobel gathers herself and steps out into the late afternoon.

The thing waits outside, its face betraying no intent, no emotion. There are no fleas or lice anywhere about its person. She has no idea how she knows this, only that it is true.

'Forgive me madam, I noticed you earlier in the grip of some seizure or malady. If you will forgive the impropriety, permit me to introduce myself. My name is Aphrêm and I am at your service should you require assistance.' He bows formally and proffers a *visite bilete*, newly fashionable amongst the Guild-brothers of the town.

Isobel finds, with detached curiosity, that she feels no trace now of the ancient wrongness that forced itself into her mind not fifteen minutes before, as if the creature can mask its nature. Collecting her wits and her manners, she acknowledges the bow.

'Thank you for your kindness sir. It was but a passing sensation, a feminine weakness.'

She takes the card and her finger brushes his. Immediately the certainty of danger returns. It takes all her strength not to flee from the thing in front of her, the thing which looks at her. She knows from the heart of her being that fleeing would be the worst thing she could do, that flight would trigger immediate chase. She knows, too, that her Sight has changed somehow, and become something new.

'You have a question, madam?'

Her tongue trips ahead of her brain.

'Yes. Forgive me sir, but what are you?'

There is the hint of a furrow, reminiscent of a horseshoe, on his high forehead, a slight dilation of his pupils, and she thinks his head cocks to one side by a fraction of a degree.

'Why madam, an apothecary, as is written on the card you hold.'

She looks at the card for the first time. The obverse bears his name and profession, the address of his business, and another address: a house called The Leyes, some distance south of the town walls she thinks. On the reverse is an exquisite, hand-coloured, Chinese design featuring a Buddhist monk and a fox. She has a vision of a beautiful river of gold and stares at the card until she slips it into a pocket beneath her apron.

'Forgive me, sir, I must about my business.'

As she walks away, thinking of the discussion she must now have with Margaret, Bethia and Allisoun, she is unsure if the discomfort in her back is from climbing the steep gradient of the West Bow or because Aphrêm's eyes are fixed onto her retreating form. She remembers now what the scene between Aphrêm and Thomas reminded her of: a shepherd, selecting a bleating and gambolling yearling lamb to butcher.

At the Bowhead she turns right, and the sensation in her back ceases as her agitation grows. Ahead she sees a multitude of High Streets receding from her, all occupying the same space yet somehow differentiated, like the glazed layers of a painting, colours and highlights dancing on the scumbled ground beneath. Men and women of many eras are engaged about their business. Reflections in windows to her right move of their own accord in contra-motion to the objects they mirror. In the distance, the heads impaled above the Tollbooth turn to face her and open their empty mouths in silent entreaties. She is aware of every living and dead eye upon her, of every shadow cast by objects that are not in the sun.

She raises her pomander and inhales the calming aromas of aloes and nutmeg, balm and musk, but her rising panic does not abate. On the other side of the street, a man and his bairns wave from the entry to a close. It is John and her six dead bairns by him. She grasps that they are warning her of something, just as all strength in the muscles of her thighs disappears. She feels herself falling into a swoon, her fingers curling tight into her palms as the deep beckoning nothingness refuses to be denied.

Aphrêm attends her. Agnes, wife of William Blackwood and her stepdaughter by John's first wife, is also there, concern all across her face, though not in her eyes, and insists she will guide her stepmother home. Agnes helps Isobel to her feet and they walk, slowly, towards the Tron. Aphrêm remains close by, in case, he says, there is a relapse and he has to administer medicaments, which he should be delighted to do *gratis*.

Everyone on the street watches their progress, until the small party arrives at Isobel's house where Thomas meets them at the door, a look of fright on his dark face. As Isobel is led inside by Margaret, she turns to thank Agnes, and sees a gleam in Aphrêm's clear eyes.

Thomas is an excellent study, and learns the secret uses of calamint and penny royal, rue and savin; how to form pessaries for use in intimate moments of passion, or poultices for application to the nethermost part of the belly; how to boil certain leaves in wine. The relative merits of mugwort and other *artemisiae*, and the uses of feverfew and lady laurel, are topics on which he could discourse at knowledgeable length should he wish.

Aphrêm tells him of Joseph, his aboriginal correspondent in the Royal Colony of Virginia, who sometimes sends rare and powerful seeds from the Indies. Joseph also sends interesting samples from the Americas, this time a mixture of liana and leaves known to the indigenous inhabitants as *ayawaska* that, when boiled into a tisane, is reputed to aid reflection on the divine. Aphrêm offers a sample, and sells Thomas tobacco leaves of higher quality than any of Yansone's illicit imports.

As late summer approaches, Thomas grows more agitated as his mistress Elspeth's pregnancy follows its natural course. Aphrêm's price gnaws at him, though he doesn't doubt that he will pay it. Pretending to administer a curative to relieve her pains and ease childbirth, he gives her his first attempted 'remedy'. The effects are apparent within the hour. He has miscalculated the quantities: Elspeth collapses in agony, the babe coming too soon. Losing his composure, he sends Elspeth's maid to fetch Aphrêm, whose premises are nearby.

Aphrêm assumes professional charge. He is the very model of care and concern for Elspeth, for whom, he advises, blessed eternity approaches. He applies a poultice to ease her pain. As Elspeth slips into the sleep from which she will not wake until Judgement Day, her waters break. Her contractions proceed at pace: this is not her first child. Within the hour, a boy is delivered, stilled born says Aphrêm, and Elspeth passes beyond worldly cares. Aphrêm, regretful and solicitous, offers to remove the tiny corpse.

Aphrêm leans towards Thomas, who is alone in his thoughts. The captain, sure that he sees the bairn's leg twitch within the cloths in which it is wrapped, looks up.

'Excellent,' says Aphrêm in a confidential tone. 'Our covenant is sealed'.

It is 17 August 1643.

Thomas withdraws from society in the succeeding weeks, though he fulfils his duties adequately. Margaret, Allisoun and Bethia are served as heirs to John Burdoun. The family obtain a decree against the Earl of Morton for payment of old debts. They don't celebrate. Deteriorating relations between Thomas and Isobel mean he dons his uniform and is off on martial business, sheathing his sword away from the marital bed.

Montrose, once the great Montrose, now the turncoat Montrose, Lord Lieutenant of Scotland and traitor to the Covenant he signed, is slaughtering true Scots in the cause of King Charles. Thomas returns to arms with relief and, to the satisfaction of Allisoun, is appointed a Major in the Earl of Lanark's Regiment. Thomas is off to Hartlepool and Newcastle and away from Aphrêm. He yields to the charms of a woman, but is armed now with an extensive knowledge of ways to prevent his seed taking root. He serves with distinction, until he is captured at Newcastle.

Often, in the dark of night, he sees the child, his son, its leg twitching in Aphrêm's grip.

Thomas is not given to imagination, but sometimes he glimpses another life, on the banks of the Clyde, teaching his boy to fish, instructing him in the gospel, watching him grow. He sees the long unfolding of choices not made, and mourns the memory of a life that will never be.

Sixteen forty-four begins and runs its course. Thomas is freed. Aphrêm is engaged by the town to certify that mariners and merchants trading from Leith or Newhaven are free from contagion. Rumours of the pestilence are rife, and vessels from Newcastle and other suspect places are prevented from entering the harbours or putting men or goods ashore elsewhere. The fears are justified. As another year turns, the King is defeated, Montrose's star wanes, and pestilence runs like quicksilver through the streets and tenements of Leith, entering Edinburgh in triumph, finding lodgings within the town walls. It is a sociable guest, treating rich and poor, high and low, with gregarious magnanimity.

Isobel teaches her girls the ways of the world and business. Allisoun is gifted with numbers and learns how to prepare ledgers and understand what lies behind the figures there. Isobel tells them also of the Sight, and swears them to secrecy for fear of the prickers of witches. She reasons something lay dormant in her and was quickened by her encounter with Aphrêm. She grows accustomed to sharing the streets with the dead as well as the living, though she tells no one. Nor does she talk of the other presences she sees, mysterious, not blank horrors like Aphrêm but creatures of a different continuity, with deep connections to the Earth, who all ignore her. Allisoun has always seen these others, Allisoun who often holds her hand.

'What are they mother? Why do they ignore us?'

'I don't know, dear. Perhaps they are our good neighbours. I feel no threat.'

'I should like to know more about them.'

'Maybe you will, but be careful: observing them may change them, fix them in time and place, somehow, in ways they don't want to be fixed.'

'Can they help us kill it?'

'Kill what?'

'Aphrêm.'

'Why would we kill it?'

'Because of what it is going to do.'

One of the beings, green of eye, clad in a fine green kirtle that transforms into a green silk shift as light as dandelion seed, stares at Allisoun. Allisoun shakes her head at a strange sensation of dizzying drowsiness. When the feeling passes, the green lady is nowhere to be seen.

Isobel and Allisoun watch witches, confessed and convicted, led to Castlehill to be strangled at the stake and their bodies burnt. They see no evil in them, and only once sense power in one, who turns resigned eyes towards them in the moments before her death. Allisoun is silent for a long time afterwards.

The pestilence takes a firmer grip, and the people of Leith and Edinburgh leave, if they can, or stay on in penury and near famine. Isobel and Allisoun keep off the streets, lest the lingering dead overwhelm them. When it is over, Isobel and the Burdoun bairns still live, as does the Major. As does Aphrêm.

Young Margaret broaches the topic of young men to her mother, rueing their absence, carrying her virginity in her purse like a silver coin burning to be spent. Isobel's advice surprises her: 'Swive for passion, marry for security. With luck, you'll find both with the same man.' Allisoun confides that she has sinned in thought because her attraction is to other girls.

'I wish you joy,' replies Isobel, 'but do not speak aloud of it, and be ever thankful Leviticus is silent on the subject.'

New burgesses are enrolled to replace those rotting in plague pits, and the Kirk in government turns to its loyal servants to aid in the struggle against Cromwell. Major Weir is in demand. His memory of scripture is perfect and he is eloquent in public prayer. His reputation for piety grows. Isobel will have none of it and none of him. Thomas can always find an outlet for his virile passions, with his devoted sister Jean if nowhere else.

At the head of Libberton's Wynd, waiting for a hanging, Thomas is waylaid by the surprisingly strong Aphrêm.

'Major Weir: how very good to see you again; how very agreeable that you survived the pestilence. Have you forgotten our covenant?'

'Forgotten? No sir, I assure you full true it is rarely far from my thoughts.'

'Excellent. I am surprised, then, you have not delivered any further fruits of your labours.'

'There have been no further fruits, sir. Of late my seed has failed to take root.'

'Such is chance, Major, such is chance, especially for one who reads herbals. Tell me, how is your lovely wife?'

'Isobel is well, though ill disposed towards me, I fear.'

'A pity. I want a child of her womb.'

The sound of blood in his ears is all that disturbs the silence which falls on Thomas.

'We have an agreement, do we not, Major? Sealed in the blood of your son. Surely you did not think I would be satisfied with only one child? That was the initial consideration of our contract; I now require further payments to account, and my need is very specific: I wish to pluck the fruit of your wife, failing whom one of her natural family. Her daughters, perhaps. Yes, one of those charming girls got on her by John Burdoun. Major, I have faith you will succeed in this.'

'This is a terrible thing you ask of me, Master Aphrêm. An abomination in the Lord's sight.'

'Is it Major? Is it really? What did that old dolt from Tarsus say? *Whom He did predestinate, then He also called, and whom He called, then He also justified.*

'By-the-by, I heard a story recently. Some years ago, in Waygateshaw, a girl came upon her brother and sister in the family barn, intimately entangled. The sister, sixteen years old, I believe, was mounted on the brother and they were enthusiastically, not to say noisily, swiving. The girl did her duty and advised her parents, and the wanton sister was sent away. Who knows what became of the brother. I shouldn't think he'd wish this episode known, especially if he had a position of prominence. That offence ends in the flames.'

'A curious account, sir. Who would believe such depravity?'

'Always a pleasure to talk, Major. I should let you about your business: no doubt you have much to consider.'

Thomas's sister, also named Margaret, last seen telling tales at Waygateshaw, has married Alexander Weir, a merchant in Carluke, and is now in Edinburgh where Alexander is a bookseller. She avoids Thomas, whom she loathes, but by chance Thomas sees her and Alexander deep in conversation with Aphrêm. Thomas, on private business for the Estates, expects personal catastrophe at any moment. There is no comfort in scripture. He can see no way to deny Aphrêm short of accepting disgrace and bringing about his own death.

At last, he gathers together certain herbs and tinctures, and prepares a decoction which Margaret Burdoun, now approaching sixteen years and quite the young lady, is induced to drink. Thinking they are alone in the house, he pulls aside her shift when she is unconscious. Passionless, he defiles her. There are no whispered encouragements, no intimate caresses of new lovers, no shared smiles as they catch private memories in each other's eyes. There are no gentle explorations of each other's bodies, no meeting of minds in moments of joy as his seed is planted.

Isobel discovers them, too late to save Margaret's virtue, just as her daughter wakes. Margaret wails but Thomas slaps her with a force that shocks in the awful silence of the room. Isobel hurls herself to claw his face but, with battle-practised precision, he takes hold of his walking-staff and swings. The knurled blackthorn pommel hits Isobel's temple as a swat hits a fly. A muffled crack, and Isobel collapses. Thomas turns to Margaret.

'Be silent if you wish to avoid being whipped from Castle to Netherbow. I will be master in this house. I have friends in very high places who will believe any allegation I make against you. You are mine to command: is that clear?'

Isobel wakes, a poultice on her head. She cannot move her neck and knows the damage to her skull is too severe to survive. Once, a visiting merchant gave her a nut, brought from distant islands. The nut was filled with a sweet liquid which one drank after striking the outer shell just *so*. She knows her shell has cracked, falling against the corner of a dresser in a dreadful accident, her neighbours are told, such a shame, and her so young with those lovely girls to bring up. Margaret, withdrawn, and Bethia and Allisoun, distraught at near fourteen and fifteen years respectively, are at Isobel's bedside.

Isobel calls Thomas, who stays in the house to guard his charges against escape.

'You will suffer for this breach of the covenant between us. You will rise high in the eyes of your betters, but the day will come when you burn for your sins. Your name will be blackened the world over by means you cannot begin to imagine. This I have seen.'

'Burn, madam? Seen? What devilry is this? Your brains are addled. I shall not burn, for I am sure of my salvation in the Lord.'

'You poor fool. Ask your friend Aphrêm what I mean, Aphrêm the stepping-maister to whose jolly-tryp you dance. Salvation? By their fruits shall ye know them, sayeth our Lord: your works proclaim the path you have chosen. Listen to me: when snow is on the ground in April you will burn at the Gallow-lee where crowds will taunt you and jeer. When the hangman takes you to be strangled, when you see the tar and coals and torches, you will remember today, and despair of salvation. The flames will take you and your murdering staff, and your ashes will be scattered on the wind without hope of resurrection.'

Margaret, Bethia and Allisoun stay in the house as their circumstances reduce, while Thomas's name rises. Margaret is summonsed to his bed daily until her monthly curse does not come. Two months later, Aphrêm visits and enters uninvited.

'Thomas: you have something for me?'

'I do not.'

'The girl Margaret expects your child?'

'She does, but the seed is recently rooted, it is too soon to be sure of the outcome.' Thomas is in the shadows, smoking his pipe, unable to look Aphrêm in the face. In another room, the sisters listen in silence.

'Very well. 'Tis a pity the dam died, but I will take the girl Margaret.'

'What? That is not our covenant: the babes you said, the babes.'

'And I will have them. How better to preserve my investment? Fetch her.'

'Aphrêm, I—'

'Fetch her or I shall take her. You know the consequence of disobedience.'

A year passes with no word from Margaret who, it is told, eloped with an English soldier who got a child on her.

Bethia is engaged as a maid by her virtuous grandfather John and his formidable second wife Barbara Hamilton.

Allisoun has vanished.

There were reports of Allisoun in Fife and Perthshire. A girl of her description was seen taking ship for Virginia, or possibly Bruges, though it might have been Reval, Cadiz or Bordeaux. Hamburg is mentioned. Thomas suspects Aphrêm has taken her, though the creature denies it, saying he is otherwise occupied with Margaret, a fine broodmare which will shortly be put to stud again to preserve its interesting bloodline.

Thomas lodges at Widow Whitford's house in the Cowgate, and continues his intelligence work for the Estates, taking care to ingratiate himself with the Town Council. In October he is elected to have the charge of the Town Guard, new-formed by Lt. Col. Affleck, whom he replaces. His payment of 11 pounds 2 shillings and thrupence per month makes up for moneys he is still owed for former service. He finds better lodgings and a housekeeper, Bessie Wemys, whom he wastes no time in bedding.

Amongst Isobel's possessions he finds Aphrêm's *visite bilete* and the address of The Leyes. Despite meticulous searching of registers and archives, he can find neither charter nor seisin for the property, which he thinks might be by Carterhaugh, nor reference to Aphrêm in any other records, including the rolls of burgesses and Guild-brethren. There is no record of him having permission to trade in Edinburgh or any other burgh in the Kingdom. Thomas does not need his long years in intelligence to know that this is remarkable, particularly for a foreigner, as Aphrêm surely is.

He has no time to investigate. Come the new year, the King's head is removed at Whitehall, a cruel necessity, says Master Cromwell. Charles II is declared King at the Market

Cross, but amongst the shipmasters and traders of many nations passing through Leith, the talk is only of the execution. The idea that a people might kill their King is not to be contemplated by businessmen who value certainty. The mood is uneasy, especially amongst pious Covenanters like Thomas. The fortifications of Edinburgh and Leith, long in need of repair and maintenance, are strengthened against a day which all expect to come, and Thomas is hard at work.

It is 1650 already, and the great turncoat James Graham, Marquis of Montrose, is brought to Edinburgh for sentence and execution. Thomas is appointed, with Wallace and Colville, to stay with the condemned in the Tolbooth.

Thomas, Captain-Lieutenant Thomas, Major Thomas, who lost too many comrades in the Covenanter cause to Montrose's treachery, takes every opportunity to disturb the condemned man's final hours.

'Major, sir: it would gratify me greatly if you did not smoke tobacco during my prayers.'

'What care I for your gratitude? Tomorrow you will swing from yon gibbet and I will still smoke my pipe in the cause and interest of Christ.'

'Have you no decency sir, even as I prepare to meet God?'

'You made your choices, Mr. Graham, and God deserted you as an apostate and a dog. If you will excuse me, I believe my pipe desires a fill.'

The whole town hears of this. Montrose's old friend and lawyer John Nisbet marks it and does not forget.

Melrose dies in scarlet and lace and dignity, with ribboned shoes over silk stockings, before the large crowd gathered at the new-built scaffold on the High Street. His head soon stares down at the same crowds from its spike on the Tolbooth, beneath which Thomas stands from time to time smoking his pipe.

Thomas exults in the death, even as he gives thanks most earnestly for his own salvation.

Thomas's services are required again as fortifications continue to be repaired, from West Port to Netherbow, despite Cromwell's forces not having left England.

One morning an early visit to Leith takes him and a guard by the Gallow-lee, where an unfortunate is in his final moments, the wirrying garrotte around his neck, the fire well ablaze.

'Who is that poor soul, I wonder?'

'Fiddes, sir. A ploughman from Restalrig. Carnal relations with his master's cow, I believe.'

'A cow? May the Lord have mercy on his unfortunate soul. Whatever could possess him to do that?'

'Who can tell what filthy lusts lurk in the hearts of men sir. Still, at least there are no children at the end of it, eh? No children at the end of it!'

'Indeed, sergeant, when you put it that way, no children.'

'Do you have children sir?'

Thomas watches Fiddes die, and spurs his mount to ride on. He has no wish to watch Fiddes burn for want of children.

Jean comes from Dalkeith to live with Thomas in rooms off Stinking Close by the West Bow. She brings with her a loom and an astringent tongue, and soon comes to his bed, though she always preferred the barn, she says. If she and Bessie are jealous of each other they do not say, and Thomas enjoys them equally.

It occurs to him he has not seen or heard of Aphrêm for some months. Out of uniform and under cover of darkness, Thomas reconnoitres the Grassmarket and Cowgate to find the apothecary's premises closed and barred. He goes home with an unfamiliar lightness in his heart, which Jean and Bessie both observe, and are the happier for.

His intelligence work keeps him occupied. Jean has noticed his lack of diligence in the study of scripture, and is surprised to find herbals and a pharmacopoeia in his small library. She buys him a gift.

'A collection of Mr. Gillespie's sermons? How thoughtful.'

'It can sit on your nightstand, and it's just the right size to go in your bag when you travel.'

Thomas can think of better things to do about the country than read sermons.

Free of Aphrêm, he takes to considering the fate of his soul again. He is certain of redemption, of course. Though he is a murderer twice over and a rapist, he has faith in his Lord's covenant of salvation. But he is haunted by the twitching leg of his unnamed son by Elspeth, and the blank despair on Margaret's face as he gave her to Aphrêm. He opens the book at random and reads,

> *refusers of the covenant and railers against it are justly censured, but withal, if wickedness and malignancy be found in any that have taken the covenant, their offence and censure is not to be extenuated, but to be aggravated.*

He never opens it again.

Neither Jean nor Bessie is likely to bear children but he takes no chances. He reads herbals when he finds them, and listens to stories told in Leith by mariners and whores, women taverners and returning merchants.

In the bottom of his private box he keeps the sample of leaves from the Amazon which Aphrêm once gave him, an aid to prayer and meditation, Aphrêm said. He has never tried them, but today he brews a very small amount, well diluted, and sips with caution, grimacing at the vile bitterness. He is disappointed to feel no effects and drinks off the dregs. He settles into his chair in front of the fire to read his daily Bible passage, which is the Epistle of Paul to the Christians in Corinth, at chapter 13.

Though I speak with the tongues of men and of angels, and have not charity, I am become as sounding brass, or a tinkling cymbal. And though I have the gift of prophecy, and understand all mysteries, and all knowledge; and though I have all faith, so that I could remove mountains, and have not charity, I am nothing. And though I bestow all my goods to feed the poor, and though I give my body to be burned, and have not charity, it profiteth me nothing.

Burned: the word sits proud on the page before him, hovering above the paper like a kestrel above a doomed shrew, shifting pinions and tail. Thomas blinks his eyes and shakes his head.

Burned: the word will not release him from its talons, its beak tears his flesh. He feels vertigo, though he sits in his chair.

Isobel's last words ring as bell changes in the steeple of his mind.

His son's leg twitches.

'Excellent,' says Aphrêm.

When I was a child, I spake as a child, I understood as a child, I thought as a child: but when I became a man, I put away childish things.

He is a child again, named Thomas for his father and grandfather, emulating their ways, learning the noble Borders arts of betrayal and deceit. It is not deeds that matter before God, he is told, but faith: faith alone.

'The same old story,' says a voice behind him, a woman's voice. She does not show herself no matter how he twists and turns. Her disgust is tangible, he feels it slither over him. The patterns of the flames in the hearth configure and transform into shapes that suggest meaning, though he can't interpret them.

Flames.

Burning.

Every moment of his life crowds into his present. Every person he has known, every choice he has made, every person he has killed, is laid before him. Whiskers of fine silk connect every figure and every choice, inexorable and inescapable, though space and time follow no obvious chain of cause and effect. Faith alone, not good deeds, he says to himself, but he knows that he has neither; and if he has neither then what hope has he of redemption? How can there be salvation for such as him? What will keep him from burning?

He is in awe of the immanence that challenges him. In the patterns of possibility, he glimpses the transcendent, and has no other name for it but God. He sees the whole and looks to scripture to interpret what he sees.

The presence offers no further opinion; his audience is over.

When Jean comes home, she finds him still in his chair, eyes closed, Bible open across his knees. She approves. He has possessed her life and her body since she was sixteen and she regrets nothing, save for his wayward piety. They will visit Dalkeith later, he on Estates business, she to see a distant relative. They should be preparing themselves, but she lets him rest a while longer. She finds his cup and the box of strange leaves beside it. Curious, she makes herself a brew, much, much stronger than his. She gulps at it and, too late, tastes it earthen bitterness. She pours it away and rushes to the bucket to vomit.

Once her sickness is past, Jean prepares for the arrival of the coach. By the time it arrives she is seeing visions. Colours flow. Objects lose solidity and speak to her. They say they have no reality but are just energy states in motion, probabilities arrested by her sight. She doesn't understand. Sounds echo and decay, repeating over each other in discordant polyphony. Thomas talks to her. He is a void surrounded by a halo of uncertain hue. His body recedes in foreshortened perspective while his nose looms immense in front of her, as though reflected in a convex glass. The sounds of his mouth are those of gulls nesting in a deep cave: harsh, discordant squawks that rebound once, twice, thrice off the walls.

In the coach she closes her eyes, but the motion rekindles her nausea. The coach is huge and black, drawn by six magnificent coal-black mares with haughty demeanours and braided manes. The coach and horses burn with red and orange flames. Yellow sparks flash where hooves strike the ground. The trees lining the road lean in, peering at her with ligneous eyes. Flies impact on her face. She senses a female presence though she cannot see it – it is always behind her.

In Dalkeith, Jean is found a shady spot outside while Thomas meets intelligencer colleagues and obtains the latest dispatches from England. The news is not good for the Covenanter cause: Cromwell's army has won decisively at Worcester. Thomas must return to Edinburgh immediately with this news. Jean is still gripped by visions, but there is no choice but to leave. On the return journey Jean rambles that she was commanded to speak to the Queen of Pharie, and asks why the horse is burning so.

Burning: why must it always be fire?

The next morning both wake late, in separate beds, separate rooms. Thomas feels inner contentment, despite the news of the defeat. Jean is agitated. When she taught in Dalkeith, she often had visitors to her rooms after she prepared omelettes with wild mushrooms. The visitors came in many forms, once even as a fox, and all told her wild and wonderful tales of hidden worlds around her, and of True Thomas who walked between them. She knew the tales for deceits to trap the virtuous, and the visitors to be emissaries of the Devil.

Nothing confirmed her faith more than to be tempted by spirits as the Lord was tempted in the wilderness. She encountered the transcendent, and has no name for it but Satan.

From that morning, Thomas finds more room in his life for godliness and prayer, she for bitterness and fear.

It is 1669. Thomas and Jean still share rooms in the West Bow, but live as sister and brother only. He is seventy but in good heart. He clings to old ways despite the restoration of the monarchy and the promotion of the enemies of his beliefs to political power. And he still touches the transcendent. He tries to live a prayerful life and bring comfort where he may. The prayers flow from him as a spring of living water, and he is gentle despite his grim features. Angelic Thomas, he is called.

Jean sees the Devil everywhere.

Bethia Burdoun, now married with children, keeps her own counsel but will, when it suits her, let slip information about what Thomas did to Isobel and Margaret twenty years before. Old ears are eager to hear it, biding the days until the long debt falls due.

Winter hardens. Thomas is on his way to a conventicle, where he will lead prayer, when he is seized from behind and pulled into a dark vennel.

'Hello, old friend,' says Aphrêm. 'How very good to find you still alive. A man of prayer now, I hear. The godliest of the Bowhead Saints. A survivor when so many Covenanters are in the ground.

'Do you remember *our* covenant, Thomas? Did you think me gone forever? I need you again. I require another babe of your wife's blood. One of her daughters still lives here. Attend to it. You know the consequences of refusal.'

'I am old, Master Aphrêm, my body fails me. Are you unable to steal babes for yourself?'

'Where would be the fun in that, Major? Far better to enjoy your torment; far better that you are blamed and I am not. Let me know when it is done. My sister will collect the bairn.'

Thomas is released. Aphrêm is nowhere to be seen.

Pleading illness, Thomas walks home, shaken. He opens the locked cupboard at the back of which lies his old box, buried under books and papers. He takes out the last of the *ayawaska* and for the first time in many years makes a brew. He sees again all the moments of his life. Isobel and Margaret stand before him, with Elspeth and his babe. The presence is with him again, silent, questioning, challenging. He recoils from the lick of the flames that wait, the condemnation that will come. He knows the choice he has to make. And what his decision must be.

A deep peace suffuses him as sleep comes. As he slips away, he hears Montrose, reading the poem made the night before his death.

Let them bestow on ev'ry airth a limb;
Open all my veins, that I may swim
To Thee, my Saviour, in that crimson lake.

His son's leg twitches. Isobel says 'you will suffer, Thomas. You will rise high in the eyes of your betters, but the time will come when you burn for your sins. Your name will be blackened the world over by means you cannot begin to imagine. This I have seen. When the snow is on the ground you will burn at the Gallow-lee where the crowds will taunt and jeer at your passing. When the hangman leads you to the stake to be strangled, when you see the tar and wood and torches laid out before you, you will remember what you have done today, and despair of salvation. Then the flames will take you and your murdering staff, and your ashes will be scattered on the wind that blows up from the Forth.'

He must put away childish things. He thinks of faith and works, and the blood in which he swims, though whether to salvation or damnation he does not know. He fears his piety has come too late.

'Too late? That's not how time works,' says a female voice behind him. 'There is more to Being than Time; more to existence than past and present.'

'Isobel said I would burn, without hope of salvation or resurrection'.

'Isobel saw much, but she did not see everything.'

Thomas sleeps a dreamless sleep. At the next prayer meeting, instead of his usual declamation, he sits in a chair in the centre of the worshippers, puts aside his tall hat, and lays his cape on the floor at his side. Closing his eyes, gathering his conviction, he leans forward on his staff and says:

'Friends, I have weighty sins in my heart and on my conscience. They must out. I beg leave to confess my manifest sins to you, though what I tell you means my death.'

Aphrêm watches the flames consume Thomas's remains, but does not wait the full seven hours it will take the corpse to burn away. The crowd soon thins; one burnt old man is much the same as any other. But I stay well into the evening, stay until the hangman rakes over the dying embers. The hangman keeps glancing at me as I step from foot to foot to stave off the cold of snow.

'Who was he to you that you wish to see his ashes?' He shovels the dust into a sack.

'He was my stepfather.'

Unseen by the executioner, Isobel and Margaret stand by me. I see no remnant of Thomas in this or any other world, though my Sight is weak.

I turn to go home, where my husband and bairns wait. There I will take my pen, and ink as black as any crow, and write a letter of thanks to Sir John Nisbet, friend of Montrose, persecutor of Covenanters, and His Majesty's Advocate, for his successful prosecution of Thomas. And a letter to Allisoun with news of Thomas and Aphrêm.

And tonight I will leave a token of thanks to my good neighbour for telling me much of this story, and for her other Gifts.

TWO SPIRITS

Great-great-grandma Sarah had three older brothers. The eldest, Robert, died in a phosgene gas attack at Cambrai in November 1917. His last letter home hinted at what was about to happen: the family Gift in action. He went and did his duty anyway, for which I want to slap his silly face in pride and frustration.

The other brothers, David and Michael, were twins, born in February 1898. I knew a fair amount about David, or thought I did, but nothing about Michael after 1919 when he and David were demobbed. David married and had one child, Charlotte, who I was named after.

Michael disappeared.

I know this because I tried to trace my family tree and my greatest disappointment was my inability to crack the mystery surrounding Michael's disappearance. I'd put what I knew of our family history on various online sites, looking for help, but had no replies.

Aunt Charlotte, my first cousin three times removed, though we never called her anything but aunt, was a harridan, a loathsome creature who found fault with everything I did, never bothering to disguise her contempt. Worse, she doted on my sister, Mary, who received lavish birthday gifts while I was lucky to get a card. One year, when I did get a card, she hadn't managed (or bothered) to sign it.

On the last Sunday of every month, we would all go to Aunt Charlotte's house for a sandwich tea. I hated those ordeals. Her house smelled of stale piss, but my parents insisted we go and accepted no excuse short of serious illness. Faking it was impossible, of course.

Charlotte's health failed while I was a teenager. Mary was already away at university, so help with Charlotte's care fell to me. This meant dropping round on my way to and from school to tidy for her, pushing round an ancient vacuum cleaner that smelled of wet labrador.

Charlotte wore a calliper for most of her life, a gift of the polio that almost killed her when she was little. Latterly she was confined to a wheelchair. Attending to her personal hygiene was embarrassing for us both, but, oddly, we got along much better once we worked through our mutual awkwardness. Despite what happened later, I don't think to this day that she ever liked me much, even though we found something that, ever the optimist, I like to think might have developed into friendship had she lived longer.

As my oldest living close relative, born in 1926, Charlotte told me a lot about the lives and loves of our family through the second half of the twentieth century. She didn't like any of them, and her portraits of relatives and in-laws were often etched in acid. She laid the acid on thicker when I laughed at her character assassinations. I said she should have been a writer. She didn't reply, but bestowed the closest thing to an approving look she ever gave me.

After she died, I found her unpublished manuscripts, increasingly bitter tales of encounters with fairies, told as if autobiographical, and folders of rejection letters. Surprisingly, there were no notebooks, drafts or journals, and her old diaries were only for hairdresser or dental appointments.

She didn't say much about herself, but was more forthcoming about her parents. She claimed not to know anything at all about Michael. She didn't believe her father was a twin until I showed her the birth certificates. I think she told the truth: Michael was erased from family memory with a thoroughness that could only be deliberate. Those who knew him are too dead to ask, especially if your Gift is as weak as mine. Charlotte was also unhelpful about her early life, saying in those days well-behaved middle-class children were seen and not heard, and most definitely not told anything 'juicy'.

I found her sudden death much more upsetting than I expected. Then her lawyer said she'd named me her sole beneficiary in the will I didn't know she'd executed, upsetting Mary, Mum and Dad.

She'd inherited her suburban bungalow from her parents, which they owned outright after coming into money early in their marriage. There were also substantial old investments that sustained Charlotte in comfort all of her life, and would do the same for me if I decided to stop working for a local property company. Charlotte found me that job: she said there was a vacancy and they took me on after no more than a short interview.

I hadn't discussed sexuality, let alone gender, with my parents, and it was great to have somewhere of my own to bring lovers. It's not that I'm promiscuous, or anything like it, but company helps me tune out the noises at night: the slithering brush of leaves against the windows, the creaking pipes and floorboards, the falls of dust in the space between the walls, the sounds of memory trickling into history.

Charlotte's disability kept her out of the attic. I doubt anyone had gone up there since her mother died, and probably for several years before that, because she, too, was infirm in later life. The Ramsay ladder worked, and I poked my head through the hatch into a wonderland of dust and mummified spiders. The ancient light bulb still worked too, and, once the attic was cleaned and vacuumed, I found a well-organised history of the mid-twentieth century middle classes.

The bookshelves were full of worthy volumes presented as school prizes, and low-brow novels, including a large number of spotted and mildewed Agatha Christie and Ngaio Marsh first editions. There were toys, dolls, boxes of cufflinks and collar studs, pen nibs, dolls houses, photographs (framed and in albums), filing cabinets full of household papers, receipts, invoices, and accounts, and all sorts of other paraphernalia and junk. It took three weeks, working in the evenings and at weekends, to go through what was there and sort out what I wanted to keep, what to send to sale rooms or charity collections, and what to throw out.

Toward the turn of the year, when autumn rain turned to winter snow, I checked inside the roof for leaks, poking into the angles and corners by the eaves. That's where the box was tucked away between the joists behind a built-in bookshelf in the corner farthest from the hatch. It was metal and padlocked, with no sign of a key. Excited for valuables. I rushed downstairs and cut the shank of the lock with a hacksaw, ruining two blades.

There *were* valuables, but not what you might expect. Inside was a large, sealed envelope with no writing or other marks on it. On top of the envelope was a copy of *The Machine Gunners' Pocket Book* of 1917. I opened the envelope. Inside was a series of letters from Michael to David, dated between 1919 and 1926, all sent to an anonymous accommodation address in Edinburgh. The postmarks were from across America.

And there was a series of professional photographs, each in a card sleeve with a tissue-paper cover. The photographs were of Michael with Charlie Chaplin, Buster Keaton, Edna Purviance, Mary Pickford, Ben Turpin, Mabel Normand, Fatty Arbuckle and a slew of other silent movie stars I didn't recognise and whose signatures I couldn't decipher. On the reverse of each, presumably in the hand of the pictured actor, was a personalised inscription to David. I don't know much about that stuff, but I did think they might be worth something. My fingers tingled when holding the semi-formal shots of a very young Fay Wray at the beach wearing not much more than a smile and a yard or so of carefully draped crêpe de chine. It was signed by both Wray and the photographer.

No one had ever mentioned these before. Maybe no one knew about them except David, who disappeared behind German lines in 1942. There was mystery there: his service records for both World Wars are missing, as are Michael's for WW1. Another relative, Captain Walter Pitcairn, my second cousin twice removed, also died in WW2. Charlotte thought Walter was something in intelligence, and was there when they discovered the concentration camps, but I haven't traced that branch of the family yet.

Michael's handwriting was a louche, loping scrawl in faded blue ink, and difficult to read. I asked for a long weekend from work. The owner, an odd old man called Ephraim, wasn't available. His assistant, Margaret, was not only happy to let me have the time off, but, when I told her about Michael and the Hollywood connection, was fascinated to find out what the letters said. My colleague Ryan was happy to cover for me and pick up a little overtime into the bargain.

I hadn't expected it to be so easy to get the time off. Margaret is pleasant and easy to work for, but has a reserve about her, a quiet watchfulness that can be unnerving. There's something not quite right about Ephraim and

Margaret. Maybe that's why they're management and I am just a trainee.

Anyway, this has all been a way of introducing the transcribed letters.

25 December 1919

At Sea

Ahoy! And Merry Christmas!

Well, what a farrago of nonsense, not to say unpleasantness, that was. You would have thought after risking the lot for King and Country and making it through the 'flu, not to mention the attentions of the shrinks, the old folks would be so delighted to see us again that any of my little *improprieties* would be overlooked, especially after Bobby copped his packet.

Apparently not.

Have they spoken to you again yet? How convenient that I should simply disappear.

Bitter? Me? Yes, actually, I am. I didn't think Ma and Pa would go so far as to approve, but I did think they might turn a blind eye for once, if only out of gratitude for the return of two thirds of their complement of sons. Still: no good crying over spilt milk, eh? I'd rather be in Blighty but here I am, out on the mid-Atlantic in December, disowned, dishevelled and dyspeptic, cast onto the cruel seas of fate.

O! Me miserum!

Never fear: I have landed on my feet. There is an absolutely *charming* young waiter in the first-class restaurant to whom I poured out my sorrows over left-over Montrachet and oysters. And his old chap! My God it's a thing of beauty, a real liver lifter. I don't know if travel really does broaden the mind, but it certainly broadens the sphincter!

Pip Pip! I'll send you a proper letter from New York once I am settled and have a return address.

Don't do anything I wouldn't do!

Your brother

Michael

14 September 1920

Dearest David

Thank you for your last and your concern. Yes, I am growing used to exile, after a fashion, but it's good to hear how things are at home, particularly with Sarah. If you could find a way of assuring her of my affections without giving the game away, I should be grateful.

Sorry not to have replied *toot-sweet*, as the Froggies say, but things have been decidedly rum.

I am loath to write this, but I think our mutual friends will have to be told.

God, David, I thought all that Excalibur stuff was behind me.

I got out of that situation in New York and used some of my immoral earnings to beat a hasty retreat to St Louis. I didn't expect a problem finding work or, failing that, a *patron* to cover my expenses in return for discreet favours. I had a quick short arm inspection too, just in case I had any unwanted souvenirs of New York which, thank God, I had not. Things were looking promising until some hoodlums took a fancy to my wallet and duffed me up rather. The medics did enough to patch me up then tossed me out.

I couldn't find casual work in the following days, walking wounded and all that, and I'd no money to keep my lodgings, and for obvious reasons would not accept the offer of a cheap room in the landlord's cellar. So I gathered up my pack and found a billet, dug in under the stanchions of a railway bridge. I laid doggo there for a while. It was worse in France, of course, and at least there weren't Alleymen lobbing whizz-bangs at me. Not too many of the recently dead hanging around either, which was a blessing. The odd thing was, my first night in that little fox-hole provided me the best night's sleep I've had since we first went to the front, as if I'd come home to my childhood bed. God knows why, after Wypers.

I dreamt of Bobby, too. I don't remember the detail, and it was just a dream not the other stuff, but there was comfort in it.

Heaven knows I have no cause to remember the trenches with fondness, but I think I left something behind there. For a short time in that hole I almost thought I had it back, as though whatever I am trying to put behind me is the very thing for which I am searching. As I said, decidedly rum.

And there was a coyote. David, it was magnificent, sitting there as bold as you like in a railroad siding, its fur mesmerising, the dusty shades shifting with the dappled refractions and reflections of the early morning sun. No mange I could see. There was white fur around its muzzle and around its eyes. At first I thought it was a large dog because it looked like it was wearing a collar, but it was just darker colouring around its neck. It stared me straight in the eye before it padded off into the shadows.

A girl was bunkered a hundred yards or so from me. I noticed her because it was obvious the poor thing was up the duff. She was of African family, young, under twenty at any rate, in shabby clothes. She made no attempt to speak to me or anyone else. No sign of any young men visiting, though I noticed one or two of her ancestors trying to get through to her.

A scuffle broke out soon after sundown on my fourth night. A man and a woman were hauling the preggers lassie off towards a black motor car, a limousine as they call them here.

It was *them,* David. I'd know their 'feel' anywhere even if it weren't for the ears.

I'm sorry to say I panicked and made a dash for it. Stupid, of course, although I hope understandable. One of them turned and came towards me, a ruddy great knife pulled out of a sheath on her belt.

I ran like billy-o in the opposite direction. She didn't run but, somehow, gained on me. I thought I was a goner, like poor old Bertie Jenkinson and that odd chap from the café at Amiens.

I managed to grab a handrail and scramble aboard a goods train pulling out of the yard. She stopped and jotted something down in a notebook, then turned back the way she had come.

I hopped off at the next chance, a marshalling yard somewhere, crossed the tracks, and clambered onto another train heading off in a different direction. I changed trains and direction again around two hours later, and then sat pat until evening when it slowed outside a town. I don't know which town. I jumped off and walked parallel to the track for a while, keeping under cover until I came to the edge of a large goods yard where a lot of other fellows were gathered around a fire.

I was in such a blue funk I'm surprised I got that far. Those *things*, well, you know what I mean. I suppose it proves once and for all the Yanks were mistaken (or lying) when they said it was strictly a European problem.

Three black limousines drew into the goods yard. Damn me if the occupants didn't jump out and start to search the train I had just got off, while a couple of bruisers went to the crowd round the bonfire.

I made myself scarce and set up as per field training. They searched every wagon, then reported back to an individual who had stayed by the car. It was the creature with the knife. She had a child with her, a female of her own kind. I couldn't risk scanning her, but I could see the ears in the half-light even at that distance. They stood for a full minute, peering into the darkness all around. I dropped and could sense their gaze as it swept over my head. I had not the slightest doubt they were hunting me.

I held my position for five minutes more, until a commotion made me raise myself to a low crouch to see what was happening. Several railroad bulls arrived and set about the hobos with staves, laying into them hard.

I backed into the night, at a crouch. I was 200 yards into the trees when the first shots echoed in the night.

Christ, David, it was the front all over again, clinical, casual, routine: the arms reaching for heaven, bodies slack, eyes vacant, take no prisoners, leave no witnesses. The bulls finished off any who still twitched, then wandered off, leaving the earth to soak up the poor sods who copped it, just like those Bosche lads we did for at Bapaume while they cried for their mothers.

I know you'll have to pass this information on, but I'm not ready to face the Excalibur mob again, any more than I need to encounter PTAs again. I'm going to disappear for a while after I send this, as much to avoid old comrades as old foes. I'll write again when I'm able.

As Ever

Michael

3 December 1920

Dearest David

It seems a while ago now, but I promised you a further letter and here it is.

I've had plenty of time to reflect on what happened and what it might mean for me given all that happened before. I daresay I'll write some more about that one day, but for now I'll keep this factual. Just as I did in my last, I assume 'old colleagues' have an interest in what I write and have set it down accordingly.

After the carnage of the railroad yard I lay low. I had no idea what the creatures were up to, and of course they might have human familiars. I was very hungry. I stayed on foot and managed to steal food from farms. I was filthy, so I stole clothes too before bathing in brackish water, well off the beaten track. It might have been easier had I used my Gift, but, well, that's a hole I don't want to go down again.

Eventually I jumped on a northbound train, then another going westwards, into the evening sun. I reckoned the risk was slight, given I looked like a typical railroad bum, bearded and scruffy and no doubt smelling pretty ripe as well. I settled down in a corner. When I woke I wasn't alone.

He was in the opposite corner of the boxcar from me, looking me over like a critic examines a painting, appraising, keen eyes behind the fringe of his shoulder-length hair which, unlike mine, was clean and glossy. I pulled my knees to my chest and looked back. After a time he tossed an apple at me and, without a word, wrapped himself in a blanket, put his head on his pack, and fell straight to sleep.

He was nothing like the caricatures. No feathered head-dress or buckskins, no war paint on his cheeks, no moccasins on his feet. Just another working stiff, as they say here.

The boxcar kept up a loud rattling on frankly haphazard tracks through unidentified terrain. Despite the noise, the clatter and sway of the carriage lulled me towards sleep and I almost didn't hear the two men who ran along the roof and swung in through the open door. They made no threats, issued no taunts, didn't say anything at all actually. They ignored my sleeping companion. They couldn't both rush me in the space, so one came straight at me with a knife.

The old training kicked in. He made an amateurish slashing motion and I grabbed his out-swinging forearm, stepped through, and twisted the arm as far as I could up his back. He screamed and let go of the knife which I caught and sliced through his throat as I kicked the legs from under him.

The other fellow's revolver had snagged on his belt so I rushed him, stabbed the knife up beneath his ribs and twisted the blade. It was over before I had time to think. I took his gun and ammunition. and put them and the knife on my pack. I fleeced them for cash, and pocketed what they had.

They were human. Their ghosts stood over the corpses with comical surprise on their faces.

My new companion had not moved except to open his eyes and watch the fight. I got the oddest impression I'd passed some sort of test. He stood up and dropped the thugs' bodies onto the track. As the train rounded a long curve, damn me if I didn't see that coyote again, I recognised the collar fur. It trotted out of the trackside undergrowth towards the still-warm corpses.

'That coyote will make short work of them,' I said.

He looked at me with curiosity.

'What coyote?'

I'm afraid I'm out of paper and want to get this off to you as soon as possible. I'll write again as soon as I have opportunity. I don't know when it will reach you, but all best wishes for Christmas and the New Year.

Your Brother

Michael

30 September 1921

Minneapolis

Dearest David

My apologies for not writing sooner (has it really been a year?) but I've been somewhat peripatetic. I hope you weren't too worried by my silence. Alas, I can't provide you with an address for correspondence yet.

I'm delighted to say there's been no more unpleasantness. I still jump at shadows from time to time, but so far so good. Silly, really, after everything we did. Or maybe not. I remember those other poor fellows up at Craiglockhart.

I'm employed, though I dare say Ma and Pa would not approve. Joe, my Indian companion from the train, was on his way to a travelling carnival and circus. He performs under the soubriquet 'Injun Joe' and seems content for everyone to call him that. I picked up work in the same troupe on his recommendation, which seemed to carry some weight.

My duties vary, mostly labouring, putting up and hauling down the big top and other sideshows, and some gate work when the crowds get too rowdy, giving any trouble makers the bum's rush. Don't believe all you might have heard about prohibition over here: there is plenty of booze for those who want it, which is nearly everyone. For some reason, Joe thought I should try some kind of mentalist act, but I couldn't face the thought and faked my way through failing an audition. The last thing I want to do is to encourage this wretched family curse.

Anyway, after my last, we travelled together as far as Rapid City, South Dakota, where Joe met some of his own people, a meeting from which I was politely excluded. From there we made our way by horse to where the Circus was set up, before coming back east with them by train.

The carnies are fabulous people, David, figuratively and literally. Ma and Pa would be horrified to know who my companions are: giants and dwarfs, women (bearded, bald and tattooed, choose any two from three), men with vestigial tails, animal wranglers, bear wrestlers, acrobats, wire-walkers, card-sharps, a mind reader, a fortune teller with a touch of the real stuff about her, and clowns. Wonderful people all, with a great camaraderie; grand companions as we criss-cross this huge country.

My pay isn't brilliant, but food and accommodation are provided so I can't complain. Also, I have found it easy to find *companions* on my travels, many of whom are happy to pay for the privilege, especially in the more puritan towns. Anywhere with a surfeit of churches pretty much guarantees rough trade and a healthy supplement to my income, often lifted from the collection plate by the preachers. Imagine what they'd make of that at Greenbank!

Joe, with whom I share a billet but not a bed, knows my nature and seems remarkably unconcerned, saying only that I have two spirits and should take care to be true to both.

I'm not sure if we'll winter here, but if we do I'll let you know an address for return letters.

Your Brother

Michael

17 July 1922

Montana

Dearest David

In haste.

It was midnight on the outskirts of Helena. I was under starlight when an engine roared up from the town. A black automobile, driving with dipped lights, sped towards us and, so help me, every sense I had told me the child from the hobo jungle was in it. This time I had no escape route.

I crouched in the shadows of a caravan, frozen, trying to pretend I wasn't there, trying not to think about Ypres, and what we found. When the limousine drove by without slowing, I made up my mind PDQ and grabbed my old haversack into which I stuffed some essentials. I still had the gun and the knife. Joe wasn't there and wouldn't notice my absence for several hours, he was used to it. I checked the tank of a motorcycle and set off in the opposite direction to the limousine. I kept my lights off and used dead-reckoning until I reached the road heading west.

I stopped once, to write this note, which I will post at the next opportunity.

Will it always be like this? Will I always be running from them?

Your Brother

Michael

PS Thank you for your last, which eventually found me. My congratulations to you and Isobel. Please accept my genuine best wishes for your future life together.

15 September 1922

[postmarked Oregon]

My Dearest David

Once again, my apologies for tardiness. As you probably guessed, I went to some lengths *again* to make myself scarce. This is to let you know I am safe and well.

I do not enclose a return address – I do not want to let my whereabouts out of the bag, and you shouldn't rely on the postmark.

I have had no further encounters.

Despite the difficulties which it should cause, I am giving serious consideration to a return to Blighty. Also, despite the promises I swore when we were demobbed, I have reacquainted myself with the Gift, which brings surprising comfort. There is a deep peace in the heart of this country: sometimes when deep in meditation, I feel I am in touch with something ancient and abiding, which brings welcome respite. I don't suppose what we did, what happened, will ever leave me, nor, perhaps, should it. But for the first time I allow myself some hope I might be reconciled to it.

Now the hard part, although, as I come to write this, I don't find it as difficult as I expected. I was not as honest with you as I should be. Nor as honest with myself. Since Ma and Pa threw me out, I've had dreams most nights, and some days too if I let myself drift. They are always the same, the same as the ones I had in the hospital, always that damned cellar and what we found there. But this time we couldn't get away.

Since St Louis, the creature with the knife and the strange child have always been there too.

Anyway, since tapping into the Gift again, the dreams have stopped. Well, almost.

There are odd perspectives to be had, working in the great redwood forests: I often wonder what it would be like to be as old as these trees, to live through time while all about is constant change. Is it really constant change, do you think? Or do things really just stay the same and only seem to change because our lives are so short and we mistake transience for long-term shifts? Is it the Gift prompting these thoughts? I don't know.

Sometimes, I think Bobby is with me. Ridiculous, of course, I am far, far from where his spirit lingers, but I feel his presence sometimes. You remember how he used to be, especially after he discovered that damned Indian treacle.

Your Brother

Michael

16 March 1923

[postmarked California]

My Dearest David

Once again, my apologies for a long gap between letters. What can I say? I lay doggo in the backwoods and kept a very low profile. I've worked my way south towards the sun. It was a hard winter and I shall be glad of the warmth.

Anyway, this lets you know I'm still alive. There have

been no further incidents and the Gift continues to bring comfort.

Your Brother

Michael

31 October 1923

Hollywood, Los Angeles

My Dearest David

I think my luck might be turning!

After my last, I grew rather tired of the backwoods life, and a conviction grew that, instead of running and hiding from things, I should begin to move *towards* something, though I had no idea what.

The isolation meant I managed save positively *loads* of cash, enough seriously to consider jacking it all in over here. I finally ditched that old motorcycle from the circus and splashed out on a new machine of my own. I know you won't be interested in the details, but it is an absolute smasher! Amusingly, after my time with Joe, the marque is *Indian*. I chose it with long distance riding in mind.

I rode south and picked up a hitch-hiker on the way, a sweet young thing called Wilma off to audition for the motion picture industry in Hollywood. We got quite chatty, especially when she worked out I wasn't a threat to what remained of her virtue. The stories she told me about actors! I was shocked, David, shocked! Even I, decorated veteran of innumerable depravities. Well obviously I had to come and see for myself.

I found work with a company that services the swimming pools all the film stars and executives regard as *de rigueur* for an agreeable life. In the heat I would turn up at the house in overalls and promptly strip down to shorts and singlet while working.

Bingo!!

After all those months labouring I am in pretty buff order, though I say it myself, and everything Wilma said was true. My God, they were all over me. After a long drought, a veritable flood. Men and women both, and you wouldn't believe who I'm talking about! Well, I soon found myself *very* popular once word of my tastes got around. I was even offered a screen-test by one particularly tasty young director whom I encouraged to have his wicked way with me on the couch in his office, common practice, you may be surprised to hear.

No go on the screen idol front, I'm afraid, but if you look closely at crowd scenes you may spot a familiar face!

I can make a *much* better living catering to the 'needs' of the industry than I from cleaning their swimming pools. Suffice to say, there is plenty of scope here for an enterprising young Scot to establish and develop a thriving business and rake in the clams.

My address is enclosed and also some photographs of some of the stars. Not all of these are my clients, but you can have fun divining which amongst them is!

Your Brother

Michael

17 October 1924

Hollywood, Los Angeles

My Dearest David

Many thanks for your last and the photographs from your wedding: you both look simply *ravishing*. I had one of them framed and it has pride of place on my office wall, where I see it whenever I look up from my desk.

I very much regret I was unable to be there. I had a notion to attend in some sort of disguise, but of course that would be impossible. I hope the gift I sent will go some way towards setting you and Isobel up in the style you deserve.

I'm pleased you appreciate the photographs, even though you cannot share them. I enclose several more, including one with that insufferable little prick Chaplin who seems to think an autographed photograph is a fair price for my silence on other matters, which it is not. Also, amongst the many hucksters, charlatans, chancers and cheats out here, there are some, usually the technical bods, who actually care about their craft and have pretensions to art, and I enclose one or two early portraits of a teenage aspirant by one of them, a fellow called Mortensen who turns out clever work when he puts his mind to it.

Business is thriving. The town is always full of young men and women who will go to *any* lengths to establish a foothold in the 'movies', and I can cater to the most *esoteric* requirements of my clientele, although I draw the line at some requests. Some of my clients have no scruple about taking advantage of their young admirers, and for some the younger the better, I regret to say. I simply *refuse* to supply those needs, though I confess I have on occasion allowed my silence to be bought.

Does that shock you? It shocks me. I have since learned, I am happy to say, the Gift is useful for selecting both 'employees' and clients.

I've put aside any thoughts of returning to Blighty for the moment. Although this is a pretty disreputable business to be in, I am accruing far too much moolah to walk away. The stock market here is absolutely *roaring* ahead with no signs of stopping and I already have a quite satisfactory sum invested on the New York Markets. I reckon I should be able to come home in style around 1930, only six years away now. I have a mind to earn enough to retire early to a life of genteel debauchery somewhere in the Home Counties, if not Morningside.

My best wishes to you both.

Your Brother

Michael

17 September 1926

Hollywood, California

My Dearest David

Many, many congratulations. Charlotte is *such* a lovely name. I hope you and your family continue to thrive.

It is with some trepidation at such a happy time that I raise other matters, and yet I must. It relates once again to our war service and to earlier events. Although you never confirmed it, I continue to assume you retain contact with our former comrades. As you know, I hold them in no particular regard (I know that's a bit rich from someone in my business), but even greater than my distaste for former comrades is my dislike for those *creatures,* and what follows may, or may not, be relevant intelligence.

I have a high turnover of 'employees'. Some find the requirements disagreeable and go home; some find success on the screen and try to pretend this is due to their acting talent alone; some, alas, come to unpleasant ends. Never doubt, David, that this town is anything other than a gigantic bordello, saturated in alcohol, narcotics and desperate egos. The addled corpses of the bright and beautiful are daily found abandoned in motel rooms, or at the foot of that damned new sign on the hill.

At any rate, I'm accustomed to employees moving on. Most have the decency to let me know they are leaving, even if only to secure any fees I owe them.

A steady number of women leave, temporarily or permanently, because they are up the spout. If the putative father is sufficiently *stellar,* the studio may pay for a private clinic to attend to matters. In those cases I always know of the progress of my employees. Lately I have found a rise in the number of such women who simply disappear. I only noticed because, in all cases, they were girls for whom I had no family information. Perhaps others wouldn't have thought it significant; my Gift said otherwise. So I made a point of keeping a particular eye on the girls of whom I knew little, and tried to get more information from them about their backgrounds and, to be indelicate, their next of kin.

Two months ago, another of these girls disappeared; eighteen (she said), pretty, rootless, and pregnant. I tried to find her with the Gift without success. Wherever she was, she was beyond my meagre reach. But I did feel a familiar presence at the outer edge of my perception. It was just the faintest touch, but quite unmistakeable.

There's something else.

I grew curious about my old circus companions, and hired a private investigator to see what he could find out for me. I handed him a pack of lies about wanting to check the references of a potential business partner. He made the strangest report back.

It seems that our company had a dark reputation for leaving mysterious disappearances in its wake, especially of pregnant girls in nearby towns. Eventually word reached the owners and the show closed, and the performers went their separate ways. You'll be ahead of me, no doubt: I put two and two together and made Ypres. With each passing day my certainty grows that the creatures harvest children in America too.

One other thing. Last Sunday evening, I was by the pool reading the trade papers when there was a disturbance in the surrounding hedgerow. The coyote stood there watching me, the very same coyote from St Louis and the train: I know its markings. It watched me for a while then loped away.

The upshot of all this is that I am setting my affairs in order and will soon leave Hollywood. I will advise of my plans in a further letter. For obvious reasons, I felt obliged first to set this down.

Your Brother

Michael

21 September 1926

Hollywood, Los Angeles

My Dearest David

Since my last, events have moved at quite a lick. My financial affairs are in order, and I have arranged the sale of my business interests in their entirety to a competitor. It was not difficult: I have always supposed that my life here might come to a sudden end for one reason or another, and it seems I was right.

My attorney will put my property on the market and has instructions to remit all of the proceeds of sale, which I expect to be substantial, to you. I've also liquidated my stock holdings. I should be grateful if you could put some of it into trust for the benefit of Sarah, and some also into another trust for Charlotte and any other children who bless your marriage. My attorney, whose business card is enclosed, has a copy of my Will, which I executed yesterday.

What has happened?

After posting my last, I took it into my damn-fool head to send my driver away and walk back to my office. I had only a moment's warning of the two thugs lurking at the entrance to an alleyway. I dealt with one of them quickly, but his colleague was smarter, and this time there was no snagging belt. A pistol was already drawn and aimed at me while I tackled the other chap. It was obvious I was a goner, and I smiled, I think, at surviving the trenches only to buy it from a bullet in a back-lot. In the same moment, as though it mattered, I took in all of the squalid circumstances of my death, the obscene daubs on the brick walls, dog-dirt amongst the litter, the strange beauty of flowering weeds rooted in the gutters above me. I remember the look on my assailant's face when he saw me smile. He hesitated, and that was fatal.

The coyote took out his throat.

The dead men had no wallets or other identification, so it looks like a professional job, presumably set up by some new fellows trying to move into my business.

I wasn't surprised when the coyote appeared again at my house later that evening. I *was* surprised it brought Injun Joe along too.

I sat on a low wall on my patio as Joe told me a lot of things, of which I have time to write only a few. It seems we both had our secrets: amongst his own people he is a person of some importance, the word he used was shaman, and he said he recognised me as a kindred spirit from the beginning. This was confirmed for him when I saw the coyote and he could not. The coyote is an animal of very great significance for his people, it seems. The meeting in Rapid City after I met him was to discuss what to do with me. They decided to watch me for any further signs of abilities. He did not expect me to leave abruptly (I haven't yet told him why I did) and has searched for me ever since. He came to Hollywood when he spotted me as an extra in a movie. The coyote showed itself and led him to me.

That's the gist of it at any rate. I'll tell you the rest when I next write.

I told him I was moving on. I told him of my Gift (I did not mention the family). He made an offer which, as some of my shadier associates would say, is hard to refuse: to take me to a gathering of his people, where I could meditate with them. All he will tell me of the gathering is it will be in a sacred place in the High Sierra, in a grove of ancient yew trees his people have tended for centuries, if not millennia.

I told you in previous letters of the comfort I have found in the Gift. I've begun to trust in its judgement. Perversely, after my previous attempts to ignore it, it was silent on the decision I had to make, although I perceived uncertainty about where this will all lead. I found the uncertainty intriguing.

So I will go with Joe to this ancient yew grove. We leave first thing in the morning. I will arrange for my assistant to post this, and I shall write again as soon as I am able.

Your Brother

Michael

That was the final letter. I didn't know what to make of it all – not just Michael's story, but the implications about his military service, the Gift, and David. I picked up *The Machine Gunners' Pocket Book* and flicked through its pages. Further pages were neatly folded in a paper wallet stuck inside the back cover. David's signature was on the upper right of the first page of the *Pocket Book*. One of the documents, unsigned and undated, was in the same handwriting. It read:

At 19.30 hrs. we received an order to hold our position and dig in. Due to persistent heavy rain, the trenches were flooded and the berms treacherous, making digging impossible. Visibility was poor, estimated 15 to 30 yards (variable). There was sporadic sniper activity by the enemy and some whizzbanging. The men were lacking food, sleep and ammunition with no prospect of re-provision.

In accordance with sealed orders, I proceeded alone to reconnoitre the immediate vicinity. Circumstances were not ideal due to both physical conditions and the overwhelming presence of the recently dead. Assessment of the disposition and intentions of the enemy proved impossible.

Pursuant to Standing Order 14/5/d – Supplementary, of April 1915 (as amended), I record hereby my awareness of an unidentified presence within the range of my perception. The contact terminated abruptly.

My brother Michael, joined me and we conducted the investigation together. We found the remains of a farmhouse and outbuildings, reduced to charred rubble. Both Michael and I felt the site was of significance.

We uncovered the entrance to the farmhouse cellar. Inside we found what I presume to be the former inhabitants of the farm: an adult male and female, both in advanced stages of decomposition. Each had been decapitated. Present also were the remains of five children (four male, one female), similarly mutilated and also in advanced states of decay. One child, an infant, was alive but enclosed in a contraption of brass and leather which held in place what appeared to be syringes and tubes through which its blood was draining. The contraption was operated by a PRIORITY TARGET ALPHA which I exterminated forthwith.

Michael moved to examine the infant, but was attacked by a second PRIORITY TARGET ALPHA that emerged from a recess. I killed that creature too, but not before it had sunk its teeth into Michael's neck.

We left the cellar with the infant, still in the contraption, and the heads of the two creatures.

I exercised my delegated authority to return to EXCALIBUR field command to make this report and await further orders. Michael was moved from the field hospital to be repatriated as a matter of urgency to specialist facilities in Craiglockhart, Edinburgh. The infant, the contraption and the heads of the creatures were remitted to the custody of EXCALIBUR Command.

I ordered an artillery bombardment to sterilise the discovery site.

Respectfully submitted, etc.

Clipped to the manuscript were a death certificate for Michael, a telegram advising the Menzies family of Michael's death in combat, and a letter of condolence from his commanding officer. None were signed or dated.

A quick search on the internet gave no leads to Excalibur Special Operations, and Dad said they meant nothing to him either.

Margaret called to see how the transcription had gone. It turns out old Ephraim is something of a silent movie buff and is quite keen to see the letters and photographs too. They were insistent. I remembered their extended earlobes, and, following a strong instinct, packed a bag and left by train for London.

This morning, on a whim, I bought a cheap phone and called the public contact number of the Security Services. I said I'd found papers indicating my relatives were involved in military intelligence, and that they might be best placed in an official archive. The person on the other end of the line thanked me and said she'd alert the archivists. She had never heard of Excalibur but that wasn't unusual given the poor records from the period.

It wasn't more than twenty minutes later someone called back asking me if I could drop by MI5 headquarters this afternoon with the letters, to meet an archivist. I'm about to go there now, but not before I've called in at an auction house to have the photographs appraised and valued.

SOFT SINGS THE RIVER

It happened like this.

Ba Ren sat down to rest in the shade of a banyan tree. He was tired and overheated. His coarse robes chafed his dry skin and made weeping lesions that stung his dusty flesh. Perhaps the hallucinations would soon come back.

He untied his shabby pack and examined the contents again. However often he looked, it did not get any better; his spare robes were as filthy and infested as those he wore. He fingered the rough-sewn seams and hems, checking the weave, sweeping away the lice and their eggs he found there.

There was movement to his left, a lizard, about a foot and a half long, dusty of skin and black of eyes. The beast stood still, aware of him. It was the first living creature, apart from birds, Ba Ren had seen for days.

'So, Mr. Lizard, I am in a quandary. What do you think I should do: stay here and die of thirst, or walk to yonder mountains and hope to find water on the way?'

'Mountains, Mr. Monk? My eyes are too small and close to the ground to see that far.'

Ba Ren looked at the creature.

'My fever is returning; I could have sworn you spoke.'

'Of course I spoke! You asked, I replied. What should I have done?'

'You might have ignored me. Forgive me, I've never heard of a talking lizard before.'

'Well that's hardly my fault. And anyway, who would tell their friends they'd met a talking lizard? No one would believe them.'

However much Ba Ren considered it, and he'd considered it many times, he could not think of any notable ability he possessed, despite long years of training, despite endless privations and purgings of body and mind, despite all the manifold precursors of Enlightenment. He was sure he would remember if he had spoken to a lizard.

He was not Enlightened either.

And he was hungry. Although he found fasting and abstinence difficult, divine irony decreed he was now a living embodiment of the ascetic ideal: gaunt and hollow-bellied, skin as cracked as the dry mudflats shimmering away into the hazy middle-distance. He ought to meditate, but meditation was hard, more so when his mouth and throat were parched, when the ache in his empty stomach was permanent, when his head pounded. As he did every quarter hour of every day, he agonised over whether if it would be wrong to kill the lice infesting the cloth; once again he decided, to his regret, it would, for all things have their place in the circle of life.

Ba Ren and the lizard studied each other in silence, the creature's face impassive save for the slow flicking of nictating membranes. The lizard, it seemed to him, was much more appetising than the handful of lice he let live. He suppressed the idea, trying to blank his mind lest the gods hear, then was embarrassed by his superstition.

He had not met another human for two months, he reckoned, and hadn't seen much other life either, apart from the scrubby vegetation that somehow clung to existence.

Even scavengers were scarce, the ubiquitous black kites seen only as distant specks in open blue skies.

'I don't know, Mr. Lizard, whether you spoke to me, or if my brain is addled. In either case, greetings: it is a pleasure to meet a fellow survivor. How have you managed?'

The lizard shifted its balance, its tongue flicking to test the air.

'I have certain advantages. I can survive far longer without water than you, and there is no shortage of flies and insects for me to eat. Frankly, I am much more surprised to see you: you are the first living human I have seen for a long time.'

Ba Ren didn't understand why he, alone of all the monks, survived the great pestilence. His brother monks were much worthier: more noble in their devotion, further advanced along the path towards Enlightenment. But every single one died in the first week of the plague. Their deaths were quick, often less than a day after the first symptoms manifested. They were moral, learned and pious. They faced their end in virtuous ways: with courage rather than weeping, with calmness rather than distress, with prayer rather than curses.

It made no difference: they all died.

He was no better than a journeyman monk, his teachers said. Ba Ren the Dreamer: devout, diligent and harmless. He was easily distracted when meditating, renowned for fumbling clumsiness as he did his chores around the monastery. There was no meal he could not burn, no ritual he could not garble. He could not discern eternal truths in the words of the scrolls. His singing was a quarter tone flat amongst the rich tenors and baritones of his fellows.

He endured fever and delirium for four days, then woke on his pallet to find himself alone. Perhaps there was a reason why he was spared, or perhaps it was chance. He did not know.

'Do you have a name, Mr. Lizard? I am Ba Ren, and am pleased to make your acquaintance.'

'No. We lizards have no possessions, not even a name to call our own.'

'Then you are a better monk than me. Perhaps that is what I have done wrong: I have clung to my name.'

'What is this 'wrong'?' Said the lizard. 'Either you are alive or you are not; you are hungry or you are not. What has a name got to do with it?'

'Perhaps I shouldn't be surprised by your question: you are just a lizard, after all, and I have spent many years trying to meditate on these things.'

'Just a lizard? Just a lizard? What do you mean by that?'

Ba Ren paused and stared through the liquid horizon, remembering.

In the first days after waking, he expected some relief to come from beyond the monastery walls. The complex was remote and supplies came only once every week, so he was not concerned. He set about his duties with his usual diligence, setting pyres for the bodies of his brothers, burning incense to their memory, praying for their safe passage to the next life. He slept more than usual and his dreams were fevered because the sickness lingered, but there was sufficient stored rice and grain to feed him, and the well gurgled and gushed when he pumped the lever.

After two weeks of solitude, the time had come to pack food and a flask of water and make the descent to the nearest village. The rough path meandered alongside a stream, which seemed less forceful than usual as it ran over and between boulders. Red-whiskered bulbuls washed and preened in shallow pools, scattering into the higher branches of rubber trees at the sound of his footsteps. The flecks of light dancing in the splashing water reminded him of something, though he could not pin down the memory;

something from home, before the monastery. Generations of monks had created and tended famous water gardens along the route of the path, forcing harmonic order onto the landscape, domesticating the chaotic precision of nature. He did not approve, but never found the courage to say so.

The village held only distended and burst corpses, their stench heavy in the foetid air. The remains were defiled by vermin, many of which also lay dead and bloated.

Wrapping a damp cloth around his mouth and nose, Ba Ren built several pyres and dragged the decomposing bodies to them. All afternoon the smell of burning flesh embraced him as a mother clings to her child in a crowd. The sickly perfume permeated to his clothes, infusing his sweat as he climbed the long path back to the monastery. When he could suffer his stink no more, he immersed himself in a pool, scattering carp and terrapins. The cleansing flow of a cascade parted about his head and sluiced away the aromatic remnants of the dead.

For a further week he observed the daily rites in the temple and tried to meditate, preparing simple meals only when needed. But, at last, he decided to walk to the nearest other monastery, fifty miles away. He secured the temple treasures as best he could, and made his final bows to the great statues of the Buddha and the bodhisattvas. He asked for the protection of the Guardians of Heaven and all the immortals. He took particular care to cover the magnificent fresco of scenes in the life of Queen Maya, the virgin mother of Buddha, the like of which was to be found nowhere else east of the mountains.

His first calling to become a monk came in a vivid dream. He couldn't remember the details when he woke, yet it made a deep impression on him. He woke knowing he wanted to follow a reflective path. Something about the fresco reminded him of that forgotten dream: the flow of the scenes, perhaps, or the way the pattern of the gilding led the eye into and around the panels.

He packed food and water and set out down the hill again, wearing clean robes and a broad-brimmed hat woven from bamboo leaves. He did not notice the stream was less forceful than on his previous walk, that the pools where bulbuls bathed were shallower. Late on his fourth day of walking he reached the other monastery. It housed only the dead.

Nauseated by the condition of the bodies and the foul smell, he apologised to the dead and to all the immortals in the Jade Emperor's heavenly realm, and abandoned his attempt to build funeral pyres. This complex was better appointed than his own and boasted Imperial connections. It had an elaborate roof design with glazed *wenshou* protecting the ridges. The dragons were impressive, but he always smiled at the figure who led the zoomorphic procession, the bureaucrat, with the Buddha-ears of the immortals, riding a giant cockerel. Even his grandmother, who knew everything, could not explain that one.

It was a shame to do it, but he fired the whole monastery. At a safe distance upwind, he lit incense sticks and bowed before the blaze, honouring the dead. He left the sticks upright, their stems stabbed into the sandy soil.

'I am not doing very well, am I Mr. Lizard? For so long I have had no one to talk with, and now I am tongue-tied. As for names: all of my life I have sought Enlightenment and one-ness with the world around us. My teachers instructed me to let go of myself, to lose my ego, to see the Buddha in everything and everyone, and I have tried so many ways to do that. I meant by keeping my name I have clung to my sense of self-identity, and thus have never lost my ego. So perhaps I should throw away my name along with these filthy rags, and live out the rest of my days, which are probably few, naked, without the baggage of self.'

Ba Ren had set out to search the plain for other survivors. But every village or monastery he found contained only corpses: he soon learned to identify settlements from a distance by the carrion eaters circling on the thermal uplifts above them. Always, he made his respects to the dead when he could, but, as the days turned to weeks, he avoided habitations.

He did not wander in straight lines, but circled and criss-crossed the land, keeping to the shade where he could, as the sun blazed in an endless, cloudless sky. Weeks of wandering along or near parched water-courses were interrupted by recurrent episodes of delirium. He gathered food when he could. His vows prohibited meat, but he was not tempted: any meat he found was always putrefied, swarming with flies and maggots.

'That all seems arse-about to me, if you don't mind me saying so. Is that a human thing or just between you and your teachers?'

'I am a monk. I don't spend much time with humans who are not monks or teachers. Otherwise I might be tempted to break my vows.'

'What are vows?'

'Vows are promises, commitments to do, or not do, things which might block the path to Enlightenment. I accepted a life of poverty and chastity and I gave up eating meat.'

'Well, thank you for that, at least, although you wouldn't like me anyway. There isn't much meat on my bones, and the kites all say my kind taste awful.'

'The kites talk to you?'

'Duh! We all talk, it's only humans that have a problem there, possibly because of that ego thing you talked about.

Even the creatures we eat, we take care to treat them with respect. It's hardly their fault they are prey.'

The plain, once fertile and rich, was a dustbowl. Grasses and crops, bushes and trees were withered and brown. Streams and irrigation channels held only the slightest trickle of water, usually undrinkable because of bodies upstream. He could not survive much longer should nothing change, and was not confident he could travel much further, even with the aid of the long staff he had found. If rescue was coming it would have arrived by now.

The plain was once a vast glacial-scrape basin, and was surrounded by low, eroded hills with mountains beyond, refracted through the heat haze in shimmering purple and blue. There was still snow still on the high peaks to the northwest: taunting, beautiful. Snow meant melt-water, fast and refreshing.

'So, how's it going for you, then, the poverty and chastity thing?' said the lizard.

'At the moment, they are not temptations I have to endure.'

Ba Ren's stomach ached. His voice rasped across his dry throat.

'Chastity means no sex, right? Rejecting meat and sex seems like trying to ignore your own nature. I'm not sure what good will ever come of that.'

'That's right, no sex. We must transcend the base desires of our bodies. As for meat: my papa was a hunter and I was never hungry for meat as a child. But when I decided to seek Enlightenment, I had to put away childish things. I put aside worldly snares to focus on deeper truths.'

'And your fellow monks? The ones who also renounced these things? Where are they? Did it do them any good?'

Celibacy and shame had many times left Ba Ren lingering on his pallet to hide his early morning erections, ashamed of his erotic dreams of the mother of Buddha. He picked up a stone that fitted neatly into his hand, and ran its rough edge along a seam of his spare robe, scraping out the remaining lice.

'What is this Enlightenment, anyway? I am not familiar with that word.'

'According to the Buddha, Enlightenment is knowing what has to be known, abandoning what has to be abandoned, and building what has to be built.'

'I hear the words, but I don't hear meaning when they're joined together like that.'

'Sometimes, Mr. Lizard, I am of the same opinion.'

Ba Ren often doubted his calling. Papa wasn't happy with him when he announced his intention, neither was Mama, but he was young and stubborn. Memories of that day bled through into many nows.

The theory of poverty and chastity were much more attractive than the reality. Sitting starving and shaven headed by the side of a road while pretty girls skipped past without giving him even a glance, was unpleasant. The moral superiority of his brothers was intolerable. He was old enough to know there was no shame in returning to his parents and admitting his folly, and yet he stayed, always hoping to glimpse a different path to Enlightenment.

Then the plague came.

'So you abandon things that are part of your nature. Who decided eating and reproduction aren't important? Your teachers sound to me like they've got ego problems, trying to guide you to this Enlightenment by ignoring what you are. You would be better off staying true to your nature and finding your place in the great order of things. Without food and fucking there would soon be no more life, which would be a sad state of affairs if you ask me. But what do I know? I'm just a lizard.'

Ba Ren threw his spare robe over the lizard and brought the stone down, hard, on the creature's head.

'My apologies Mr. Lizard, but I find your arguments convincing. Forgive me, I must kill you.'

The lizard was right: there was little meat on its bones and the taste was bitter, but Ba Ren tore at it with his teeth and ate it raw, black eyes and all, leaving no waste for the hungry scavengers in the sky.

Besides, talking with a lizard was a pretty crazy thing to do.

'Good point,' said the lizard.

It was cool to walk in the night, with a full moon to light the way. He managed almost five miles before the lizard had its revenge. Ba Ren's diarrhoea stank and the cramps in his stomach and bowels forced him to the ground, doubled over. He had seen enough dysentery to know he had to replace the fluids or he would join his dead brothers. With each contraction he was sure his insides were trying to squeeze out.

The karma was not lost on him. He did not believe in supernatural punishment, but was amused by this new example of divine irony.

Three times he cramped and shat what little was left in his guts, without the strength to squat. Towards dawn he found a tree with condensed moisture on its leaves; he licked and sucked them dry. He drank from a thin brown rivulet that slunk through a muddy channel.

He slept until noon and rested in the shade until evening, in contemplation. He had broken his vows. The lizard died so he might live. He'd tried to see the Buddha in the lizard, but he'd killed and eaten it all the same. He wasn't sure he cared much, and couldn't decide whether to be pleased or distressed by that. It was easy to be obedient and serene in the monastery, with the routine rhythms of rituals and daily life, less so in a time of trial. He'd broken his vow, and was still alive because of it.

And what was the consequence of disobedience? His shit fed countless ants and insects, which would in their turn nourish other creatures, and life would continue. It was catastrophic for the lizard, of course, but all part of the circle of life. One day soon his own carcass would be a harvest feast for scavengers – something he approved of in theory, but was happy to delay.

There was a noise over his shoulder: another lizard was camouflaged in the roots of the rubber tree that gave them both shelter. Ba Ren thought for a while, then tossed a stone at it, sending it scuttling, away.

'Have a good life, Mr. Lizard,' he said. 'Put in a good word for me with the kites, and try to see the Buddha in all things, if you can.'

The hills around the rim of the plain held clean water in shaded groves. Exhausted, he knew he must not drink too much at once, though he longed to gulp down huge draughts. There were scrubby fruit bushes too, and he nibbled berries, aware of every sharp pang in his protesting belly. A pool was substantial enough for him to strip off and immerse himself. He soaked his robes, holding them downstream, hoping the vermin infesting the ragged cloth had the sense to escape.

As evening wore on, he drank more water, always in small sips, slowly rehydrating his near-skeletal frame. The next day he found an abandoned farmhouse, little more than a shack, with food in the larder. He set and sparked a fire in the hearth, and made a bowl of rice and brewed a bitter tea. He found clean clothes in a press, and ointment for the raw sores on his skin. He burned his old rags, apologising to any lice that had not taken his earlier hint. He trimmed his wild hair and beard then shaved his head completely. He lay down on a clean pallet and fell into a deep sleep.

He woke at the noise of an animal snuffling around outside. The sounds were light, no heavy footfalls. The bottom of the unlatched front door scraped a slow arc in the dirt floor. A fox stood silhouetted against the open doorway, ears pricked forward, nose held upright.

'Please, come in.'

Startled, the fox stepped back.

'You are safe: there is no harm here. Please, come in and be comfortable where you may.'

And the fox did come in, and curled up in a corner of the room.

When he woke again the fox was gone, leaving only its impression in the dust of the floor. He rested all of that day. His head was tense, as though another bout of fever or delirium was imminent. He moved only to steam more rice and brew more tea.

In the corner of the room stood a makeshift altar, dedicated to Xi Wangmu, the Queen Mother of the West. Shrivelled remains of peaches lay in front of it, and a small supply of incense sat to one side. He knelt and made his respects, bowing and offering thanks that he had survived to find this place.

He tried to think about what he should do next. There was nothing for him on the plain, but he did not know these hills or the mountains behind them, though he'd been told that beyond them a great trading route took silk to far western lands and brought horses back. He supposed it must be late autumn now, and crossing the mountains in winter was not a happy prospect. He was still pondering when he tried to stand and was overcome by dizziness. He found his bed and was asleep well before the twinkling heavens revealed themselves at dusk.

He was again woken by a noise. Lifting his head with care, unsure of his condition, he looked for the fox. Instead, a young woman stood in the doorway. Silent, she entered and curled up on the floor, in the same place the fox had lain the previous night.

The tides of memory beached him on his grandmother's knee and the tales she told him as she sliced fruit and vegetables and rinsed rice. Her stories warned of fox-spirits, and the dangers of inviting them into your house. His head ached, and he was still dizzy. He fell back into unconsciousness.

When he woke he was alone. She was the first human he had met in weeks and they had not exchanged a word. He couldn't decide if she had really been there at all, if his mind had concocted the whole thing, like the talking lizard. But the next night she came again. This time she sat at the end of his bed.

'You are kind, sir, allowing me to sleep on your floor. Might I do anything for you?'

She was backlit by moonlight shining through the open door. He could make out the contours of her body in the drape and fold of the opaque material of her gown, imagine the upcurve of her petite breasts, see the pebble of a nipple pushing against the cloth. He had the first stirrings of lust, and looked away.

'Thank you, but I ask nothing. You're welcome to share this hut and my food and water. Nothing is needed in return.'

'I have things to share too: I give them freely, like you give your kindness.'

'Thank you, daughter, but I can't.'

'You have a wife? A fiancée, perhaps? You hope to find her still alive?'

'No, that is not it.'

'Then what? Am I ugly? Do you prefer young men? Why do you reject me?' She looked away. Moonlight refracted through her tears. He tried not to watch the movement of her breasts under the robe. She stretched, as though uncomfortable. The arching of her back pushed her nipples, now ripe, against the taut silk. Her robe parted above her knees to expose her thighs, smooth, inviting, leading his imagination into wet shadows.

'I ... No. None of those. I am a monk; I can't accept your gift.'

'But who'll know? There is no one left to see, no one left to criticise you or chastise you, or whatever it is they do to you. There's only us here, now, under this roof, before that altar, in the moonlight.'

'I took vows.'

'What is a vow worth when there is no one left alive?'

'What is a vow worth if I can break it when I think I won't get caught? Will it speed me along the path to Enlightenment? You are very beautiful and I want you very much; no one has ever offered me their body before. But as much as I want you, as much as I don't want to die without knowing that pleasure, I would like to know Enlightenment more.'

'Have you never broken a vow?'

'Only once: I agreed with something I ate. Why do you cry, child?'

'Because my mistress will be displeased. Do you have a name, Mr. Monk?'

'I used to, but I lost it while out walking. It didn't seem worth going back to look for it.'

'Careless of you. I'd better leave you to your search for Enlightenment then.'

'Please stay. I'd like it if you stayed. I've had no companions for so long now, I forgot what it's like to have someone nearby.'

She settled down beside his pallet and fell asleep. After a long time, he slept too.

He woke to feel her hand under his blanket, warm and soft, cupping his balls while his body betrayed his best intentions. Erect at her touch, he pretended to sleep while she held him firmly, moving her hand with rhythmic insistence: coaxing, gripping, teasing, pleasing. He did not know her name. *She is a fox-spirit*, his Grandmother's voice said. *She'll steal your strength*.

A vision of mother Maya took him, and came with sudden, urgent release. He could not restrain his gasp, the overwhelming pleasure, the sense of correctness.

'Thank you,' he murmured, as her hand caressed him and changed into a paw as her furry muzzle and rough pink tongue darted around his cock and across his lower abdomen, licking him clean.

'You could have had all that and more,' she said, as she trotted out of the door, brush held high behind her. 'It is a pity you are such a good monk.'

When he woke again, drained, satisfied, regretful, there was only a slick wet patch on his mattress to remind him of her gift. He didn't understand why he was crying.

He fell back to sleep and into a dream, the same dream that had hovered on the edge of his boyhood long ago, a memory not quite lost, not quite found.

He stands by a river of gold. It is not really gold, it just looks like gold: the yellow gold of sunrise, the red gold of sunset. The light folds in on itself, flickering. Call it time, call it life, call it possibility, always splashing and flowing, falling and tumbling in cascades and cataracts, streaming through countless channels. Wild, never landscaped.

Sometimes he has seen this river in the shapes behind his eyelids in the half-moments between sleep and wakefulness, when the form of the day is still uncertain and open to suggestion. In those moments he sees the light splashing in the spray of the river's rapids, solid and certain in time's chaos.

This time, the dream did not fade as he emerged into consciousness.

The fox stood at the door, waiting. She took several steps before looking back. He understood: he should follow. He looked around the hut for clothes, but they were not his. His staff leant against the wall by the door; he left it for the next traveller. He walked out naked.

She led him along an ill-defined track by what was once a lively stream, but was now a gentle flow of brackish water, overhung by trees, in which song-birds trilled and fluted. Blue magpies grubbed out insects and larvae with their scarlet beaks. Sometimes she was fox, sometimes woman, brush twitching, hips swaying. The memory of her hand and paw, muzzle and tongue was fresh and arousing. He did not even know her name.

The river of gold ran through everything in his sight, obliquely at first, then with clarity. He stopped and watched with a delighted smile, entranced by the dream state insinuating itself into his physical world like an after-image in his eyes from staring for too long at reflected sunlight.

They reached a shadowed grove where peach trees flourished in a broken ring around a pool on which lotus flowers were still closed against the night. She stepped aside.

She touched his hand as if by accident and whispered, 'I'm sorry.'

On the other side of the pool stood an ancient yew. In a canopied bower under its branches sat Xi Wangmu herself, her leopard skin cloak, complete with tail, draped over her shoulders. Below the cloak she wore a white silk gown, the bodice embroidered with diamonds and rubies, hems chased with emeralds. She wore her strange ornamental headdress, decorated with representations of the fabled peaches of immortality. She had the Buddha ears of an immortal. Her teeth were white and sharp, like those of the tiger, as legend told.

The monk stopped at the outer edge of the grove, curious about the eddy it made in the river of gold, as though the place were peripheral to the flow rather than part of it. Light coursed through the lotus flowers and up the trunks and along the branches of the peach trees, pouring into the fruit, but it did not flow into the yew which stood isolated, unilluminated, seemingly in an area of still water.

'Well, nameless monk: what are we to do with you?' Her voice oozed like sap down a lacquer tree in autumn, a rich alto, resonant with scents of resin and eternity. 'You alone managed to survive our cull, which is remarkable, and declined the charms of my hand-maiden, which is unheard of. You are a singular human, and singular humans are interesting. And a problem.'

The river of gold became more intense, no longer an overlay but the main focus of his sight. Xi Wangmu was not in its current, but part of some other, dark river. It seemed to him they were at a confluence where waters of different density or salinity from separate headwaters flow together through a common channel, but do not merge.

His grandmother had a story she would tell him at bedtime. In the Jin dynasty, she said, there lived a woodcutter named Wang Zhi. One day, he went to Lankeshan to gather firewood. An old man and a boy played Go by a rock next to a lake, so he laid down his axe to watch the game. Hours passed, until the child said you should go home now. Wang Zhi picked up his axe and found it tatty and rotten. He felt strange and hurried home, but when he got there everything had changed and no one recognised him. He asked the elders of the village about shops and houses he knew, and they said they were demolished centuries ago. Wang Zhi had been in the immortal realm, where one day is many years on earth.

He took a step back, but his way was blocked by two others, also female, also borne on the currents of the dark river.

'I am sorry, Mr. Monk. You have travelled far to get here, but this is the end of your journey. Please forgive me, but I must kill you.' The Queen of Heaven stepped from her realm and walked towards him. 'You have survived much, but we must have your body and blood to understand why you lived when the rest of the herd did not. It is not your fault you are our prey.'

Ba Ren looked up. Beyond the sky, golden threads joined the myriad stars, the warp and weft of heaven's loom, the great tapestry in which all things are made. All possibilities were everywhere in the golden ocean, the tidal reaches of all pasts and futures, bound together in the great spume and foam of consciousness.

He was a spark of life in a greater flame. He burned in the flame.

His earthly desires were just a lesser part of a greater joy, a distraction from the flow of the river of gold. He abandoned them.

Before him was the palace of eternity in which all life resides. He built what had to be built, its foundations and roof-beams, its tall walls and cloistered corridors, its screens and buttresses.

Smiling, he allowed himself, the least of monks, to be caught up by the cleansing flow of light, whose waters sung soft anthems and antiphons of welcome.

The bright flame of the fox-spirit flew free from the shackles that bound her to the earth, and was joyful.

He rose above the grove while below his body glowed, brighter, then brighter still, until, at last, his earthly form discorporated into the eternal now, and the lotus flowers opened their petals to bloom, blissful in the morning air.

COYOTE IN THE CORNER

You're a God-damned witch, that's what Mama said.

She didn't always say that stuff, she used to say she loved me, but that was before she caught a bad dose of religion from Billy Graham, and Hank hit her one too many times so's I had to kill him. When they took me away, she told them to bury me deep dark down in their deepest cell, right down there where the sun don't shine, 'cos I'm a God-damned witch like the rest of my God-damned family.

It was 1954 and I was fourteen years old.

Hank wasn't my papa. Mama said Papa died in the war and left us like the God-damned selfish man he was. I've always known that ain't right, that Papa is still alive somewhere, even though Mama truly believed all the days of her life he was dead. She met Hank, whose name was Harald but nobody ever called him *that*, not even *his* Mama who called him a God-damned, no-good waste of space asshole, at a victory party in George Square in Glasgow after the Germans lost. They got married and we came here with him. When we got here he wanted me to take his name, Pedersen, but I said no, and that was the first time he hit me. Mama shouted at him to stop, so he turned around and punched her and said the God-damned kid's gotta learn some God-damned respect and so do you: can't run a God-damned family without some God-damned respect.

That was when I decided to kill him one day. I was six.

Hank took us to Minnesota to display us to his family as his spoils of war, but we soon took off down the Mississippi and then up the east coast until we finally fetched up in New England. We never stayed one place for long: Hank would find work on a boat or at the docks and then get fired, and we'd move on to the next port, until I guess he got blacklisted everywhere. Mama cried all the time and that just made Hank go out drinking more and come home late, when he came home at all. I learned to make myself small and not say anything, even when he hit Mama and then they went to their bedroom and I'd hear him grunting and the bed springs creaking. And then he'd snore while Mama cried some more then went to the bathroom. By then Coyote was my friend, but I didn't tell Hank and Mama because they couldn't see him (of course they couldn't see him, he's far too real to be seen).

I met Coyote in Minneapolis in Spring 1947 when I was sitting down by the Milwaukee Road waiting for the Twin Cities Hiawatha to roll past to places with names so exotic they made my mind ache: Red Wing, Winona, La Crosse, Oconomowoc, until it reached Chicago 420 miles later. This was just before the Twin Cities Zephyr on the old CB&Q line got wrecked at Downer's Grove. Rabbits hopped around the scrap of wasteland I was at, enjoying their freedom to do exactly as they God-damned pleased. I had a ham sandwich with me. The ham was mostly gristle and the rough bread was smeared with lard rather than butter, but Mama made it and it was very good.

Coyote looked like a scrawny old dog. He watched me from scrubby wasteland and I broke off part of my sandwich and held it out. He came over, scattering the rabbits to their burrows, and something happened, something in my head, like a door opened to stuff I'd forgotten even though I never knew it in the first place. Coyote, no ordinary beast, accepted me.

Coyote helped me start to understand this new world.

There's something about America, in the soil and the air and the never-ending skies. It makes you want to take a train to nowhere and sit on your God-damned ass all day whittling sticks and watching rabbits until magic happens and you're King of the World.

America insisted itself on me the moment we walked down the gangplank, when it was all still exciting and new, and Hank hadn't hit me or Mama yet. It was in every branch creaking in the wind and the warm rain on hot days, the smell of the rivers and the sea, the touch of ferns and grasses. America was everywhere in the trees and lakes and streams and the teeming abundance of life, ancient life that ignores humans completely, even as we bulldoze the land and fill it with gravel and concrete and build roads over it.

Coyote walked right out of that America, the America most Americans don't know, even though it infuses the air they breathe and the water they drink. He ate the scrap of sandwich and nuzzled me with his dry nose and licked my fingers and let me scratch his ears.

Sometimes I was only in school long enough to get registered before we moved on. Hank never bothered. He said I didn't need schooling 'cos I was a God-damned stupid little asshole who would come to a bad end and good riddance. Granny, who was odd, and her sister Bella, who was even odder, taught me letters and numbers when I was small, so I could read the comics and papers and magazines that lay around the place. Mama didn't like Granny or Bella; I think she married Hank just to get away from them.

Libraries were my refuge, a sanctuary where I could read all day and make winsome faces for the librarians and let them fuss over me and bring me cookies and soda even though they weren't supposed to. It's easy to read lots of stuff when you don't have a teacher telling you you're not old enough. I didn't understand everything I read, but so what? I wasn't going to be doing any God-damned comprehension tests or book reports. The most interesting books in libraries are often those that are pristine and unread: there is untamed wilderness there, prairies and mountains, unexplored and undemarcated, like America before Lewis and Clark or Mason and Dixon.

A line by Thomas Wolfe hit me, like his head lifted up from the ink and off the page and his mouth said the words straight out:

The rails go westward in the dark. Brother, have you seen the starlight on the rails? Have you heard the thunder of the fast express?

My fast express thundered deeper and deeper into the heart of the elemental America, the America I travelled in dreams with faithful Coyote as my guide. But mornings were a succession of two-room apartments, always on the wrong side of the tracks.

Nothing seemed to trigger Hank's last blow-up, though there was never much need for a trigger at all. We were living in the shitty end of Boston and I'd been out playing hooky at the library. Mama was crying in her room hiding the swelling under her eye. Hank had gone out to find some whiskey and drank half of it on his way home. Mama had been to hear Billy Graham a few days before and I guess she must have gone forward to acknowledge Jesus as her Lord and Saviour and received a laying on of hands and the Gift of the Holy Spirit. Maybe it was the Holy Spirit who emboldened her to talk back to Hank.

Anyhows, Hank laid into her hard and I wanted it to stop and wanted him dead, dead, dead; really, really wanted it like I'd never wanted anything so much before. Next thing, Coyote was on him, tearing and ripping at his throat, massive paws planted on his chest, blood and saliva dripping onto cheap linoleum. It took Mama a moment to realise Hank wasn't hitting her any more but was sprawled on the floor in front of her, twitching his last, his ghost just standing there by the table, surprised. She couldn't see where Coyote had mauled him, but she knew he was gone. Then she looked at me and pointed to me eyes and screamed and screamed and screamed.

'You did this! You did this! You're just like them, you've got their eyes like your bastard father and his bastard family.'

She was going to hit me too, something she'd never done before, but her breath just hissed out of her like she had a slow puncture, and she flopped on the floor next to Hank and cried, until the neighbours came in to see what all the screaming was about.

And that's when Mama pointed at me and told the neighbours I was a God-damned witch and I'd killed Hank, and she sat rocking backwards and forwards, banging the back of her head against the thin plaster-board wall and speaking in tongues in a language even Coyote couldn't understand.

I figured she'd be happy Hank was gone.

The police wouldn't let me stay with Mama, and they wouldn't listen when I told them my name: they insisted it was John Pedersen. So I said it God-damned wasn't and they hit me and told me to watch my filthy mouth and learn some God-damned respect. They were just like Hank.

They couldn't hold me because the next day the doctors certified Hank was full of whiskey and died of a massive heart attack and it was like all his valves and stuff inside had burst and they'd never seen anything like it. And they couldn't send me down for being a witch, not even in Massachusetts. Then they asked where I went to school and I said I didn't and they decided Hank and Mama neglected me. They asked my Mama to take me back home, but she said she didn't give a good God-damn what they did with me because I was a God-damned evil little witch and the Bible says at Exodus chapter 22 and verse 18 *thou shalt not suffer a witch to live,* and if they wouldn't do the Lord's work then I was their God-damned problem.

So they filed me away in the Youth Service Board Detention Center where they put all the other kids they didn't know what to do with.

They put me straight into a dormitory just before lights out. I wanted to cry myself to sleep but the other kids were listening in the darkness and would make fun of me, so I kept it all in. Coyote stretched out next to me on the iron-framed bed. He was in my dreams too, and we followed the starlight on the rails like the wise men following the star. That was the first night he let me ride on his back. We chased reflections all the way into the heart of America. We ran to a place with a broad clear lake and Coyote dived right in with me still on his back while we went right under. The shock of the cold water felt real, all the panic and pleasure of total immersion in the cleansing waters of the dreamscape.

I came up for air, snorting bubbles, and looked back at the trees we'd come through. From the shadows, figures looked back at me. They had Granny and Bella's eyes, witch's eyes, and if I wasn't one of them before, I was now.

My mattress was wet when I woke up. All the other kids gathered round, holding their noses and laughing. A nurse came to take me away for a scrub shower and a fresh change of clothes. I stood there scrawny and naked under the cold water as she worked stiff bristles into my complaining skin. She asked if my name was John Pedersen and I said it God-damned wasn't, so she hit me on the ass with the back of the scrubbing brush, and I called her a God-damned asshole bitch and she skelped me again, harder, and said I wanted to watch my God-damned filthy language. Then she whacked me one more time because she chipped a nail on the edge of the brush and that wouldn't have happened if I wasn't such a God-damned insolent boy, and what kind of a God-damned Limey accent was that anyhows?

Five minutes later I stood in front of a fat man who wore a light coloured three-piece linen suit, with a pocket watch and silver-dollar fob on a double Albert, and spit-polished leather shoes. He had a shiny face and kept licking his lips with the tip of his pink tongue. He named me John Pedersen too, and I said I God-damned wasn't and he picked up a long cane and swung it hard against my leg. The tip hit me right where the scrubbing brush landed; my skin split just before outrage at the pain coursed through me. Coyote, in the corner, was alert and silent, waiting for a sign, but it wasn't time for someone else to be dead, dead,

dead yet on my say-so. So Pink-Tongue lived to name me again as John Pedersen and I said again I God-damn wasn't and looked him straight in the eye, trying to look as Coyote might when stalking prey.

Pink-Tongue stared back, surprised and maybe confused, and maybe something that might have been fear, or maybe my eyes had opened onto beckoning blackness, the chasm behind a witch's eyes. Maybe he heard Coyote's warning snarl. Whatever, he didn't lift the switch again.

'We'll speak again tomorrow, John Pedersen. Some time alone might help you consider the consequences of your attitude.'

They put me in an isolation room down in the basement, which they said was punishment, but suited me just fine. The wet mattress was in there with me too, just me and its stink and the stone floor with no blanket to warm me. There was no food. On a low shelf by the door was a Bible to nourish my God-damned soul, but there was no light to read it by, even if I wanted to.

But Coyote let me ride on his back as he ran into the deep dark American night, where the moon had not yet risen above mountains silhouetted black on black against an endless sky. Behind the rush of the wind voices whispered, muttered, called out, but there wasn't any meaning in the half-heard sounds that might have been words.

The next morning the other kids stared as the masters paraded me into the hall as an abject specimen of the depths of depravity to which children will sink if they didn't mend their ways.

The food was horrible, but Mama always said you never know where the next meal is coming from, so I wolfed it down. I was hungry, but remembered my Dickens and kept it to myself. The others at my table looked like they wanted to ask me questions, but strict silence was enforced.

Breakfast ended with a prayer asking Jesus to watch over us and try and find it in Him to redeem our squalid existences. To help Jesus out, Pink-Tongue called six boys out to the front. He slipped his suit jacket off and draped it on the back of a nearby chair. He instructed each boy in turn to hold his hands up, left under right. Each boy received four hard stokes of a thick cane, though their misdemeanours, if any there ever were, remained undeclared. With each stroke the fat man's tongue danced across his lips. He had the same swelling in his pants as Hank when he took Mama to the bedroom and made her cry. Pink-Tongue regarded the room, the cane still angry in his hand.

'John Pedersen!'

Every face turned except mine.

'John Pedersen: stand up and step forward.'

I did not.

A master picked me up as easy as you like, and threw me at the wall. My face slammed into the painted stonework. A boot connected with my kidneys as I slid to the floor in my own blood and vomit.

'Answer your betters when you're spoken to, you God-damned piece of shit.'

Coyote's hackles rose and he tensed to pounce, but again I stilled him and got up. I looked at the master and Pink-Tongue, spat, then turned my back on them and sat down at the dining table, wincing.

I didn't feel the blow to the back of my head that knocked me out.

I knew something happened while I was out. I knew even though I came to in pain, panicking at the mask over my face, seeing the relief on the faces of the attendants as they regulated the oxygen flow from the tank at my side. A nurse said I'd swallowed my tongue and gone dark purple and had a seizure right there in the dining room, and the masters had all got into a hell of a commotion that I might die, until one of the cooks had known what to do. But that isn't what changed: when I opened my eyes the world looked less solid, like everything was an infinite chain of possibilities, forced into stop-motion animation by my looking at it, resentful at being constrained by my eyes.

And the people looked different: they all looked less solid too, and had halos or auras around them, all of varying colours and intensities. All of their lives were right there in front of me: the spark in the infant, then the choices they'd made and their regrets and secret desires, right through to the creased and crumpled ways they would die. They were embryo and corpse and all the possibilities in between, and all the witches' eyes in my head shone with approval.

Everything clicked back into focus after a while, but the sensation lingered, as did the glow of the auras.

'We'll soon have you fixed, John Pedersen,' said the nurse, not the one who had scrubbed me the day before, not thinking I might not want to be fixed.

'That's not my name.' Her aura showed she was kind, or that's how it seemed. 'Hank Pedersen wasn't my papa. Papa didn't come home from the war.'

She gave me a surprised look, gentle too, maybe she'd been warned to watch out for my God-damned filthy tongue, and cleaned the dried blood from my face.

'Well, your nose isn't broken, but you'll have a nasty looking bruise there for a while. Let's get you tidied up. I love your accent, by the way.'

The hues swirling around her deepened, and I wanted to say it was OK and not to be lonely and not to cry, but I didn't. Just like I didn't tell her I knew her name was

Martha Feldman and her brother Saul was ripped apart by a Japanese mortar shell in a makeshift trench down below Kakazu Ridge and died so fast he hadn't even known about it for five whole minutes, but just stood there outside of time looking down at where his skin flapped like an empty raincoat on the bright red soil. I'd never even heard of Martha or Saul or Kakazu Ridge before. She was close to me as she cleaned my injuries, close enough to smell cloves on her breath. She probably was only just a few years older than me. In one possible future, Martha and I lay side by side under a blanket looking at the stars.

I looked in confusion at Coyote in the corner, but he just flicked his ears and scratched behind his jaw with his hind paw.

They put me back in the dorm that night, with a clean mattress, not long before lights out. The other boys were quiet, unsure what to say. I guess none of us ever had a real friend and I sure didn't know how to go about making one.

'My name is John,' I said.

Coyote curled up, rested his snout on crossed forepaws and went to sleep.

We rode together on the fast express on starlight rails. The train was modern like the Twin Cities Hiawatha but with the big lounge right up front, and it hauled wagons not coaches. We sat right up there on top of the Skytop, moonbeams streaming through Coyote's fur. All around were ghosts of hoboes and hitchers, America's flotsam and jetsam, carried around the networks forever in the clickety-clack rhythms of bogies on the track, or at least until the day when trains don't roll no more. They were all of them sitting on the roof with us, or riding the rods or clutching the ladders and steps of the old wagons: sticks, pegs, blinky and wingy, lefties and righties, blind, mad or drunk, or just spouting the wisdom of the wheels for anyone inclined to listen. The towns and marshalling yards in our path clung tight to the hem of the rails as moss clings to light in a cave, holding their breath as we thundered through, hearing echoes of the dream of expansion that built America, reminding them of all that was there before, what's still here if they could only see it, echoes of the yearning to be free from themselves, the birth right that haunts the soul of suburbs.

On we thundered, through the vast heartlands that separate the seaboards, the dead casting aside empty rum bottles, blind drunk on the joy of their phantom existence. The track was forever built out ahead of us, answering an imperative only the train could disclose. Then up we rose, up and over the lakes and prairies, disturbing the deep rest of ancient spirits, here long before men crossed the land bridge from Asia; up and across the Great Divide until we reached the far mountains, home of wolf and bear and all the unknown that stay in the shadows and out of the sun. There, in the High Sierra, was a grove, and at its heart a great blackness, and from the blackness a voice called out words I didn't know, but I knew they were meant for me.

Coyote's eyes glinted yellow in their dark orbits. He'd brought me here on purpose: this was a place I would be one day, far, far away from the mundane America where my body slept.

In the morning, my face had healed. After a tepid rinse in the communal showers, embarrassed to be naked with the others, especially as I was still thinking about nurse Martha, we all trooped single file to breakfast where the whole ghastly routine started again. Six boys were summoned by Pink-Tongue and six boys raised their hands to receive the cane: *swish, whack, swish, whack.*

'John Pedersen, come forward.'

I did not.

'John Pedersen has ideas above his station, everyone. His mother said he was a witch and he used magic to kill his father, right before she threw him out of the house, that's how special *he* is.'

Laughter bubbled round the room. My skin tingled as I flushed red; I wanted to be somewhere else. I told Coyote *don't kill him, just frighten him.*

I stood up and looked at Pink-Tongue, my head cocked. I looked out from the blackness behind my eyes. Pink-Tongue's aura was muddy and congested – how did it get to be so God-damned twisted? The swell in his pants was obvious: his aura centred there. I remembered Hank and Mama and the grunts and tears and a wave of disgust washed over me. I'd seen Leon Mandrake or Harry Blackstone working an audience in picture books, and raised my hands to shoulder height, like them.

The boys and masters laughed, and I guess it looked pretty God-damned ridiculous. Nurse Martha, standing near the door as if trying to sidle out, turned away.

'Mister Pink-Tongue, you need to have some God-damned respect: how d'you expect anyone to answer if you don't have any God-damned respect?'

I thrust my hands up and forward, fingers splayed: theatrical. Coyote leaned in close and snarled in Pink-Tongue's ear, clamped his jaws around the wobbling throat, tightening his grip by slow degrees. So help me, I smiled as Pink-Tongue choked and gasped, eyes bulging, face purple, tongue-tip frantic.

Nobody laughed now. Chair legs scraped on the hard parquet floor as they all hurried to get away, but I wasn't interested in them. Voices rose in shouts and screams and masters and nurses ran to Pink-Tongue to help, all except Martha, who never took her eyes off me. I kept the pose for maybe thirty seconds, then swept my hands down to my sides with a flourish. Coyote released his grip and Pink-Tongue fell to the floor. I spat, and sat down.

Pink-Tongue was still choking as he was helped away, and now *I* laughed to see the spreading brown stain in the seat of his fine suit pants as the smell spread through the hall.

I poured a glass of milk.

They moved me the same morning. I asked if I was going home, but they didn't speak as they stuck a needle in my arm and fastened restraints and huckled me into the back of a wagon.

The muddy courtyard was surrounded by low-built farm buildings. There were inner and outer perimeter fences, maybe three or four times the height of a man, with coiled barbed wire along the top. Dogs patrolled between the fences, and I felt the dull red of their malice even from a hundred yards away. The whole God-damned place smelled of pigshit.

The buildings were scrappy, but the door was thick and strong and the locks and chains bright. A sign, hand-lettered in black on a white background, read *Welcome to the Loving Arms Attitude Adjustment Center for Deviant and Delinquent Adolescents;* and below that *Suffer the little children to come unto me. Matthew 19:14.*

My room was almost square, with basic furniture. In

the corner farthest from the door was a sink and a toilet. A mirror, bracketed to the wall, reflected light from the high window back into the room. The walls, solid brick and painted pale green, were otherwise bare. I checked a chest of drawers, despite my handcuffs, and found clothes that were too big for me and a King James Bible. I opened it at Exodus chapter 22, and there it was at verse 18, killing witches. At verse 22 it said *Ye shall not afflict any widow, or fatherless child. If thou afflict them in any wise, and they cry at all unto me, I will surely hear their cry; and my wrath shall wax hot, and I will kill you with the sword; and your wives shall be widows, and your children fatherless.*

A man and a woman came into the room. They looked like they wanted to make sure I got the message they'd take no shit from the likes of me. Their faces were made for disapproval, faces that, like owners and dogs, had grown to look like one another. They stopped short when they found me with the Bible. Just dumb luck on my part, I guess. Anyway, their auras, which had been a kind of blue-grey, softened, and I got an idea.

'Sir; ma'am.' I put on the winsome face that charmed the librarians so, and it worked somewhat. They were confused. I guess they'd heard pretty wild stories about why the detention center had got me out as quick as it could.

'Well now, son: you're reading the Good Book there.'

'Yes, sir: Exodus: the Lord saving his people from captivity.'

'Praise the Lord for his mercy and grace. I'm Mr. Young, the principal, and this is Mrs. Young.' Mrs Young didn't look like I'd have her approval any time soon, Bible or no Bible. 'At Loving Arms we do the Lord's work of salvation,' he said, unlocking the handcuffs. 'Where are your belongings?'

'I have none, sir.'

'None?'

'Mama threw me out without a thing, Her husband died and she said I did it.'

'What did the judge say?'

'Ain't seen no judge, sir.'

'When was this?'

'Three days ago sir.'

They shared a look.

'When can I go home, sir?'

'The Detention Center say you're a dangerous troublemaker.'

The Detention Center folks were God-damned liars, but I held my tongue and asked 'what is this place?'

'*Loving Arms* is part of a non-profit based in Delaware called the Yewtree Foundation. Yewtree takes in boys and girls like you all over the country who have been lost or abandoned or thrown out. Our chairman, Joseph, is really keen to meet you, said you are just exactly the kind of child he's looking for. He's a real Red Indian, how exciting is that?'

I smiled at Mrs. Young and pretended interest, but said 'I just want to go home.'

'This is your home now.'

They pulled the door behind them. There was no handle on the inside. I was locked up with God-damned holy-rollers. Coyote was in the corner, as usual, but he was asleep and no use at all.

They gave me a tour later, but I didn't pay much attention to the showers and the classrooms and stuff, only the library. It was mostly creeping-Jesus stuff. There was no sign of a librarian, and the books were racked randomly, but the room was bright and airy and had the heady smell of bindings and ink and dry paper.

Out the back door was the pigshit smell. There was a large vegetable garden we were supposed to tend as part of our education. Beyond that a fenced yard contained kennels. I walked out past the enclosure and across the field towards the perimeter fences.

'The fuck ya think you're going boy? Looking to leave? You all do when you get here.'

He was nondescript, medium height, with the build of a lightweight boxer. His voice was rough but measured. His aura shifted and folded around itself in unpredictable ways.

'Gonna show you something, boy.'

He led me to some rabbit snares. Three of them were sprung by fat bucks, hopping and pulling, straining to get free. With a deft, practiced move, the man grabbed a buck by the scruff of its neck and hoisted it up, freeing the wire loop with his other hand. Tongue between his teeth, he whistled one sharp note and three mean-looking mastiff crosses were there at the other side of the inner fence in seconds, snarling and growling: expectant. The dogs were rakish, ribs showing, welt marks livid across their backs.

'Dogs's just like boys: if you want their God-damned obedience and respect you have to whip 'em and half-starve 'em, then give 'em a treat from time to time so they'll thank you.'

He tossed the squealing rabbit over the fence.

The dogs had it before it touched the ground, ripping and tugging at the fur and sinew, their snouts red with gore as they gnawed the fresh bones.

'Just so's you understand, boy, you don't get out except through the gate. Carter's dogs ain't choosy 'bout what they eat. Now git your ass back where it belongs.'

The Hiawatha arced yellow, grey and red across the sky above our heads. Light blazed from its windows. Coyote and I ran over constantly-changing terrain, grass to rock, sand to marsh, steel to water. Shadows flowed with eyes and voices. Red-eyed and pink tongued mastiffs bared their teeth and tore sinew and cartilage from terrified rabbits that had Hank's face and cursed me out for killing him and Mama screamed I was a God-damned witch and should be put down like a rabid dog.

From away over the horizon, a black grove in the Sierras enticed me, its gravity drawing me to whatever waited in its heart, the voice that called me, though it didn't know my name.

The call was still strong at breakfast. I was supposed to sit a test, I guess an IQ test, but they weren't ready and left me alone in the library. The random arrangement of the books on the shelves annoyed me. I made it past five rows of holy-roller volumes then found a tatty old pamphlet introducing the Dewey-Decimal system. By the time they remembered me two hours later, the call of the grove was forgotten and I was well on the way to a shelf plan for the books. I wasn't doing any harm and didn't need any supervision, so they just let me get on with it for the rest of the day. I was so absorbed I almost forgot where I was. Then I looked out of the window at the dogs and wire.

I wanted to go home, but the food was regular and good, or at least better than Mama made, and the water was hot. Summer would soon turn to fall and the sky would fill with the honks of the first Canada geese. I had to head west to the grove but it made no sense to risk it if the weather was turning, and anyways I didn't know where I was going or how to get there. I looked at Coyote for help but he just looked bored, like the question made no sense.

If this was a God-damned school story I'd tell you about the other boys there (and they were all boys at *Loving*

Arms, no girls), but there's nothing to tell. I got used to making myself small when Hank was around and I pulled the same trick again, keeping my head down and staying out of people's way until they stopped seeing me at all, I guess. Mr Young seemed grateful for the work I did in the library, and I enjoyed chores in the vegetable garden. I didn't need anything else: I had Coyote.

Mr. and Mrs. Young were pleasant enough, but they kept an eye on me 'cos they said their boss had me marked as a favourite. That annoyed Mrs. Young, though she never said why. Whenever I asked when I could go home, their answer was always the same, *this is your home now*. But my home was never surrounded by fences and dogs.

One time, Carter, who Mrs. White called Sergeant, caught me eyeing up the boundary. Next time he came past he waved, plucked a rabbit from the game sack slung over his shoulder and tossed it over the wire to waiting jaws. He strolled away laughing.

The teachers were an odd crowd, mostly well-meaning I guess, quite young, like they'd just qualified and couldn't get hired anywhere else. English classes were a God-damned breeze when the teacher found out my reading was years ahead of the rest of the class. She let me alone to read a book while she concentrated on teaching others their ABC. And I was old enough to know she was kinda cute, like nurse Martha. Her name was Helen Miller and I guess she was my first crush.

A brain doctor came by one time and asked me a load of questions about growing up, and showed me some pictures and asked me to say what I saw, and wanted to know if I'd ever seen Hank and Mama naked together and what they were doing. I remembered Hank grunting and Mama crying and told him to keep his God-damned dick in his pants and mind his own God-damned business. I didn't see him again, and Mrs. Young warmed to me a bit more after that.

We had a math teacher, Mr. Stuyvesant, who was OK. He tried his best to teach us arithmetic and geometry and stuff. He studied at a fancy university and seemed to think we were some sort of good deed he should do, but I guess it helped pay his way too.

I was kept behind in his class one day for some God-damned thing or another, trying to work out some problem he'd given me about triangles and circles. Meantime he wrote stuff on the blackboard, odd squiggles and symbols. Some looked like math, some like the Greek letters I'd seen in one of the holy-roller books, others made no God-damned sense at all. Coyote was curled up in the corner of the classroom, I guess math and Greek don't interest coyotes much.

Anyways, Mr Stuyvesant was stumped and kept staring at the board, so I stared at it too, and the God-damnedest thing happened: the squiggles and Greek seemed to shimmer and rearrange themselves right there on the board. There was a pattern there, or more truthfully, a whole lot of possible patterns, but one seemed more 'right' than the others. I had no idea what it all meant or what he was trying to do, still don't, but I figured out where the problem was, where the flow seemed to bunch up and double back on itself in a tangle and come out of the other end all wrong. At the bottom of an odd shaped squiggle like a f, or one of the holes in a fiddle, Mr. Stuyvesant had put the number 24. I rubbed it out with my fingers and chalked in a shape like a snake eating itself that seemed to me to fit there, though I'm God-damned if I know why. My triangles and circles refused to shimmer or do any useful God-damned thing at all. Mr Stuyvesant looked for a long time at the board, then at me, then scribbled stuff down fast on his pad of paper, his aura ablaze with swirls and eddying hues.

'Why did you do that, John?'

'It seemed to fit, Mr Stuyvesant.'

'It surely does, John, it surely does. This is going to blow the socks of my professors, and get you some attention too.'

'You mean like more math?'

'You'd better believe it, buddy.'

But it didn't. Mr. Stuyvesant packed up his notes and left. He was in a hurry, I guess, and his motorcycle tyres lost their grip on a dusty road so's he smashed into a fuel truck coming the other way. There wasn't nothin' left of him or his notes when they finally got the fire out. The next day the school cleaners wiped the board clean for a math class that never came, and the snake ate itself for nothing.

When Mr. Young told us about Mr. Stuyvesant resting in the loving arms of Jesus at breakfast, we all bowed our heads and muttered *amen*. Then Mr. Young said

'We have a visitor from the Yewtree Foundation this morning boys. She's coming to check our progress and decide which of you are ready to move on. Her name is Maria and I'll thank you to keep civil tongues in your head.'

Mrs. White took me aside.

'Maria is particularly keen to meet you, John. She has special instructions from Joseph. Be sure you're easily available.'

I was in the vegetable garden, tidying up the beds, thinking about Mr. Stuyvesant and his squiggles. Maybe they were important, but lots of important things like that were lost when people died. They all hit me from nowhere and smacked me sideways, the lives unlived, the possibilities never made real. The woman who invented the working anti-gravity device that took humanity to the stars didn't get born: her parents were murdered at Buchenwald and Flossenbürg without ever meeting each other. The man who found a cheap, easy way to produce unlimited fusion power was all burnt up as a baby at Nagasaki in August 1945. I asked Coyote if he had anything to do with Mr. Stuyvesant hitting the truck, but he was too busy licking his ass to answer.

The gate opened and a long black car drove in. Mr. and Mrs. Young went to greet it as the driver opened a door.

Maria was very tall, quite pretty I guess, but her ears were odd, like they were longer than normal. Her hair was almost to her ass, held back by a barrette. She was dressed all in black from throat to toes, and over the top wore a knee length fur coat, unfastened. The blackness of the High Sierra grove wrapped around her. A loud chorus of the black eyes in the forests and mountains of my dreams sang out that she was walking death, or worse.

I ducked where I couldn't be seen. Coyote growled, hackles raised, yellow eyes fixed on the woman. The Youngs and Maria went through the front door. The gate was wide open behind the black car. It was time to go, ready or not.

There was no growl or bark or anything, just the blow of the dog hitting my back out of nowhere, paws pressing, teeth worrying at my upper arm, biting hard through my jacket. Its canines broke my skin and its head started tearing at me, ripping through my sleeve.

'The fuck ya think you're going, boy? You ain't going anywhere near that gate 'less you want to lose some flesh.'

Behind Carter the other dogs were poised, wet lips drawn

back from teeth and gums, bursting with hate and fury. I kept my chin tucked into my chest to protect my throat as best I could, and called out to that God-damned Coyote for help. But the God-damned faithless bastard had left me to face this all on my own.

I had an empty pressure in my guts, chaos in my head.

The Youngs shouted at me, but the *thing* Maria arrowed towards me at a speed I couldn't believe.

When the mastiff took its chance to try for my throat, I surrendered to the abyss, staring at Maria. And so help me I laughed, hysterical I guess. With her long ears and brown hair and fur coat she looked just like a God-damned giant rabbit. Imagine: a God-damned giant rabbit coming for me. It was the funniest God-damned thing I'd ever seen, funnier even than Pink-Tongue crapping his pants.

And that's what saved me, the sight of the rabbit: something must have transmitted to the minds of Carter's dogs and they were away and onto her/it before Carter could do a God-damned thing about it. I was still laughing as Maria screamed and fell and her throat was bitten out as the mastiffs ripped in.

A roar of approval sounded deep in my head, and a great cry of rage from an age-old inhuman chorus. There was a mighty shout out from the heart of the black grove. Maria heard it too, maybe the last thing she heard, and I caught an image in her mind of a circle of ancient yew trees surrounding a sacred place. And a name.

When Hank died, his ghost stood there looking bewildered, but Maria twisted away into nothingness like black smoke in a summer breeze. And I kept God-damned laughing, though I dearly wanted to stop.

Her driver ran up with a shotgun and took out two of the dogs, but it was far, far too late. I studied the surviving dog like it was one of Mr. Stuyvesant's squiggles, tracking the patterns in its dull aura. I reached out to rearrange the swirling colours, fixing them.

The driver just stood there with the shotgun broken open, feeling in its pocket for cartridges. The Youngs hadn't got there yet and were gasping their way through the mud towards us. Carter was with his two dead dogs, crying, sorrow turning to hatred when he saw my eyes.

'I heard rumours about you, boy, 'bout how you near killed someone down at the Detention Center, how you killed your Pa. I heard tell 'bout how you're a God-damned witch. I don't hold with that shit, but you're goin' to fucking catch it now.

'Take him, boy!'

But the surviving dog didn't move. I pursed my lips and whistled and it trotted to my side. Carter made to rush me.

'Why you ...'

The dog growled, teeth ready to snap and tear. Carter got the message. I didn't feel sorrow for him, for what was I if not a fatherless child? What was I if not afflicted?

'It's OK, boy,' I said, scratching the dog behind its ears. 'He ain't nobody worth a God-damned thing.' I turned to the Youngs. 'I'm afraid I have to be going now, I've got things to do.'

A click and catch: the driver pointed a loaded shotgun at my head.

'My mistress came a long way to acquire you. Walk slowly to the car. Leave the dog. You,' he gestured to the Youngs, 'Bring my mistress's remains.'

I called for help: now would be a good time for the Lord's wrath to wax hot. The hidden America stirred. Motes of light streamed through all the living things in the field: through the scraps of grass in the mud, the seeds lying dormant beneath the surface, the insects swarming around the dead dogs. Coyote was back, tongue lolling from the side of its mouth, sharp yellow eyes and black pupils taking in everything.

Around the feet of the driver the earth tumbled and rolled; roots and tendrils pushed through the surface and grasped his ankles. Crawling things, centipedes and millipedes, spiders and beetles, swarmed around the creature's legs. Biting insects gathered themselves into a swarm and flew around its head, nipping its skin. It waved its arms to beat them away, but dropped the shotgun which hit the ground butt first and discharged both barrels. A gaping hole opened in the chest of Mr. Young, a great spray of his blood catching Mrs. Young and Carter.

The roots got fatter, stronger, as they squirmed up the driver's legs, over his hips and waist and around the body, tightening their grip all the time. The flowing stream of light around the dark core of the thing was beautiful, the eddies and currents in the stream, like the flow of squiggles on the blackboard, like the aura of an uncorrupted human.

I was so enthralled by the beauty of the lights I didn't notice I'd stopped laughing, and hardly noticed the bodies of Maria and the driver as they were pulled down through the mud into the deep earth below. When it was all over there was no sign they had ever been there.

Mrs. Young slumped in the mud, her husband's head in her lap, his blood and mud soaking her skirt. She was crying. I touched her head, explored her possible futures and they were mostly good. I was glad.

Sergeant Carter was nowhere to be seen.

And Coyote? He looked so God-damned pleased with himself, though I couldn't figure out why. Funny how I'd never noticed before that Coyote had no aura at all. I hadn't forgiven him for abandoning me, but then again I'd got out of the mess myself and maybe that was his point.

Teachers and the other boys swarmed out of the school. In the distance the gate stood open.

'Well?' I said to Coyote.

He and the dog trotted along beside me as I walked right out through the gate and down the road. My arm stung where I had been bitten, but it would soon heal. I had to go and see my Mama first and check how she was doing, but then I had to go to the deep darkness of the distant grove.

I'd find a way westward: I'd listen for the thunder of the fast express, follow the starlight on the rails. I didn't know what waited for me, but I knew who was trapped there, who was calling me: his name was Michael.

THE FOURTH CRAW

Look, I didn't want to be there in the first place. I don't mean on the dockside watching them hoist the body out of the water, that's no one's idea of a fun day at the seaside; I mean I didn't want to be there at all. I didn't want to be back in Scotland. I didn't want to be that me. I didn't want to inhabit that name, that identity. I'd tried to be someone else for five years with a quiet life at the Treasury, an office of my own, my secretary Esme, a comfortable chair, and time to grow into a name. I didn't have to kill people and live with all the consequences of that. The me by the dock was the someone I'd tried very hard not to be any more.

The local police weren't too happy about me being there either. It was bad enough I'd seen inside the shipping container, worse when they found the floating body, as if it were their fault and I'd caught them red-handed. They never like to think someone might know more than they do, or that they might just be front of house, going through the motions, checking tickets and selling ice cream without ever seeing backstage at the matinee. Every so often one cast a furtive look my way, wondering who I was and why I was there.

The sea spilled from the sodden clothes of the poor soul they lifted from the Clyde, draining over water-white wounds where his head and hands once were. Had he been happy or sad? Did he have big dreams as a child? Did he achieve any of them? Why did he die? Fuck knows.

The uniformed lads didn't have a problem: a sergeant came over.

'Do you need to take a look, sir?'

'What's to see?'

The flesh of the corpse's wrists and neck looked like upturned crabs at low tide, pierced by black-backed gulls.

'Nothing special, if you ignore the missing bits.'

'This the first?'

He patted his uniform pockets for cigarettes, then thought better of it.

'We pull them out every week, usually sad bastards who've had enough and top themselves. Or unlucky drunks who got pissed and fell in. Ones wi' bits missing? First I've seen it in twenty-five years.'

'Could he have floated down from Glasgow?'

'Mebbe, but you get to know what they look like when they've been in salt water. So I'm guessing he's come in on the tide. No' long dead though, I reckon.'

'Why?'

'He's in a bad way, but no' as bad as he'd be if he'd been out there a while.'

Over his shoulder I could see the plain-clothes guys giving him filthy looks for fraternising with the likes of me.

'What was he wearing?'

'Brown overalls over jeans and a sweater. Rubber soled boots with a steel toecap.

'Any labels?'

'No idea: we haven't looked yet.'

I looked out at the choppy water, at the gulls flying into the breeze, their wings struggling to do more than hold them in the same place.

'Any gossip?'

'Nothing to hang an investigation on. Probably drugs, one way or another though.'

Most things are these days.

'You'd best get back, Sergeant, your colleagues will lynch you.'

'Nae danger, sir. McPherson's the name should you need anything.'

I walked back with him. I had no reason to do that, nothing to see or do, I just wanted to mark my territory. I called McPherson when we were in earshot of the others.

'Could you make sure I get a copy of the mortuary report? Probably no link to the container, but you never know.'

I gave him my hotel address and walked back to my pool car. Forget your Aston Martins, they'd given me a two-year old dark green Hillman Avenger while the police swanned about in shiny 2 litre Mk. 3 Cortinas. The radio came on when I turned the key; Noddy Holder sang *Mama Weer All Crazee Now*. I turned it off.

A sharp breeze rolled across the water; the scudding clouds turned to darker tones. The weatherman said to expect early sleet in the Highlands. All the joys of the Clyde Riviera were mine to enjoy: no wonder we invented whisky.

Movement across the estuary caught my eye. The dorsal fin of a Polaris submarine slipped out towards the Atlantic, wet slate against the vermilion smear of distant hills.

Hawking's office hadn't changed much, still the same regulation issue furniture that favoured function over aesthetics. A substantial desk came with his grade, and a conference table with eight chairs, and two battered leather armchairs that glared at each other across a scuffed coffee table. Standard civil service pale green emulsion walls, unadorned by art, home to a venerable cast-iron radiator encrusted in decades of cheap white gloss that kept in the heat. The plumbing clanked and clattered even though it was August. A scuffed path ran across the carpet between the desk and a document safe that squatted in one corner of the room.

Relentless afternoon sunlight angled through venetian blinds covering casement windows, casting whispering shadows in the corners of the room.

There were no personal items. Even his pen and stationery were standard HMSO issue. A bottle of Stephens blue-black registrar's ink sat next to an Anglepoise lamp to the right of a large blotter: the top sheet was destroyed every evening.

He looked less cadaverous than the last time we met, more jowly, hair a touch greyer, hairline further up his temple. His eyes were still the same, a gateway to the devious old sod who lived behind them. His suit was good quality, but off-the-shelf. His shirt and tie came from a high street shop. The tie was pastel yellow with no link to school or regiment. Only his shoes hinted at his history: black oxfords shined to a parade-ground finish, well waxed in the welts, with recently replaced commando-style soles.

Once, several years ago, I'd tried to find out more about him. I reckoned I was discreet until he pulled me aside.

'Best give it a rest, old chap,' he'd said, 'you'll only do yourself a mischief.'

I kept digging of course, he'd have no use for me if I hadn't, but I didn't get far. It was as though he didn't exist before 1945.

'You got the message then? Good show. Just milk in your tea? Good, good. No, no! The armchairs today, my boy. I have a job for you, and you're not going to like it. No, not going to like it one little bit.'

Too bloody right I wasn't. I'd had a hard enough time getting out of Hawking's clutches in the first place. I told him so, but couldn't puncture his glee.

'Take it as a compliment, dear boy. We have a little problem and you're just the chap to tackle it.'

The tea was too hot and strong to do more than sip. I waiting for him to say more, but he was in no hurry. I couldn't blame him: I'd never told him the real reason I'd left, hadn't told anyone, not even myself at first.

'Why me?'

'I need an old hand on this one, someone sensible, someone who's been around the block a few times.' He gave me a direct look with an attempted smile. He'd probably read somewhere it would help mollify me. It didn't.

'Yes, but why *me*?'

'Pragmatism, just pragmatism: you're available.'

'You never put me on routine jobs. I've been off the roster for five years.'

'Not quite: you're on the reserve list and all that, and you still get a salary supplement.'

'You're kidding! It's about enough to get me cod and chips and a pint of bitter every fortnight if I'm lucky!'

'It's the symbolic value that counts, taking the Queen's shilling don't you know? And there's something else: I need someone who'll fit in with the locals.'

Oh shit.

'Something's cropped up on the Clyde. We need a Jock for this one, and you're the best I could find in a hurry.'

'No.'

'Now, listen....'

'No. You know why as well as I do. You're yanking me out of retirement for a wee frolic *doon the watter*, with only the remains of my Scottish accent as a justification? This stinks.'

He fixed me with a glare. He wanted me to ask him what the job was, show that I was interested.

'Treasury treating you well, are they?'

'As a matter of fact they are, yes.'

He grunted. 'Well, you'll be back there soon. I've already arranged your leave of absence. Paid, of course.'

I tried to raise a single eyebrow in disbelief, something I'd seen on a science fiction show on television and rather liked.

'I'm a long way from agreeing to do anything yet.'

'Spare me the insubordination routine.'

'I don't recall subordination as a quality you encouraged in the field.'

'Don't be asinine. You don't have a choice so let's get on with it.'

I could have made a grand gesture and walked out, but it would do no good. Hawking would just make life very difficult indeed for me until I capitulated. I'd done it often enough to other poor buggers on his behalf.

'I want three things.'

'Do you now? What?'

'My full operational allowance restored and back-dated for the five years I have apparently been yours to recall. Payable as a lump sum, tax-free and up-front. An established identity that won't compromise my day job. And I want out for good.'

'Done! Now then, you'll want to know what this is all about.'

'Heroin? Good God, man: are you crazy? Where would you get heroin on a submarine at sea? And where would you have chance to hide it or inject it? The notion doesn't stand up to a moment's scrutiny. '

The Navy lads are twitchy about their submarines, or maybe it's about what the subs can do if the order is ever given. They're not especially fond of us since part of our job is hitching a lift with them for reasons that we can't explain, disturbing the routines and rhythms of their hermetic worlds, eating their food, farting in their oxygen supply, and generally getting in their way. They also suspect we get paid more.

I had questions to ask, questions which would put them on the defensive. I could have asked them in London, but would just have got the usual guff from the Admiralty. I had a better chance of getting straight answers at Faslane, HMS Neptune to the pedantic, home of the third and tenth submarine squadrons. The base Commander was well warned I was coming, and I dropped in to see him as a courtesy, though he wasn't who I really wanted to speak to. Unfortunately a large-scale exercise meant a lot of the crews were either at sea or far too preoccupied to have time for the likes of me.

'I didn't only mean serving submariners, Commander. There are a lot of other personnel here.'

'Mr. Chambers …'

'Major.'

'Yes, *Major* Chambers, I don't know what sort of operation you think I run, but I assure you that we have no problem with heroin or other narcotics here.'

I tried the eyebrow trick again and waited.

'Yes, well, there were some unfortunate stories of marijuana, particularly when the Yanks were around, but those were isolated incidents, Major, and dealt with firmly. Lessons were learned.'

'Commander, please understand my position. Intelligence suggests the Soviets are involved with local criminal elements, supplying narcotics in return for information. You might be right and there's nothing in it, but I have to investigate.'

'Oh I understand, Major, and you'll have my full co-operation. I just don't expect you to find anything.'

'Thank you, although in my world *not* finding anything can be as interesting a result as finding it.'

I stood up. I wanted to give the impression that *my* interview with *him* was over, but he was too experienced in ward-room politics to fall for that.

'Sit down, Major. Smoke?' He offered a packet of Players No 6, an oddly below-decks choice for an officer. I shook my head. 'Look, Major, we're talking of a service that for two centuries has strung out its fighting men with rum. Chaps on subs are a strange breed. They're immensely proud of their dolphins and don't like criticism. They spend weeks under the Arctic with only each other for company. The quacks will tell you all about isolation and confinement and the removal of the usual day and night routine. In some of the older subs the air can be pretty stale with God knows what in it.

'They're watched all the time. They don't readjust quickly to life ashore. They might miss births or deaths of close family, and they can never say where they went or what they did. Did you hear about that American boat, the Tautog?' I'd heard the rumours. 'Nearly a nasty business, like the Thresher and the Scorpion. Our lads don't see their Russian counterparts as enemies, there's something between them, a shared fear of sinking so far down you'll never be found again.'

He used the stub of his cigarette to light a second, and crushed the first in a Newcastle Brown Ale ashtray.

'So, Major Chambers: if you ask me if they've a reason to look for a needle to hide in, yes, of course. That's why we pick them carefully and watch them. We watch every whorehouse between here and Edinburgh. As the Yanks say, we don't have a drugs problem, just the occasional people problem.'

I winced at the phrasing. In reality the Americans were worried enough to offer an amnesty and guaranteed medical treatment for any Navy man owning up to drug use.

'I appreciate your candour, sir.' I said, forcing myself to look suitably appreciative. 'But our intelligence could equally cover wives left behind, administrative staff, logistics people. I have to be thorough.'

'Yes, yes, of course. Who do you want to speak to?'

'Regulating Branch and the Chaplain.'

He looked at me for a few seconds.

'Regulators I expected, but the Bish? His lips are sealed, you know. Should I warn them to expect you?'

'I'd be grateful.'

He stubbed out his cigarette and rose, making it clear who was dismissing whom.

The Regulators went out of their way to be helpful in all ways they could, except any that might reflect badly on them. They were disinclined to tell me anything that might contradict the Commander's assertions. I got nothing, which was more than I expected.

I was surprised to find the chaplain's office was so business-like: I'd expected something more obviously ecclesiastical.

The padre ('Call me Bob, Major, everyone does') was rangy but looked like he kept himself fit. He maintained a luxuriant beard below thinning red hair, and no doubt relished his vaguely piratical air. I dare say he thought having 'character' would make him more accepted. I wasn't sure if the suggestion of villainy was enhanced or offset by his dog collar and dark grey suit.

We faced off over a couple of mugs of instant coffee, a far cry from the fresh beans I got in London.

'So Major, how can I help?'

'We've received some intelligence. I'd like your opinion on it.'

'It implicates someone in my flock?'

'Not specific individuals, no. It's more general. The suggestion is that a foreign power is providing heroin to people associated with Neptune in exchange for secrets.'

Bob picked up his mug and held it in front of his mouth for a time, eventually taking a sip, scowling at its heat.

'A naval chaplaincy is a unique thing. We're responsible for several thousand souls, some at sea, some not. We see pretty much everything you'd see in a normal parish, with the added load of caring for submariners. And there's Polaris, why it is here and what it might do one day. Most are only nominally Christian, and it's usually routine hatching and matching, with the odd despatching.

'They're young. They can take long periods under water, but inevitably they sometimes feel lonely and isolated. When they get back it's hard to adjust, especially if they get it in the neck because of Polaris. And mostly they do OK. But not always.

'If you come back from a six-month cruise and find your wife four months pregnant, what do you do? Or your dad was buried two months ago? And they're sailors, you know? Home on shore leave with a thirst, and an itch to do what sailors have always done.' He took another sip of coffee.

'So you haven't had any heroin problems on the base?'

'I didn't say that.'

He looked at an indefinite point high above my right shoulder.

'Have you heard of rites of passage, Major Chambers?'

I had, but I wanted him to tell me about them. 'It's an idea in anthropology: you go on a ritual journey and the person who comes out the other end isn't the same as the one who goes in. Something like that happens to submariners: the journey changes men. They come home with the same face and the same name, but something is different. So if you told me that some of them tried heroin I shouldn't be surprised, and with the numbers we have it's pretty much certain some will, or someone in their family has. But I haven't heard of any particular problem, and sooner or later one of the chaplains or parish ministers nearby would hear of it and tell me.'

'Could you tell me if you had, or if you heard anything?'

'Not if it identified an individual. We're about the only people in the Navy with a duty of absolute confidentiality. But I'm happy to poke about and let you know if anything turns up.'

'A message for you from the Chief Constable, sir. They've found something down at the container port at Greenock he thinks you may be interested in.' The WPC handed me a slip of paper with details when I got back to my hotel.

The policeman at the gate checked my ID and waved me through. He wasn't to know that the papers and the scuffed wallet were only issued the week before.

I looked for the senior officer amongst the collection of police cars and ambulances. he introduced himself as Inspector MacLeod, a tall fellow with greying curly hair and the stance of a street-fighter. My ex mother-in-law had thrown me warmer looks. They'd waited for me for an hour and a half.

'You'll be wanting a look.' A statement drawn out like he was working bacon gristle from between his back teeth.

A large shipment of what looked like pure heroin had been found between bulkheads in the engine room of the *Equestris* during a random Customs search. When they searched the unloaded containers, they found the women's bodies.

They were huddled together, all clothed. Judging by the smell, they'd died several days earlier. Packing cases behind them once held food and water. Scattered around the floor were electric torches, syringes, spoons and charred matches. Track marks pocked several arms.

God knows what the temperature was in there during their voyage. The stench was awful, just like '44 and '45.

The radio crackled in a panda car.

'Sir, they say there's a body in the water.'

MacLeod glared at me as though I'd arranged this just to spoil his day, then detailed a couple of cars to check on the floating body. I took a final look at the container and decided to follow them.

'Carry on, Inspector,' I said, just because I could.

The hotel was anonymous, which suited me fine. It was someone's townhouse in the 19th century, and hinted at mercantile grandeur if you looked hard, through half-closed eyes, on a foggy night. It was quiet, with only a few travelling salesmen in the other rooms. I dropped into an armchair with a cup of tea and glanced through last night's Evening Citizen. The news hadn't improved and I wasn't interested in football chatter.

Glasgow was a long way from Neptune and Greenock, but it gave me the space to think through what I'd learned, even if I wasn't sure what that was. I reckoned the padre's denial of any major problem was definitive.

Through the window I could see the Queen's Park and the hills beyond. Sometimes, if I let my imagination wander, I fancy I can see pathways shimmering just below the threshold of normal perception. I could make out a line coming over from where Stirling should be towards Provan, or thereabouts. I conjured a vision of the topography before we humans made our mark, the raw sinews of the country beneath the stretched skin of civilisation, before we gave it names and changed its face.

Civilisation my arse: tell that to the bodies in the container, and in the boxcars in railway sidings all over Germany, and the cellars outside Rome. All the corpses and flies, and always that smell. Those memories were from the first me, before my family were told that I was killed in action, before someone else came back from the war instead of me.

This was the first time I'd come back to Glasgow, city of my birth, city where my parents and siblings still lived for all I knew. I once had a wife here, married in haste in '40, and a son, whom I'd never seen, born six months later. This was the place, the dear green place, to which Hawking once promised never to assign me. This was where old school friends might bump into me on the street and think they'd seen a ghost, and they'd be right.

Someone told me once that your cells die and regenerate all the time, and by the time you're my age you don't have the same body you began with. I'm not the mewling scrap of skin and bones whom my parents named for my grandfather's father, not the bairn who went to school, not the bairn who went to war, not the person who came back; not the man you think I am. And yet, despite my best efforts, despite all the names and identities, I still feel the same, most of the time, I think. But how can I be the same if even the brain I think with is a replacement?

All the people I've been have done things, most of them unpleasant, in the name of Her Majesty or her father before her, all in the cause of civilisation. No one would mourn me if I died right now: they'd done all their mourning in 1945.

There was nothing on telly except a folk singer. He wore tartan trews and a billowy, black linen Jacobite shirt, surmounted by a rough leather waistcoat. The tartan was redundant in black and white. He strummed a shiny Gibson 12-string guitar and drained the life-blood out of a medley of children's songs. I turned him off, but the damned ditty stuck in my head:

Three craws sat upon a wa'
Sat upon a wa'
Sat upon a wa'

I told myself that I shivered because of the sudden stuttering rattle of a shower blown against the window, not the other memories, the ones my mother did her best to whip out of me.

Damn Hawking to Hell and back. Like the first craw, I couldnae flee at a'.

McPherson waited in a greasy spoon in Greenock. Breakfast was fried square sausage and two fried eggs served on fried pan loaf slices: if they could fry the tea they would have. I'd already had a quick scan of the newspaper front pages in the newsagent next door. The headlines were all about Munich, nothing about the women or the heroin. Domestic stories were pushed well inside and weren't much more than the weather, the future of Clyde shipbuilding, a missing German businessman, and football, always football.

The sergeant opened a leather briefcase and handed me

a manila folder containing photographs, carbons and third-generation photostats.

'This is what we've got so far. Nothing about our floater, a bit about the ship. Nothing about the girls yet.'

'How many were there?'

'Thirty-four.'

'Jesus. Anything in common?'

'Naw, but who knows? If you don't mind me asking, sir, whit's this all about?'

There are only two real rules in my game: don't blow your cover and don't involve civilians in operations. The sergeant counted as a civilian.

'I'm looking at whether there is any chance that drugs could get through to the submarine base.'

'It'll be a bit more than that if the Chief Constable has your back, sir.'

That's sergeants for you.

'Yes, it'll be a bit more than that, but it's why I'm interested in the heroin rather than the girls.'

'You might want to have a think about that, sir.'

I looked quizzical but didn't insult him with the raised eyebrow treatment.

'We don't have much trouble with the Navy boys and drugs. Mostly they just get pished and fight the Yanks. But they spend a lot of time wi' whoors, and my money says those dead girls were whoors. And they were using. So mebbe if I was guddling for sailors, I'd tickle them wi' women.'

'That's a bit of a stretch to make them addicts, though.'

'You wouldn't need to, would you sir? Just take some photies or Super 8 and blackmail them. Hypothetically, of course.'

Beyond the café window, the sea and sky were the colour of scuffed brown corduroy.

143

'There's another thing, sir.'

'Yes?'

'The shipping line says that container came from the Bosphorus, from Odessa. I thought that might be relevant. Hypothetically.'

Out on the river, random shafts of sunlight broke through the clouds, picking out highlights on the wave-tops, yellowy-white foam on the brown and grey of the water.

'The Navy say they keep an eye on every brothel between Faslane and Edinburgh. I don't suppose we could make a list of the places they usually go, could we?'

Sergeant McPherson smiled and produced another manila folder from the briefcase.

'Ah, well: I'm glad you asked me that, sir. If Mr MacLeod asks, by the way, you didn't get this from me. It includes the east coast, too, for when the Navy is in the Forth. The ones wi' the red asterisk use girls from overseas.'

'Why bring them in a container? There must be easier ways. So why don't we work out where the girls were going and see where it gets us?'

'We?' He favoured me with a raised eyebrow. 'That's polis work that is, sir. We'll get onto that and you do whatever it is you do.'

Whatever it is I do. Maybe it's because what I do is bound to who I am that I don't know either who I am or what I do.

I took the long way back from Greenock, round the coast. I bought an ice cream cone and a newspaper in Largs and sat on a bench, watching car ferries shuttle to and from the Cumbrae Slip, while the Keppel took the longer route to Millport, and the Waverley and Queen Mary II cruised to more distant resorts.

Once upon a time there was another me, a child, excited to go doon the watter at the Glasgow Fair with his parents

144

and sisters, when the Broomielaw bustled with merchantmen, the yards built ships galore, and the big Clyde-built liners raced across the Atlantic. Back when Glasgow was the second city of the Empire and the maps were tinted pink with the certainty of supremacy and 'Clyde-built' meant something. That wee boy from the tenements, the boy with a giant toffee apple as a treat from his Aunty Bella's sweet shop in Rothesay, how did he get to be me?

Only Polaris went doon the watter now, off to cruise under the pole for as long as there is ice to slide under. If SRI was right, that might not be much longer.

Another vista flickered in front of me, a Clyde without shipyards and no people on the shore, the sea level creeping higher every year. I blinked in the breeze, and the vision was gone.

If I'd planned my time better I might have taken a cruise from Largs, but I hadn't and, anyway, the sky in the north was still dark. On a whim, I took the road over Fenwick Moor towards Eaglesham and pulled into a layby by a small hill. I sauntered up a top that was too slight to be called a summit. Despite warm sunshine, the breeze was stiffer up there, whipping around my face. But there were no distractions of modernity to disturb the peace. I looked out over the expanse of scrub and bog and could have been anyone: a spark of consciousness under an uncertain sky; a scrap of life dancing like cotton grass in the wind.

Far off, an aircraft, a Viscount by the look of it, rose from Abbotsinch. A few moments later the faint drone of its turbo-props reached me. The spell was broken. I eased myself into the car and back into Major Denis Chambers, whoever he was. From their perches on a dry-stane wall, the crows were coarsely *caw*-ing. I didn't look to count them.

I made a short call to London from a phone box in Eaglesham to pass a request to the local control officer. I needed an assistant.

I met her in Edinburgh, in a café near the Netherbow, where the site of the old gate into the City was marked by brass plates set in cobbles at a junction.

She was the only other customer. We did the usual recognition two-step. She was in her mid-forties. I assumed she was single as she wore no rings and had no marks on her fingers where a ring might normally be. Her clothes were Morningside-sensible, smart, if slightly dated. She wore flat shoes, and those odd uplifted-almond shaped horn-rimmed spectacles. Her hair, light brown with undisguised hints of premature grey, was pulled up into a bun, again smart, but practical rather than severe. Not much make up, only lipstick. Control said simply that she held an honours degree in Law from Edinburgh University and had served in signals intelligence, though in what capacity was unsaid. Her name, or the one I was given, was Anna Mill.

'You have some research to be done, Major?' Her voice was well modulated with an intriguing undertow of earthiness, an underlay of accent. I handed her a copy of one of the documents Sergeant McPherson gave me the day before, and let her scrutinise it while I added two cubes of brown sugar to my coffee. 'That's a list of establishments visited by submariners from Faslane.'

Anna raised her eyebrows, the ghost of a smile on her lips.

'Do you mean brothels, Major?'

'The same. I'd like you to find out what you can about them, who owns the business, who owns the buildings, if there are any securities over them, and so forth.'

'What are you looking for?'

'I have no idea. I'm just poking around to see if there is anything to see.'

'Might I ask the context?'

'You heard about the container in Greenock?' Her eyes grew more alert. 'The working assumption is that the women were brought here as tarts. The police are on it, but I'd like to dig around. To be honest, it might be wasted effort, but you never know.'

'Is this a records search only, or do you want me to go and have a look?' There was that same hint of a smile. I found it rather attractive, suggestive of the private woman behind her professional face.

'Let's stick to the records. The Navy watch the buildings and we may as well keep this to ourselves.'

She put the paper into her shoulder bag.

'Is there anything else I should know?'

'Only where you can find me.' I gave her the address and telephone number of my hotel. 'How long do you think you'll need?'

'All being well, I can get the property stuff done at Register House in a day, another day to get copies of any interesting deeds. I'll let you know about the rest, but probably three days should do it. A week at the outside.'

'How do I get a message to you?'

'Best to go through channels. I'll be in Register House or other offices in working hours.'

I paid for the drinks and held the door for her. She gave a wave to the woman behind the counter as she left: a regular, then.

'Can I give you a lift anywhere?'

'It's OK. I can walk from here.' She offered her hand. 'I'll let you know how it's going.'

Her hips swayed as she walked away from me, and I decided she had been schooled in deportment. She went up St Mary's Street, over the junction at the Netherbow, and onto Jeffries Street, where she got into the driver's side of a new-looking Hillman Imp.

I couldn't face driving straight back to Glasgow, so I walked up the Royal Mile, across the junction with South Bridge, and up past St. Giles Cathedral. I savoured the magnificent yeast and roast-malt aroma of the Edinburgh breweries. I had time to find a decent pint amongst the chemical monstrosities that pass for beer these days.

I could sense history all around me: you can't walk up the Mile without perceiving the ghosts of its long, bloody, past. Aunty Bella in Rothesay used to say she really could see ghosts, especially the phantoms of sailors who walked out of the sea in the bay at low tide, and the shades of fisherman gathered round the pier. When she told us, her eyes would grow wide and a hatch would open onto a deep upwelling of something intoxicating. My mother always shushed her and told her not to frighten us, which I found odd. Among my many childhood fears, ghosts were never a concern: I saw them all the time, but didn't ever tell anyone. The first, and only, time I told mother it triggered a whipping and the ridiculing pity of my siblings. Bella always seemed to have a soft spot for me, though. Ma said she couldn't think why.

Maybe it's because I was thinking of Bella that I had the oddest sensation that I could see the past overlaid on the present. The vision hung fractured and ambiguous as presences faded and mingled with the crowds around me, neither fully here nor completely absent. Heads spiked on top of the long-demolished Tolbooth looked at me in hollow-eyed mockery. I shook my head to dismiss the sensation, and, like the locals, spat on the Heart of Midlothian to ward off the shades of the past.

Up at the Lawnmarket, near the West Bow wellhead, I noticed I had a tail. She was good, and I'm not sure exactly what tipped me off. Most of us in the game develop an instinct for this. Astronomers compare plates of the same part of the sky looking for what changes; we look for what is constant amidst the change.

She was strikingly tall, wearing clothes that could have come from the back pages of *Melody Maker*, a dark suede maxi-coat with sunflower patches, buttons open from crotch-height to reveal tan leather boots, black tights and a pink mini-skirt. She wore a purple beret over long auburn hair. Unlike the usual hippy-stuff, her gear was properly cut and had quality about it. She could have wafted through a continental terminal, bound for Milan or Rome, and looked at home. She stayed well back, but always kept me in sight.

I tried the usual routines, slipping in and out of shops, doubling back and dropping down Advocate's Close to Cockburn Street then working my way back up to the High Street and slipping sideways into the door of a pub. None of them worked. Sooner or later I spotted her again, out there amongst the living and occasional dead.

I wasn't sure how to play it, to engineer a confrontation or make myself scarce. There was a time when I wouldn't have hesitated, but I'm 53 and out of the game. I had to assume she wasn't alone, and I half suspected she knew I knew she was there, yet still made herself known. Either she wanted me to know she was following me or she didn't care. Either way I didn't like it. I went back onto the street and flagged the first cab I saw. I took it to the

West End and called Control from a phone box. I told them where I had parked the Avenger and that it was probably watched, then caught a train from Haymarket to Glasgow.

Around four, reception called to say they had a package for me. It contained the keys to another dark green 1970 Hillman Avenger, and directions to where it was parked. They also handed me a sealed letter. In my room I made a pot of tea, and sat as still as I could, letting my mind go blank, willing myself to forget the spiked heads on the Royal Mile, staunching the flow of images from my deep past, suppressing what I didn't want to remember, denying life to the long dead. I didn't want anything to do with the dead.

I opened the letter: the Chief Constable requested the pleasure of my company at 18:00 at the Jail Square mortuary.

The Chief Constable was an enigma – a devout Christian, fond of salmon fishing, he's forever 'the Hammer' to Glasgow's neds. He was a naval rating at Normandy and spent his early policing years in the marine division. A man to treat with respect. I arrived at the mortuary where a constable ushered me instead into a chamber in the High Court next door.

'Ah! Major Chambers. You know Inspector MacLeod and Sergeant McPherson, and this is Detective Superintendent Walker. Sorry to haul you in, but the Russian Consulate asked for a meeting. Your Head Office thought you should attend. The meeting is at seven and we thought it would be sensible to square our stories and get the latest from the mortuary, which is why we're here and not in Pitt Street.'

'How were you intending to introduce me, sir?'

'That's part of the reason I asked you here early: you and I are the only ones who know why you're here.'

MacLeod, Walker and McPherson leant forward slightly. The Chief Constable had Special Branch experience, so he wasn't about to let any secrets fly free.

'Probably best if you introduce me as plain Denis Chambers up from London, with an interest in the international aspects of the case.'

'Fair enough. Now, Alex: what's the latest?'

The *Equestris* left Odessa, Walker said, with the container, on Sunday 20 August. It reached Rotterdam and changed crew on 31 August. The container remained on board, and the ship left again on Saturday 2 September, arriving at Greenock two and a half days later. The container was therefore on board for sixteen days. The condition of the bodies suggested death, probably of asphyxia, was before the ship arrived in Rotterdam. At least ten bodies had track marks. No identity papers were found. Their luggage, such as it was, was consistent with them boarding in Ukraine. No personal items apart from clothes and toiletries; no jewellery.

The heroin in the bulkhead, packed in fifteen transparent packages, was near one hundred percent purity. No link so far to any current members of the *Equestris*'s crew, who were from a variety of nationalities, but background checks were still in progress. The ship remained at Greenock, despite the protests of the owner's agents.

There was no progress with the body pulled from the Clyde and no known link between it and the *Equestris*. The crew members who boarded in Rotterdam were present and accounted for.

'And the container?' I didn't look at the sergeant.

'What about it?'

'Somebody was supposed to collect it, I assume.'

'Ah, well. Yes. The manifest names a haulier. The name is false, the haulier doesn't exist, and the delivery address is an abandoned warehouse in Leith near the docks.'

'May I have a copy please?'

The constable who had ushered me in knocked and said that the consular representative, Mr Lasarev, had arrived slightly early.

'Of course, show him in constable. Gentleman, I believe he is interested only in the women – best not mention the heroin, eh?'

We all stood as the Russian came into the room. He exhibited just the right mix of insouciance and deference as he shook the Chief Constable's hand and gave a very slight formal bow.

'Thank you for seeing me Chief Constable. I hope I haven't taken up too much of your time.'

'Not at all, it is our pleasure.' He made the introductions. Lasarev shook each of our hands in turn, offering the same slight bow.

'Gentlemen, shall we get down to business?' He spoke in almost accent-free English. He hitched his suit trousers and ran a hand over his cropped hair as he sat down. 'Chief Constable, gentlemen, you enquired about a vessel called the *Equestris* which sailed from Odessa two and a half weeks ago. I believe a number of deaths are involved, but your constable wasn't at liberty to say more than that. The ambassador asked me to find out what has happened, and, naturally, to offer assistance.'

'My apologies for our reticence. Our enquiries are still at an early stage, and there's a lot we don't know. Superintendent Walker can tell you what we have so far. It is not pleasant.'

Walker gave a detailed summary and spread some

photographs on the table. I watched Lasarev: he was the perfect model of an attentive listener. He had a small pocket notebook and a propelling pencil on the table in front of him, but made no notes and kept his eyes fixed on the speaker. He looked briefly at the first two or three photographs, but didn't examine the bundle.

'Thank you, Superintendent. I understand perfectly why you were reluctant to set hares running, that is the correct expression? You will have our immediate help in obtaining records from Odessa. We will alert our police regarding reports of missing women. I am particularly disturbed that some used narcotics: this is something on which we have very strict policies.' He turned to me. 'Forgive me Mr. Chambers, I am not clear on your role in this.'

'I'm here to monitor international aspects and report back to the Foreign Office if anything requires diplomatic assistance.'

'And is there anything?'

'Not yet, no.'

'Thank you. If the Chief Constable will permit, I suggest that you and I talk privately, and establish proper channels.'

'Of course.'

He knew I'd agree to meet, I still owed him a drink or six from the last time we met, ten years before, in East Berlin, when he wore a Red Army lieutenant-colonel's uniform and called himself Salkov.

I asked if there was anywhere nearby I could get a decent meal without exceeding my *per diem* expenses: man cannot live on Stakis Steakhouses alone. I bought a newspaper, and found a bar. It was a decent place, with an old-fashioned, disreputable air. The long mahogany counter bore the stains of decades of spilled pints and burning cigarette ends. The bar stools, all in a row, were set tall so that the patrons' shoes rested on the brass foot rail. An ornate gantry, also mahogany, held spirits, blended whisky mainly, with a couple of malts for the choosy, as well as gin, vodka and several rums. There were mirrors etched with the names of forgotten breweries: photos of local lads made good at the boxing or the football hung like dusty trophies, the glass nicotine-stained. Like all the best bars it smelled of spilt beer, smoked tobacco and stale old men.

My heart jumped at the traditional Scottish tall beer founts, but they all served fizzy keg creations. I bought a Guinness.

There were a few others in, all men, some with long scars on their cheeks, probably not earned in Heidelberg or Jena. They glanced at me as I came in, but didn't talk. The newspaper didn't say much, though I lingered on a reported claim by the Israelis that they were interested in Eberhard Graf, the missing German businessman. Mossad suspected that his real name was Wilfred Ehmann, a long sought-after guard at Treblinka.

Fifteen minutes later Lasarev walked in. He gave me an expansive smile and a loud *Tovarishch,* which earned a lot more than a quick glance from the bar. They probably thought I was a Union official getting my instructions from Moscow Central. I bought him a pint of heavy, and we took a table in a corner.

'So then, Mister *Chambers,* how surprising to see you again: we thought you had retired.'

'So did I. Funny how that happens.'

'Well you are looking well; the Treasury obviously agrees with you.'

'You're well informed. What do I call you now? Is it still Sasha?'

'Why not? What's in a name anyway?' He took a sip of the beer and grimaced. 'You should come back to Berlin, or Budapest maybe, where there is still real beer.'

I waited for him to get to the point.

'So then, *Denis*: if you are here, someone must think we are involved in something. Do you think we are?'

'I don't know what to think, although now that you've shown up, I'm wondering.'

'Quite so. We shall each have to say we met an old friend and then there will be real interest from on high where there was only suspicion before.'

I studied the line of optics behind the bar.

'Only if I tell them. We heard a rumour some of your friends hoped some of our sailors might tell stories to young women, especially if they were photographed in the act.'

'My friend, that explains your government's interest. It doesn't explain why they sent *you*.'

'There's no mystery, I was available.' I tried to sound sincere.

'So, someone tells this spy story and, presto! A box full of dead girls from CCCP is found on a quayside, and they decide to pull you away from your desk and your quiet life to see what's going on?'

'That's about the size of it, Sasha.' I had no reason to correct him.

'Well, who am I to question your story? My superiors will think it thin, though.'

'They'll be right, but it's the only story I've got.'

'And if you have a better story, will you tell me? For old time's sake?'

'That depends on the story. Will you tell me if your friends are working on our sailors?'

'That depends if they're my friends or merely fellow countrymen.'

155

I asked for a number at which I could get in touch with him.

'I think we have the basis for a mutually beneficial understanding. Another beer?'

He raised his glass in salute and grimaced.

'I have learned new phrases from your television since I came here. Listen: Scotland! Your weather is rotten and so is your food. But your beer, your beer is ... Pish!'

He roared with laughter. I took it as a no.

On the way back to the hotel I stopped at a call box and rang Control. I passed on the name of the warehouse in Leith and asked for it to be added to Anna's enquiries. I didn't mention Sasha.

I slept in, and stayed in bed, lying on my back, hands behind my head. I had nothing to go on, no evidence of anything untoward, except I was followed in Edinburgh, and the Russians had sent Sasha to nose around. Somebody, somewhere, wasn't telling me everything, and that somebody was Hawking.

I couldn't work out what to do next without news from either Anna Mill or Sergeant McPherson. I didn't want to go back to Faslane without anything to work with. And I was irked by my retreat from Edinburgh.

I drove into Glasgow city centre. I went to a bank and cashed a cheque for the lump sum Hawking had arranged, then crossed the City and parked round the corner from a car rental agency. I left Glasgow in a rented Sahara beige Ford Escort 1300XL, for which I paid cash.

I drove straight through Edinburgh, down to the foot of Leith Walk and over onto Constitution Street. I parked just beyond the junction with Queen Charlotte Street, and picked a small holdall out of the back.

Leith was once an important European port, but each year the trade in Leith dropped off with the coming of container ships to the Clyde. Even the railway station at the foot of Leith Walk was closed, only used for maintaining diesel locomotives. The sun was bright, but the tenements around me loomed brown and black. The port was still out of sight as I walked along Bernard Street towards the Shore, where the ribbon of the Water of Leith ends its meandering trek from the Pentland Hills. Despite the soot and smoke in the air and the filth in the water, I could smell the sea. The cries of gulls, and a massed chorus of clackers in a school playground drowned the sounds of traffic and light industry.

I had a Nikon F 35mm camera in the holdall, with 35, 50 and 135mm lenses. I'd really wanted to road test one of the new Olympus SLRs, but stores weren't having any of that. At the Shore, I loaded some Tri-X and spent a while making sure I was seen photographing the waterfront and generally acting like hobbyist photographer.

Two new-looking padlocks on chains secured the doors of the warehouse. The roof and walls were sound, none of the windows broken. The unkempt courtyard had none of the usual accumulated detritus of empty industrial spaces. It took me a while to notice there was no graffiti. That alone was enough to make it unusual: it wasn't unkempt enough.

The main doors were on runners rather than hinges. The runners were untarnished and well-greased. Tyre marks in the dirt suggested at least one vehicle had been in the building in the last couple of months or so.

I looked for any access down the sides, but the way was blocked by eight-foot-tall corrugated sheeting, bolted to a hidden framework and topped with coils of barbed wire. I took a few photos then walked on down the street, taking other, random, shots in case anyone was watching.

I tried to access to the rear of the building, but couldn't. Whenever I approached through a close or a side street I found a tall and substantial stone wall, which looked nineteenth century to me, also topped with barbed wire. From what I could see of the windows, they were inset behind recently-painted vertical metal bars. Short of shimmying down a line from a helicopter, I couldn't see any way in or out apart from the front door.

Whatever else it might be, it was not abandoned.

I worked my way back to the car. I rang Control from a call box in case there were any messages. I was told to wait where I was, and five minutes later Anna called me back.

'Major, I have some of the information you asked for.'

'Can you suggest when and where we could meet?'

She named a café on Rose Street in two hours

I bought a copy of *The Scotsman* and went straight to Rose Street and found the café. There was another tearoom just along and on the opposite side of the street, where I snagged a window seat, ordered a pot of tea, and settled down with the paper.

Right on time, Anna walked along the street and entered the rendezvous. She carried a leather attaché case. I gave it five minutes, until a familiar figure appeared on the opposite side of the street. It was my tail from the previous day, wearing exactly the same clothes. She didn't see me and kept walking, stopping further along the street, apparently window shopping.

I borrowed the telephone and a directory.

'It's me. You were followed.'

'Oh I doubt that, Major. I was very careful.'

'Your tail is waiting further up the street from you. Could you leave the attaché case with the manageress there and go? I'll pick it up later. Keep an eye out for a very tall woman in a dark maxi-coat over a pink mini-skirt, wearing a purple beret over long hair.'

'Did you notice anything else about her?'

'No, should I have?'

She hesitated 'Your description reminded me of a former colleague.'

'Former?'

'She died.'

'OK. I'll contact you via Control later.'

Five minutes later, Anna left the café and came along the street towards me. I stepped back into the shadows behind the door. I still had the short telephoto lens on the Nikon and took several shots as Anna kept walking, past me, then past the watcher, who waited a short time before following. I gave it another five minutes before retrieving the attaché case. I found the car and drove off. I stopped in Corstorphine and 'phoned Control from a call box. I confirmed I had the case and said this time it was Anna who seemed to be the subject of the tail.

Anna was thorough. The case contained copies of title documents with her typed notes and analysis.

Of the brothels specialising in foreign girls, eight were in the west, four in Edinburgh. Six of those in the west were in townhouses or flats and changed hands several times in the last decade, usually transferred between limited companies. Four of the properties were in the same ownership since the nineteenth century, two in the west and two in the east.

Title to each of the four was in the name of a different Trust, and registered between 1880 and 1882. Anna noticed all of the titles were registered by the same firm of solicitors,

Uddart and Maule, Writers to the Signet in Edinburgh. Each property was also used to secure loans at various times up to 1950, and all of the securities were granted to the same creditor, a further Trust administered by Messrs Hardaway and Scheidt, solicitors, Newcastle upon Tyne. All were originally sold as development sites. As usual, the titles were feudal and contained conditions imposed by the feudal superiors. The superior was the same in each case, yet another Trust, the Third Aphrêm Family Trust. Anna hadn't tracked down the original trust deed, but the beneficiary seemed to be connected to a property at The Leyes, Selkirkshire.

The Leyes was now owned by a company registered in Germany, Carterhaugh Estates GmbH. According to the telephone directory, it was a stables and rescue centre for retired pit ponies.

The warehouse was held on a very long lease, granted for 900 years and one day, in 1785. The first tenant was the Endeavour Whaling Company, which, judging by various securities granted over the years, changed its name several times and was now Endeavour (Holdings) Ltd. The 1785 lease was granted by The Equestris Trustees who had themselves taken title, in 1784, from The Second Aphrêm Family Trust.

Anna managed to get time on the mainframe computer and ran all the names and addresses she found in the documents through a Soundex search of the archives. Aphrêm in conjunction with The Leyes raised a flag to refer to a restricted file from 1946. That file was empty except for a cover sheet directing all enquiries regarding those names to the War Office with the reference of either or both Operations EXCALIBUR (1916-18) or LANYARD (1943-45). The sheet was amended in 1964 when War Office was scored out and Ministry of Defence written in.

The person to whom all enquiries should be referred was Hawking.

I was a captain by '44, a real rank earned in the field under my real name. I joined up on a commission thanks to the University OTC, and was posted as a subaltern to Army Intelligence, probably because I was good at crosswords and had reasonable German and passable Russian. We were Mrs Astor's D-Day Dodgers; we fought our way through North Africa, then Sicily and worked our way up the ankles of Italy. I had various duties, usually the ones that others found unpleasant.

Most of the prisoners we took were squaddies. We'd try and get out of them whatever tactical stuff we could: movements, supply lines, food and ammunition reserves, and the like. Officers were higher value, but would give up information without too much effort on our part. Often calling for a fictitious Polish officer would frighten them into talking straight away. Sometimes we acquired SS and Gestapo officers who would not talk at all without 'persuasion'. They were my job.

Strictly, we weren't supposed to do anything physical to get them to talk, but there were lots of things we weren't supposed to do that I did anyway. This meant I questioned them somewhat more intensively than was gentlemanly. Sometimes it meant expediting their demise.

Listen to me, drifting into the euphemistic. My job was to interrogate people and sometimes kill them. And I turned out to be good at it. I always knew what was needed to break them, always knew the best line of questioning. They said I had a gift for it.

I had no guilt about killing them either: these weren't

reluctant squaddies or conscripts, they knew exactly what they had done, were proud of it, even. I could have done without seeing their outraged presences hanging around after I bumped them off, but if you try long enough and hard enough not to see, then eventually you won't.

Don't expect me to apologise. It was war. We left a lot of boys behind in shallow graves. I like to think that many more made it home, on both sides, because of what we did. What I did.

By June '44 we were in *Campagna Romana*. The idiot Clark disobeyed orders and chased the glory of 'liberating' Rome instead of tackling the bigger problem of the German 10th Army, which promptly moved north where it could kill more of us. I was quartering the plains and driving up into the hills with Sergeant Douglas who had been with me since Sicily, another sergeant who forfeited his first name on promotion. Partly we were on the lookout for any German stragglers who might have information, partly we were trying to link up with partisan groups.

It's no great hardship to be in Italy in summer, of course, so long as you aren't fighting for your life. War for me meant long periods of loafing around interspersed with intense bursts of things sensible people would find distasteful, if not abhorrent.

I was never happier.

Despite the war, it was still Italy: olives grew on the trees and grapes on the vine. A kind of normality was reasserting itself, albeit slowly. The air smelled of oregano, lavender and rosemary. The few days I was there followed a pattern: scorching hot days, with thunderstorms rolling off the Sabine hills in the early evening, leading to long, humid nights. It was one such evening, after the thunder and rain, we found ourselves in a town I'm still not allowed to name.

The town, laid out long before the Romans pretended to Empire, stretched along the elongated spine of a ridge, part of a promontory bounded on three sides by cliffs. Scratch a metre or two beneath rough, cobbled streets and you'd find pre-Etruscan cart ways, climbing towards the central piazza. Residents, in no great hurry, made their way through alleys and arched passages to their homes. Under terracotta roof tiles, the walls, pockmarked by recent bullets, were washed white, pink and ochre, occasionally smeared by russet stains where collaborators were shot. Last year's wine matured in cool cellars, while S*angiovese, Montepulciano,* and interloping *Lacrima* ripened over pergolas and in garden vineyards.

In *La Rossa's,* over cards and cold beers, the talk was all of war and whether we liberators could be trusted. As always, the cry was to punish the guilty, but all over Europe it was the innocent who died – quickly, slowly, cleanly, appallingly. Modern warfare made sure the innocent were more efficiently targeted: a school here, a hospital there, evisceration everywhere. The accidents that always happen when you drop bombs on inhabited areas. It never matters which side you are on when the shrapnel comes your way, the gas slips over the back of your throat, the bread knife hacks your gizzard. And always it is the fault of the other side, never, ever, the fault of the side that pulled the trigger, no sir, sounds like sympathising to me, sir, please step this way while we ask you some questions ...

On the other side of the piazza, at the high point of the ridge, stood a *castello.* It had a late medieval look, with old glass windows set in Romanesque arches, recessed below machicolated battlements in the French style. The massive front gates lay smashed, off their hinges, and we drove through the open archway.

The heart of the *castello* complex was an ancient tower that climbed above ornamental herb gardens and courtyards. The open spaces were lined with lemon and orange trees. All the culinary aromas of Italy concentrated there, before they rose to the sky, past the swallows dipping and diving through swarms of insects, up to where a solitary eagle rode thermal contours only it could sense.

The main garden was an exact dodecahedron, and the most ancient part of the *castello* complex. A well preserved and maintained Roman mosaic formed the pavement of a cloistered walkway that enclosed a lawn, in the centre of which was an ancient yew tree, planted when the site was first dedicated to some forgotten deity.

The interior was abandoned in haste, by the look of it. Sergeant Douglas and I took a look around, picking our way through the chaos left by looters, to see what, if anything, could be found with intelligence value. He took the main rooms, I went off to look in the cellars, not expecting to find much more than some decent wine the Germans and the looters had missed.

Instead, I found most rooms untouched, and filled with elaborate and very old furniture that could have gone to a museum. I gave everything a cursory look over. I felt an odd sensation, one that I've had once or twice in my life, a feeling of dislocation and discontinuity, as though I was missing something obvious. I kept going until I found the main entrance to the cellars. The door was unlocked. I flicked on an electric light switch.

There was no wine. This was where the Gestapo and Kappler's SS interrogated allied POWs, partisans and any other unfortunates who came to their attention. The rooms were organised with the precision of an industrial laboratory; it wouldn't have surprised me had white lab coats still hung behind the door. I recognised the purpose of the tools systematically arrayed on shelves and racks: I might use them myself in the appropriate circumstances, with the appropriate prisoner. I felt a certain sense of professional admiration.

In the corner of each room, opposite the interrogation area, was a desk and chair. I tested the drawers of one desk and found it unlocked. Inside were pens and ink, rulers and boxes of paper-clips, still shiny, as well as ledgers and scrap paper. The ledgers contained intact records of interrogations: intelligence gold.

Another drawer held dog-tags or regimental insignia from prisoners, along with other personal items: lockets, spectacles, fountain pens, watches, wallets, photographs, engagement and wedding rings, and gold teeth, neatly segregated into male and female and placed in individual compartments.

Beyond these rooms were cells, roughly constructed in the ancient vaults. Most were empty but there were bodies in six of them, hanging by their thumbs from piano wire. All had been tortured; all killed by a single shot behind their right ear. The bodies, male and female, were naked. They had all soiled themselves several times before they died. The stench of shit and death was beyond nauseating. My professional admiration evaporated. This wasn't extraction of military intelligence from high-value sources, this was depravity.

In the wall furthest from me was an opening. There was no door. An unlit corridor was beyond, and, at the threshold, a very light breeze flowed from the darkness, smelling of dampness, mildew and old blood. The blackness was as tangible as toothache. I checked the battery in my torch and entered.

The sense of dislocation grew stronger, as though I'd left the world behind. It wasn't just the smell and the damp, it was a more pervasive sensation that everything around me had shifted out of kilter, and I was somehow walking between the interstices of two entirely distinct realities.

I put my hand out to steady myself, but pulled it back when my fingers touched the slick wetness of the black walls. Why did I keep going? Because the smell of corruption told me that something was down there, more tortured bodies, perhaps, remains that should be given a decent committal and a memorial stone. That's what I told myself, anyway.

As I passed a deep alcove on my left, I felt the touch of a rifle barrel in the small of my back.

'Walk on for two more paces then stop and place your torch on floor. Don't look back and don't speak unless spoken to.'

The accent was Scottish, Edinburgh, and commanding. I did as I was told.

'Good chap. Now: who are you and why are you here?'

I gave my name, rank and serial number.

'Well now, that's something I didn't expect. Tell me, who is your father and what is your mother's maiden name.'

'My father is John Pitcairn, my mother is Christina Menzies.'

'And your mother's father?'

'Frederick Menzies.'

'Then you may relax, Captain. My name is David Menzies and we are cousins: your great grandfather Walter was my grandfather. You didn't tell me why you're here.'

'I've already told you rather more than I'm required to, Mr. Menzies, and I might ask you the same.'

'That would be Colonel Menzies, and I have a rifle pointed at your back.'

'Aye sir, and I have a pistol pointing at the back of your head. Let's be sensible, shall we?' How Sergeant Douglas had got there so quietly is a mystery to me to this day, but he had. 'Perhaps, sirs, we should all step back out of this corridor to where we can all talk like officers and gentlemen. Colonel Menzies, sir, your rifle please.'

'I have no rifle, just a length of lead piping which I am putting down now.'

'No hasty moves now, sir, and there'll be no misunderstandings.'

'Sergeant,' I said, 'I'm about to pick up my torch and turn round. I'd rather not go back to those cells. We can chat here, where the air is a little fresher.'

No one looks their best in an ancient corridor lit only by a hand torch. Even so Menzies was an odd sight. His uniform looked made for someone three sizes larger. His silver-white hair was roughly cropped as if hacked with a blunt bayonet. It was his eyes that caught my attention, not just because they were unnaturally prominent in his gaunt face, but because they were the same as Aunty Bella's in Rothesay, the one who saw ghosts of sailors walking from the sea; the same eyes that sometimes looked back at me from the mirror when I washed and shaved after shooting a prisoner. Whatever else he was, Menzies was family.

'At ease, Sergeant, I'd like to hear what the Colonel, my cousin, has to say for himself.'

Sergeant Douglas lowered the service revolver but took a step backwards, keeping his options open.

'So,' said Menzies, 'you have a touch of it too.'

'Pardon me? A touch of what?'

'Do you know much about our family history?'

'No: my parents say very little about the family; the only one we ever see is my Aunt Bella.'

'Bella? She was probably the strongest of us all.'

'She has a tobacconists and confectionery shop in Rothesay. What do you mean strongest?' But, as I asked, I remembered her eyes, and the deep well of *something* there.

'I think you know.'

This wasn't a conversation to have in front of the sergeant.

'About your question: we're scouting for anything Jerry left behind, and looking out for partisans. We found this place an hour or so ago. I followed my nose down this corridor.'

'I'm looking for something else. There's more in play here than you know.' His face became distracted while he talked, and I sniffed a whiff of mania about him.

'I can't join in with personal—'

'This isn't personal you damned fool; this is as important as beating Jerry. Back in the day we used to call them Priority Target Alpha. I have to go down here, but you don't. There's plenty back in the offices to keep you occupied.'

'I can't finish my job without knowing what's down here.' I glanced back at the sergeant. 'You can stay up and start recording what's in the office if you want, Douglas.'

'Begging your pardon sirs, but not fucking likely. I'm with you.'

'One other thing,' said Menzies. 'If anything happens to me down here, make sure a report gets back to the War Office. The operation is called Lanyard. Mention that, and someone will get back to you.'

'What is Priority Target Alpha?'

'I hope you don't find out.'

The chamber contained what looked like elaborate medical equipment. There were strange contraptions of brass and leather, from each of which snaked several rubber tubes. These seemed to mean something to Menzies, but all he said was 'Why is it always children?' Around the walls were a dozen cribs, containing blood-stained mattresses over which lay unbuckled leather restraining straps, though why you might want to restrain a baby is beyond me.

I don't really know what it is I see when I see ghosts, but whatever they are I interact with them: seeing, hearing, talking, though not touching or smelling. Whether they're souls, or spirits, or echoes, or something else, who can say? Despite my best efforts to ignore them, they're real. I'd never felt them so powerfully before; I staggered, leaning against the architrave for support. I was surrounded: remnants and reminders of the humans who had died in this room, bound into the strange contraptions, every last one of them an infant, formless and terrified, in a residual existence they could not understand.

I wished I had a way to free them, to exorcise their spirits and bring them peace, but I didn't have even the first idea of where to begin. Menzies must have seen my reaction, though he made no comment. Sergeant Douglas looked inscrutable, well used to the ways of officers.

An open door led from the chamber into a cave. Cool air blew through the door, and I hurried towards it. It was as well we had the torch: a metre beyond the door was a chasm that almost claimed me. I lay on my front and peered over the edge, shining the light into the depths. The beam wasn't strong enough to reach the bottom; the smell told me all that I needed to know.

Turning sharp right from the door, a ledge ran around the rim of the abyss and, eventually, onto the open side of the cliff that formed the east face of the promontory. A track led down through the deepening twilight towards the plain. Menzies sat for a moment on the remains of an old wall just beyond the entrance.

'What did we just find, Colonel?'

'You don't need to know and you wouldn't believe me without asking lots of questions I don't have time to answer. If we get back to Blighty look me up, remember Lanyard, and I'll tell you everything. Or ask Bella. I'd like to know you better, but I have to follow this trail.'

We shook hands and I watched him set off into the darkness, surprisingly agile.

'What do you make of that, Sergeant?'

'Fucked if I know, sir.'

We walked back the way we came. At the lip of the chasm I motioned Douglas to go ahead. I waited. Spectral figures of murdered women and children rose from the blackness and floated in front of me.

'Your babies are inside: take them home.'

There was a rush of movement, then nothing: no presences at all, only a distant memory of the sobs of reunited mothers and bairns echoing around the spaces behind the walls.

I liberated a brace of untouched cases of grappa and went back to the interrogation rooms. I selected some tools and, weeks later, took unprofessional pleasure in using them on Gestapo and SS prisoners, telling them how much I admired German precision instrument making. I also requisitioned stationery, pens and ink. I still have the tools. I keep them in a safety deposit box in a London bank. And I still write with the fountain pens, though not at work – the inlaid SS flashes and Reichsadlers wouldn't go down at all well in the Treasury, or at least not with the junior staff.

My report didn't mention Menzies or Lanyard at all; I wrote only that we found what might be a medical facility below the interrogation cells. We made an inventory of everything and packed the ledgers and the prisoners' personal effects off to HQ. On the third day I went back down through the cells, now mercifully cleaned up, and through the corridor. The chambers were completely stripped. There were no cribs, no brass or leather or any tubing. No one would say who did it. I asked in *La Rossa's*, but they all looked the other way.

I got on with the war and never met Menzies again. Sergeant Douglas was killed in action shortly afterwards in a skirmish with the German 10th Army Clark allowed to escape. By the time we found the concentration camps and the wagons full of bodies in the railway sidings, Italy, my distant cousin, and operation Lanyard, were forgotten.

Until now.

I bathed and went to the sink to shave, memories of Italy rippling through my mind. The face looking back from the mirror was the young man I was, not the man I am. I closed my eyes and splashed cold water on my face and round my neck, but when I looked up, his face was still there, wrapped around my bones, my tendons, my cartilage.

I met Sergeant McPherson for a late breakfast and an update. On the café radio the pipes of the Royal Scots Dragoon Guards played *Amazing Grace*. Memories of Highland regiments and the lads I'd buried rushed back. McPherson caught my mood. He was too polite to say anything, he had a touch of it too, he was the right age.

'Africa. Italy. Germany.' I said.

'Singapore. Burma.' He looked out of the window. 'There was a pipey, from the Gordons, played over every grave on the railway. Every fuckin' day: *Floo'ers o' the fuckin' Forest*. I hate that fuckin' tune, cannae listen to the pipes: cannae no' listen.'

I had the full fry-up for breakfast again, I hadn't eaten the night before. McPherson watched me get torn in. He didn't have much news.

'And the women?'

'No' much sir. The post mortems say twelve, maybe thirteen, had track marks. The lab might tell us more in a couple o' days. It looks as though they suffocated. There were air-holes cut into the container, which would be fine if it was stowed in the open air, but it wasn't, it was in the middle of other containers. The lassies could have banged the walls and shouted all day. No one would hear them: they were dead the minute they got on the boat.'

'Any confirmation they were Eastern European?'

'No, though that Russian bloke is as good as his word and the polis in Ukraine are trying hard. But you know how it is, sir: people go missing all the time. Think of all the kids that run away from Glasgow for Kings Cross. If we canna look after our own, why would we think they can look after theirs?'

'Anything from the brothels or the Navy?'

'Lots of co-operation but nothing else from the Navy. No co-operation from the whoorhouses. If there's a connection we huvnae found it. We had some clerks look through the port records, though. They reckon in the past six months four more containers went to that warehouse. We've asked Dundee and Edinburgh to have a look, but it's a big job.'

'So we're getting nowhere?'

'No sir, and unless you can get answers from the dead lassies, we're not going to, either.'

I wiped egg yolk with fried bread, and swallowed down the last of my tea.

'Could you do me a favour?' I handed him three exposed rolls of Tri-X. 'I took a trip to Leith yesterday. There's some photographs of that warehouse. Could you have one of your lads process these and let me have eight by tens?'

'Just the warehouse?'

'All of them: might as well.'

I took the ferry to Bute. Rothesay Bay was as green and lovely as I remembered it. The island, swaddled by the hills of Argyll, pulled heartstrings in ways Kenneth McKellar and Moira Anderson would envy. I walked, promenaded I suppose, along the Esplanade. The pre-war gentility I remembered had gone, but locals and day trippers shopped for groceries or bought trinkets and sweets, or relaxed on the grass in the Winter Gardens. Pop music blared from café jukeboxes: someone had a silver machine, apparently. Teenagers in high-waister jeans tottered around on platform shoes. Holiday shops did a roaring trade in buckets and spades, beach balls, sailing boats, and crab fishing nets.

Bella's old shop was now a sad-looking general newsagents. The tobacconist side of the business hadn't meant much to me as a child, although the smell of Latakia pipe tobacco will transport me across the years in an instant, but the confectionery business was the thing. It was Bella's boiled sweets and tablet that ruined my teeth forever.

I had no purpose, I just let my feet take me where they would, which was higher, to where I could look over the bay and out into the Firth, trying to imagine it in its heyday, the big ships in the main channels, and the yard-owners' yachts, built by their own workers, cruising further out, out where the workers could never go.

Bella was beside me. She looked exactly as I remember her from when I was a boy, when she would be in her twenties. I tried to remember when she had been born, around 1900 I think. I couldn't think of anything to say except the obvious.

'I didn't expect to see you.'

'I could say the same. Killed in the war, weren't you?'

'The wee boy you knew was, yes.'

'What took you so long?'

'I didn't want to come back - couldn't come back.'

'I knew you weren't dead, though; I never told anyone – not your ma or your sisters or your wife or your son. That's why I waited.'

'Emily? And John? What happened to them?'

'She met an American sailor in 1946 and moved to Minnesota. We had a couple of letters then never heard from them again. It broke your ma's heart.'

I looked away, anywhere but at her.

'In the war I met a cousin, in Italy, David Menzies. He said there was something about our family, and something about you.'

'He told you that, and you never thought to come back and find out more?'

'It was complicated. What don't I know?'

Bella's eyes focused on a distant nothingness. Her hair, fine as it was, did not move in the light breeze whispering around us.

'I'll tell you this, the rest you'll need to find out for yourself. There's a Gift in our blood. Some have it stronger than others. You have it. David and his brothers had a lot more.'

'David said you were the strongest.'

'Did he?' She gave a slight smile. 'Your ma, bless her, had it too but hid from it: denied it. She was aye stopping me telling you stories; she didn't want the Gift to waken in you.'

'How is she?'

'Killed in a car crash seven years ago.'

My gut tightened.

'All those years and all she had were some photies and your medals. She lost her son and grandson. Don't go greetin' for yer ma' now, it's way too late.'

I looked away again. I always looked away.

'What is this Gift?'

'Remember when you were a wean and we used to go walking?'

'With the dead sailors? Yes.'

'You only remember the sailors, not our good neighbours? What a waste you've made of yourself. For those of us with a moral compass, the Gift imposes a duty. David, Bobby and Michael did their duty.'

'David mentioned something about a Priority Target Alpha. What was that?'

'A predator that farms us like cattle and picks off the vulnerable. We've watched them for 300 years, since one took two of us in Edinburgh. It called itself Aphrêm and stole Isobel Mein's lassie Margaret, and Margaret's unborn child.'

Children, why is it always children? This was absurd: we were talking up a side street in Rothesay about predators amongst us, like we were in a cheap tartan copy of a Hammer horror film.

'What happened to David and his brothers?'

'Bobby died a hero in the First World War, Michael disappeared in a scandal not long after. David came and went as he pleased: he went to America but no one knows what happened to him then, not even me.'

'What did you mean by *waited for me*, Aunty Bella?'

'I was with your ma in that car.'

'But—'

I spoke to the breeze and the empty street.

I found a pub and ordered a double malt and a half of heavy, and sat in the snug. I felt sprockets and gear-trains revolving around me, arcs and courses turning around uncanny axes, re-calibrating my understanding, nudging me in directions I didn't want to go. I sank the beer and added the dregs to the whisky, watching the swirl as the liquids mixed, losing myself in the viscous patterns and the scent of the esters.

'I forgot to say,' said Bella, sitting beside me. 'Ask Anna Mill about what I told you, she'll put you on the right track.'

'Which bit of it?'

'Any of it or all of it: you decide.'

I poured the liquor down my throat and made my way to the pier and the ferry to Wemyss Bay on the other side of the Clyde, the side where McPherson told me I needed answers from the dead.

The 'Gers were playing Partick Thistle at Ibrox and I was in the wrong place as 35,000 punters tried to leave. I was hungry: the fried breakfast was a long time ago. I didn't fancy another Steakhouse meal, but the alternative was a pie supper from a chippy and I didn't want any more fat. I spotted an Indian place. I'd had better, but it was tasty enough.

I learned long ago the best way to think about a complex situation is not to think about it at all, but to let things whirl around somewhere in the back of my head. Sooner or later something will pop out. By the time I'd finished the pakora and was eyeing up chicken dhansak, the only thing I'd really settled on was that I had nothing to connect any of what was happening to Faslane. I'd no evidence of a heroin problem amongst submariners. Everything else was for the police and there was no reason why I couldn't wrap this up and get back to the me that waited in the Treasury.

Except I'd somehow picked up another tail: old me was hanging around, haunting every mirror, taunting me with my own memories.

I met Emily at school and always fancied her. I bumped into her one evening when I was home on leave from basic training. We went dancing and then up the back of a close after a few beers. Next time I came home there was an obvious bump and she was adamant it was mine, so we did the decent thing. We both knew, everyone did, that a ticket to the front might be one-way. If the worst happened the baby would be legitimate. Better an orphan than a bastard.

Neither of us loved each other really, but we were young and had feelings and were well disposed towards each other. It might have worked out, who knows? But then my war kicked off in earnest. In '45 I was offered a life that fitted better who I'd become, a life that didn't sit well with domesticity. I jumped at it. Rather than lingering unhappiness for decades, it seemed less cruel to allow Captain Walter Pitcairn MC to die in action and to make a clean break. I was pleased Emily met someone else. She'd be 53 now, and John 31 or 32, probably married with kids of his own in America.

I left the car where it was, a ten-minute walk from the hotel. My path was masked from the hotel both by the curve of the street and by trees and ornamental shrubs lining the pathway. I spotted out the watchers before they saw me, just as they were changing over a shift. I watched through a gap in branches as one young man swapped places with another in the front seat of a blue Morris Marina. The one leaving walked off, away from me. As he passed a brown Cortina, its occupant gave him a wave. I found a pen and a scrap of paper in my jacket and jotted down the registration numbers.

I walked towards the hotel. The guy in the Cortina recognised me. I crossed to where his colleague was parked with his window open, smiled and waved at Cortina man, grabbed the collar of the other guy, and smacked his face off the door frame.

'You'll need to be better than that, sonny,' I said, tossing him a handkerchief for his nosebleed.

In the hotel, the receptionist gave me a package and an envelope. The envelope held a note, unsigned, undated, saying *please phone home*. I opened the package in my room. There was a compliment slip from Sergeant McPherson, processed negatives, trimmed and put into transparent sleeves, and a set of eight by ten prints. I looked at the pictures I took when Anna left the café. The six prints were pin sharp and nicely exposed. Anna's back was clearly visible. The tall woman in the maxi-coat wasn't there.

The attaché case was a bit obvious but it was all I had. I put the papers and photographs into it and left, using all the tricks I could remember to shake off any tail. Eventually I worked my way round to the car and drove around at random, watching my mirror.

I stopped when I found a telephone box.

I dialled a London number, let it ring four times then replaced the receiver in the cradle. I waited thirty seconds then called a different number which picked up on the second ring. I pushed the coins in.

'Yes?'

'Calling home.'

'Ah! So good to hear from you. How are things?'

'Hard to say: I haven't found anything.'

'Are you ready to come home?'

'No. There's something odd going on.'

'How so?'

'I picked up a tail. I don't know who, or why, but I'd like to know.'

'Connected to your questions?'

'Possibly.'

'Hmm. Any overseas interest?'

'Co-operation from the relevant consulate, nothing else I can see.'

'Well, keep at it. Treasury don't expect you back for a couple of weeks, so take your time. What have you planned for tomorrow?'

'Sunday? In Scotland?'

He was still laughing as he hung up.

I rang McPherson to thank him for the photographs, and asked another favour: I gave him the registration numbers of the two cars.

I drove out to Pollockshaws and caught a train to Glasgow Central. The attaché case went into left luggage. On the return trip I parked in a side street and approached the hotel with care, but no one was watching.

I wasn't joking: what can you do in Scotland on a Sunday when nowhere is open and you really don't want to think too much about what your dead aunty told you? I'd seen something in the paper about a child in a toy dinghy carried out on the tide, helpless: a familiar feeling.

The ebb and flow of the war washed me into many odd coves and backwaters, and most aren't in the official record. You might think the horrors of the camps would dominate my memories, but they don't. The smell never leaves, the gagging on the foul taste of putrefying meat in the back of the throat, nor the memory of gritty dust thrown to the heavens from the crematoria chimneys, swirling in the breeze, coating your skin, gathering in the seams and hems of your fatigues, drifting into your nostrils and mouth. But the scale of the suffering and horror and my overwhelming pity were too much for memory. It became just background to me after a while, a commonplace. Like a battlefield surgeon has to shut out the immensity of the carnage to make clinical decisions, so I had to keep a professional focus. I had to blank out the squalor of the living and the suffering of those dead who still lingered in the foul miasma. Sometimes I sang for them, or maybe for myself. McPherson wasn't the only one, I'd got sick of the lament too, heard it too many times from too many pipeys, sung it too many times:

The Flooers of the Forest, that focht aye the foremost, the prime o' our land, lie cauld in the clay.

It was at Bergen-Belsen that I finally learned how to block the dead from my sight: I couldn't bear the look they gave when I met their eyes. That was also when my talents as an interrogator began to fade – read into that what you will.

And my job changed. I was no longer required to extract intelligence and execute the detainees. Now I had to identify individuals with desirable skills and knowledge who might be of some utility to the Empire, and spirit them away from mob vengeance with new names and identities.

The Yanks were much more committed to it than us. They wanted Nazi intelligence on wartime communist espionage networks: they were already gearing up for the Cold War. Plenty of German generals survived the attempt on Moscow and had information about conditions out East, so they were shipped over to PO Box 1142 for a new life with the poor and the huddled masses yearning to be free.

Weapons technology? The Apollo missions? Thank you to the rocket scientists from Peenemünde, and to Operation Paper Clip that gave them such well-rewarded lives in Long Island and Florida, far from Nuremburg and Mr Pierrepoint's busy noose, a world away from London, where their V1 and V2s had fallen.

And there were the others: the experimenters, the poisoners, the chemists, the torturers, the butchers. All relocated. I helped do it. I found assets and whisked them away to His Majesty's zone of influence, failing which, to ensure our valued friends and allies didn't get their hands on them, I killed them.

There was a lot of it about. The killing didn't stop on VE day: the revenge, the reprisals, the madness, the suicides, no one talks about it. Old men and boys were beaten, mutilated, murdered. Best not to talk about the women. The camps didn't close down, not when there were plenty of POWs to be put to work, starved until they weakened and died. It wasn't the war criminals who suffered. Of course not. They had already presented their *curricula vitae* to eager new employers. One nasty piece of work, Friedrich Buchardt, oversaw the deportation of tens of thousands of Jews and Gypsies from Lodz to Chelmno, then managed exterminations in Belarus. He landed a cushy berth with MI6 until '47 when he went to work for the Americans instead. Useful in the fight against communism, you see.

We had a long history of this, at least since Guy Liddell took himself over to Berlin in 1933 to meet the head of Abteilung 1A and enjoyed congenial dinners with Ribbentrop, all to set up an exchange of information about communists who Abteilung 1A, soon to be called the Gestapo, was committed to eradicating. Fascism, said the head of MI5, was just a natural response to communism.

Hawking already used that name by the time I met him in '45. He ran part of our operation to salvage what we could from the ruins of the Reich. He was the same then as now: efficient, calculating, ruthless. Quite why I appealed to him I'm not sure, but I dare say my by-then fluent

German and Russian and willingness to kill people to order had something to do with it. He offered me the alternate future, the one that didn't include my wife and child, the future I chose.

And for the next twenty-odd years that's what I did, found old Nazis, offered them a job or gave them a quick death. Latterly, there were no jobs available. That was my moral compass, Aunty Bella, that was my duty. I'm sure the floo'ers o' the forest would be proud.

Is it any wonder I never went back to see Ma? Is it any wonder I changed my name so many times?

Knocking shops don't keep the Sabbath.

I'd woken up certain that it was time to do something. I'd been too passive, questioning, researching, observing, reflecting, getting nowhere. Time to mix it up. The place I wanted was up the far end of Great Western Road. Eastern European and Russian girls worked there. Traffic was so light I spotted my tail before I'd even left Glasgow city centre.

In the reception room, the erotic and the suburban collided in an unholy clash of chintz and corsetry. I was given a photograph album to pick a girl, like picking underwear from a mail-order catalogue. Natasha was the only Russian available. Five minutes later I was in a small room with fibre-glass curtains, a double bed and a wicker chair. Under the chair was a small pile of well-creased and thumbed dirty magazines with Dutch titles. I doubt anyone spoke Dutch but, then again, I don't suppose they were there to be read. The wallpaper was crimson flock with paisley patterning, like it was stolen from a job lot bound for a curry house. On the walls were three *faux* gilt frames surrounding eight by tens of naked women in uncomfortable-looking poses. A bowl on the windowsill held a *potpourri* of rubbers.

I wasn't aroused in the slightest.

My tail was parked about fifty yards along the street, the driver still in the car.

The woman who came was somewhere in her mid-twenties, thin, with shoulder-length dark hair. She wore improbable lingerie under her translucent nylon robe. Her lipstick was an intense scarlet; kohl wrapped around her grey eyes like lead came wraps around stained glass. Her eyes were wary: appraising. She came in with a sway of her hips, her hands moving to her lapels to remove the robe, trailing cheap eau-de-cologne in her wake.

'Keep it on,' I said in Russian. 'I'm here to collect.' She took a step back towards the door. I was too quick and grabbed her wrist, pulling her roughly towards me.

'Don't be stupid. I get what I want, you get paid, and everyone is happy. You even keep your knickers on.'

'But I have nothing more since last time.'

'Don't give me that.'

'I don't know you. I don't know what you want. You should leave.' Her accent was hard to place, though I'd guess at Leningrad. She tried for the door again but I pushed her onto the bed.

'Really Natasha? There are always more containers, more girls where you came from.' Her trembling increased.

'I can't give you what I don't have.'

'All those talkative sailor boys and nothing to show for it?'

Her trembling stopped. Her stillness was so complete as to be disturbing in itself.

'Sailors? What have they got to do with it?'

I pushed back the sleeve of her robe. A cluster of needle marks was concealed by makeup. She flinched.

'Well, well. Sampling the merchandise? Don't be silly Natasha, you know what we can do. I just need the films and photographs.'

But I'd already lost her. I never expected to get a pitying look from a junkie in a brothel, but every day brings its own surprises.

'You made a big mistake coming here.'

'Really? Why?'

'Just go.'

Once, I might have tried to force the issue, but it would be wasted effort. Besides, all I wanted was to poke around and see what happened next.

'If that's how you want it, Natasha. Next time, I won't ask so nicely.' Her eyes held mine, flickered a brief moment of doubt.

'There won't be a next time.'

I looked in the mirror as I drove away, expecting to see a car make a U-turn to follow. Instead a second car, already facing the same way as me, pulled out. I stopped at lights and checked the mirror again. The driver of the first car walked into the brothel, probably not for a Sunday afternoon quickie.

I stopped at a telephone box and checked in with Sergeant McPherson.

'I traced those numbers sir. They don't exist.'

'I'm sorry?'

'The numbers aren't on record; fakes by the look of it.'

I made a second call, then drove to the city and parked in the new Anderston Centre. I found a recess behind a parked van from which I could see without being seen. My tail parked on the opposite side of the same level. He walked to the Avenger and looked about, shining a torch into it. He spoke into a walkie-talkie, then walked to a pedestrian exit. His radio crackled again as he went through the door.

I took the stairs up to the next level where I'd left the rented Ford Escort, and drove east.

Lasarev tapped the window and got in.

'So, you have news, *Major*?'

'Nothing positive, maybe a hint or two. The usual. And you?'

'You go first.'

'I spoke to a prostitute earlier, a Russian girl, in a brothel our sailors use. She seemed to know nothing about blackmailing sailors, but she's involved in something that frightens her. Your turn.'

'My friends don't have any operations as you describe at Faslane. There are other ones, but you probably know about them already.'

'And your fellow countrymen?'

'Nothing they admit to.'

I gazed out over the Forth to the glow of Edinburgh on the opposite shore.

'Yet the girl wasn't surprised I spoke Russian. So what is going on?'

'That, *tovarishch*, is as mysterious as why you were assigned to this.'

'Yes. About that: you might be able to help me there, Sasha.'

He raised a single eyebrow in the way I still hadn't mastered.

'Now you have my attention.'

'I need to know what's in a couple of old War Office files without letting my own people know I'm interested. Your friends can probably do it.'

'Why don't you ask your own friends?'

'Because I don't have any.'

He laughed.

'And what do I get in return?'

'You might find out why someone is exporting girls from Odessa to die in a metal box. And you might find out why someone wants me involved. And you'll get the beers I owe you.'

'What's in the files?'

'I don't know, but I want to tell you a story about something that happened in the war, in Italy.'

The news on the car radio was confused, fractured, but I got the gist. A car bomb, they suspected.

I parked half a mile away from the hotel and slipped into a bar for a pint and a whisky. I downed them quickly so there was alcohol in my bloodstream and on my breath.

The police were searching my room, forcing my suitcase. McPherson was one of them.

'Fuck me, sir, you're dead!'

'News to me. When did I die?'

'This evening. They're still picking bits of you out of the concrete at Anderston. The Hammer's daein' his dinger!'

'Nice of him to care. What happened?'

'Your car exploded. The press want to know if it was yon Fenian bastards. Where were you?'

'I had a couple of drinks too many and came back on the bus. You'd better let the Hammer know that I'm still here, and I'll need a secure line to my boss.'

'Bit of a fuck up old chap?'

'I can't see how it fits: it's too amateurish.'

186

Hawking grunted.

'Well someone obviously wants you out of the way.'

'Happy to oblige, I never wanted to be here in the first place. And Box 500 will be all over it, so our involvement will be known.'

'The word is out already. I'll fly cover. What's your next move?'

'More of the same: try not to die.'

'That would be helpful. Have you any idea who did this?'

'Not a clue.'

'What about that tail in Edinburgh?'

'Unexplained. I'll pick that one up tomorrow.'

'Yes, well: whatever you're doing, do it better.'

I'd only just got to sleep when Inspector MacLeod phoned and asked me to come in and tell him about the unidentified naked woman, bound and gagged, in the boot of the Avenger when it exploded.

There won't be a next time, she'd said.

'Never seen her before.'

The working assumption was the bomb had gone off as it was being planted. Natasha died in the blast, if she wasn't dead already, but was protected by the back seat and bodywork from the same fate as the bomber.

'I don't like you, *Major*, or whoever you are. I didn't like you before and I like you even less now.' MacLeod was pacing the interview room, throwing me glowers that no doubt made his usual interviewees quail.

'I'm not here to be liked, Inspector.'

'What *are* you here to do? Something about heroin and Faslane? Sounds like a cover story to me.'

'Are we going to get to the point soon? I'm tired and I have a busy day tomorrow.'

'The point is you show up just as we find thirty-four dead lassies and a floater and next thing I know your car blows up with a woman in the boot. This is my beat, Major, and I don't need this bollocks messing it up. I like it even less than I like you, which is saying something.'

'And the heroin.'

'What?'

'In your list: you missed out the heroin on the *Equestris*. And you missed whoever it was got themselves spread all over the car park.'

'Look: we're supposed to be on the same side: can you throw me a bone at least?'

Don't blow your cover. Don't involve civilians. Simple rules for complex times.

'Try this: my hotel was watched, two guys in a Cortina and a Marina.' I dug the scrap of paper out of my wallet. 'These were the registration numbers.' MacLeod noted them down.

'Past tense?'

'I spotted them and gave one a bloody nose. I haven't seen them since.'

'Is it too much to hope they had Irish accents?'

'I'm sure I can remember that particular telling detail if required. Any developments with the rest?'

'Nothing on the floater: his clothes could come from any chandlers in Europe, and there were no distinguishing marks on his corpse. Same with the heroin – nothing to show where it came from or where it was going. The Drug Squad lads haven't found any disappointed buyers yet. The girls haven't been identified, despite the best efforts of our Russian comrades. The lab reckons they were all only just out of adolescence. Also, they all probably gave birth sometime in the past few weeks or so: all standard, no caesareans. That might help in tracing them.'

'Are we sure they died in the container, that they weren't already dead?'

'You're a sick bastard. As sure as we can be, they were too far gone to be sure.'

'Can I go?'

'Of course, wouldn't want you to lose sleep before your busy day.'

It was 11 September, my sixth day in the field, and all I had to show was a bombed-out pool car and thirty-seven deaths: a quiet Monday night in by Glasgow standards. I called Control to say I was going to hire a car and charge it to Her Majesty, which I did – a Ford Capri. I got it from a different company to the one where I got the Escort.

I spoke to the Customs guys who found the heroin. I didn't get much out of them except some eight by tens of the stash as they discovered it, twenty transparent packages taped to the bulkhead in five rows of four.

'Call-Me-Bob' confirmed that he'd picked nothing up on the Neptune tic-tac.

And I saw a dead man in Victorian clothes on the third-floor landing of my hotel before breakfast. It wasn't anyone I recognised and I wasn't happy to see him.

In my room I splashed my face with cold water. I didn't know who looked back at me from the mirror: it was my face, but not a me I'd met before; not a me I wanted to know; not a me with an office and a secretary; not the me who didn't see dead people any more. It was a me who looked furious about something, but he wouldn't tell me what it was and I didn't want to ask.

I met Inspector MacLeod at lunchtime in a West End bar. Holy of holies! It served beautifully kept, cask Belhaven 80/- from a McGlashan font: I'd found my new favourite place in the city. I said so and MacLeod smiled before he remembered he was supposed to be a hardman.

'Are you certain about those registration numbers?'

'Yes, why?'

'They're ours.'

'Ours?'

'Ours: flagged in the registry as Drug Squad pool cars. I checked the logs: on the night in question they were signed out by two individuals I happen to know are undercover officers, who've both disappeared. Can you think of any reason why Drug Squad might have an interest in you?'

'Maybe. Can you remember how many packets of heroin were found on the *Equestris*?'

'Fifteen. Why?'

I took the folded eight by tens out of my jacket pocket.

'Because Customs found twenty.'

'Shite. Fucking shite.'

'I thought that'd make you happy.'

'Fucking-fuckity-fuck-fuck-fuck. Who've you told?'

'You.'

'Who do you plan to tell?'

'That depends what you do.'

'Why would they take an interest in you, though?'

'Because I'm an outsider, investigating heroin and Faslane. There's something else.'

'Am I going to like it?'

I gave him an expurgated account of my visit to Natasha, and the chain of logic that took me there.

'Good thinking, I'll give you that.'

'Not mine; it was Sergeant MacPherson who came up with the idea.'

'MacPherson? What the fuck has he got to do with this?'

'We were chatting after he gave me an update on the investigations.'

'And you didn't come to me?'

'He's more approachable.'

'Aye. MacPherson is certainly approachable, but I have my doubts he's entirely clean. Nothing overt, nothing obvious, but no' quite right either. When did you plan to tell me about the Russian bint?'

'I hadn't planned to tell you at all. I talked to her about something else entirely.'

'Fuck's sake! She's killed in your car a couple of hours after you pay her a visit and you weren't going to tell me? We are on the same side, right?'

'You asked me that last night too: you tell me. Another pint?'

'I suppose that Russian bloke will have to know about Natasha.'

'I suppose he will, when you finally identify her. At the moment you only have my word. Who knows how long it will take you to verify it.'

'Where were you when your car exploded?'

'In the pub, I told you.'

'No' for all that time you weren't, you weren't pished enough. Where were you?'

'Gone to see a man about a dog.'

'That's no' very helpful.'

'No, I don't suppose it is. Look, the main rule in my game is never to involve outsiders in operations. You're an outsider. I'll tell you this much: I was ready to pack up and go home until Natasha was killed. That stunt was stupid and amateurish. I thought I was here chasing fairy tales, but now I know something's going on. That kid was frightened and now she's dead because I went to see her. I need to know if it concerns me or not.'

'And if it doesn't?'

'Then it's a police matter and I can go home.'

He grunted, swigged his pint, surveyed the spirit gantry.

'The pathologist says the women couldn't have been dead before they were loaded onto the ship because they all had some of the food in the container with them in their stomachs.'

'Did they test the food? For sedatives or anything?'

'You're a suspicious bastard, aren't you?'

'I try.'

At the Registrar's I found the record of my mother's death in July 1963. I ordered a copy of the death certificate and gave my hotel address. At the library I searched the newspapers and found a funeral notice with the name of the cemetery and a note of the principal mourners, my father John, my sisters Jane and Mary and their respective husbands.

The grave was easy to find, nestled in a pleasant churchyard with neat lawns with well-managed evergreen and deciduous trees around the perimeter: oak, horse chestnut, and beech, with a scattering of silver birch. A fine rowan grew at the main entrance, the traditional protection against witches. Blackbirds and song thrushes were everywhere. I was pleased to see the headstone and plot well cared for. I placed my flowers alongside others, still fresh. My father's name hadn't been added to the gravestone, but mine had. *In loving memory of Christina Menzies, died 18 July 1963, aged 65, beloved wife of John Pitcairn; and to the memory of her son, Captain Walter John Pitcairn MC, killed in action, Germany, 11 April 1945, aged 26. Always remembered.*

There were dead people all around me; I was surrounded by ghosts.

'Why have you done this to me, *tovarishch*?'

'What? What's happened?'

'I asked one of my young friends in Leningrad to access those files: he reported they didn't exist. Twelve hours later my young friend was dead in a road accident and I am ordered to report back to Moscow to give a full report, along with anyone else my friend contacted in the past two weeks.'

'You're sure it's related?'

'I have no doubt. And your story from Italy convinces me.'

'How so?'

'Because I heard such stories before, from an old comrade who fought on the road from Moscow to Berlin, who transported Nazis to the gulags. He told me of strange things found in isolated farmhouses and *Schlösser*, in railway sidings and underground complexes; told tales of creatures that stole babes-in-arms and took their fluids using devices as you described, creatures that hovered around extermination camps and consorted with the doctors and guards.'

'These creatures set up the camps?'

'Oh no, my friend, the camps were a human creation. We do not need monstrous creatures to create such horrors. *Nyet*, the creatures were parasites on our own barbarity. And before that I heard the story first hand from a Nazi. I thought he was insane. He was one of those who would play games with the occult. His name was Ulrich Huber: SS-Oberführer Ulrich Huber, but he worked with political intelligence rather than doing any actual fighting.

'He was a fanatic, an enthusiast for the extermination of undesirables. He inspected death camps to ensure they worked at maximum efficiency. He did not care for inflicting suffering or for sadism, only for death. He was impressed by Henry Ford and his ideal was the perfect production line, with raw materials arriving in an orderly manner to process into product as cost-effectively as possible. He was obsessed with achieving optimum capacity against theoretical models of materials management and productivity. A good German industrialist in every important respect.

'When he discovered these creatures, he was incensed: not only were they not Aryan, they weren't human, and he fixed on finding and eradicating them whenever he could. He said the creatures are physically strong, intelligent, extremely well-connected within human hierarchies and protected by human familiars. He claimed he'd shot and cremated thirteen of the creatures by the time I questioned him. He wanted me to understand that they were a greater threat to humanity than all of the Jews, Gypsies, intellectuals, homosexuals and communists combined, and that Stalin and Truman must take all necessary steps to eradicate them.'

'When was that?'

'Late '47, early '48 perhaps. I recommended he was either summarily shot or committed for forced labour. I have no idea what happened to him.'

'How many others have you told about this?'

'Are you crazy? Look at what's just happened to my friend Evgeny. You understand what this means?

'We're compromised. What will you do?'

'If I would be able to live, I will go to ground where I can. You should do the same: someone has already tried to bomb you, yes?' I noted his rare grammatical slip.

'I'll give it some thought. I'll leave a message in Stockholm, in the old way.'

He walked into the evening. I considered SS-Oberführer

Ulrich Huber. As it happens, I do know what happened to him. He was spirited into the American sphere of influence and I killed him in Bremen in October 1948 on the orders of Hawking. I dropped the weighted body into the Weser, outside the city, taking care to dress the corpse in deckhand's clothes and remove the head and hands.

On the train back to Glasgow I pondered Huber's fascination with industrial processes. Across the aisle, a heavily bearded young man with long hair and wire-rimmed national health spectacles read Bram Stoker's *Dracula*. The whole vampire thing always struck me as odd, all that messing around in graveyards. If they were smart, vampires would set up a proper supply chain to secure supplies of strategically important raw materials, such as blood, and establish effective ways to dispose of the evidence.

The dead girls had recently given birth.

Children. Why is it always children?

Perhaps they'd hide their supply chain in plain sight, in trade and transport channels. Like container ships.

At Queen Street Station, I called Control and asked them to thank Anna for me: I wouldn't require any further services from her, then I went to meet MacLeod for a pint.

'How did you know?'

'Know what?'

'About the food in the container.'

'I didn't. I'm just a suspicious bastard like you said.'

'Well you were right. There were traces of taxine in the food and once they knew to look for it, they reckon some of the women showed signs of—' he checked his notebook, '*taxine alkaloid ingestion*. They only found it because one of the boffins is interested in obscure poisons.'

'What's taxine alkaloid ingestion when it's at home?'

'Apparently taxine is a poison derived from yew trees. In the right doses it's deadly, but they think there was just enough to weaken the women rather than do them in: it has to be deliberate.'

'So they were never being trafficked for prostitution at all: they were murdered and left for someone to find. Why bother with all the rigmarole? Why send them here?'

'Your guess is as good as mine. We only found them by luck, who knows what was supposed to happen?'

'It was definitely luck was it?'

'Yes, it was a random search by Customs, MacPherson was very clear on that.' He closed his eyes for a moment. 'MacPherson: shite. I'd better ask the Customs boys, who, by the way, are still smarting over the loss of five bags of pure heroin from our custody.'

'Any further forward with that?' MacLeod looked pained.

'The two Drug Squad guys are still missing. We think one of them, Dougie Fraser, is the one who blew himself up with your car, based on clothing fragments. Jim Shields is nowhere to be found. He hasn't been back to his flat because there's too much there to incriminate him, savings accounts in various names with several thousand on deposit, and details of an apartment he bought for himself in Spain. Spanish police say it's locked and hasn't been used for six months.'

'Any press interest?'

'A couple of duty reporters, nothing heavy. We've told them we're checking out links to Northern Ireland but we think it's probably gangland drugs stuff. They're only interested in Cod Wars right now anyway.'

I raised my glass to salute the Icelandic Navy.

'So how long are you sticking around for?'

'Long enough to be sure about the bomb and Natasha.'

'And Faslane?'

'Nothing in it. Wherever the heroin is going, it doesn't seem to be there.'

'And all the other stuff?'

'I'm curious, of course, but it isn't any of my business.'

'Good. So you can fuck off and I can do some old-fashioned policing.'

'You reckon you'll get to the bottom of this lot?'

'The bent Drug Squad, aye, but the container? Not a chance, we haven't anywhere near enough to go on. And we're no closer to working out where that heroin was from or where it was going. We had some Interpol interest in the floater though.'

'What's their angle?'

Seems they've a unit that tracks floaters. They used to get two or three a year, every year since the war. They found them in Europe, South America, even Australia: same MO, sailor's clothes, head and hands missing, no identity ever confirmed. They were quite excited: it seems ours is the first for five or six years.'

'Best of luck to them. What about that warehouse in Edinburgh?'

'Nothing to see. The local force watched it for a while from down the street, but there was no sign of anything going in or out.'

'It doesn't hang together, does it? Why put thirty-four women in a box in Odessa then post them to a warehouse in Edinburgh, making sure they are dead before they get there? There's a bigger picture.'

'Of course there's a fucking bigger picture, but fuck alone knows what. So we'll file the lot, floater, dope and corpses, in case anything else turns up. What else can we do?'

MacLeod had a partial answer next morning.

'I checked with Customs. It wasn't a random search:

they were tipped off. We were meant to find that heroin.'

But I'm a suspicious bastard. What if the heroin were bait, and what if we were really meant to find the girls all along? What if this were a classic Haversack Ruse to see how we react? I felt the pull of that chasm below the *castello* when the spectres flowed around me to reclaim their children, the dislocation, the scattering of space and time and consciousness.

And I knew why the face in my mirror had been furious.

'Just calling home.'

'My dear chap: what's the latest?'

'I'm packing up, there's nothing for me.'

'The bomb?'

'An unfortunate misunderstanding. Some bent Drug Squad boys thought I'd stumbled across their operation. They got silly and tried to frame me. One blew himself up another is missing: the local coppers are onto it.'

'And those poor girls?'

'Not for us: their cases are open, but the only lead takes you to an abandoned warehouse. So with no evidence at all of heroin use around the subs, I'm done.'

'And the other matter?'

'Attended to.'

'You saw the news? The Israelis?'

'Yes. Can't see how it's a problem though.'

'Quite. So what are you going to do now?'

'I've got a week left of the holiday you so kindly arranged for me. I'm going to take it.'

'Anywhere nice?'

'The Highlands: maybe take a ferry to the islands. I've never been up there and this seems as a good a time as any.'

'I envy you. By the way, did you talk to the Russians at all about this?'

'Russians? No. I met their consular rep., but then nothing. Why?'

'Their man seems to have done some private sleuthing and might be a problem. Anyway, I'll need your report and expenses chitties, soonest. And let me know where to find you if I need you.'

I went to a bank and withdrew all the cash I could, then took a cab to near where I'd left the Escort. I drove to Edinburgh, parked in the New Town, then walked to Waverley Station and caught the next available train to Peterborough. I'd kept a flat there as a safe house for fifteen years. I burnt everything relating to Denis Chambers and took a suitcase from the back of a closet. In the case was a fresh identity, clean clothes, bank documents for a savings and a current account, cash, and an untraceable handgun with silencer and ammunition. If necessary I had two further safe houses, one in Paris near the Place d'Italie and another in Rome.

I made no attempt to go to London. The next morning I caught the first train back to Edinburgh, hired a Morris Marina and booked into a B&B as Thomas McCaig, commercial traveller for a paint company. I did not try to recover the Escort. I left the Marina, as shitty a car as I've ever driven, at the B&B and took a bus to Leith where I made my way through back streets to the warehouse. I wore plain-glass spectacles with a large frame, and a battered trilby. Hardly a heavy disguise but it might throw off a casual observer.

I watched the street for two full hours until I was sure there was no active surveillance in place. The parked cars were empty, there was nothing unexpected in the windows of surrounding properties, most of which were boarded up.

There was a fresh 'For Lease' sign in front of the warehouse. I took details of the agency handling the transaction. The courtyard looked a lot tidier than it had. The main door was ajar, the chain loosely threaded through a handle with both padlocks clipped to one end.

I looked inside. It was empty except for dust. Light filled the open space, revealing old stone walls, well pointed, and a concrete floor. There was only one other door, in the wall furthest from me. *Déjà vu.*

In the far corner, by the other door, a man in brown overalls swept the floor, shepherding dust towards a shovel and a large dustbin. He turned and started towards me.

'Can I help you?' he called. 'I'm afraid there's no one else here at the moment.'

'I saw the notice and wanted to take a quick look at what was on offer.'

'Viewing is by appointment only.' He kept coming and my senses went into overdrive. *There is a Gift that runs in our blood*, Bella said, a Gift that my mother didn't want to waken in me.

Too late.

Myriad possibilities surrounded this moment. I could see the flow and interaction of my consciousness with the space around me, the boundary where air and floor stopped and 'I' began, a permeable boundary fixed only by the act of observation that is awareness of self. The entity moving towards me was *wrong*, a manifestation of something other, as though its reality was fixed by some other flow of consciousness, some other gestalt. It was both real and a nullity, it existed in our space but was entangled with another.

It moved with shocking speed, hands crabbed into claws, a predator's eyes, teeth bared in a snarl. It knew me for what I was even if I didn't know myself. I dropped and rolled out of its way, and tried to trip it as it passed but it was too fast, stopping with dismaying agility. It put itself between me and the door, and came for me again. I tried the same trick, feinting to roll left but rolling right, but it was too smart, and caught me a powerful kick in the ribs, then fell on me.

I squirmed out from under the fall, wincing at the pain in my side, feeling every one of my years. I tried for the door but the creature was too close. Its fist connected with my jaw and it grabbed me from behind as I was off-balance.

I threw my head back, hard, and felt its nose break, but also its teeth cutting my scalp. Its hold loosened just enough that I might break free, but I had no chance. It tightened its hold again and I could do no more than clutch for balance at the chain on the outside of the door. As the creature pulled me back, the chain came with me.

I hauled, feeling the heft of the metal in my hand, and raked the heel of my right shoe down its shin. Its hold loosened again, and I swung the length of chain. The padlocks cracked hard into its temple, stunning it. I wrapped the links around its throat, stepped round it, and throttled all life from its inhuman carcass.

It died as a twisting fold in the threads of the fabric of human space, a ripple in the warp and weft of possibilities.

I doubt the fight lasted more than a minute.

Breathing hard, with a painful rib and a slow trickle of blood down the back of my head, I dragged the corpse across the warehouse floor to the open door in the far wall. Beyond was a storeroom, at the end of which, under a propped up hatch, were stairs into silent darkness.

I felt in its pockets for keys and anything else I could find, retrieving a wallet. I heaved the body down into darkness and closed the hatch, bolted it shut, and placed random packing cases over the top. I locked the storeroom door and slid the keys back through a gap beneath it. I picked up my hat, and wrapped the chain around the outside handles of the main door, as though it were locked. Then I got as far away as I could get on foot, the trilby at a rakish angle to hide the blood on the back of my head.

On Constitution Street, a graveyard slept behind a wall, though I felt the empty stare of long forgotten cadavers deep below the pavement.

Instead of the obvious route up Leith Walk, I took Easter Road, quieter, more ancient. Again, I sensed times overlaid, an infinite succession of moments anchored to the physical, as faces from the deep past and possible futures breezed past me, scraps blown on the breeze of an infinite now. I went up by the old execution grounds at the Gallow-lee, long buried under buildings, where the heat from the flames of all those burnt could still be felt. There, I sensed the questioning gaze of two powerful spirits, women, in archaic clothing.

They offered a cautious welcome to a prodigal son come late into his inheritance.

I walked over the top to Abbeyhill and came to the foot of the Royal Mile at Croft-an-Righ, the King's Croft. The energy lying dormant in the rocks and stones and forgotten watercourses beneath the tenements and cobbled High Street, the many realities abutting and intersecting, nearly overwhelmed me.

I didn't want to be picked up as a random drunk and questioned, so I flagged a taxi to my B&B, where I gingerly washed my hair and took a long bath before falling into a deep, dreamless sleep.

I woke twelve hours later, and was careful to shave so as to leave sideburns and the beginnings of a moustache. I didn't catch the eye of the face in the mirror: I wasn't ready for that yet.

Downstairs, in a small lounge, breakfast was fried eggs on toast and a pot of tea. The news was on the radio. The floater in the Clyde had been identified as Eberhard Graf, the missing German industrialist. Police were urgently seeking Major Denis Chambers in connection with Graf's murder. Chambers was believed also to be involved in the murder of a Russian student, Evalina Yelagina Fyodorovna, in a car bomb incident in Glasgow. Major Chambers, thought to be an alias, was possibly at large in the Highlands, was armed and under no circumstances to be approached by any members of the public. Unconfirmed reports from the Metropolitan Police said Nazi memorabilia was found in Chambers's London flat.

I told only one person I'd be in the Highlands, the same one who sent me on this assignment, the one who wanted to see if the supply network operated by the creatures he protected was secure against the likes of me.

One of the other guests was playing loud blues-rock on a cassette player. *I've been framed* ... wailed a Glaswegian voice. You and me both, pal.

When did Hawking make the link between me and my family? What, or who, led him to set me up? How many of these creatures did he get out of Germany? That could all come later.

I drove to St. Mary Street. It took a while, but eventually a familiar Hillman Imp pulled up and Anna went into the coffee shop with her passenger, a woman in a green mini-skirt, with eyes green enough I could see their colour from fifty yards. When she left, alone, I followed until, eventually, she went home to a ground floor flat in Marchmont.

After ten minutes I knocked at her door. She said nothing when she opened it, but didn't seem surprised to see me.

'Hello Anna,' I said. 'My dead Aunty Bella said I should ask you about Isobel Mein and my family's Gift.'

'You took your time about it; they're goin' daft trying to find you. You'd best come in.'

London in the sleet was miserable. It was cold in April's northerly winds. It was Friday and my fourteenth evening on the streets, blending into the exodus from Whitehall and the great departments of state, trying not to attract the attention of the extra constables, more in evidence after the IRA bombs in March.

It didn't help that the streets of London are infested with ghosts. The outlandish costumes of the Carnaby Street years were gone, but it's still hard to tell the living from the dead when they are all around you in the half light, tricorn hat or no. It was one of the things Anna and I had talked about that first evening.

'Could you tell me more about the woman who was following me?' Anna asked.

'Tall, with auburn hair. Hippy-ish clothes but well cut, not cheap. A dark suede maxi-coat with sunflower patches, leather boots, calf length, black tights and a pink mini-skirt. Purple beret. Why?'

'She was a colleague for a while and we got friendly, or as friendly as you get in this game. Her name was Joanna, Joanna Caulfield. She disappeared three years ago, presumed dead.'

'What was she working on?'

'I don't know, it was well above my grade. I think it was something internal to the department, but the lid was screwed down tight, and even tighter when she vanished.'

'How do you know about Bella?'

'Because we're distant cousins, Major, and I make it my business to know about our family.'

A few days later, Anna and I went for a drive down to Selkirkshire.

'*Why come you to Carterhaugh without command from me?*'

'*I'll come and go,*' young Janet said, '*and ask no leave of thee.*'

'Pardon?'

'It's from an old ballad: Tam Lin,' I said.

'I know the source, I just didn't expect you to sing it. We're in deep ballad country here, Tam Lin, True Thomas, Thomas the Rhymer...'

'And The Leyes, where Aphrêm lived.'

'Yes, The Leyes. I thought you might like to see it, or at least drive past it.'

'I thought it was a stables now?'

'It is, but we, I, think there might still be a connection.'

'Why?'

'A gut feel, based on movements around the place from time to time – the occasional limo. coming and going, young women who are seen around the property for a few months, clearly pregnant, who disappear. Something isn't right.'

Why is it always children?

I remembered brass and leather and the cradles.

'Are you OK?'

'No. Maybe. Just remembering something David Menzies said about children.'

'David? You didn't tell me you met him. When?'

'Italy, June 1944. Why?'

'He's the great enigma. The last known sighting of him was 1942. He was listed as missing behind enemy lines, presumed dead.'

'Trust me, that means nothing. You corrected yourself just then, you said *we* and changed it to *I*. Who're 'we'?'

'That's a long story.'

'How long?'

'Three hundred years and counting.'

'Best get started then.'

'Right. There's someone you need to meet, a neighbour, a good neighbour, you might say.

Now I see the dead everywhere. It's not too bad as long as they don't notice me, don't try and ask me favours. Whitehall is something else: there's a greater density of the dead here, clinging to faded dreams of Empire, straining to sing *Rule Britannia* with spectral vocal cords. The offices are full of them, still clocking in every morning at 8.30 prompt, leaving for the suburbs again at 17.00, not realising they've been promoted to another department, another ministry. I don't know what tethers them there when eternity is theirs to explore. Perhaps they don't have the imagination to leave: as in life, so in death.

Hawking was good, too old a pro to stick to a routine. He'd done something different every night when he left the office. On four occasions he'd left in an official car, but most evenings he left on foot by a nondescript door in the back of the Foreign and Commonwealth Office building, though that isn't where his office is. He didn't have a set time to leave and didn't use a predictable route. He never used the same underground station on consecutive evenings, and sometimes took a bus.

But his options were limited for the first quarter mile or so of his walk, and one evening or another, his route would bring him up Whitehall to Trafalgar Square and I would pick up the tail there. He hadn't done that on the previous thirteen evenings.

I wore blue overalls under a donkey jacket. I had Doc

Marten's shoes with steel toecaps, and a woolly hat, with a brim I could draw down over my brows. I was bearded.

Around 18.15 it looked like it was another wasted evening but then Hawking was there on the other side of the street, striding into the wind. He cut an anachronistic figure in his suit and bowler hat, but his bearing was military and he ignored the chill, declining to unfurl his umbrella.

I stayed well back, kept to shadows when I could, merging with clumps of pedestrians when I couldn't, doing nothing to draw attention to myself. Hawking turned onto the Strand, and crossed to turn up Bedford Street, then Floral Street and, eventually, onto James Street and into Covent Garden Underground.

I half suspected the wily old bastard would slip out the other entrance, but he took the lift down to the Piccadilly Line. Smart: the lift made it harder to be followed. I eased through the queue to get into the next lift. I thought I'd lost him, but spotted him towards the middle of the crowded Eastbound platform. I timed my walk through the crowd with the arrival of a train, and slid a long knife deep into his lower back at kidney level, slicing sharply sideways and up. His cry was lost in the clatter of the bogeys as I pushed him onto the track.

I walked on without looking back as the first onlookers screamed. I took the Long Acre exit. The knife went into a litter bin, my gloves into another. I slipped up an alley and took off the donkey jacket and overalls, under which I wore an off-the-shelf three-piece suit with office shirt and tie. I lost myself in the pre-theatre dinner crowd.

The next morning a short note in the *Times* said Police were treating the death of a senior civil servant in Covent Garden as suspicious and appealed for witnesses to come forward.

They can appeal all they like, they won't find me. My alibi is solid: like the fourth craw, I wisnae there at a'.

LIGHTEN OUR
DARKNESS

I love churches. Not drab modern prayer-houses, or back-room chapels, or those dreadful American monuments to ego and greed, I mean proper churches with chancels and apses, lady-chapels and stained glass, and an aumbry for the reserved sacrament.

I love to sit in the midst of humans in the darkening chill of a winter night, when psalms and anthems roll over the ridge of the reredos like clouds over a mountain range. I revel in cascading voices illumined from within by candlelight and prayer, that smell of beeswax.

Father doesn't like me to be in such close proximity to them, but indulges what he calls my *youthful idiosyncrasies* and says *it's a phase she's going through, they all do*. He even cracked a joke about it: *don't pray with your food dear,* and chuckles when he repeats it, which is often.

Over the years, I've sought out ecclesiastical buildings wherever we've been, from the mighty cathedrals of Reims and Chartres to the great basilica of Hagia Sophia, and in Cairo, Moscow and Odessa. And, of course, in York, Gloucester, Salisbury, Durham and my favourite: the austere beauty of St Magnus Cathedral in Kirkwall, where the very stonework transports you to a more brutal age while elevating your soul to the hope of eternity.

Despite all his long years, my father has never accepted that humans, our creations after all, our livestock, as he never ceases to remind me, are capable of creating beauty. He sat with me once in Orkney listening to Peter Maxwell Davies conduct his *Martyrdom of St. Magnus*, but said it was just noise (*croaks and discords* he said). Even the great choral works of Palestrina, des Prez and Monteverdi leave him unmoved. I remember one evening in St Mary's Cathedral in Edinburgh, listening to a choir sing the few known works of Robert Carver. The voices of the sopranos and countertenors carried my heart high into the vaulted roof, rising on whispers of incense.

Ergo, bone Jesu, propter nomen tuum salva me ne peream et ne permittas me damnari quem tu ex nihilo creasti—

Father just snorted and said that humans are not pets, as he always does when he gets exasperated with me, as if I didn't know that, as if I haven't known it my whole life.

It's nothing personal. He, more than most, has good reason to keep to the old ways, the old rules. My cousin, who lives in one of the human cities, often claims that some of them can be decent, and he's right, but it rather misses the point, doesn't it? The rules aren't there for fun, they were made for very good reason: when we are discovered, humans will always try to eradicate us.

Every so often there's agitation for change, and a cohort denounces the rules as crude and barbaric. They preach a doctrine that we are all creatures under the same skies on the same earth, and that we are all made 'equal', though by whom or what is never said. Even they aren't so reckless as to invoke the old gods. These *naïfs* insist that farming of humans is 'murder' and that humans have 'rights'. Sentimental nonsense, of course, but the rhetoric of the modernisers appeals to the young, or some of them at any rate, and occasionally to misguided idealists who should be old enough to know better. They don't last long, just long enough to see the error of their ways and gain an intimate, and fatal, understanding of the law of unintended consequences.

To most humans, we're just monsters from stories, stories which grow more elaborate as the years pass. This is no bad thing: however ridiculous, their popular entertainments about us serve a useful function. Taming us in stories distances us and encourages humans to disregard their tacit knowledge that we are here. That's why we seeded the stories in the first place, one of our more successful strategies to cope with their uncontrolled proliferation and the consequent risk of our discovery. It's quite amusing how far the stories penetrated their culture and now flourish without our help: Lilith, Lestat, Matthew Clairmont, Spike, Angel, Byronic anti-heroes or anthropomorphised archetypes all. And those films with fanged women in diaphanous nightgowns drifting around misty cemeteries and always ending up naked? Hilarious.

As their shamans, seannachies and makars grow ever more creative in telling and retelling the myth, they grow further and further from the truth about us, and leave us free to slip unremarked through the interstices of their imaginations: fleeting, transient, always here but never there. Presence and absence are just matters of perspective.

And yet there I sat in a church, listening to sung evensong, feeling the gentle pull of the familiar call and response, led by the blind old priest, long past retirement, who cared for the souls of the small flock, reciting from memory words he could no longer see.

O Lord, open thou our lips;
And our mouth shall shew forth thy praise.
O God, make speed to save us;
O Lord, make haste to help us.

I'm attracted to the high church – none of that primacy of the Word nonsense beloved by those dour Reformers with their endless exegesis of minutiae. There is a splendour in ritual, in the old liturgical soft-shoe shuffle, a splendour that transports. I think it's to do with the use of all five primary senses to produce something greater than the sum of the parts, that ineffable sixth sense of apprehension of the numinous, of the immanent, the encounter with the divine.

Does it surprise you that I speak of the divine? I don't know why it should. We have been on this earth a long time and have long memories. We have seen many things that are difficult to explain without invoking the idea of other realms, other realities. That's another reason I like ritual, treading the boards to play my walk-on part in the divine comedy. It's why I like the flummeries and fripperies of the high churches, the scripted choreography of the costumed *pierrots* in their sanctuaries, chasing the spectrum of the liturgical seasons, mining silver at the rainbow's end for their chalices and patens, and gold for the embroidery on their chasubles.

I'd settled on Anglican as my denomination of choice. It wasn't a random selection. The liturgical density of the Orthodox churches is a fascination and a joy, but a little goes a long way: too much is like binge-eating baklava. Rome has its attractions, but also an abiding tone of smug superiority that puts me off. And there's the guilt thing, and the apostolic assertiveness, and enough narcissistic

212

self-abasement to torment the tits off a tortoise.

On the whole I find the Anglicans more attractive because, and I appreciate the irony, they operate on a more human scale, and the Episcopal Church in Scotland is the most human of them all.

Lighten our darkness, we beseech thee, O Lord; and by thy great mercy defend us from all perils and dangers of this night; for the love of thine only Son, our Saviour Jesus Christ. Amen.

The words tripped off my tongue as they always do; I reflected on their simple beauty, as I always do; and I reflected that I am one of the perils and dangers warded against, as I always do.

I stayed in my pew while the humans filed out. Father and I have long kept the family tradition of meditating together in the heart of the sacred yew in our garden, and it's easy and natural for me to linger in the embrace of the small church and reflect on the service. Tonight it was the ancient words of the *Nunc Dimittis* that snagged me like a thorn catching a cardigan, tugging at my threads.

O Lord, now lettest thou thy servant depart in peace according to thy word.
For mine eyes have seen thy salvation

Yes, let me depart in peace.

For I'm not at peace. I am very far from peace.

The priest stood nearby, in his cassock and a pair of worn loafers, waiting for me, though I didn't know how that could be.

'May I be of comfort, daughter?'

I started, alert.

'I've a lot on my mind, Father. Forgive me asking, but how did you know I was still here?'

'There are several ways of seeing, not all of them need eyes. Do you want to talk? I need to lock the church but I can offer tea and an understanding ear, if you want.'

I should have said no, I know that. I should have declined politely, gathered my coat and bag, and gone home.

But I didn't.

I made the tea, despite his protests. I take pleasure in little acts of kindness. As it brewed in a china pot sitting on a doily (Portuguese lace if I wasn't mistaken) on the table in his library, I looked around the shelves.

'Help yourself if there's anything you'd like: I can't read them anymore.'

How did he know I was looking? I wanted to find something to take, out of some perverse desire to please him, but there really wasn't anything there that caught my eye. I poured each of us a mug and added milk and sugar to his.

'You come to services here sometimes, but we haven't been introduced.'

'My name's Margaret. Do I call you Brian? Or Father Brian? Or ...?'

'Whatever you're comfortable with.'

'I'm curious. How do you know I've been here before?'

'You always wear the same perfume: subtle, musky, pervasive without being overpowering. You sing contralto and favour harmony over melody. Your phrasing is distinctive, as though your breathing is too slow. I probably wouldn't notice in a bigger church with more of a congregation, but there we are.'

'I'd no idea.'

He smiled. 'When I interrupted you in church, I got the impression you were deep in thought.'

'I was meditating. The words of the *Nunc Dimittis* seemed especially real tonight.'

'Meditation is a lost skill amongst modern Christians I fear.'

'Oh! Sorry – I'm not a Christian, though I have an interest in the religious.'

'How odd: I am a Christian, but not especially religious. Why were the words real for you?'

'Departing in peace. I'm not at peace.'

'Do you know why?'

I knitted my fingers into my hair, pulled them out again, like an embarrassed little girl caught being foolish.

'I think so, though I'd prefer to work my way around to that.'

'That's only human.'

Deep breath time, a deep breath as I break one of the rules, one of the more important rules.

'Well, that's the thing: you see, I'm not human.'

I'm not sure what reaction I expected, but I didn't expect the one he had: complete acceptance. I watched the mug in his hand, but there was no tremble. His poise was not disturbed at all.

'I suppose that explains the breathing. Tell me about your meditation.'

Why didn't he question me about *me*? Why didn't he react?

'The *Nunc Dimittis,* the words of Luke:

O Lord, now lettest thou thy servant depart in peace according to thy word. For mine eyes have seen thy salvation; which thou hast prepared before the face of all people; to be a light to lighten the Gentiles and to be the glory of thy people Israel.

'Is salvation only for humans, do you think? Is it given to creatures like me?'

'May I ask why you're interested?' Again, he didn't pick up my cue.

'Because … Because my conscience is … troubled.'

He sat back in his scuffed and sagging armchair. I had the distinct impression he was staring at me through his sightless eyes, considering me, weighing his answer; though not, I think, judging me.

'I don't know how to answer. I wonder why it's important to you. A troubled conscience, yes, I understand; but why salvation if you're not a Christian?'

'Doubt.'

'And if you're not human?'

'Humility: we don't have a monopoly on knowledge.'

'Doubt and humility are good; better than arrogance and certainty.

'The answer I want to give you is no, salvation is not just for humans, but I don't know how to back that up except, I suppose, from the idea of Grace. Our loving Father will not turn away from those who seek Him. I don't believe it matters whether you're a Christian or, as you say, human. What matters is that He accepts you.'

'Even if I don't deserve it?'

'Especially so. Who can possibly deserve it?'

I sipped my lukewarm tea, Outside the world red-shifted into a glorious sunset.

'That begs the question, rather, doesn't it? It presupposes a fault, an idea of sin as something more existential than just bad behaviour. It presupposes that we, or humans at least, are fallen.'

'Or it can simply be a metaphor for the state of not being divine.'

'That's not how it's usually understood, though, is it? The over-riding premise is the unworthiness of the profane.'

'There have been many interpretations; there are many rooms in this mansion. I prefer an interpretation which accepts and does not condemn.'

'You're evading the question.' I smiled. 'I understand why. But if it is just a metaphor for not being divine, why say the words of the Nicene Creed every Sunday?

> *I believe ... in one Lord Jesus Christ, the only-begotten Son of God, Begotten of his Father before all worlds, God of God, Light of Light, Very God of Very God, Begotten, not made, Being of one substance with the Father, By whom all things were made: Who for us men, and for our salvation came down from heaven, And was incarnate by the Holy Ghost of the Virgin Mary, And was made man, And was crucified also for us under Pontius Pilate. He suffered and was buried, And the third day he rose again according to the Scriptures, And ascended into heaven, And sitteth on the right hand of the Father. And he shall come again with glory to judge both the quick and the dead;*

'That's quite some embellishment of the metaphor. Are you really a Christian, Father?'

Was my question too direct? I did not want to diminish myself in his regard.

'I have doubts, of course. When I was first called to ordination I was full of all the certainties of a young man. After all these years, after all that I have seen, the joys and pains, the harvests and hunger, the love and grief, after all of the devotions I've made and the sermons I've preached, I have no certainty about anything. Except my faith. I believe I have met God, and I act in the faith of that belief as a disciple. I act as I believe He wants me to, with compassion. I don't really care about the details.

'I'm not a dogmatist. I have no interest in elaborate theologies, I've seen enough of those vanity projects. I believe simply that if we open ourselves to an encounter with the divine, then it is a transformative thing.'

Silence insinuated itself, punctuated by the ticking of the clock on the mantelpiece, its carriage mechanism deafening in the quiet of the small room.

'You remind me of something one of my great-aunts used to tell me. She's very old now, and we all think she's a bit batty, but she always said that a Buddhist monk attained Enlightenment right in front of her. She said he overflowed with light and vanished.'

'Really? I should have liked to see that. To answer your question, whether or not you believe in the idea of 'salvation' and whether salvation is only for humans or not, I believe that if you encounter the divine, the divine will not reject you.'

'And if I reject the divine?'

'Then I can't advise you. But I don't think you do, or you wouldn't think the way you do, and you wouldn't come to church so often. Your conscience troubles you, you said.'

'Yes.'

'Tell me then.'

'It's complicated.'

'What did you do?'

The final admission. The point of no return.

'I killed a girl who trusted me.'

'When you say you killed her, do you mean in an accident?'

'No. I stunned her with a taser and then stood by as she was injected with enough heroin to kill her.'

'And you did this out of malice? Out of anger?'

'No. It was the last part of my initiation into adulthood. If I hadn't done it, I would shame my family and break a line of tradition that stretches to the dawn of memory. But I had a free choice, so the responsibility is mine. Have you read Van Gennep, Father? I killed her and everyone treated me like I'd become something different. But something else changed too, something inside, something Father didn't expect: I became more aware of my doubts. It's like what physicists call a step change, a new equilibrium state.'

'What was her name?'

'Eleanor.'

'And you feel guilt?'

'Oh yes: so much. And I have to keep it hidden from my family, especially Father. He's so proud of me, it would break his heart to know of my weakness.'

'Weakness?'

'Remorse for the death of a human. It would be unacceptable in my Father's sight.' My fingers caught my hair again, the hair I kept long to hide the prominent earlobes which signify so much amongst us.

'Initiation is a strange thing. People think it is binary, that you go from A to B, child to adult, single to married. But it isn't like that. It's just a milestone. The journey goes on.'

'Father Brian, would it shock you if I said that I have a great appreciation of Judas?'

'Iscariot? The betrayer? That depends why.'

'Because he's at the heart of the story: without him there would have been no crucifixion and so no resurrection. Judas had to betray Jesus for the rest to happen. Jesus knew it too. Judas's encounter with the divine didn't go so well: the logic of the Gospels is that Judas was collateral damage.'

'That's, er, an unorthodox view, and assumes Judas actually existed, which some doubt.'

'Yes, but the writers of the Gospels tell it as true, and were content to portray Judas's death as a necessary sacrifice for the greater good. Just as they built the Passion narrative on an act of divine child sacrifice.'

'I'm not with you.'

'John 3:16, what is that except child sacrifice by God? And since He is unlikely to be sacrificing His own son to Himself, it looks like an act of ritual magic, sympathetic magic, the sacrifice itself has inherent power as a ritual act.'

'Well, John is often seen as an oddity amongst the Gospel writers.'

'Of course, but I see it all over the world: when Christians hold up signs in sports arenas, or when posters are put on noticeboards and wayside pulpits outside churches, all emblazoned with *John 3:16*, all celebrating cultic sacrifice.'

'The writer of John places that in the context of a long discussion culminating in assertions about God's judgement. Nicodemus tries to trick Jesus on a theological point and it should be read in that light, not necessarily taken literally. The writer is putting a theological argument into Jesus's mouth to make a point that Nicodemus would recognise by reference to his own tradition.'

'So you don't believe in Christ's sacrifice and the Last Judgement?'

'I believe meeting God necessarily forces us to judge ourselves. You mentioned an ancient tradition, so old and yet hidden?'

'Oh no, it's not hidden, you just have to know where to look, and how to look. It's hiding in plain sight.'

'Hiding in plain sight where?'

'Oh, there's the book of Genesis, chapter 5: all those old men – Adam who lived to be 930, Enosh 905, Jared 962, and the rest. The names have changed, and who they really were has been lost, but the essential record is true. The funny thing is, humans wonder how Adam and the others grew so old, while we're sad that they died so young.

Have you ever read the *Journey to the West*? Where Buddha lives with the pantheon of Immortals? Or the ancient tales from Ugarit and Mesopotamia that hide behind the Old Testament? There we are: mythologised and distorted, but there all the same.

'We created humans the way a farmer breeds for certain traits then maintains a bloodline. We created you, bred you to look like us, to be almost identical, but to carry the nutrients we need to sustain our long lives. We made you for food. Set you into herds and farmed you through the generations.'

'The vampire myth. You're a vampire.'

'No, that *is* a myth, a story we put about to hide ourselves in your imaginations. And now you look for us as creatures from stories, hiding in the darkness, when we live with you in the daylight. And we don't even need to farm you anymore, you do it for us. You're so wasteful of your young, we have easy pickings amongst your cast offs and discards. Even Eleanor: humans did much worse to her than kill her. We take the children you discard and abandon. If you don't care for them, why should we?'

'For blood?'

'No. Or not nowadays. Several hundred years ago we discovered that very specific extracts are sufficient as a dietary supplement. So we don't hunt now, except when we make the passage to adulthood. Then we must identify our prey, nurture it, and take responsibility for its sacrifice. My prey was Eleanor. I gave her every reason to trust me, to be my friend, to share her heart with me and love me. And she did. And then I killed her, even as she named her new-born after me.' The last rosy beams of sunlight angled up towards the ceiling above Father Brian's head. He made no immediate reply.

'Would you care for another cup of tea, Father?'

'Yes. I rather think I would.'

I returned with a fresh pot, two clean mugs and a packet of digestive biscuits. I poured for him and added milk and sugar. He hadn't moved from his chair: brave of him, although he couldn't have gone very far.

'You asked me why you should care about children whom humans abandon, but you do care, don't you? You feel remorse. Is it more than a farmer would feel for taking a lamb to slaughter?'

'Yes, I think so. I don't have the same remorse when we extract what you would call stem-cells and the donor dies. Despite Father's warnings, I bonded with Eleanor.'

'But you killed her all the same.'

'What else could I do? Now I wish I hadn't. She'd had such a shitty life and we rescued her and I gave her hope. She should have had her chance of life and her chance to give her daughter the childhood she was denied. All those possibilities are gone, all those worlds, all those generations of descendants who might have been and will never be. Because of me.'

A revelation shook me.

'Oh! This isn't remorse, it's shame.'

'And her daughter? The child Margaret?'

'Oh, already processed.' I broke a digestive into three pieces in my fingers and dunked some in my tea. 'After my initiation, Father and I followed the old rite, the old memorial, with a sip of Eleanor's blood.'

I nibbled the biscuit and raised the cup to my mouth. '*Mortuus est ut nos vivamus*. This we do in remembrance of her.'

Father Brian took a long drink of his tea. 'My dear, I can't help you depart in peace or settle your conscience. That's between you and God. That you are troubled is a

222

good start. But God offers his Grace freely, and as His minister I have heard your confession and will offer such absolution as I can.'

'But that's the thing isn't it: what if your Christianity is right and when I die I am not forgiven?'

'You believe in an existence after death?'

'Perhaps. I don't know. I believe my great-aunt's story, and we have seen other ... hints that physical death is not the end. But that's all we have, stories and hints.'

'Do you fear death?' I nodded. 'Then you must come to terms with what you have done, with your shame, while you live, and reconcile yourself to the prospect of non-existence, which waits for us all. We are not so different in the end. But it isn't God's forgiveness you crave, is it?'

He bowed his head.

Almighty God, our heavenly Father, who of his great mercy hath promised forgiveness of sins to all them who with hearty repentance and true faith turn unto him: Have mercy upon you; pardon and deliver you from all your sins; confirm and strengthen you in all goodness; and bring you to everlasting life; through Jesus Christ our Lord. Amen.

'The rest is between you and God. Tell me dear, where do you live?' I hesitated. 'Come now, we both know I won't survive this meeting: indulge my curiosity.'

So, he'd worked it out, accepted it.

I liked this human.

'When your eyes still worked, did you ever go on a train and see abandoned branch lines curving away into the trees? Or see white vans on country roads and wonder how they got there and where they were going? Have you ever listened to the news headlines and had the feeling there was something secreted behind them? Have you ever had those jolts where your mind seems to jump within and between moments with a stutter, a strange discontinuity? That's us. We live where your ordered lives shade into randomness, on the boundary between meaning and nonsense. Hiding in plain sight.'

His eyelids drooped – he was an old man after all, and we had been talking for some time. He yawned.

'Forgive me my dear, I'm very tired. Don't you fear you'll be discovered?'

'Oh yes. It's happened before and we defended ourselves. So we cull the herds from time to time. Some of us think the time is overdue for another cull, that we have been too *laissez-faire* since your seventeenth century and have put ourselves at risk. And your surveillance society is a threat: your drones and cameras and satellites are very dangerous for us.

'There is another thing. Are you familiar with a trophic cascade, Father Brian? It is to do with the effects on an environment when the apex predator is removed, or removes itself as we did. And what has happened is humans destroying the biosphere we share. We can't allow it to continue. So a cull is coming, and it will be severe. We call it the Gaia Cascade.'

'And I won't live to see it.' His head was now leaning to one side, a dribble of spit rolling down the right side of his chin, as his body sought the sanctuary of sleep.

'No, Father Brian, I'm afraid you won't.'

'I've lived a long time, though I am no doubt a child to you. I've expected death to come calling for a while now. I am ready. How will you do it?'

'I already have. The first pot of tea contained a poison, the second an accelerant. You're a good man, Father, and there will be no pain. You can let go now. I'll stay with you, and hold your hand.'

'There is one last thing you should know, then. Salvation

is not a magic trick worked by God: change is required – sacrifice.'

His fingers found mine and he relaxed into unconsciousness, which became a coma. I sang as I held his hand:

Magníficat ánima méa Dóminum, et exultávit spíritus méus in Déo salutári méo. Quia respéxit humilitátem ancíllæ súæ, ecce enim ex hoc beátam me dícent ómnes generatiónes.

I sang until his lungs stopped breathing and his heart stopped beating and he was just a sac of discarded flesh.

I washed and tidied the tea things and put the biscuits back in a cupboard. I took his mobile phone from my pocket and laid it on the table beside him. I plugged the landline back in. I made quite sure he was dead and kissed his brow.

A full moon shone from a cloudless sky. The Sea of Tranquillity, where men once walked, was sharp and clear. What would it be like to walk on other worlds? Why did humans do it when it never once occurred to us?

Two miles down the road I met Father's limousine where my driver waited patiently. It would be a long journey home through the night. I looked across the valley to where the church sat, the light still on in the rectory library. I can't go back there again for another twenty years in case I'm recognised, assuming there is anyone left after the Gaia Cascade. Time enough for sacrifice then.

I liked Father Brian: he was a kind and gentle man. I should have liked to know him better, talked to him about the Moon and sacrifice. It was a pity he had to die, but rules are rules.

THE BEAST ASTRAY

Mama wasn't home, not where I'd killed Hank leastaways, just strangers who never heard of her, and said to get the hell off their property or they'd call the cops, and why wasn't I at God-damned school anyway fer Chris'sakes, the God-damned kids today have it easy, not like in our day, no sir, we'd've gotten whipped for playing hookey and God-damned right.

I'd only been gone four God-damned weeks.

The cops'd haul me in front of a judge as an absconder and a God-damned juvenile delinquent just as soon as they'd given me a good kicking. And not just the cops, there was Joseph who owned the Loving Arms Attitude Adjustment Center for Deviant and Delinquent Adolescents who'd sent the *thing* Maria for me. Mama's was where they'd look first. When I said I was going back, Coyote gave me a look to say I was a God-damned dumbass for even thinking about it. But where else would I go but to my Mama?

A blackness passing on a moonless night touched the edge of my mind: a *thing* was close. Another was nearby, in a different direction, like their jaws were closing on me, tongues licking, breath hot, teeth sharp.

And now I needed to get to the other side of the God-damned country where Michael's call rose and fell in my head all the God-damned time and I didn't know how to get there and those things were after me and I couldn't wave goodbye to Mama or give her a hug or blow kisses and promise to write home because she wasn't God-damned there and I never did find out where she was.

It's not as though I hadn't gone to enough God-damned effort to get there; not as though I hadn't saved Mama from Hank; not as though she had no God-damned reason to be grateful to me; not as though I'm not part of her; not as though I didn't love her or anything. I didn't ask to come here when she married Hank and ran away from Glasgow, leaving me in the middle of God-damned nowhere with nowhere to go. It's not as though it wouldn't be nice if she could tell me what I God-damned am and why I'm made this way, and why she thinks Papa is dead when he ain't.

We went north on the B&M. Random flecks of yellow and gold in the trees reminded me of light refracting through the spray of a fast stream, like a river ran beside the track.

I was very hungry.

I fell asleep watching the golden river, and woke to the sound of a train inspection at the Canadian border. We slipped into the undergrowth.

We took random trains south then west after that. We tried to get on them while they stood in a yard, but I figured so long as they were slow enough that you could count the lug bolts on the wheel, it was probably fine to clamber aboard, even for Harry. We ate whatever I could steal. I stole a hunting knife and some matches from an unlocked workshop one time, so I could gut and cook the rabbits that Harry caught. I wasn't a good camp cook at first, the wood was damp, the meat near raw with skin hot enough to burn my fingers.

We didn't meet any other people at all. I kept as clean as I could, but even though the season stayed warm, the rivers ran cooler, and the dry leaves of the fall ain't great for wiping your ass.

Anyways, we pitched up in Racine, Wisconsin and I knew then exactly where to go next. The C&NW Twin Cities 400 stopped there on the line from Chicago to Minneapolis. I learned that ways back when I was even smaller than you are now, before I killed Hank, when I first met Coyote. And if I got to Minneapolis, I guessed I could find Hank's family and rest up for a few days there if they'd have me, and maybe even send a letter to Granny and Aunty Bella. That train did 400 God-damned miles in 400 God-damned minutes, and if that ain't worth God-damned swearing about then I don't know what is.

Harry growled. I thought the cops had caught up, but the man wore a preacher's cross on his lapel and a bigger wooden cross on a cord around his neck. The respectable twinsets and hats told me the women with him were part of his flock. Their auras looked normal enough so I figured they were OK, as long as they didn't see it as their duty to turn me in. I wasn't in a hurry to be talked at by holy-rollers and all, but they might have hot food and maybe a bath, so I wasn't going to be God-damned stupid about it. You take it where you find it, right?

I scratched Harry's ears. Coyote slunk around in the shadows somewhere, behind some old pallets in the goods yard.

'Good evening, young man. We're from the First Church of Christ Redeemer, may we offer you help?'

I put on the face I used with librarians and with Mr. and Mrs. Young, before Mr. Young got himself a hole in his chest and Mrs. Young sat crying in the mud all covered in his blood.

'We're lost, Father, me and Harry here.'

'No need to call me Father, son. Pastor Nicholson is fine. This here is Miss Archer and Miss Cunningham. We can give you a bed for tonight and a place to wash up. Then you can tell us your story before you go on your way. How old are you, son?'

'Sixteen and a half.'

'So young to be alone,' Miss Cunningham said.

'My Papa died and Mama is ill so I'm going west to live with my uncle. But, well, what with the doctor's bills and all, Mama has no money, so …'

I guess I was convincing, what with the tears and all.

'Oh, you poor thing,' said Miss Archer. 'Let's get you both into the warm for a hot meal, you and Harry.'

Harry, who'd have ripped her throat out a few days before, acted the fool, rolling on the ground for his tummy to be scratched, making snorting noises, tongue lolling from the corner of his mouth. The pastor and the women were charmed. Coyote looked disgusted.

The bath was hot and the food good. I expected they'd preach at me, but they didn't. I slept in a good bed with clean sheets. Harry slept on a blanket at the foot of the bed dreaming of rabbits, I guess. Coyote lay in the corner with his head on his paws, watching me.

I dreamed I rode the footplate of a trans-continental express. It had carriages and wagons in all kinds of gauges and livery, with a Hiawatha Skydome at the rear. Two huge E4 Hudsons hauled our ragged entourage, sparks and steam and smoke flying into the cold night air as we powered across the heartlands. It was like we were flying and there were troop ships and tramp steamers pulling away from the Broomielaw down below, and the train flew down the Clyde, doon the watter, over the Queen's and Prince's Docks and shipyards and tall cranes, past the mouth of the Kelvin, to Greenock then Dunoon, then Rothesay, where ravens circled. A voice on Children's Hour on the radio sang the best God-damned train song he knew.

I stood on the wide Atlantic and the broad Pacific shores ...

The river was in constant change, sometimes flowing through plains and forests, other times through tall tenements and bomb sites and shipyards, all jumbled together as memories out of time. Eyes watched: Aunty Bella's witch's eyes, my eyes, the eyes of primal spirits, their slumber disturbed by the clanging bell and flickering Mars Light. Ahead of us, a man in pain on an ancient tree, pricked and penetrated like a pin cushion, spine arched, throat exposed, incoherent syllables straining through the wire binding his jaws.

The thunderous pistons pounded and we shovelled more and more coal into the firebox, hurtled ever faster to our destination. The driver had one hand on the regulator and one on the whistle. The driver was Mama, who turned into Martha Feldman, and into Miss Archer, who all spoke in the tongues of men and angels, while the rough pick and strum of an old guitar drove the locomotives into the tunnels of the night.

I woke up wondering what the hell I was, what I could do, with no one to ask. Honking automobiles, the whistle and rumble of locomotives and the clang of their bells tumbled through the open casement window. I had another hot bath, and put on the clean clothes left out for me. I followed my nose to the kitchen, where Miss Archer gave me a warm smile and a hot breakfast. Harry was there before me, enjoying a bowl of dogfood and meat scraps. Coyote had disappeared.

Pastor Nicholson came by half an hour after I'd eaten. He looked older in daylight.

'Do you want to tell me your story, son? You don't have to, but I'd sure like to hear it.'

'Ain't much to tell, sir. Papa died in the war in Germany and Mama met her new husband and brought me to America. But my step-daddy died and Mama can't look after me right now, so I'm heading west to see my Uncle Michael. We ain't got no money, so I'm getting there the best way I can, riding the rails.'

'Oh, that's horrible,' said Miss Archer.

'What about schooling?'

'I've had some, but we never stayed in one place too long. I read a lot, and did some math at my last place.'

'Any jobs you can do?'

'Well, I can tend a kitchen garden, gut and cook a rabbit, and I can organize a library around the Dewey-Decimal System. And I have a way with animals I guess.'

'An interesting combination, son. Would you be willing to help out around here for a few days and then we can maybe help you on your way?'

I couldn't think of a way to get out of it, and anyway a bed and food were too good to turn down.

'Why sure.'

'What's your name, son?'

'John, sir. John Pitcairn.'

'Well, John, if you could help Miss Archer here with some chores, we'll see about finding you something else to do when I get back.'

Miss Archer, who seemed to me to dress about twenty years older than she really was, looked happy with that arrangement too. She had dark hair pulled into a knot, and a pale complexion. She had an odd, closed-up way of walking, like she was trying to hide her curves, holding her shape in check so's not to offend the Lord, though why he'd be so God-damned offended I couldn't figure. I didn't know why she touched my arm so often, or looked at me from the corner of her eyes quite so much when she thought I didn't see. But she was chatty and friendly and confided her name was Eliza, though I mustn't call her that in company in case people said she was forward, whatever the hell that meant.

She watched me later, too, when I had my shirt off after a morning in the yard splitting logs with an axe, then bustled away, embarrassed, when I looked back. But her gaze had lingered, and I found that disconcerting, in a nice way.

And, you know, I guess it would have been a good place to stay for a while, if not for old Mrs. Harrigan, who came by with food and clothes to donate to the Church.

Eliza barely had time to say *Hi Nancy*, when the old lady collapsed to the floor. Her aura was distressed, swirling in rapid eddies and vortices with worrying dark patches appearing there, blue, purple and black. I didn't think about what I was doing, I just hurried over and held my hands above her, easing the flow of colour, sensing the blockages in her arteries, encouraging them to dissolve into her bloodstream without breaking into fragments. I can't explain it any better than that, not then anyways, and not really even now.

Mrs. Harrigan opened her eyes as Pastor Nicholson and Miss Cunningham came in and saw me there, Eliza at my side.

Coyote, at the door, gave me an odd look, quizzical, surprised, hackles up. I couldn't blame him: I didn't know what had just happened either.

I shouted across the chasm between us: *what am I, Mama? Am I a God-damned witch like you said? Who am I? Why don't you want me?* But the only answer was the noise of the locomotives and wagons outside.

Miss Cunningham took Mrs. Harrigan home, and Pastor Nicholson sat next to me.

'What did you do, John? How did you do that?'

I turned my eyes to him and he pushed his chair back so fast, the legs scraping on the hardwood floor.

'I don't know Pastor. I've never done that before.'

'What are you child? Good Christ, what have we brought into our house?'

Harry came and sat next to me, licking the hand that dangled down by my side. Coyote was in the corner now, and didn't take his eyes off me. In the depths of my mind, a train whistle blew, an incoherent voice rose and fell, and, over the top of it all, my Aunty Bella sang beside my cot:

Three craws, sat upon a wa', sat upon a wa', sat upon a wa'

Eliza stood behind me, her hands steady and firm on my shoulders.

'You did a good thing, John: you saved Nancy's life. I don't know how you did it, and I don't care. That was a good thing, and don't you doubt it.'

'Yes,' said Pastor Nicholson, composure regained, though he would not look me in the eye. 'Yes, it was a good act, a blessing. But it changes things. You can't stay here, John. You'll have to be on your way.'

'What? Now you see here Alex Nicholson, we can't just throw this boy out after what he did!'

'I'm not throwing anyone out, Eliza, but think about this: Nancy Harrigan will tell everyone she knows what happened and about her miracle healing, and they'll tell everyone too, and the story will grow and grow. By nightfall every crank and charlatan in the county will be at our door. Then we'll have reporters show up and the story will be all over the State and then the country. John will be public property before he knows it, and any chance of going to his uncle will be gone.'

I searched the possible futures, let the probabilities play out.

'Pastor Nicholson is right. I'll bring trouble if I stay.'

I didn't say that in most possible futures the *things* found me there and killed anyone who sheltered me.

Eliza stifled a sob with a lavender-scented handkerchief. She had to be healed too, though I couldn't figure out how to cure her malady.

I laid my hands on her head and let her aura mingle with mine. Oh, the passions trapped in her heart, her yearning for another life far from Racine. She hoped I'd be the one to release her, even though she'd only just met me. She didn't know I was only God-damned fourteen going on fifteen, didn't know I'd lied about my age – how could she? She burned for all she wanted to be but didn't know how to become.

'Be well, Eliza. Know your heart, listen to it, and follow it.'

I kissed her forehead, and took the door into the corridor to my room. Harry didn't follow, but lingered in the kitchen.

'Do you want to stay here, boy? You have to promise to take good care of Eliza for me now, like you took care of me.'

He trotted over and allowed me to scratch under his jaw and round his ears, then lay at Eliza's side. All this time Pastor Nicholson and Miss Cunningham watched in silence. I guess they had nothing to say.

They gave me a small suitcase with more clothes inside, and some spending money for food. And they gave me train tickets from Racine to Chicago, then for the California Zephyr from Chicago to Oakland, where I'd told them Michael lived. That would be near a three-day journey if I went all the way. I don't know how much those tickets cost, but they gave them freely when they didn't have to.

It was mostly businessmen on the train to Chicago. The Zephyr was different. Most of the folks on the platform looked well-heeled and dressed to show off. The men all wore worsted wool suits with sharp-creased pants, white shirts and coloured neckties, and were topped and tailed by sharp-brimmed hats and polished shoes. They sweated in the unseasonal warmth. The women were all heels and hose and skirts cut just under the knee, with blouses and topcoats and hats even I could tell were better than the ones Mama cried over in the Sears Catalogue. Their kids were all dressed like they were going out to Sunday lunch at their aunty's house. They clustered round colour-coordinated luggage and were fussed over by conductors and porters.

None of them even noticed I existed. I guess I looked lost until an official-looking woman standing by the rear coach of the train noticed me. She wore a blue two-piece suit over a monogrammed white blouse. Pinned onto her neatly-cut hair was a military-style hat with a Zephyr pin. She said she was Nellie, my Zephyrette. She was kind, and took the time to settle me into the shining steel coach, and showed me where to put my little suitcase, despite all the well-heeled folks tutting and clicking their fingers for her attention. She was polite to them, but gave her time to a veteran, with a duffle bag and a fancy walking cane, who needed her help more. He had a ticket for the same carriage as me.

The towns rolled on into the evening: Mendota, Kewanee, Galesburg, until we crossed the Mississippi and into Iowa while I was eating supper that cost me just over a God-damned dollar. Sometime around eleven, we crossed the Missouri to reach Omaha, Nebraska before midnight.

By then me and Coyote had the Vista Dome upstairs to ourselves. When we took long curved bends, I could see the train stretched before and behind me. I caught the reflection of starlight on the rails, felt the rumble of the fast express, remembered Wolfe and something about us being always strangers and alone. He got that God-damned right.

We clattered over a cantilevered iron bridge across shining water, travelling ever deeper into lands I'd read about or seen in dreams.

I didn't want to sleep. I wanted to see everything even though it was dark, but I slept through the rest of Nebraska and woke up as we pulled into Denver at 8.20 the next morning.

The second day, life on the Zephyr found a clickety-clack rhythm. There were card games everywhere, and various characters wandering the train, looking for God knows what. I watched America go by, wishing I could find a place where everyone wasn't smoking. I scanned anyone entering the coach to be sure they were human, opened my extra eye to watch the flickering auras come and go. Nellie came by every couple of hours to check on me. Sometimes she talked to the whole train over an intercom, but often she sat with me and pointed out landmarks as we rolled by.

A couple further up the carriage cast disapproving looks from time to time, like I was beneath their God-damned notice. They were in their fifties, I guessed, and looked like they wanted to be in there with the smart set, but couldn't afford a private cabin. They called each other Sam and

Marcia. I ignored them. I figured if the worst that happened was a few looks I'd be happy. If only they knew what I was, maybe they wouldn't be so God-damned snooty. I fantasised about what I could do to them if they slighted me, until Coyote's fur rose and he started growling.

We crossed the Continental Divide in the Moffat Tunnel, then ran alongside the Colorado River for 235 more God-damned miles. The sunlight reflecting off it put me in mind of the river of golden leaves back in New England.

Nellie fixed it so's I had supper in the first, cheaper, sitting again, and I studied the timetable, trying to work out where best to get off. I asked Nellie where the best stop was to see the Sierras because I had a mind to come back hiking one day. She suggested Portola or Oroville but an excursion from Maryville or Sacramento would work too. I noted this down in pencil on the timetable, but wasn't any better informed.

I caught a last glimpse of the Colorado at Westwater, Utah, and was ready to sleep again when we pulled into Salt Lake City about twenty after ten.

I dreamed, but I can only remember snatches of imagery: a train, Michael crying and surrounded by mountains, and Aunty Bella touching her finger to my forehead, singing: *the first craw was greetin' for his ma, greetin' for his ma …*

I woke with wet cheeks.

For all the 2100 miles we'd travelled, I never once sensed anything out of the ordinary. That changed at breakfast. I couldn't pin it down, but it wasn't one of the *things*. Something was trying to check me out. I withdrew into myself. Coyote was agitated. There was no one new in the carriage, just the same passengers, the attendants and Nellie.

I was already on edge when I caught on that, not only had I missed the chance to get off at Portola, but also two *things* now were on the train where they hadn't been before. One was at the front and one at the rear, and I was smack-dab in the God-damned middle.

The train was already rolling and the next stop was three and a half hours away. We had 116 miles to travel, through Feather River Canyon without a stop. The Vista Dome had only one entrance and exit. I guess there were washrooms but I'd have to come out of them sometime. I looked to Coyote for ideas, but he wasn't there.

I wished Mama was with me to tell me what to do and keep me safe and to hold me tight and tell me everything was going to be alright, but she was just as gone as Coyote. Just as gone as everyone said Papa was.

A man walked by in a sports jacket and cravat, slicked hair, paunchy: human. Two children, a boy and a girl, played at a table down the aisle, ignoring their parent's orders to *hush*. A man with a camera tried to judge exposure with a light meter, cursing every patch of shade and shadow that threw his readings off. Nellie worked her way from the far end of the carriage, sharing a word and a smile with everyone.

Behind me the veteran's eyes were closed. His aura was unusually controlled. How did he do that? Did he even know he did it? A porter, jowly black face above his pressed white jacket, tidied away pillows and blankets.

There was a commotion up the aisle. I half rose to see Sam, slumped in his seat, his aura fading, Marcia was frantic, shouting for help. I didn't even think about it and ran forward. I put my hands over him, just as I had with Nancy Harrigan.

Sam slipped away, his pale figure emerging beside his prone body. I didn't have the strength to save him.

'Not yet,' he said. 'Please, not yet. We've only just got married.'

His heart had a fading, irregular pattern of beats through clogged valves and a ballooning artery wall. I allowed our auras to mingle for a moment, giving him a little strength. I tried to sense the ancient America again like I had at Loving Arms. I brought to mind all the lands I'd seen in my dreams, the eyes looking up as the trains I rode flew high over them, but I couldn't wish them into reality however much I tried.

Instead, I found something unexpected, sinewy and powerful and silvery-bright, made of steel and iron and wood and glass that traversed the whole God-damned country from Oakland to Chicago every two and a half days, soaking up elemental energies from the plains and mountains, from the water and the air, from the fires of old steam locomotives, from the twin diesel electric units that hauled her now. It grew from the great network of rails. It connected America from one station to the next, a powerful Being whose strength would only wane when the day came that the railroads were neglected and the heart of America was abandoned.

The California Zephyr give me a little of her power, loaned Sam some of her life and strength, Sam whose shade faded as his body started to breathe again.

I was exhausted.

Thank you, I said to the Zephyr.

I said to Marcia, 'He loves you very much and doesn't want to leave you. I helped him stay a while, but I've only bought him an hour or two without a doctor.'

Nellie took charge.

'Thank you, John. I don't know what you did, but thank you. I've called for help. Meantime, ladies and gentlemen, it would be for the best if we all took our seats and made some room.'

'Nicely done. I haven't seen or heard of that before.'

The veteran sat in the empty seat by mine. He had my eyes: witch's eyes. He was Family.

'Who are you, mister?'

'David Menzies. We're cousins I think, but we have other things that concern us right now. Are you alone?'

'Just me and Coyote.'

He recoiled.

'When did that thing attach itself to you?'

'He's my friend, the only God-damned friend I've got. I know him, but I don't know you. What you got against him?'

'My brother met it, then disappeared. I don't trust your Coyote.'

'Well you'd better start, mister, 'cos he's right behind you and don't look too happy.'

'What? Where?' He couldn't see anything. 'Oh, I remember now; Michael said that only he could see the beast unless it chose to manifest itself.'

'Michael?'

'Yes, my brother. Why?'

'Someone called Michael is calling for me from up there somewhere, up in the mountains.'

'And you can hear him? We need to get off. Now.'

'There are *things* on the train: one up front, one behind, coming this way.'

'You feel them too? Good. Now: what's your plan? How are you going to get off the train?'

'I don't have a plan. I don't know if I can call on the ancient spirits again, not on a train with all these people, and the Zephyr has already given me some of her strength.'

'You and I have a lot to talk about. Right, here's the thing: we need to even the odds and find a defensible position. Take my arm and lead me to the washroom up front there.'

'But there's a thing coming that way.'

'Yes, that's rather the point. Did you ever meet Bella, by the way?'

'Aunty Bella? In Rothesay? She's my Granny's sister. She used to sing to me when I was small; she taught me to read.'

'That sounds like her. I think I met your dad once. Nice chap.'

'Everyone says he's dead and that's why Mama got married again.'

'But you don't do you? You think he's still alive.'

'I know he is.'

Marcia clung to grey-faced Sam, and mouthed *thank you* as I passed. The other passengers looked out of the window or read their books, but wouldn't God-damned look at me. We crossed into the next carriage. Coyote followed, yellow eyes taking in everything.

'Where are you going? There are people back there asking for you,' Nellie said.

'I'm helping this gentleman to the washroom, and I'm trying to avoid attention.'

Nellie gave me a long look.

'I can't keep it quiet, too many people saw. But I can try and have them leave you alone for a while.'

We were at the end of the carriage when the things found us.

'Into the Vista Dome. Now.'

'But there's no way out of there.'

'No, but if we're smart, they won't get in either.'

There were footsteps on the stairs. My special eye opened, and the world changed, just like when I woke up and could see auras. The thing on the stairs, in its neat suit and black Oxfords, was an emptiness. It had a look on its face I'd seen before when Pink Tongue chose boys for a beating.

Coyote snarled, and the thing looked round. It was enough. *Snck,* the outer case of David's walking cane fell away. *Ssszt,* a razor-edged sword sliced the thing's throat. The return swing took off its head.

The corpse toppled into the stair well, its head rolling into the lounge below. Twin jets of blood hosed from its neck, drenching its companion, a female that threw a child at us, the girl who'd played with her brother. The child hit the glass roof of the Dome and fell to the floor, unconscious, but alive. We ducked, and the creature bellowed as it jumped, not bothering with stairs. David had no time to set himself to swing that God-damned sword.

The thing was in mid-air when Coyote leaped and clawed at its legs with a giant paw. It crashed, hard, to the deck, but rolled and stood upright, ignoring David.

'Joseph wants you, little human.'

A switch in my head flipped, a door swung open. Bella was there, and Granny, and others I didn't know. Their strength poured into me, tingling through muscle and sinew and bone. All the moments that brought me there, all the possibilities for the future: they were all parts of the same thing. A long chain of eyes receded into deep history, and the faces of powerful ancestors looked back through time to claim me as their kin, as their heir. One had bright red eyes and scared me.

And the spirit of the Zephyr, scion of a greater entity living in the rail roads and rutted wagon trails, investing America with strength and unity, binding together all of the limbs and organs of the Union, touched me. I shivered in the static charge of every electron ever stripped from its silver skin as it powered through American air. I heard the voices in the singing of the rails, in the clackety clack of the bogies of every train that ever passed over this great land, the chants of uncounted generations who'd wandered the country, the great spirits of earth and air and rivers and forests, the ancient powers deep in the wilderness, curious about the steel lace laid over their resting places. All the accumulated energy in the rails.

I couldn't stop my arms rising from my sides, any more than I could control the corona of my hair around my head.

The power took form and shape, gathering the forces together. Without hesitation, I discharged it all as a single bolt into the creature.

The thing rose into the air, already dead. Its body jerked and spasmed in the lines of force running around and through it, its ruined spine arching and curling into impossible shapes, disintegrating, atom by atom, draining into a vortex of black emptiness twisting in time and space.

All scraps and traces of the blood and corpse of its male companion were drawn into the nothingness, every scrap or sign that either of them had ever been there, until the void snapped shut with a soft plop.

The Zephyr slowed for us on the great curve around the edge of the Feather River Valley. David and I jumped into the morning sunlight, as the hum and ring of the tracks decayed. Without warning, I was lost in a vision of a future with no railroad, where everyone drove automobiles that only they occupied, an America where countless millions withdrew into solitary selfishness while the steel ribbons that bound the country together rusted into memories and museums, and a great dream died, taking its power with it.

I buzzed with the energies that lingered in my system. Coyote stayed close, head cocked, ears forward, yellow eyes shining. There were things near.

'Lead the way,' I said.

We had no boots or wet-weather gear, no food, no water. I soon dumped my case, keeping only a sweater to wear at night, my knife, and my matches.

David kept his backpack and cane. Nothing seemed to make him happier than to be out in the middle of God-damned nowhere, without gear or direction, though he didn't hesitate to break into a hut we came across and steal windcheaters and waterproofs.

'Can you tell me about Papa?' I asked, to take my mind off my protesting legs and lower back.

'Walter? I only met him once, in Italy in '44. I was hunting our non-human friends, as was he, though he didn't know it. We were only together for a few minutes. You look like him you know, and he certainly passed the Gift to you.'

We followed Coyote along a rough trail into a cluster of pine and spruce, all the time climbing higher.

'Mama called me a witch.'

'Well, that's not a useful name. Our family's origins in Scotland are lost in history, but we had the Sight, the ability to see the future, and maybe see other things too. Not everyone in the family has it, and even if you do it might not be very powerful. One of our ancestors ran into one of those creatures and it triggered some kind of change in her. That's the gist of it, at least, as far as I understand it.'

The image of a green-eyed lady flashed before me then was gone.

'No: there was someone else.'

'I dare say. I don't know everything, I'm not sure if even Bella does. Anyway, ever since then we've watched them, and hurt them when we can. But they seem also to know about us, to hunt our family. So I went underground.'

I stopped, breathless in the thinning air. I cupped my hands and sipped clear water from a rivulet that flowed across our path. I spread my waterproof on the chilly ground and sat down, my back against a fallen tree trunk.

'What are they?'

'I wish I knew. They've been here a very, very long time, though, and regard humans as their property. They prey on children, usually babies. We don't know why for sure, but they extract something from babies' bodies. I've seen this. Your father saw it too.'

We climbed above the treeline to a panoramic view of the wilderness to the south. Coyote showed no signs of slowing, but breakfast was a long time ago, and I was done in. I had to sit again.

'I've never seen anything like what you did back there. What did you do?'

'It wasn't really me, it was the train, and all the power of the hidden America coming through the tracks.'

'But how did you know how to do it?'

'I didn't. It happened before back at Loving Arms when one of those things came for me and the soil swallowed them up. I just let it happen. How come you just so happened to be on the same God-damned train as me?'

'I wondered when you'd ask that. Bella said I had to come and look for you. She's very powerful, you know, when she says you have to do something, she means it. She sees things, makes connections others can't, although she can be strange: when I left her, three rooks were preening their feathers on a wall behind her shop. She roared with laughter and wouldn't tell me why.'

A shadow moved a hundred yards ahead of us, a cougar slipping into the shadows.

'I had to set up a new identity and get a passport and sort out money before I could get to New York. And when I got here it took me a while to pick up your trail: all we knew was Hank was from Minnesota, and we had the address some letters had been sent from. Then I heard rumours and found that Loving Arms place and I put two and two together and hoped it was four. I couldn't work out how you got away. Now I've seen you in action I understand. Then I heard a story about a healing in Wisconsin and was on my way there when I had an overwhelming conviction that I should take the Zephyr instead. So I did.'

'How d'you hear about Racine?'

'Like I hear everything: by listening to crazies and sifting it through the Gift.'

Coyote watched from about a hundred yards ahead, impatient. I ignored him.

'Everyone in Glasgow is convinced Walter died. They had the usual telegram and then his personal effects were delivered. He was a hero, you know, Military Cross.'

'Why did he just abandon us? Heroes don't do that.'

'My bet is that he did it to protect his family, like I did.'

A chasm opened under my tummy.

'You abandoned your family?'

'Yes. My wife and daughter in Edinburgh.'

I had nothing to say to him after that. An unaccountable yearning to comfort his daughter came over me. Maybe, like me, she knew he was alive but couldn't understand why. Maybe she didn't understand what she was, who she was, either. And David was wrong. Walter disappeared for some other reason entirely: darkness surrounded him.

The chilly air cooled our sweat as he strolled and I trudged over rough terrain. I managed to keep going for another couple of hours until we found a spot David declared to be ideal for a billet, that's what he called it. He fished around in his pack, took out two pieces of wire, and said he'd be back soon. I gathered kindling and sticks for a small fire, which was well set up when he returned with two rabbits.

The ground was hard and the air cold, even with the radiant embers and my jumper. I was too exhausted to do anything but sleep well. I woke to the keening screech of a red-tailed hawk, loud in the sudden silence of songbirds. David was already up, performing exercises.

'Who is Michael?' I asked.

'He's my twin brother. He was in hospital after the First War after a run-in with those creatures. We called them Priority Target Alpha then. He came here in 1919 after a huge row with our parents, met the creatures again and had to run for it. We thought he'd be safe here because our Yank oppos. swore blind there were no such things in America, said they were a European problem. In the end he made an absolute packet in Hollywood, but disappeared in 1926. In his last letter, Michael said he was coming up here with someone calling himself Injun Joe to a sacred grove.'

'Why didn't Michael's Gift warn him?'

'Maybe it did and Michael ignored it, he hinted at it.'

'What did he say about Coyote?'

'Not much, just that only he could see it. He said it brought Joe to him just before he disappeared. Coyote is a trickster, you know, to the Indians. *The* Trickster, actually, like ravens. Powerful, not to be trusted.'

'Coyote is my friend; he was with me when no one else was.'

Engines droned above the clouds, an omen of change. How can things stay hidden when eyes are always watching?

Coyote took us down a track we would have missed without him. I was tired, and stiff from climbing and sleeping rough. The wailing in my head was too loud now, too loud to let me rest. The scent of resin God-damned near suffocated us as we dropped below the tree line and walked across a carpet of needles. We pushed through low hanging branches, until the trees thinned and Coyote led us through rock formations.

At last, we waded a cold stream to a raised platform of grass and moss, speckled with small white and yellow flowers. Sheer rock faces surrounded the platform. A stream flowed over a cascading series of waterfalls at one end, and flowed around the edge in a deep channel, before tumbling out again.

A massive yew stood between us and the waterfall. The tree was hollow. Around the edge of the platform were younger, but still ancient, yews, exact copies of the eldest, growing from spurs, all carefully tended.

Human bodies were displayed on the trees, positioned to be seen by anyone entering the grove. Most were rotted to bones, stitched together by the remains of their clothing. Scraps of leathered flesh hung in ribbons, swaying back and forth like bunting in a gentle breeze. A grinning skull was shelter to generations of sparrows; its brain cavity overflowed with grass and twigs.

A desiccated husk of a body, dry-cured by three decades in the mountain air, was skewered on the most ancient yew.

A branch grew through its mouth, the jaw forced further apart every year as the wood thickened. The mandible had snapped in two places. Green, needle-like leaves and bright red berries wrapped around the remains of the face like an Easter bonnet

We'd found Michael Menzies.

He wasn't dead. Frantic eyes were in continuous motion, up, down, left and right in his ruined skull, connected to the last of his self-awareness.

Shafts of sunlight picked out flecks of spray where the stream butted and splashed against rocks and stones. Light flowed all around and through both me and David. But it did not flow through the yews, and it did not flow through the creature who emerged from the hollow heart of the tree that held Michael.

'Oh now, how wonderful, this *is* a curiosity. Michael swore he'd told me all he had to tell, and I believed him. But he never said he had a twin. You surely must be his twin.'

David's thumb moved to the catch on his sword stick. His aura flared, then settled as he struggled to control himself. Pretty God-damned impressive.

'Injun Joe, I presume? Michael told me about you in his letters.'

'Letters? About me? Oh, this is fascinating; simply wonderful. What things you will tell me. And I see you share his taste in boys, unless ...' He considered me for the first time. 'I've seen your face before, recently, haven't I?'

Coyote paced the grove at the edge of my sight. I cursed my own denseness: Joe, Injun Joe, Joseph; one person.

'You're the young man from Boston, John Pedersen, the one I'd secured, the one who got away. The killer. You must tell me how you managed that. In fact, I'll insist upon it

We've been looking for you. And now you both walk into my little fly trap together.'

'Fly trap?' said David.

'Of course: anyone who can hear Michael is drawn here, and anyone who can hear Michael is someone in whom we are very, very interested. You'll both join him up there soon, you know, after you've told me everything. Then there'll be three little crows perching on my tree.'

Three craws sat upon a wa'

My Gift stirred.

I called on whatever spirits inhabited the mountains and the tickle of their curiosity fluttered in the granite shield rock. My ragged hair shifted about my face. I warmed to heat far below me, fires deep under the Sierras and Yosemite, and the Cascade to the north. The water around the grove ran faster, chattering and tumbling, throwing off ever more sparks of light.

I concentrated on the horror of Michael, hoping I could do something for what was left of him, to ease his pain, bring him peace.

'No, Joe. I don't think that's what's going to happen,' said David. 'I think Michael's suffering ends now, as will you.'

The sheath of the sword stick fell away to expose the polished blade, glinting in the sunlight. Joe's nostrils twitched as he crossed the space between them in an instant and struck David's head, hard, with a backswung fist.

'I smell the blood of my fellows.'

David crumpled. Joe admired the sword as he stood over David's prone figure.

Grass twisted and coiled into skeins that writhed, serpentine beneath Joe to tie him, to hold and consume him. The soil shook and boiled, liquefying. Joe stared at me, David forgotten.

'Oh my word: we only ever heard of this power in Allisoun and now here you are in my grove. Ephraim will want to dissect you while you live, to learn all he can before he lets me put you on my tree. What a glorious fate you have; what juicy flies you will draw to me.'

I wanted the earth and the elements to consume Joe, but his will was focused on survival. And he was God-damned strong, not like the creatures I'd killed before.

He took a step toward me, then a second, and I was in real trouble. I couldn't keep up the effort for long, but couldn't run away either. I wasn't fast enough. And I couldn't leave Michael and David. Or Coyote. I had no chance.

Why did Mama abandon me to this? Why wasn't she there to hold me tight and tell me it would all be fine, that the hurt will go away. Where was my God-damned papa? My last moments were full of rage at them, at my whole God-damned family and our God-damned Gift.

And then someone else's rage joined mine, and another's, and they were in my head. Men rotted in the mud of a battlefield, bodies ripped apart by shrapnel and shell. A farmhouse cellar was a hell where blood drained from babies. I stumbled through tunnels and caverns in Italy and death camps in Germany. I smelled the stink of corpses swinging in the rain beside the roads to Moscow.

Another joined, God-damned powerful – the red-eyed woman who scared me, whose hair shimmered in a halo about her, wielding a mighty sword, red light shimmering and flickering along its blade.

We let out a great howl of hatred for Joe and all his kind.

My body remembered the Zephyr's energy, how I'd shaped its force. I opened myself to the force of our rage, targeting it.

And I let it go. I set it all free on Joe.

Coyote yelped and howled as I'd never heard him before. All the futures from these moments sprung into being, our triumph and our failure, all the things that might be, all those that must never be, horrors still to come, horrors we couldn't avoid but could only prepare for.

The ancient spirits of the mountains answered me now. The ground at Joe's feet renewed its twisting turmoil, but instead of twined grass he was seized by the roots of the yews themselves. Ligneous tentacles forced their way beneath his flesh, through the soles of his feet, into his calves and thighs, threading through his body.

And the red-eyed woman, whose name was Alison, laughed and swung the sword, its red energies shading to black as they hissed and bubbled through the space occupied by Joseph's body, warping the air around them, draining his life force into infernal dimensions.

I felt Joseph's final horror, his outrage at the yews that betrayed him, his fear that his uncountable years of life had ended, the scream building inside him but never uttered as roots burst through his mouth, down his nostrils, sprouting leaves through his eye sockets, out of his ears, hoisting his ancient body up thirty, forty feet, until, as each questing tendril tried to claim him for itself, he was ripped apart.

The golden light I had seen so often leaped and surged, reclaiming the grove, flooding through the trees, lightening their darkness, reconsecrating them to the Earth's purposes.

I was utterly drained, the red-eyed lady had gone, but I couldn't collapse: I couldn't ignore David and Michael.

David's temple was crushed beyond healing. Blood trickled from his nostrils and ears. He struggled to breathe. A figure appeared above me: Michael. He took his brother's hand and helped him to stand, but it was David's spirit that rose, discarding his broken and unwanted body.

They hugged each other and waved to me. Hand in hand, their spirits were suffused with swirling specks of golden light, growing brighter as they folded into a dimension I couldn't see, dissolving into an eternal Now.

I had one final request for the yews and the ancient spirits of the mountains. The branches bearing human skeletons crashed to the earth. The soil rolled and twisted, drawing all the remains, including Michael and David and Joseph, down to their deep rest, to become one with the soil and rock, forever a part of the High Sierra.

I slumped at last. Coyote padded over. I thought he meant to lie by my side, but he breathed hot as he licked my face once, twice, then disappeared into me, returning whence he came, making me whole: man and beast as one.

Local people carried me to safety and nursed me back to strength. They wanted to know what had happened, how I defeated Joe, but I couldn't tell them in words. I stayed with them all winter, learning from them, living their life as best I could, until, in Spring 1955, we gathered in a sacred place. We shared a drink they brewed and my mind roamed to many places that day, far and near, past and future. Part of my journey was in their company. Coyote guided them through my memory, all my past and future.

Later, I climbed alone to the grove. It was quiet, with no sign that anything had ever happened there. I left it to the trees and flowers and birds. I've never gone back.

A week later, I walked out of the mountains to the Feather River Valley and bummed a ride on a goods train as far as Maryville. From there I walked into the wilderness until, near the foothills of the Cascades, I found the right spot to set up home, a secluded place where only beasts and birds went. I cleared some land and built a shelter. Soon, the local forest people brought me food and seeds, and I planted a garden. I did not use the Gift at all, until a mother brought her sick child to me.

I had many requests for healing, and answered them all, learning more about the Gift I'd been born with. In return I was given fruit and vegetables and occasional books.

Three years later, Eliza walked, upright, into my homestead with Harry. I would have built her a shelter of her own, but it was easier for her to join me in mine.

Martha came too one day. She said a coyote appeared in her dreams and led her to me. The night she arrived we lay side by side under a blanket as the stars rose.

And that's how we got to be a family, me and your moms. We know what's going to happen and we can't stop it, but we'll face it together and never abandon you, 'cos that's what mamas and papas do.

Sometimes I wonder what Mama would say if she saw us now.

She'd probably say I'm a God-damned witch.

The Fearefull Aboundinge

Gabriel, Michael, Raphael, Uriel laid their swords on the brows of Mama and my sister Margaret, who glowed the gleam of all their glad goodness and sad sorrows, their hopes and desires, their delights and fears, all laid bare until their light spiralled away into the spaces between us, folding the afterglow of their memory into my heart.

And Bethia, barely Sighted, family growing. She received the blessing of a normal span of sorrows and joys, sickness and health, all the benedictions of the mundane.

When their faces, blank like a child's slate waiting to be marked, stared at me, it seemed death had come, that it was my time to follow Isobel and Margaret to whatever is after this life, to travel to the unknown realms and cities glimpsed sometimes at the edge of my Sight, places I hear whispering to each other in the night, suspended in the air like the scents of rosemary and thyme on sunny summer afternoons.

The angels stood at the cardinal points of the compass, their raised longswords an arched canopy in the heavens. Light tumbled from the apex into empty air, and from the cascade stepped forward a fifth seraph, mighty amongst them: Samael, archangel of death, his face suffused with terrible, predatory love. Samael wielded a double-handed claymore. Its monstrous blade met a downturned guard of gold, its plain, turned-yew handle stretched to the stars.

The sword terminated in a bone pommel, carved with exquisite images of souls in torment, writhing and swarming like maggots on a rat's corpse.

Samael's eyes were empty, as though the angel were an automaton wound into motion by some celestial hand. A bright red flame ran along his blade. I knelt before a block on the scaffold before me, and exposed my neck to accept the killing blow that must come. But the blade nuzzled the nape of my neck like the lips of a nervous lover. Power burned into me and through me, incandescent, surging, tingling, firing every organ of my body.

A vast crowd gathered at the Mercat Cross to see my head strucken and spiked, and all the spectators, cheering, jeering, laughing, applauding and weeping were me, Allisouns who might have been. Beyond all of me were the mewling spirits of my children stilled-born, their malevolence palpable.

And when I woke, soaked with sweat, wet in my privy parts, I understood I was appointed to a task. I knew it again and again and again, every night I had the dream.

I compensated for the roll of the ship in the estuary's swell, no longer sickened by the motion despite my condition. I relished the shock of the chilly, damp air. The distant smell of filth and humanity carried on the onshore breeze told me I was home. At flood tide we put into the ancient port, past corpses swinging from the gibbet on the shore, their rotting flesh luminous pink and purple in the early morning light.

Porters and stevedores hurried to welcome us, keen to offload the French wine, butts of sac, Spanish and Rhenish brandy, Mumm Bier, and other foreign delights we carried from Camp Vere. A screeching choir of seagulls spiralled about our masts. The dead clung there, desperate to find their way back to anywhere they might call home.

A deckhand, McGhie, caught my eye and stumbled back, crossing himself in the Popish manner, muttering in Latin. My eyes burned the bright red of Samael's sword, pierced by deep, black pupils.

Edinburgh hadn't changed, it never does. People came and went, fortunes were made only to be lost, bairns quickened and died. An acrid miasma hung about the Netherbow, where charred remains of eight tenements smoked, a week after the fire that destroyed them. Surviving buildings huddled together for warmth in the chill spring air, curled tight around narrow closes and vennels, their rooms packed with women and children.

Both living and dead thronged the High Street. There were few amongst the living in the Guid Toun to remember me, and those who did weren't likely to recognise me. The dead had their own concerns.

I didn't tell Bethia I was home. I couldn't involve her in my stratagem for fear of risking the lives of her and of my nephews and nieces. She never queried the roads I'd walked. She knew nothing of Samael, nothing of what I'd done, what I'd become, nothing of my children.

My gown was good quality but nondescript. Around my head was a satin chaperon, unadorned, of muted hue. I carried letters of credit drawn on agents of substance in Amsterdam and London, and had no difficulty obtaining funds from Edinburgh's merchants, albeit at a somewhat steeper discount than the market justified. I acquiesced in their greed as though I were a meek and ignorant woman, though I longed to wring their plump necks while their eyes protruded and their bodies struggled, to laugh at their confusion when they found themselves dead. Perhaps I would kill them later when my task was done.

I said I was Allisoun Raune, relict of Kaspar Raune, bookseller and general merchant of Württemberg, felled by pestilence while fleeing the French. No one questioned it. I found acceptable lodgings opposite the Bowhead, close to where Thomas and Jean Weir spent the final years of their miserable lives. I regret I did not take personal revenge on Thomas, but Bethia did well to manipulate old Nisbet when her chance came.

The credulous spread stories now of Weir the Wizard and his magic staff, tell tall tales of lights and noises emanating from Weir's house, of infernal shrieks in the night. Nonsense: my shitten arse holds more magic than Weir ever knew. Weir, whose master was not Satan but the creature called Aphrêm.

Aphrêm who stole my beloved sister Margaret, dead near 25 years.

Aphrêm whom I had come home to destroy.

I was of age, not that they cared. It was easy to find a skipper who'd take me away for the price of his hands in my unstrung bodies, his tongue on my paps, and such quaint delights as I rationed for my passage. I had a little money saved, was schooled in my letters and numbers as a good merchant's daughter should be, and could seek the advice of the dead, for what little return that bought. I saw others too, neither human nor creatures such as Aphrêm, but some other order of being. *Good neighbours* my Mama called them, *guid wychts*, creatures of myth, like the *sidh* my Papa told of in the glens beyond his family's lands in Strathearn. I ignored them and their overtures.

Each day I expected to be found by Aphrêm or his ilk, and made my way from town to town, never staying long, eking out my savings.

My first kill was a sad disappointment – a man of course, I rarely kill women. He was drunk. He tried to drag me into an alley in Bruges, tarse already free of his breeches and half-hard in his ink-stained hand. Were he sober he might have had his way, but he stumbled and lost balance. I pricked him with my small knife as I'd seen a swineherd slaughter a piglet: seize the head from behind by the chin, reach around the throat, thrust the blade deep beneath the ear, and pull back hard to slice the gizzard. I was too enthusiastic and felt the tip of the knife scrape his spine. He was dead moments after he touched me. Only novice's luck kept me out of the first gush of his blood.

In the moments after his death, while his body spasmed and jerked, his tarse spurted too, so he achieved his intention at the last.

His purse was weighty and jingled handsomely. I took the coins and tossed the leather pouch into his gore. I wiped my blade on his breeks, taking care to keep my petticoats out of the spreading red pool.

I slid through the shadows to my lodgings, and slept sounder than I had in months. I rose early, refreshed. The town was already awake: carts and barrels rumbled through the lanes, owners shouting and whistling while their dogs ran barking ahead. A far greater spectacle lay before me: in the square in front of the Market Cross, the past bled through gashes in the membrane of time. Over and over, men and women were strangled and burned as sorcerers and witches and willing consorts of the Devil. The flames crackled and spat. The crowd laughed and cheered the end of each life. The hot air was thick with scorched hair and flesh, the acrid stench of fat dripping through the pyres, the slow-burning tallow of evanescent candles.

Restless presences surged about me. I asked them for guidance, for direction, but got no answer. That's how the dead are: useless.

I was in a state of heightened excitement, much more conscious of having become a woman than the afternoon I surrendered my useless virginity to a first mate in a skipper's cabin in Leith. I set myself to search for opportunities amongst the traders.

I avoided booths where Scots clustered and was soon amongst the Irish. I had little experience of the Irish: I don't know their language, and my family had philosophical objections to Papists, unless there was good business to be had, it being a central Institute of Reformed theology that the finer points of doctrine always yield to the pursuit of profit.

At one booth vehement words flew in Eirse.

I said good morning, in English. A handsome lad with soft features turned his face to me, his deep brown eyes appraising me from head to toes as though valuing a beast at auction. I should not have been at all surprised had he examined my teeth and slapped my flanks.

'Begging your pardon, our clerk was found in an alley, his throat slit, our takings gone. My brothers are debating how we might deal with the loss.'

'Oh, the poor man.' I said, shaking at the tightening between my legs.

'Someone had it in for him: they damned near took his head clean off. It's not easy to find a competent clerk at short notice, they're all thieves and robbers in these parts.

'My father was a Merchant Burgess and Guildsman in Edinburgh. I can figure accounts and pen correspondence and such like, though I lack practice.' I cast my line, looked into his brown eyes and watched him rise to the lure. I leaned closer. 'I am alone, in need of an honest way to earn money to pay my way to my father's Uncle in Genoa, where I am to be betrothed.'

'Your family provided you with no wherewithal or escort?'

'My escort drank most of my funds and nearly absconded with the balance before I lost him. I'm embarrassed to write and admit my plight to my sisters: they already think me profligate and foolish. Perhaps I could clerk for you until you find a permanent man?'

'And in return?'

'Food, lodgings, and perhaps sufficient for a change of clothing.' I gestured at my shabby gown, pointing to the frayed hems, letting my hands linger a little longer around my curves.

The trout rose to take the fly.

He was Dermid Tobin, and within the hour I was engaged as clerk by his father, Padraig, for a week's work. I named myself for my grandmother, Marioun McDullan, a name, said Padraig with approval, that was almost Irish.

After two hours with the ledgers, I found irregularities in the stock written off as natural wastage, and persistent rounding errors in the addition.

The late Wilhelm d'Ypres, he of gushing throat and over-eager pintle, stole from his master. He was clever, never stealing too much, sometimes barely enough to make it worth his while, but cumulatively a great deal. But he was not clever enough: he hadn't varied his method. When I was certain, I went to Padraig with my proof.

He took it well, for an Irishman.

Dermid conjured opportunities to visit my desk, sit next to me at table or make light conversation. I gave him no encouragement, and treated his brothers equally, but he had bitten hard on my lure and the barb was hooked deep. He was a young man with life in his veins and amour in his eyes and a charming wit on his tongue. He was a perfect nuisance.

Padraig asked if I would stay longer, for he could not imagine finding anyone more suited to preparing his accounts. I reiterated I was bound for Genoa, a tale he accepted with reluctance.

'This Italian to whom you are to be betrothed, Marioun, is he worthy of your talents, or will you fade into unwarranted domestic obscurity? You will have heard, I suppose, that Italian men make excellent sons, but poor husbands?'

Padraig, a wealthy widower, was in want of a new wife, I jaloused. There was advantage in the match, though always with the risk I would be caught tale-spinning. I agreed to stay a further month.

And as well I did, for it was in his library I found the volume that changed my life: the *Daemonologie* of His Majesty King James VI and I. In it, His Majesty gave a name to someone like me, with the ability to seek the wisdom of the dead in divining the future.

Necromancer.

His Majesty said necromancers were no mere witches, but had a different relationship with Satan. I knew enough to know Satan was not involved: there's no reason to attribute to the Devil what was normal in my nature, for what is natural surely cannot of right be called supernatural.

His Majesty was wrong about the dead, too. Those who linger here are trapped in their pasts and have nothing to say about the future.

But I liked the name: Necromancer.

There was a chambermaid in the household, Maria, a sweet girl with pert breasts and comely hips, whom I caught glancing at me several times with the same look as was in Dermid's eyes. I held her gaze for a moment longer than necessary, and we were soon lovers, wrapped around each other, finding unexpected pleasures in every cleft and fold of flesh.

Padraig came to my room late one night, deep in his cups, no doubt to persuade me to accommodate his lust. He found Maria astride my face, her haunches in my hands, my tongue dancing, her fingers reaching back between my thighs. Padraig left without saying anything, and I didn't need the Sight to know my time in his house was over.

Be thankful Leviticus is silent on the matter, Mama once said, and I was. But scriptural silence availed me naught. Padraig dismissed me in the morning. He consented to my plea that Maria not be punished on my account.

A band of merchants and pilgrims were travelling to Liège. I paid my way with some of the coin taken from Wilhelm d'Ypres, taking care to hide the true value of my purse.

As we passed through the gate and over the canal on the way out of the town, my lips still raw from a stolen farewell kiss with Maria, I looked over my shoulder to see Dermid's bewildered face, a puppy whose bone was stolen away.

The Guid Toun stinks. I didn't notice when I was small and had nowhere else to compare. After sea air, the streets smelt like cesspits. Mama carried a pomander of aloes and nutmeg, balm and musk, but I tried not to think of it: often, when I think of her, she visits, and I did not need any more of her disapproval.

I considered what to wear. I didn't have a large wardrobe, but had enough to meet my needs. I chose a German gown, in respectable black. An absence of colour is never out of place in Edinburgh, where grey is accounted gaudy. I'd taken it from a supposed witch's house while she sat in a cell waiting to be burnt. She had no further use for it.

My bodies were tied loose to accommodate my swelling belly, with smock and loose petticoats beneath and below. Neck cloth, apron and coif completed the ensemble. I chose good boots rather than shoes: a little showy, but the better to keep above the dung and piss of the streets. I decided against my travel cloak, which was warm but too worn for respectable day wear. I borrowed a basket from my landlady, and went into the chill morning air.

Straightaway, I regretted not wearing a cloak or hat. A cold wind came from the sea, over Musselburgh, skirted the flanks of Arthur's Seat, whipped over the Holy Rood and processed up the High Street like a pageant for a queen, funnelling through the closes, chilling my flesh. I envied the warm plaid worn in the Highland style by the vulgar women.

Papa said the Sight does not run true in families, but I know I got it from Mama, who'd heard stories about her forebears. I learned soon enough to keep quiet about it. My Grandfather, John Mein, and his second wife Barbara would denounce me as the Devil's child in a moment, such was their fervour for the Lord. Papa's family was closer to the Highlands and, recognising the signs in me, made a silent compact to hold their tongues.

I loved Papa. When I was little, he told me old stories in which bad things happened but good people always won no matter how great the evil they fought. I believed him.

After her first encounter with Aphrêm, Mama had a vision. By some strange alchemy, the meeting woke her dormant Sight and wrenched it into something else, something she tried to tend and grow in me.

At the Lawnmarket Wellhead, Mama had a vision of past and future High Streets laid on top of each other, as if time itself were a sailor's bottle in which, viewed from outside, the masts and spars, sheets and rigging of Edinburgh's beginning, present, and end were all visible as a whole ship.

I often think on this, for if Mama saw the future, then did it not mean the future was fixed? Or was it perhaps fixed by the very act of observing it?

It rose, dry, from the waters of the Wellhead. It was female, but not human. Her form shifted – it was provisional, unwilling to be defined, as though dreamed. Her hair changed colour and length from moment to moment. Her eyes were as green as the finest emeralds, as was her shift, translucent against the wan light of the low morning sun. Those eyes fixed on me and did not waver. She disappeared again in an instant, leaving no trace save the memory of those eyes.

I was so deep in thought my plans were nearly undone. At the last possible moment, I saw Bethia walking towards me, carrying her latest bairn. The urge to hug her close almost overwhelmed me, but I turned aside and she passed behind me. I forced my unwilling legs to carry me downhill, though all the while I longed to run to the arms of my family. I cursed the angels for appointing me to my task.

A grand crowd gathered around the head of Libberton's Wynd and by the Tolbooth, all come out for a hanging. I stood amongst them and the world shifted and turned about me. The Tolbooth disappeared; the unicorn and cross upped and crossed the street. Instead of the steep wynd down to the Cowgate, the road ran perfectly level away from me across a great bridge. Everywhere people milled around in strange garments. Women wore coloured breeches and light cotton shifts, and left their navels exposed for all to see. Some had curious painted images on the bodies, their arms and their legs, like Lithgow's pilgrims returning from the Holy Land, but more extravagant. Metal carriages rolled along the street to the music of minstrels playing pipes and *guitarras*.

The vision twisted. A great procession of men and women, living and dead, and an other-worldly retinue climbed the High Street from Holy Rood to Lawnmarket. The Nether Bow Gate was gone and the buildings on the High Street were built of stone. The living rutted like dogs, not caring whether their lover was man or woman. Some sickened and lay down to die in plain view, as though a virulent new pestilence ran unchecked amongst them.

There were four about whom the pageant revolved: the creature in green; a being like Aphrêm, but female, tall, with ornately bejewelled ears; the spirit of a young girl, recently delivered of a child, whom I perceived to be my kin, and an older man, strong in the Sight. They danced around each other in an occult masque, moving to the music of different instruments playing from unseen scores. As the image faded and the present returned, the creature in green turned to me and raised her finger as though in warning, then a second finger as if to let me know I had been warned twice.

To think she could warn *me*. I knew her kind, and they needed to be reminded of their place.

I stumbled, but did not fall. A young man from a nearby booth offered his arm to lean on, which I accepted.

retreated to my lodgings where, despite the early hour, I sipped brandy.

I watched the hustle and bustle below. All was as it should be: no strange Edinburghs slithered through the gaps of my Sight, and no mystical creatures roamed the street, or, at least, none more than usual. Bethia was there again, her basket full, stopping from time to time to smile and talk. A man was with her now, I presumed her husband William Henrysone, a merchant whom I had never met. I almost envied her domesticity. Almost.

And then, round the corner, walked Aphrêm, unchanged since the day he took Margaret away. I was seized by a gripping fear he would look up and see me there in the shadows. The only change in him was in his clothes, which were of more modern style and cut than hitherto. He hadn't aged a minute. He was tall, with a long stride. His broad shoulders bespoke his strength. I tried to see him through the eye of the Gift, but there was nothing to see, as though he were entirely cloaked.

I poured more brandy, knowing I must go out again.

My arse ached before we'd travelled a league. They'd given me the flightiest mare in the stable, the beast experienced riders declined. I patted her flanks and scratched her ears. My Gift stirred, and, to everyone's surprise, she and I bonded. I sat astride her as a man would and, determined to thole the pain, gathered my petticoats to form a cushion of sorts. My gown and cloak preserved my modesty, though I drew disapproving looks from some, leers from others.

All was well until we paused for lunch on the first day and I was too stiff to dismount. I endured their good-natured mockery as they helped me down.

At first, the journey passed without incident, and long before we reached Leuven I was as comfortable in the saddle as I would ever be.

I spurned advances by the men, young and old, and kept to myself, though they stole glances at me when they thought I wasn't looking. Let them. My eye was on Else, daughter of our leader Konrad Mohn. She was my age. I adored her flashing eyes and the fresh flower in her hair every morning. All the young men paid her court, but her eye lingered on me, and the smiles she bestowed on me were a little warmer.

The thieves chose their spot well. We stopped at a junction on the road to Liège to determine our direction, and were surrounded in moments by a motley band of seven, no doubt deserters from recent wars, armed with swords and pikes, pistols and muskets. They handled the weapons with the easy familiarity of practiced killers, expecting easy pickings. They would have had them had not a musket misfired. The ball travelled fast and true, clean through the neck of Else who fell, choking and drowning in her own blood.

Fury and grief raged through me like a squall in the Forth. I released the Gift to do as it would.

A high wind rose from nowhere. Boughs and leaves cracked and whipped in the maelstrom, branches snapped and flew. Vortices of dust rose and spun, and eldritch figures of a kind unknown to me emerged from the scrubby underbrush. The road writhed and squirmed, compacted earth twisting into tentacles that sought the brigands' legs as they shouted and milled, encircled and trapped, dancing and leaping to avoid the clutches of the questing earth. They were dragged down as nicely as if they stood on quicksand, until they were held firm by solid earth, heads and shoulders above the surface, seven saplings in the spring sunshine.

I took a bright new scythe from a merchant's wagon, and tested its weight and swing. There was a champion reaper, a kemper, on my great-uncle's land in Perthshire who made it look easy, but it wasn't, and I did not want to entangle the long, curved blade in my skirts and ankles.

I walked between the bandits, in no great hurry, tapping and tickling each neck with the blade then walking on, taking time to get used to the implement, selecting who would be first to die.

One of them, his head turned away from his fellows, couldn't see the scythe, would only hear their screams and curses and wonder what was happening. He would be last.

I walked amongst the heads sitting proud like neeps in a field, and chanted as I reaped my crop, a rhyme my uncle taught me as a bairn and got into trouble from Mama for his efforts. I found my rhythm, and sliced the first gizzard clean through.

> Tam o' the Lynn was thirsty to sup
> He cut off a head tae make his cup
> The blood poured out as the ale poured in
> 'Here's a health tae the ladies,' quo Tam o' the Lynn

The second neck was sturdier than the first – the blade caught on bone as my knife had snagged the spine of Wilhelm d'Ypres. A lazy whetstone restored the edge, whistling along the metal. I let them watch the action of my arm, my fingers testing the keenness of the blade. I couldn't decide whether it was more satisfying to slice from the front so they could see the blade coming, or from behind so they could not.

> Tam o' the Lynn he had three bairns
> They fell in the fire in ilk ither's airms

'Och!' quo the youngest, 'I've got a hot skin.'
'Ye'll be hotter in Hell,' quo Tam o' the Lynn.

With each head, each wail or whimper of terror, I remembered Maria's fingers and tongue, which became Else's fingers and tongue, and the kiss of Maria's lips, which became Else's lips.

Tam o' the Lynn was condemned to the fire
He shivered with cauld in the heart of the pyre
He sliced a lang strip of the De'il's foreskin
'That'll dae for my scarf,' quo Tam o' the Lynn.

I approached the last of them from behind, improvising a melody, adding grace notes as I pleased, letting him hear my steps. I walked past him, the bloody blade trailing in the dust before his face. I slid the whetstone again, walking slowly around his peripheral vision until I was behind him once more.

Tam o' the Lynn had nae breeks tae wear
So he killed him a ram tae make him a pair.
The fleshy side out and the woolly side in
'And the heid for a helmet' quo Tam o' the Lynn

I let him hear the end of the verse, think himself reprieved, then sent him to Hell, shuddering when his head rolled and his prayer of thanksgiving animated his dead lips. Long waves of ecstasy pulsed through me.

Else's spirit lingered by her body. I kissed my fingertips and touched her forehead.

'Perhaps we shall meet again, in a kinder world. I wish you joy of your journey and blessings along the way.' She melted into the soft glow of another world, her face turning from sorrow to wonder as she entered the light.

I plucked the flower from her hair and put it in mine.

They say we abide in the middle-earth 'twixt heaven and hell, but I see no middle, only endless transitions.

The woodland creatures were gone, back to their elfhame. The silence of the road was broken by fevered muttering. The company were on their knees with the pilgrims, lips moving. The ungrateful wretches weren't giving thanks but pleading to be saved, from me who had just given them their miserable lives.

'Else walked into the light in wonder at what she found there. In your grief, be comforted she is waiting for you in a world to come,' I said to Konrad.

His eyes stayed shut as he prayed with even greater fervency. I have no idea whether he heard me or not. I took my valise from a cart and fixed it above my saddle bags. From the discarded weapons I selected a long, vicious knife, with a carved ivory grip and a shining, razor-edged blade, well balanced in my small hands as I tried feints and thrusts.

I scratched the ears of my mare.

'I name you Else,' I whispered. She tossed her mane as I swung into the saddle.

Not one of the company, still kneeling in the dirt, red from the bloody spray, would look at me, let alone thank me or bid me farewell. The junction smelled like an abattoir in the heat of the midday sun.

'Should any of you take a notion to tell of me, I shall return from the depths of Hell itself to take vengeance on you all without discrimination. You are now each responsible for each other's lives.'

I nudged Else into a canter and left them praying amidst the bloody blooms and scattered heads. I took the southern fork, the road that did not lead to Liège.

I washed dried blood from my hair and clothes in a tumbling stream. Small birds flitted through the trees, chirruping and twittering. Bright sunlight fell in angled shafts through the tree canopy, refracting through the spray of the water. My arms and legs were warm in the light as I stripped.

My arm ached. The screams of the bandits as they watched me kill their fellows one by one rang in my ears, their frantic pleas as each twin fount gushed, prayers on lips that did not know they were already dead. I'd let each wonder if their turn was next, each one hoping to their last second that I might relent and show mercy just to them.

I walked out into the deepest part of the stream where it formed a pool, shockingly cold after warm sunlight. It was not too deep: I could stand and my head and shoulders cleared the surface. I cannot swim, but I could dip under and immerse myself in the cleansing flow, luxuriate in the sensation of cold around my head and through my hair, and revel in the joy of it.

A cluster of sunbeams played across the surface and I spread my arms to embrace the light, free of the company of men with their shifty looks and lewd gestures.

Enthusiastic applause came from the bank.

He stood by Else, scratching her ears, but his eyes never left me. He was well dressed, in an old-fashioned style, a finely embroidered doublet above green hose, an unfastened leather cape.

My Gift stirred: he looked surprised and quelled my attempt with a subtle gesture.

'Well now, what have we here? *Une jolie femme* who sees me and uses my own tricks against me. This is a most diverting entertainment.'

His English was curious, but I had the impression would understand him whatever language he spoke. I called on the Gift again, with more vehemence this time. Nothing happened.

'Now, now, my beauty. No need to be impolite. Your clothes await. Oh! But of course, you are shy: I will turn my back to preserve your modesty.'

I walked towards him, making no attempt to conceal myself as I rose clean, dripping, defiant, from the pool. Delight sparkled in his eyes, which were of differing colours, the left grey, the right green. He offered his hand as if to dance a gavotte, and I took it. He performed an elaborate bow and touched cool, dry lips to my fingers.

'Ah! You are from Alba are you not? Your very flesh declares itself. And you have met my cousin, I taste her on you. But I see you don't know what I mean. Here, let me dry you before you catch cold.'

Another subtle gesture of his fingers, and the water fell from me. I dressed and put the flower back in my hair. His eyes never left me, his gaze more appraising than lascivious.

'I do not believe I have been introduced to your cousin, though you are of the good neighbours are you not? This is the first time any of your kind have done me the honour of speaking with me.' I attempted a curtsy.

'I do so like a polite child, though, of course, you are no longer a child. The forest is alive with rumour and outrage.' He pointed to the vicious blade tied to the Else's saddle. 'A nasty weapon, but I daresay only as nasty as the arm that swings it. Are you a cruel child for all your courtesy?'

The forest vanished, and the scene at the road replayed in the air as if seen from above through a tercel's eyes. I toyed with the doomed bandits, sang my song, said farewell to Else.

'Touching: you had feelings for the girl and comforted her spirit as she passed beyond. My, my, my: you are a precious prize. You must accompany me to my hall. There are many human dead there, perhaps even that lovely girl. We can feast, we can dance, we can make love, and we can talk of my cousin.'

'Forgive me sir, I must decline. I shall be on my way.'

'Child, you misunderstand. It was not an invitation. I insist you grace my court. Look: we are here already.'

A well-pointed high stone wall stretched forever left and right. Mighty oak gates opened onto a courtyard where fair folk were about either their duties or their pleasures, it was hard to tell. Around the courtyard, banners in all the colours of the rainbow hung from poles set into the stone. The flags bore obscure crests and sigils in bright embroidery, though the cloth was faded and frayed. In the far wall, another set of gates was open, and beyond them a long avenue stretched to an azure horizon where the towers and crenellations of a stone keep could be seen. An ornate coach in white and gold stood ready, six milk-white steeds in harness, liveried footmen waiting.

'I said I decline your invitation.' I stood firm, clinging to my own world. 'A gentleman would respect my wishes.'

'My dear child, such charming *naiveté*: why ever do you think me a gentleman?'

Above the oaken gates, the sky darkened to match the glower of his face. A swirling wind like that at the crossroads sprang up, whirling around me, faster and faster, threatening to blow me off my feet and over his threshold. I reached deep into myself and found Mama, the memory of Margaret, and my hatred for Aphrêm. I imagined my feet planted deep in the solid rock of Edinburgh, my toes wriggling into the residual heat of an ancient caldera, cooled by underground springs made holy by long-forgotten blood sacrifice.

'I. Shall. Not. Come. With. You. *LEAVE ME BE!*'

The great oak doors slammed shut, stranding him outside his estate.

'Oh my cousin, what have you made?' Very well child, I release you. But remember this: enjoy our Gift, fear our malison. The hour of your greatest need will come, when our Gift falters and no one will save you. Then you will remember *Le Dauphin des Faies* and the chance you spurned.'

The stream pooled and eddied, still dappled by sunlight. But the sun had shifted and was lower in the sky, as though hours had passed rather than minutes. The flower in my hair fell out, withered, petals limp and brown. Else had wandered off, though not far. She whinnied to see me, and we left, not caring what direction we travelled. Soon, a full moon rose, and we followed it until overtaken by tiredness. The forest lay expectant and silent: watching. I couldn't shake the feeling it did not want me in it. In the gloaming, a magnificent stag stood in the far shadows.

I was stronger than at dawn: I had taken the heads of many men, and had commanded one of the good folk to leave me be, and he obeyed. I was indeed a necromancer.

It was my sixteenth birthday.

I couldn't approach Aphrêm in the street and strike him dead: I didn't want to be hanged as a common killer. Nor could I use the Gift in public without suffering the fate of a witch. My vengeance would perforce be private. I would lure Aphrêm with the fruit of my womb. I would go to his premises and seek his help, even though my visions on the High Street shook my confidence in my ability to mask my feelings.

The raised finger of warning was an odd arrogance, for re that race not like children I can command to my will and expect obedience? *Beware our malison*. The voice echoed. I dismissed the memory.

The rest of the vision interested me more: the creature, the spirit and the man, surrounded by the dead and dying. Why had I seen them? Was it a distant future fated to happen, or just one possibility amongst many? By seeing it, had I made it real? The spirit was of my kin, but how? The man: strong in the Sight, but of unknown family, who was he? The creature, a female, who was she? Where was Aphrêm?

Perhaps there are many ships in many bottles, waiting to be created by sailors yet unborn, contingent on the caprice of the universe and the sum of all the things we do.

A great cheer went up. A poor wretch was launched into eternity, dangling on the end of the tow, torso and pinioned limbs convulsing, lungs burning for breath they would never again draw.

Perhaps each time a child is born a lineage is created, a golden thread is embroidered through the warp and weft of infinite chance, unless snipped by fate, and the future is an eternity of unfinished tapestries.

I finished my brandy.

The morning was no warmer, and the chill wind carried all the foul stench of the streets. My nose and stomach protested. How different things might have been if Papa hadn't died and Mama not met Thomas Weir. I tried to warn her, but who listens to a bairn? Had Papa lived, we would be a normal merchant family, our fortunes ebbing and flowing on the tides of time and chance. Without Thomas Weir, Mama would have lived to see us grow. Margaret would not have been stolen by Aphrêm whom I, a necromancer, would not have come home to kill.

Another bottle, another ship.

Would I ever talk to Bethia again? Or Mama's sister Alison, and her family, if any of them still lived? They would be in this mass of humanity somewhere, swarming the High Street as flies swarm on dung. They probably thought me 25 years dead, as, I hoped, would Aphrêm.

It isn't far from Lawnmarket to Bow Head, to West Bow and Grass Market, and thence to Aphrêm's premises. The way was choked by the crowd dispersing after the execution. Children put their hands around their throats and made throttling sounds, imitating the condemned's death struggles, laughing and shouting. I gathered it had not been a good death: the condemned protested her innocence and cried for mercy, refusing to pray for her own soul's salvation. At last, the executioner threw her from the ladder to get it over with, delighting his appreciative audience.

Her ghost cursed still: the crowds, the assize that found her guilty, the judge who condemned her, God for the unfairness of her end, the man, more guilty than she, who lived on, and, most of all, her sons and daughters, brothers and sisters, aunts and uncles, who came out in the cold to watch her die.

The stench of human dirt was thick, the scent of Mama's pomander strong.

'Do not do this thing, daughter. You cannot know how it will end.'

I ignored her. There was a quickening in my belly, a kick. I searched for the child growing in me, the spark of life within.

'It is not too late, Allisoun. Stop now.'

But it was far too late, Mama. My course was plotted, my sails set, my bottle waiting.

The crowds thinned at the foot of the West Bow. I turned into the Cowgate. I had seen Aphrêm's premises so many times in memory and imagination, but standing by the serpent and stick fixed to the wall by the door brought my attention to the reality of the present.

I rehearsed my story for the hundredth time: I was a new widow without dependents, I required unguents and medicaments to ease my discomfort, I sought recommendations for a birthing-woman when my time came. The old scar on my cheek tightened. I drew a deep breath and went in.

A counter stood in front of a wall lined with jars and bottles, precisely labelled with their esoteric contents. The room smelled of moss and spices, of preserving fluids and unrecognisable chemicals, though I identified some specimens from my own studies. A fully articulated human skeleton, bones tagged with strips of vellum bearing Latin names, was displayed in an open cabinet, warning in its eye sockets.

Aphrêm had his back to me, the end of a siphon in his right hand, measuring a precise quantity of fluid into a glass flask held in his left. I willed myself to stay calm, to clear my mind of distraction. He turned with a broad smile.

'Ah, there you are, Allisoun. I've been waiting for you.'

My eyes darkened; my focus shifted to see the flow of life around him.

'Oh very impressive, yes, very impressive. But consider carefully what you do next.'

Through a door to my right came another of his kind, a female who could be his twin, dragging Bethia, who carried her youngest bairn in a sling.

'This is Ys, my sister, who is more than happy to snap Bethia's pretty neck if you do not do as I say. She can demonstrate with your niece if you wish?'

Ys gripped Bethia firmly around the head with one hand and snatched the child with her other. The brat squawked as Bethia tried to scream against the gag in her mouth.

I recalculated: I no longer had to worry about casting my bait, only about protecting Bethia and the child.

'It will not be necessary, Master Aphrêm. I am yours to command.'

'Excellent.'

Ys returned the babe to Bethia.

'Your sister and her delightful family will be quite safe so long as you do not do anything foolish. I want to tell you this without any possibility of misunderstanding: their lives are now in your hands, just as yours was in the hands of those merchants and pilgrims so long ago. Yes, I know about that. I know many things. Ys will release them once you and I are far from here.'

Ys looked at me with frank curiosity. She was familiar, not just as Aphrêm's twin, but also as the creature at the *danse macabre* in my vision of the future. Perhaps that was the message in my vision, the warning I was given: I must kill Ys to stop that future.

'Have we met, little human?'

'I believe so, in a vision of things that might be.'

My eyes met Bethia's. Love and despair were in her look, fear and anger, too, and a darkness in her pupils I did not remember from childhood, the darkness of an unformed Gift.

To travel alone as a single woman would draw attention and unwelcome speculation when rumours of witchcraft were afoot. I met a vagabond on the road. He eyed me with naked lust. I took him off the road to where a small waterfall poured into a pool of clean water. With a broad wink I offered to delouse him if he would do the same for me. I helped him out of his clothes and fondled his upright pintle, leading him to the water's edge, where I caved in his skull with a rock.

I slit his throat to be certain his angry ghost wouldn't slip back into his body, hid the corpse, then soaked his clothes to remove the vermin and his stink. When the clothes were dry, I squeezed dead any lice and fleas that survived in the seams, drew my bodies tight to flatten my breasts, and put his clothes on. With dirt rubbed around my cheeks and chin to suggest a beard, I drew glances but no suspicion as I travelled. I stole better, cleaner garments when I could.

I followed rumours of witches, but only ever found poor women and men tortured and killed without reason. Erasure by fire was the only thing I feared. Once, in the shadows of a tavern, a law clerk told me of the great bonfires of witches and warlocks in Scotland, led by the gleeful killers of the Kirk, whose enthusiasm for putting women to the flame in the name of Christ-crucified knew no limit.

By their fruits shall ye know them.

Then came the day I encountered a great crowd of villagers carrying improvised weapons, searching for stolen children. They saw the long knife at my side and asked me to help. As they did, a great cry went up and we followed to a low dwelling in a nearby clearing. Outside the door, sword in one hand, flaming brand in the other, stood a creature of Aphrêm's kin in a fighting stance. It would kill many of the mob before coming to any harm itself.

This was the first time I'd met one of these creatures since my Gift had grown strong. Where I sometimes saw the light of a soul in a human, there was only blankness in this creature. I could not see what spirit animated it.

With my Gift eye open, I drew upon the enduring power of the earth. In my mind I anchored myself to the bedrock of distant Edinburgh, and reached for its strength. Under the creature, the grass stirred, wrapping itself around its ankles. Shocked hesitation on its face gave me only a moment's opportunity, but I took it, long knife in hand. The thing fetched me a blow on my cheek with the back of its fist: hard, brutal. My skin split and blood trickled down my face, but momentum was with me. My blade took out its throat.

The surging cheers turned to screams and vomit in the cottage.

Five pale babes were strung by their ankles from a line of metal pegs fixed in a low beam. The bairns' blood drained through tubes in their necks, emptying into large glass vessels. All around were scattered the paraphernalia of the alchemist and surgeon: alembics and ventois glasses, leather cowls, and lengths of copper and brass pipe. Arranged on a rack were gleaming saws and knives, straight and curved, pointed and hooked.

The creature knelt in the grass that held it, clutching the wound, trying to staunch the flow of blood. With a great swing of my arm, I took its head. Kicking, ripping, tearing, the crowd mutilated its remains until only scarlet scraps remained to colour the grass.

Movement pulled my eyes to the edge of the clearing: the stag again, and, leaning with easy insouciance against a beech tree, *Le Dauphin*, who made a leg and doffed his hat. His voice was loud in my ear, despite the distance between us:

'What a pretty Gift my cousin gave you, my beauty. I begin to understand her purpose. Use it with wisdom and we may yet be friends.'

I banished him with a gesture. He gave a cheerful wave, and returned to the greenwood shadows.

I had killed one creature, I could kill more: I could kill Aphrêm. That night I dreamed of Samael for the first time.

I was summoned by a local Estate owner to receive the thanks of the neighbourhood. I went to a large farm near Trier, with a separate wine-press house and all the outbuildings needed to produce wine in commercial quantities. The owner and weingut was Florian von der Grach, but it was his mother, Anna, who greeted me in excellent English, recognised me for a woman, and asked what I did besides taking heads of monsters.

Florian, she said, was a dissolute idiot who drank the Estate's product and gambled away whatever money he had. Hearing my family background, she asked me to examine the finances of the Estate and put things right as best I could. In return, if I wished, I would have food and lodgings and a small allowance. I would have the honour of reading to her at night and grooming her hair. I was welcome to make new clothes from material in the house or alter any I liked. I would be called housekeeper, though local girls would attend to domestic duties. And I would begin by having a hot bath and donning clean clothes as my smell was rank.

Anna was imperious but good company. She was lonely beneath her hauteur, starved of the company of her long-deceased husband and ignored by Florian, her only surviving child. She was no one's fool: I think she guessed from the beginning that my defeat of the creature had been achieved with uncanny assistance, but she did not pry.

Each morning, I picked a fresh flower for my hair and thought of Else, though as months passed, I found it more and more difficult to remember her or Marie's faces. I was careful to leave titbits and presents around the outbuildings for the good neighbours, who sometimes passed on gossip. They told me of Le Dauphin, and also of Scotland and other places around the world. They would not stop talking with horror of the great witch hunts led by the viciou killers of the Kirk, and of their countless victims sent to untimely deaths. They couldn't, or wouldn't, tell me anything of Aphrêm and his kind.

When Florian finally came home, penniless, he tried to assert himself, and I gave him short shrift. In his absence I had become de facto manager of the Estate. A proposal of marriage followed, and I accepted. The indignities of a marital bed were a small price to pay for status. Besides, he was too drunk to perform most of the time. On his rare triumphs of sober manliness, I could pretend sufficient pleasure to keep him content with his lot, before the grape called him again, as it always did. A child by him was out of the question.

The first time he showed signs of wandering to whatever gambling dens he frequented, I met him at the door with my bag packed to accompany him. That was enough to dissuade him.

I cultivated information as assiduously as our labourers cultivated vines. I received deference as my right, of course, and worthies in the area sought my favour more and more as the Estate's fortunes improved. I gave financial assistance to those it was in my interest to have as debtors. I even attended church and tolerated tedious expositions from the pulpit. I flattered the preacher from time to time. Sadly, his library held no volumes on sorcery or necromancy.

The dead were everywhere with their tittle tattle, but their chatter was the usual melancholy nonsense. I looked for cunning women, but none had power. However, they were steeped in lore and story and some had books they could not read, but I could. I learned a lot about *die Hexenkräuter*, hemlock and henbane, opium, aconite and thorn apple. They told me about excretions from the skin of toads, of alerûna and the origin of secrets, and the uses of fly agaric and liberty caps. I discovered the fine distinctions between mushroom induced arousal, hallucination, and death, and how to engender all three leaving no trace.

Snuggle-toothed old Geertruyd, a notorious crone, told me of the rare mandragora found beneath gallows, infused with energy from seed that dripped from the pricks of virgin criminals at the moment of their death. She offered a lot of gibberish about how to draw the roots from the ground with ears stopped against their screams, how to draw circles around them and make incantations, and other such nonsense. I stopped listening, until she said that witches could use the energies of the dead to create unnatural children.

Tension rippled across the waters of lochans, hissing through scrubby broom and heather on the moors. Streams rose high in bleak, rounded hills and carved sacred pathways through hidden glens, cascading over ancient rock, building energies that lay dormant but watchful. It was a blessed wilderness, prone to sudden squalls even on sunny days, and held its secrets close.

Aphrêm lived here. I envied him.

We did not talk during the long journey over rough roads that bounced the carriage in all directions. I was given a cushion out of respect for my condition, but shewn no other comforts or conveniences.

The house was set well back from the road, obscured by untamed woodland. The flagstones, when I walked into a broad, wood-panelled hall, were well-worn by the passag of centuries of feet, speaking of great antiquity. Obelisk by the road hinted at ages before the memory of men and women. How long had it been inhabited? No human dead lingered to ask.

Aphrêm led me to a reception room where a great log fire blazed.

'Welcome to The Leyes. I hope you will be as comfortable here as your sister before you.'

'My sister whom you stole away.'

'Stole? Not at all, old Weir made a bargain, and bargains must be kept.'

'A bargain he had neither right nor title to make, yet you seized her anyway, a debased infeftment as you must know. How did she die?'

'In childbirth. None of her bairns showed any signs of power, alas, no matter who the sire.'

'And the bairns? My kin?'

'All put to good use, I assure you. I may still have their bones should you wish to inspect them. Now, I would have you settle in your rooms. You must be in best of condition when you deliver your child. How long will that be?'

'At Lammas, by my estimate.'

'And your first child too: remarkable. I am surprised those lusty Germans got no more upon you. Need I remind you not to be so foolish as to try and escape?'

My shoulders dropped as if in defeat. I gave the slightest shake of my head, and kept my eyes to the floor.

'Good. Your sister was quite fecund until her untimely demise. I wonder how we shall fare with you. You are much stronger, I think, like your mother, though I barely knew her.'

'Master Aphrêm, I am forty-three years old, carrying my first child. As like as not I will not survive childbirth. Tell me, are you like the fanatics of the Kirk, keen to see women suffer and die? Do you hate women, Master Aphrêm?'

'I am not. They are your own kind and do as humans always have. I am not human. I no more hate you than a farmer hates a lamb. I rather admire you in point of fact, but sentiment will not deflect me: you are not my pet, and there is a natural order to things. If you seek the hatred of women, look to your own species. Look to how you're treated by your men: bartered, beaten, battered, burnt. A canker infests your species and has throughout the eons, a canker quite as virulent as any pestilence of our devising. I have no need to hate you: you hate yourselves quite enough.'

'The Kirk claims justification from the natural order too, Master Aphrêm, men over women. What makes your order better than theirs? The women are just as dead. Justification is but haggling over the spoil-heap of corpses.'

'You are hardly innocent of killing, Allisoun.'

'In self-defence, Master Aphrêm, when threatened.'

'But that is not true, is it? Your butcher's bill is long. Your fine black gown: did you not give a woman to be burned that you might have it? I had a neighbour once, True Thomas they called him, for he could not lie. You should emulate his virtue, for your own sake if not mine.'

'You evade the question. Why is your order superior to the Kirk's? By what algebra do you make that calculation? You say that ends justify means and your ends are preferable, yet the end for women remains the same. I believe you seek a justification for your crimes as much as do I.'

'Crimes? Is it a crime against cattle to take them to market and turn their bones to soup? Is the wolf to be fyli and assized for slaughter of a sheep? I am a herdsman and you are of my herd. This has been the established order since first we bred you out of the wilderness. Do not forget your place, and all will be well between us.'

From my window, I looked through the upper branches of trees to barren moorlands beyond. I'd heard the old tale on childhood winter nights. Somewhere out there, Thomas Rhymour d'Ercildoun met the Queen of Faerie and rode off to Elfland, not to be seen again for 7 years. Here too young Tambourlaine met the Lady Margaret. This was an enchanted landscape, rich and strong, and I allowed myself to hope my stratagem might succeed.

True Thomas be damned: he could stay in ballads, where he belonged.

I was cautious. I didn't want to poison myself. My first unguents held the least quantities of ingredients. I found an excellent preparation in an Herbal: henbane, poppy and mandragora in goose fat. Smeared on Florian's prick while he lay drunk, it suppressed his urges most effectively. I took care to wear gloves and washed my hands thoroughly: my own urges were my business.

I experimented with boiling the smallest amount of mandragora in red wine, as though preparing a winter drink. I increased the quantity by small fractions, sipping a little before retiring each night, until the night my dreams became vivid and lucid.

Land stretched from horizon to far horizon, each detail sharp and clear as I flew high above, soaring towards moon and stars. I wore only a night gown but was neither cold nor warm. All creatures on the ground beneath me, foxes and badgers, owls and hawks, lizards and stoats, were clear and sharp in my sight. Whiplash snakes rolled like cartwheels through the forest, knotting themselves as their tails caught in their mouths.

Few eldritch creatures were abroad, but those who were caught my passage beneath the Moon and watched me go by. I ignored them.

My Gift eye perceived the world in strange lights, as pools and eddies of energies, some static, some intermingled but never co-mixed. Subtle gradations of colour and density marked occulted boundaries. I was pulled north and west, drawn by potent strings of belonging, to Scotland, the home from which I exiled myself. There was a great strength I drew upon: the ancient kings and retinues slumbering beneath Edinburgh, waiting for the day they awoke to reclaim their Estate. But the fineries and filigrees were all with the men. The women wore drab plaids as their winding sheets, no circlets or diadems graced their brows.

An old song called. I looked for the singer, and flew to a leaf-green grove in the clouds, where a creature sang herself into existence.

Her skirt was of the grass-green silk,
Her mantel of the velvet fine,
At ilka tuft of her horse's mane
Hung fifty silver bells and nine.

I no longer apprehended the world below me. My host remained cloaked. She did not look at me, but swept her arm around as if to scatter seed on fresh-tilled fields. The far edge of the grove transformed, sprouting landscapes as she sang.

O see not ye yon narrow road,
So thick beset wi' thorns and briers?
That is the path of righteousness,
Tho' after it but few enquires.

And see not ye that braid, braid road,
Across yon lovely leven?

That is the path of wickedness,
Tho' some call it the road to heaven.

She removed her hood and she became he: *Le Dauphin des Faies*, intruding into my dream. I rejected him again. *Le Dauphin* bowed, and only two paths remained.

Behind me, a third voice spoke, the voice of the deep spirits of the Earth and Moon speaking in unison. Creation spread below me, as though I'd stepped outside of it and all times were visible.

'Choose your path well, Allisoun, the children of the living need you.'

'And the dead, who are mine to command?'

'They are not, and never were. Their time on Earth is done. You have no power over them, only over yourself.'

I stepped from pad to pad across a lily pond. At the far shore I examined the two roads. But my sight shifted and between the paths of righteousness and wickedness was a patch of utter blackness, an absent sliver of somewhere that wasn't there.

There was a quality about the blackness, a texture and density, rich and barren, pregnant with promise and despair. It was beautiful. I ignored the voices behind me and their pathetic warnings. Did I not command a good neighbour at his castle gate? Do I not see the dead all around and listen to their chatter? Am I not a necromancer?

I put both hands into the jaws of the sliver of black and pulled them apart, forcing a gap wide enough to step through. The entrance slapped shut behind me as waves over a drowned sailor. Darkness flooded my heart, offered its weight, its energy. Like an estranged grandparent, it welcomed me home.

I woke with a pounding head, and a deep lethargy. Everything spun when I tried to stand, as though I stood on a high parapet with no balustrade, head and stomach lurching. Light streaming through the windows hurt my eyes.

I remembered the blackness, and the secret knowledge revealed to me. I had been shown the means by which I could take my revenge on Aphrêm as a necromancer should, calling on the power of Hell, demanding the obedience of the Devil himself if I had to.

The potion still worked in me, kindling my inner flame. I summoned my maid, a blackmoren girl procured out of the *Mercado de Escravos* of Portugal, and bid her to my bed, where lust took me. She complied: she dared not do other.

My confinement came soon enough. I had no idea if Aphrêm knew my plans, but he was too intelligent to question, even obliquely, in case I alerted him. I mustn't appear too subservient or calm, as that would also make him suspect me. I kept to myself as much as I could. When the weather grew warmer I explored the grounds, looking for plants that I might use. There were many Aphrêm grew as an apothecary that I did not recognise, but several could as well come from a witch's garden and lead to a burning were a sharp-eyed minister or elder to recognise them.

The grounds were laid out in four parts: his Apothecary's garden, a vegetable garden (he rarely ate meat), an orchard and, at the end of a path, a well-tended glade with an ancient yew tree at its centre. The yew held a sacred significance for Aphrêm, and he spent time there most mornings. What devotions did he observe? What faith motivated him? For he was no more a Christian than me.

My connection to the earth was fresh and vital in this landscape, but the yew was a puzzle, part natural, part intrusion from some other place. Perhaps the human world looked the same to Aphrêm. I asked him one evening, but he said I babbled like an idiot.

Nor did he understand when I asked him about the dead. The idea that an individual essence passes into another realm on the termination of the earthly body was dismissed as human superstition. He would not discuss his own beliefs or myths at all.

'You want to believe,' he said another evening, 'that things follow a predictable, orderly pattern, repeating into a consistent future. That is a typical human point of view. Your natural order is an illusion, though there *is* an order. Your dead do not transit neatly from one conscious state to another, it is the living who do that, slipping from moment to moment, believing the illusion of continuity. The dead are beyond that, if, indeed, they can be said to be anywhere at all.'

There were few visitors, though a satchel of documents arrived every Friday, and Aphrêm would disappear into his study for hours to examine them. He seemed to have no concern for what I might do in his absence and I was free to wander through the house, which seemed as ancient as the yew. Layers of history accumulated within it like rings of a primordial tree.

I asked several times about Margaret and her children, but he told me nothing at all and forgot, or thought better of honouring, his offer to show me their bones. I remembered the babies draining into jars in the forest and told him why I shuddered.

'Ah, that was you? We thought it likely, but some said it was a man, a traveller who vanished soon afterwards.' His equanimity surprised me, but he said no more.

My anxiety ripened with my child. What if I'd miscalculated? What if the child was stilled-born? What if Bethia should be hurt? He said Bethia had been left to bring up her family because he knew I would return and I was the richer prize, but I didn't trust him. I had no one to comfort me, not the shade of Mama or of Margaret, not the good neighbours. I was alone.

As Lammas approached, Ys came to the house. She ignored me. She and Aphrêm were busy making preparations for some event they did not disclose.

One afternoon, I met *Le Dauphin* on the fringes of The Leyes estate. He stood on the other side of a demarcation line only he could see and refused to cross.

'*Ma chère*, you are looking well. You mean to do this thing? There is still time to take another path. All you need do is come with me now.'

'And Bethia? It means her and her family's deaths.'

'So, there is a price you will not pay? That is good, there is hope for you. Then know this: whatever choice you make, all your family will receive our benison and protection from Aphrêm and his kind so far as we can bestow it. Continue with your plan, however, and we will rescind your Gift. This is your final warning, *ma chère*.'

'You think to threaten me? You will obey me as you are bound to, imp, or face my wrath.'

A sad smile twitched across his lips and eyes.

'I told them you would not listen. Very well, accept the consequences. Our Gift is withdrawn: we will find worthier recipients.'

Such a silence fell as I had never known. I sought my child, tried to sense the familiar mass of impatient hatred in my womb. But there was nothing at all.

294

When my time came, I hoped Aphrêm and the gathered creatures would think my agitation a natural fear of imminent pain or death. There were three of them: Aphrêm, Ys and a female called Sarah who had expertise with birthing humans. Aphrêm and Ys were only to observe. My room was prepared with clean linen and hot towels, and oils and unguents to ease my pains.

Every other thought faded when my waters broke and birthing began. Mama wasn't there, nor any whom I might want with me. Why could their spirits not be present, not even Margaret who must have died there?

The baby had not turned and the process would be difficult. I recoiled from Sarah's touch, but her calm presence was reassuring. She believed the bairn's legs were straight, and she might ease the passage. But I could not imagine a worse pain as my back seized like my insides were twisting, as though all of my insides would be squeezed out with the child, as though my hips were pulled apart by unseen hands.

My Sight awoke, though not my lost Gift. I was thrown out of my body and hovered above the bed, looking down on a Yule tableau. I wanted to stay there, suspended in nothing, while my poor body suffered, but I was dragged back to pain.

Sarah said the babe was coming and I should prepare for the worst. It all happened very quickly after that.

A slick slithering told me the child was out, arse first.

'The calf is not breathing,' said Sarah.

Aphrêm and Ys rushed to the bed. Sarah unwound the umbilical cord from the bairn's neck and skelped its rear end to shock it into its first breath.

It awoke.

To life.

To horror.

I learned my lessons well in the black world, the secret of binding spirits, trapping them, starving them. I named my first-born Legion, for its tiny frame was host to many, many tormented souls.

The souls of my other children snuffed out in the womb.

The souls of men, taken at the moment they released their living seed.

The souls of witches driven mad as they were pitched quick into the fire.

All harvested and stored in dark places, forbidden by me to move on to other realms, agitated to insane fury like a stoppered and shaken flask of fermenting ale.

Legion screeched and clawed the air, letting fly a miasma of concentrated hatred, snuffing the life from the first creatures it encountered. Aphrêm and Ys dropped to the floor, never knowing they were dead.

Sarah screamed, a piercing howl so loud it hurt my ears, and leapt back, but the child had no interest in her – its malice was now directed at one only, the one to whom it was still attached: its mother. Its creator.

Dullness gripped my mind, as though starved of air. I tried to fight, to find the power of the earth and build defences, but with no Gift I was a normal woman, abandoned to the spite of my own child.

'No: not me! I didn't create you for this!'

In my final moments, I took joy in the deaths of Aphrêm and Ys, satisfaction that they would steal no more children.

As I faded, my own heart's blood echoed in my ears, a loud thudding, insistent on life. Legion's eyes glowed red like Samael's. Yet the thudding grew louder, the hammering of heavy boots on the stair.

The door crashed open. The creature that entered snatched Legion from my breast and wrung the tiny neck. It cut the umbilical cord and dashed my bairn, my first-born bairn, hard against the stone wall, leaving a red smear of memory. The imprisoned souls burst free of their bindings, and rushed from darkness to light, leaving this earthly Hell behind.

The creature fetched me a mighty blow with its fist. As I passed into unconsciousness, Sarah named it Ephraim.

I woke: my first surprise. I was unrestrained: the second. I ached. My left eye and cheek were swollen. Several upper teeth were loose. My jaw was stiff.

'So, you wake at last.'

The voice came out of the depths of time, as dry as parchment in the desert, as rich as the fertile soils of the Nile Delta.

'You killed my children.'

'As you kill ours.' Talking took effort.

'Aphrêm was my son. I loved him for years beyond the imagination of your kind. His hair streamed in the Steppes breeze as he rode with Temujin's host, the same breeze that blew through Byzantium and Bālàshāgǔn, a breeze that whipped dust devils around his boots in Babylon, and even then he was old.

'And Ys, my loving daughter. She who sailed a hide boat from Orkney to Ireland, through Tintagel to Brittany, from Marseilles to Alexandria. Who travelled with Thomas the Apostle to India. Ys the handmaiden of her aunt in China; Ys, traveller of the Silk Roads; Ys, bringer of pestilence to the Golden Horde, emissary of Death.

'By what presumption did you do this thing?'

'He killed my sister.'

'They died for that? For the life of a single human? At the hands of your grotesque spawn? There is something unnatural about this. Something I must understand.'

'I fulfilled my task: I am ready to die.' I almost believed my own bravado.

'Oh, you will die, you may be sure of it, but not today. I do not yet comprehend what you did. I have never seen the like, and I thought there was nothing new for me under the sun and stars.'

Later, he summoned me.

'I do not know what you did. I should dissect your diseased carcass while you yet live to find the root of your corruption, study your entrails for signs of your sickness. Your spawn yielded no answers. Nor can I find your sister Bethia to examine.

'So I have considered the matter of your death. I have decided to deliver you to your own kind for judgement by your own laws.'

He ushered in the minister and elders of a nearby Kirk.

'Tell these gentlemen your name, if you please.'

I spat on the carpet and looked away. Ephraim spoke for me.

'You see for yourselves what we are dealing with, gentlemen. The woman calls herself Allisoun, but goes by many family names: Bourdoun, Mein, von der Grach and Raune to my certain knowledge. She is of good stock, but her step-father was the notorious Major Weir, who burnt for his abominable crimes. No doubt his corruption spread to her. Make your confession now, Allisoun: it would be well to avoid persuasion.'

'My confession? My confession to what? That I took the life of your children who stole away my sister? committed no crime in righting a great wrong.'

'Your sister, Madam?' An elder with a cherubic face bu keen eyes asked the question. Ephraim answered.

'She refers to her sister Margaret who, you will recal

was married away to an Englishman to palliate her incest with Major Weir, as deponed at his trial by those who knew her.'

'So, you confess readily to the slaughter of Master Ephraim's son and daughter. You were right to bring this to us, Master Ephraim.'

'There is more, gentlemen. There are rumours from Germany of her sorcery and knowledge of potions, and of unnatural lusts, though I cannot provide witnesses. It is said, too, that she dressed as a man to deceive others about her sex and true nature, despite the prohibitions of Deuteronomy and Leviticus. The birthing-woman Sarah will tell you also of the child this woman brought forth, and of the deaths of both my son and my daughter who showed her nothing but hospitality and charity in her time of need. I warn you, sirs, it is a story to freeze your souls and I can only think it the work of Satan himself.'

The court sat at night with only a judge present, for fear so shocking a case as mine would bring alarm and consternation to the lieges. I was accused of witchcraft and sorcery, of carnal copulation with Satan and the bearing of his child, and the slaughter by demonic means of Aphrêm and Ys. Testimony was brought from Ephraim and Sarah. McGhie the deckhand averred that my eyes aboard ship were as red as a demon's, that unnatural sounds came from my cabin and that I claimed to see the dead. Bethia was obliged to give an account of my childhood. She said I had a gift for numbers and accounts, which was held by the Lord Advocate to be evidence of conjuration by numerology and thus proof of sorcery. The minister and elders deponed that in their custody, and under the lightest of questioning,

I called in aid spirits, whom I called *Le Dauphin* and the green-eyed faerie, which were aliases of Satan, and that I called on my own dead mother and sister not to forsake me. I had sought to escape by the power of the Devil, who had not answered, which, as his late majesty King James had written, was the inevitable fate of the necromancer.

My doom was never in doubt: that I be taken to the Castlehill of Edinburgh and there, after a short time to make my peace with the Lord my God, my left and right hands to be stricken off for the slaughter of Aphrêm and Ys, and thereafter I be put quick onto the pyre and my body burnt to ashes.

The executioner sharpens his blade, the whetstone rasping on the cutting edge. *Tam o' the Lynn was condemned to the fire* ... The pitch and tar are prepared, the coals banked and lit. I try again and again to call on the Gift to save me. It does not answer.

A great crowd fills the empty space before me: A thousand Allisouns, five thousand Allisouns, more. All the Allisouns who might have been, all the unmade tapestries, weeping for me, cursing me, thankful my fate is not theirs.

I despise them.

Legion stands at the back, grown to a man, or woman, or child, or monster, malice palpable, though it has passed beyond this world. I never knew if my bairn was boy or girl.

Ephraim is here to see me burn. Beside him are *Le Dauphin des Faies* and his cousin with emerald eyes.

'Why did you abandon me?'

'Hark at her, calling on Satan. Wisht! Hauld yer tongue witch, save your blasphemies for Hell.'

The good neighbours, who, I realise, Ephraim can't see or hear, answer me.

'You abused our Gift: the power was yours to protect humanity from what will happen.'

'But I am a necromancer. The King said so.'

'Foolishness from an unwise fool. You believed whatever spoke to your arrogance. We warned you thrice, but you ignored us. Our Gift and benison are now with Bethia and her children, and with others.'

'The future? The great parade and the people dying in the street? Did I prevent it?'

'Ephraim has hardened his mind against humans and plans a great revenge. Because of you. You created a future that we cannot now stop.'

'Is there no mercy for me?'

'You will not feel the fire, we grant you that blessing.'

'I don't understand. I completed the task set for me. Daddy told me the old stories: he said I should remember them, that evil always loses.'

'He was right.

'And you have.'

But I hadn't. For darkness welcomed me once before, and its paths through the black lands were familiar to my feet. I looked beyond the crowd, beyond the gathered versions of myself, beyond my tormentors, beyond the angels' arch of swords, to where the future gathered, and the sliver of black beckoned.

Resolute, I abandoned my useless body, and walked into eternity.

TO DANCE THE DANCE MACABRE

I square up to death in tumbled leather brown brogues and a Harris Tweed jacket. My battered old hip flask is charged with Glenfarclas. I drink it all down in a long burning stream, eyes watering, not bothering to breathe. God, how I've needed that. This stuff will kill me, the quacks said, but a dead man walking doesn't care.

I straighten the knot in my tie. From the right-hand pocket of my jacket I take the 9mm mouse gun I kept in a locked box on top of the wardrobe. It will blow my brains out quite effectively, and this is the perfect spot to do it, before the final indignities.

The path bisects the city. There is magic here, literal and figurative. All remaining human noise disappeared when I shambled down the steps at Roseburn Cliff. Here, there is only the chatter of water over stone, antiphonal birdsong, susurrating breeze through the trees lining the riverbanks. I remember the day I first came here, the gardens tumbling down to the waterside, the brusque greetings of other walkers with their muddy chocolate labradors, the abrupt shift from town to country.

That was when there *were* other walkers, when the houses on the opposite bank weren't a chiaroscuro landscape of ash and char.

Beech and willow are in leaf, as well as hornbeam, elder and linden. There's a wood pigeon somewhere, prr-cooing a lament for humanity. A wren darts through shrubs and fallen leaves on the hillside. A kingfisher, iridescent in the sun, perches on a branch stuck midstream.

That first day I came down here, I identified one or two sites with a hint of the sacred about them, a sensation of otherness, unmistakeable if you have the ability and experience to recognise it. And some of the people I met on my walks here were not, in a strict sense, people at all.

For a man who often feels out of time and place, I was at home here. Mhairi loved it too. In those days we often took walks on weekend mornings to Stockbridge for a pub lunch. That was before pub lunches became all-day sessions for me, and Mhairi stayed at home in despairing silence.

There's a bench at the AIDS memorial below the Gallery of Modern Art, where I sit and watch the water as it flows over the weir. Ducks bob in eddies and pools, arses upended as they scrat about the riverbed. Otters are frequent here now. Downstream, a grey heron waits patiently for fish and frogs. I'm reminded of Hesse, and the chap who found enlightenment watching the Ganges, hearing the great song of a thousand voices in a single word, feeling the unity and the flow of all things. Does anyone still read Hesse? Will there be anyone left to read him?

A kestrel, female by the size of her, quarters the grassland pausing now and then to hover, wings a-flutter, using her tail for stability. An unkindness of ravens perch on the upper branches of a silver birch higher up the slope. Four of them, fat on carrion, watch me with casual indifference. No dippers today, which is a shame: I'd like to see them one last time.

I close my eyes and smell tree and leaf, river and pool, even unseasonal wild garlic and honeysuckle. The chirps and songs of small birds seem louder. Eyes open, I watch long-tailed tits and yellow wagtails, chaffinches and blackbirds flitter between bushes. A pair of goosander are at the weir now.

There was someone further round the path earlier, with Mhairi's careless gait and careworn shoulders. But Mhairi died fifteen years ago. Cancer, they said, but I know I killed her. I used the most insidious weapon of all: I drained her will to live.

She visits me often, but never here. The memories are too potent, and there are so many memories.

The gun nestles in my hand, but I'm not quite ready to die yet.

I am six years old. The police ask me questions. I try to tell them the people in the woods took Neil away. They say I am a liar and an evil little boy.

I talk to a social worker and a psychiatrist and am put in a special class at school, and no-one believes me, so I stop talking to anyone at all.

I look out of my bedroom window towards the woods. A creature in the bracken and ferns looks back at me. She has deep green eyes, like the stones in the earrings my great-aunt used to wear. She waves and winks, then vanishes.

Unseelie: the word comes.

I play alone because none of my friends are allowed to come and see me. I wish I grew up in a place where strangeness is accepted, or tolerated. Edinburgh's suburbia is sniffy about the weird, at least in public. I only learn later what happens behind the smartly painted doors of Morningside and Trinity.

I am sixteen. Neil comes home on a dew-drenched June morning. He walks through his parents' back-door like he's only been away for a couple of hours.

Neil is still six years old.

Mrs. Heaton screams and people twitch their front curtains to see what the fuss is all about.

In the street, I meet the same psychiatrist, come to talk to Neil.

'Told you so,' I say.

I am nearly eighteen and everyone is relieved I've won a scholarship to a university 600 miles away. As the taxi pulls away from my parents' house, Neil, forever stranded in his own childhood, stares at me from an upstairs window. The *unseelie* creature is with him, her left breast exposed. Neil turns to suckle.

Five years later he hangs himself from a tree with his school tie.

I am twenty-four and settling my parents' estate. They dreamed of travelling the world when Dad retired, and died together when the overloaded ferry they were on sank in a squall off Indonesia. Their bodies were never recovered. They stand hand in hand in the corner of the bedroom, watching as I pack their clothes into suitcases to give to charity, tossing their underwear into a black rubbish bag. I feel awkward handling Mum's bras and pants. I turn on the radio. A correspondent reports from Africa on outbreaks of a virulent new haemorrhagic fever in Sudan and The Congo. They're calling it Ebola after a Congolese river. I shiver at the news but don't know why. I understand now.

I pretend I can't see Mum and Dad until, at last, don't.

🦊

306

It's a breeze to shrivel the skin and parch the throat, to drive rational people to the edge of craziness, and send crazy people hunting for the fatty smell of blood hissing on sun-baked stone. As it sweeps across the *Campagna Romana*, the hot evening air gathers scents of lavender, oregano and wild rosemary, and casts them through the open windows of a *Castello*, high on the ridge of a Sabine hill.

On a plain wooden bier in a high chamber is an open wood coffin, unvarnished, without ornament. The cadaver within is too fresh to stink, though it will soon. Tall silver candlesticks are around the casket at the cardinal compass points. Pure beeswax candles burn true and steady despite the movement of air through the window.

Below the chamber, a town stretches along the elongated spine of the ridge. A road climbs towards the central piazza, where the street market is packing up, and a band unloads their instruments and amplifiers from a white Fiat van.

In *La Rossa's*, over cards and cold beers, the talk on the TV in the corner is of war and skirmishes in all the usual places. And the plague, of course, still only second in newsworthiness, the true impact not yet grasped but memories of national lockdowns strong. Talking heads talk. Images of helpless Black people, surrounded by noble White people in hazmat suits, flicker across the screen above the bar. Politicians, who never learn, assure their countries there is no possibility of further spread and all possibilities are guarded against. They are following the science, they say. Survivors thank their God for preserving their lives, the same God who kills myriad others. They say it is a mystery: we cannot know His purpose, though divine distaste for same-sex marriage might be implicated, as might Zionist and Muslim extremists. Strident voices online and in the media denounce rumours of a virus as a hoax perpetrated by the global elite to supress freedom.

None of the humans glance up to the tower, where we gather to celebrate their imminent death.

We enjoy refreshments, all local produce, fresh from the market or from private orchards, dairies, bakeries and nurseries. Olives and hazelnuts, cheeses, San Marzano tomatoes, peaches and bread, all served in Han dynasty Chinese bowls, arranged on a table made by a master craftsman in ancient Sumeria.

No meat, of course, apart from the exquisite spiced *sanguinaccio*, prepared with human blood sweetened with crushed yew berries, a recipe preserved from deep time. The dish is presented in slivers so fine that each portion dissolves on the tongue like *hostia*.

Local wines are served, fresh and unpretentious, unadulterated by sulphites. They release sustained notes of violets and roses that linger long on the palate.

We eat and drink in silence. Small talk and personal conversation will come later, after the rite. The soft shimmer of an ancient gong calls us to order, and one by one we process through an ante-chamber, up a spiralling flight of stairs, to the main chamber, into which the hot breeze still blows, the corpse hastening now towards putrefaction.

We take our habitual places in the chamber: standing by the window, sitting in high-winged upholstered armchairs. We travelled the world to be here, those who could, to represent our families. Were it not for the open coffin, we might be a party of affluent tourists in the lounge of a boutique hotel, waiting for a tour bus to whisk us off to the Colosseum and Forum, the Pantheon and the Spanish Steps, with a packed lunch at the Trevi Fountain.

On a sideboard running in an arc around one quadrant of the circular room, further refreshments are placed, arranged with ritual precision around a bonsai yew centrepiece.

Father, as Eldest, raps on the old wood.

'We are gathered to pay our respects to this human, the first fruit of our harvest. Who wishes to speak?'

'I do.'

My ancient Aunt Xi Wangmu, whom I suspect of being mad, as all the ancient ones become in time, glides over to the sideboard and pours a fresh glass of wine, pausing to select a sliver of *sanguinaccio*, positioning it precisely in the centre of a roundel of thin, toasted bread.

'Humans are strange beasts. In all my many years I have never understood what happens in their heads. Nor have I had any great love for them, even when they worshipped me as a god. We all know what we have done and why, so I will waste no weasel words.'

She places the sliver of toast and *sanguinaccio* onto her tongue, savouring the sensation in her prim mouth, raising her glass to salute the coffin.

'To humans: from dust you came and unto dust you will return. Rest in peace.'

She sips her wine.

I look at Father, presiding over us, we who put the Gaia Cascade in motion, our great cull of our livestock. I can't work out if he is enjoying this or if, more likely, he approaches it from the strict logic of animal husbandry and self-preservation. I have doubts about Father's sanity too sometimes. It wouldn't be the first time one so ancient has grown hollow, like an old yew, when the cumulative years of degeneration can no longer be supressed by human stem-cells, and decline becomes inevitable. And there is anger within him, a memorial flame to Aphrêm and Ys, of whose death he never speaks, but on which he never stops brooding.

There's a discussion he and I often had in the heart of the sacred Yew at The Leyes.

'No, we need a breeding population, and sufficient numbers to keep their core infrastructure running. That should still leave a billion or so, once their numbers stabilise,' he says.

'I can't imagine the world without them, without all the things we use.'

'I know. We grew soft and forgot the old ways.'

'Were the old ways better?'

'Yes. The balance we maintained is lost: the established order was muddled in the trophic cascade. And their technologies, this internet, this world wide web, the surveillance, they have a powerful unifying effect. It brings them together around a common source of knowledge, like Babel all over again. Nothing they want is beyond their reach. They threaten us, as they threaten the planet.'

'How did it get this far, Father? When did we lose control?'

'When the line between predator and parasite blurred.'

'We are the wrong kind of blood-sucker?'

We watched the early sun burn through the morning haar, the silence broken by the sounds of geese overhead, calling from the uncertain sky.

'We're treating humans no worse than they treat other species, or themselves. Look at them: Srebrenica, Warsaw, Gaza, Sabra and Shatilla, Dachau, Biafra... So many I can't list them all.'

'That's not a justification.'

'No. But you know very well it was a consideration.'

'To excuse genocide?'

'An emotive term. A human term. The ecological case for culling them is overwhelming, you made sure of that when you made it. And the habitat loss from climate damage is too great a threat to our survival. But you are right to doubt, Margaret: you find ethics in doubt, not certainty.'

'And what does your doubt tell you, Father?'

'That we've culled before, but this is on a different scale.'

'Something transgressive?'

'Transgressive of what? Be careful of tacit metaphors, Margaret, they betray your thoughts. How many are too many? This is a necessary correction. Look at how they live, what they do to each other, how they treat each other, how they arrogate a position of superiority to themselves. They are beasts, Margaret. Less than beasts. Empathy is a dangerous indulgence where humans are concerned. They'll be none the worse for a good culling.'

'Must it always be plagues?'

They work. Do you think the end is invalidated by the means?'

'No, but I wonder if we are invalidated by the means.'

'Look at the humans with their cattle and how they respond to Foot and Mouth Disease: do they let their moral doubts stand in the way of doing what they know to be correct? No. And neither can we.'

The calls of geese faded, replaced by the soft chirrups and trills of song birds. Somewhere, a thrush began its song as the haar evaporated. I had learned not to push too far. I am not the first child of Ephraim, but I am one of the few he'd thought worthy to survive beyond adolescence.

'We allowed Europeans to invade and colonise the Americas because we listened to our doubts, and look what happened.'

'They walked on the Moon.'

'They did, but only after almost eradicating the existing humans, and enslaving millions of their fellows, whom they traded and discarded like any other disposable commodity: slavers always understood built-in obsolescence. These are the humans who gave us Hiroshima and still thought Nagasaki a good idea. We should have dealt with them then.'

311

'Ethics is an equation then? An algebra of moral equivalence?'

'You know me better than that.'

'And if the humans fight back?'

'How can they? We've planned too well.'

'The same way they walked on the Moon.'

I support the Gaia Cascade, as its prime author I can hardly do otherwise. We must cull the numbers of humans. They threaten us, but, as importantly, they've damaged the planetary eco-system almost beyond repair. In a few short centuries, perhaps less, there will be no room for co-existence. We must reassert ourselves as apex predator and re-establish the proper relationship between us and the human. We must let the Earth reclaim itself. The responsibility for that is ours and ours alone: no-one in their right minds would invoke the aid of the old gods, just in case they decide it would be fun to help.

Then we'd all be fucked.

I married late. I was nearly 37 and Mhairi just 22. She only ever knew me as Urquhart Menzies. That isn't my birth name, it was the cover identity I adopted after India. I never told her that, and the identity was so well put together that I didn't have to lie much about my lack of extended family. She still had her real family name of McTernan.

And Mhairi was involved in operations anyway: she understood about identity and security, even between lovers and spouses, perhaps especially between lovers and spouses.

George was born prematurely in February 1991, and only survived for two days. Sarah and Marion were born in 1993 and 1994 respectively. We were happy for a while or at least I was, but I was soon deep in a passionate affair with drink and blind to Mhairi's misery until too late.

After Mhairi's death, Sarah and Marion were brought up by their Granny and Grandad McTernan, who went to inordinate and determined lengths to keep me out of their lives. And I can't blame them, though I did at the time.

I remember the morning the significance of the first virus struck me. Sunlight angled through the casement windows of my study. Glittering specks of dust hung suspended in the thick air as I settled in for another day.

Like every day, I was up and out of bed, showered, shaved and breakfasted by six-thirty. I lingered over breakfast because I found it hard to see the point in making the effort to do anything else. Apart from rising early, I've never been much for discipline.

When Mhairi and the girls were here, I had a reason to pretend to care, before my first drink anyway. But Mhairi's ashes are scattered and the girls are long gone. Their absence aches like a sensitive tooth.

It wasn't as though I needed to work. I had a pension from the government and a small retainer from them as a reservist and consultant, but what began as a convenient cover had, over time, begun to feel like my real job.

On the wall, framed certificates and front pages from my accidental journalistic career were corralled into a few square feet: special foreign correspondent, inadvertent stint as royal reporter when the shit went down in India, opinion columnist and resident curmudgeon. Then, inevitably, the lifetime achievement award' conferred, as is traditional, shortly before I was shown the door. Apparently I was too old guard for a revitalised media and comms team who wanted to run some new talent up the flagpole to see how flapped.

All was charted as dispassionately as the Admiralty record of wrecks. There were no awards for the other stuff, no medals or citations, no thanks from a grateful nation, nothing to undermine deniability.

No-one commissioned work from redundant hacks like me, even though I am two hundred and twenty-seven weeks and four days sober. I still had a pseudonymous slot in the nature diary of a national daily every fortnight, but I already had six months' worth of those written and waiting. Besides they only brought in a nominal fifty quid per piece and an invitation to the annual 'festive' lunch which, on the only occasion I went, was an utter nightmare.

I hadn't had any 'real' work for some time. My anthologies of *Strange Tales of Auld Reekie* sold well to tourists, even though they mostly contain half-truths or outright fabrications. I persevered in chronicling the weird, writing online despatches in my blog, and pitching the occasional piece to mainstream outlets.

I had plenty of hits on the site, though. Plenty of people who believed every strange story I put up there. There's no-one as gullible as a rationalist who wants to believe.

The usual cross currents and whispers of the house were silent. I turned on the large monitor I found easier to read. The many bots and crawlers I crafted and released into the wild brought me tall tales from all over the world. My former colleagues would no doubt raise their collective eyebrows at my methods, but, then, they hadn't learned their trade in one of the more obscure outstations of Her Majesty's Government.

I can't say exactly what I looked for. Like a chess master reading a position and rejecting unfruitful lines, I didn't think about what I was doing. This was about feeling and instinct, intellect could come later. I looked for things that seemed 'out of place'.

There was no shortage of material: lights in the sky, earthquakes and aliens were standards, a heady brew of signs and portents in their own right, even for those without a penchant for catastrophism. In the Heaven's Gates and Solar Temples of the world, the poison bubbled and the robes were freshly laundered and pressed.

On every continent the crazies got crazier. Rumours of conspiracies and subterfuges, all covered up by the mainstream media in deference to their Illuminati paymasters, went hand in hand with a tsunami of poltergeists and bent cutlery. An albino baby with a vestigial tail had been born to an Arrernte couple outside of Mparntwe. Floating lights and strange creatures were reported from both London Underground and Paris Metro. The ghost of Elvis was seen on the tarmac at Prestwick Airport by three independent witnesses. The lizard creatures of Buckingham Palace were in league with the hidden elite of the Knights Templar, and the elusive Cult of Diana had been heard in Sloan Square, their chant '*Gaudete! Gaudete! Diana ventus candelae est*' echoing through the metropolitan night. Speculation was rife over the role of extra-terrestrials in hiding the truth of 9:11. House members in Congress suggested that recent earthquake swarms in Arkansas were the handiwork of Antifa insurgents. White supremacists were preparing to defend the planet in the name of the Aryan race.

As far as I knew, only one of those was true.

Just another Monday morning in August, then, except for whispers of a new virus striking in Africa. What my algorithms picked up before anyone else was that the same was happening in Asia, the Americas and Europe. My queries showed a rise in questions to message boards about similar symptoms, and big shifts in stocks of specialist pharmaceuticals. There was a sharp increase in orders of protective equipment from hospitals, including in the UK, and labs everywhere were rushing to be the first to sequence the new threat. Besides, I could *feel* the significance as surely as I can see the dead.

Security chatter was increasing too – not all of my old backdoors and datasinks were obsolete. The tenor was unmistakeable: panic in low places that would soon become panic in high places.

This was why I still got paid a retainer. I called it in.

Father asked me to identify as many of the humans with what they called their Gift as I could, and either bring them over as familiars or kill them. We had already eliminated our existing familiars to ensure their silence.

'How will I find them, Father? You tried for long enough and only found a few.'

'You have the material the human Hawking gave us.'

'I have, but it is old, and doesn't cover the world outside Europe.'

'It is the best we have since Joseph disappeared. These so-called Gifted have only been an issue since Allisoun killed your brother and sister. My hypothesis is that it's only that family line we have to identify.'

'Why couldn't you find them?'

'It's a rogue talent, and it seems they took steps to hide themselves.'

'You don't think they were protected?'

'Don't be ridiculous.'

'What happened to Joseph? You never told me.'

'Something catastrophic. Some human mare at one of his idiotic schools babbled about a strange child and the ground swallowing up Maria, but she was clearly insane

I went to Joseph's grove where he kept his trophy Michael, but it was as though it had never been, just old trees in the mountains, with no memory of what it once was.'

Michael. Michael Menzies. The name sparked a memory.

'Do you remember that human child, Charlie, who used to work for us, the one who found the photographs and letters of Michael Menzies then disappeared?'

'Hmmm? Remind me, humans are all much the same after a while. Stallion or mare?'

'Not an easy question in this case. Anyway, Charlie was researching their own pedigree. If they were of the same line as Michael, that might provide clues.'

And it did. The human had put what it called its family tree on the internet for anyone and everyone to see. It was invaluable in hunting them down.

I woke the next morning with the dislocated confusion of a poor night's sleep, wondering where I was. Mhairi was there too, curled up on top of the antique mahogany wardrobe, watching me with an unblinking gaze that both comforted and disturbed.

She was of variable age: now the empty sack of skin in the hospice bed who died without saying goodbye, now the 23-year-old with the alluring wriggle and lips made for mischief, now gravid with our children, now a baby, a parcel of potential. All the times of her life were there on the wardrobe. She was solid not spectral, and the dust she dislodged made a slow descent in front of the full-length mirror.

'I've missed you.'

She made no response. Her gaze didn't falter.

'I don't even know what I could say to make it right.'

The same old one-sided conversation. My eyes welled and I blinked to clear them. I reached for a handkerchief from my bedside table. When I looked back, there was only dust floating in the air.

I kicked the duvet away and swung my legs over the edge of the bed. My dream journal was open, though I couldn't remember dreaming. During the night I'd jotted down three words to jog my waking memory: *genitive, ablative, golem*. I had no idea what they were meant to signify.

Downstairs, I drank tea and ate cardboard cereal. I tried to blank my memories, but it didn't work. The phone rang. The ringtone told me who it was, and I resented the presumption of intrusion it represented. The voicemail service kicked in after six rings, but the ringing started again as soon as the line was free.

I filled the kettle with fresh water and flicked it on. I dropped a couple of slices of bread into the toaster to brown while I prepared the tea, warming the pot before adding leaves and pouring boiling water over them. By the time the leaves had infused and I poured out a mug, my toast was thinly spread with a scrape of butter and a spoonful of marmalade. Eventually I gave in.

'Lieutenant-Colonel Menzies! I thought for a moment we were going to have to send in the tracker dogs in to find you. Or at least pop a drone or two through the letterbox.'

'Very droll. And what can I do for you?'

'Well you could open your door when I knock on it in two minutes. HMG requires your talents and I'm here to bring you in.'

'Here? Now? But I—'

'All will be explained. And put some more toast on, I'm famished.'

She had the trick, from long practice, of appearing

nondescript. Her suit was smart without drawing attention to itself, her face framed by auburn hair that could have been cut by any High Street hairdresser in the country. She wore make up designed to make her forgettable, and looked nothing like one would expect a senior member of the security services to look. Nor, for that matter, did she look much like she had the last time we'd met, when her hair was hennaed and clipped short to fit under her uniform beret.

'You're looking well. I can't say I expected to see you again.'

'Well, no. And you never would have if you hadn't called in yesterday. I heard about Mhairi. I'm sorry.'

'Thank you'.

An armoured personnel carrier squatted in the street, challenging the resident SUVs to make something of it if they thought they were hard enough. Two uniformed personnel stood by it.

'That'll have the neighbours in a tizz!'

'Do you speak to them much?'

'The neighbours? Not since Mhairi died. 'Hello' in the street, not much more.'

'What happened to you, Ming?'

'You were there.'

'Yes, but I didn't start drinking.'

'India didn't start me drinking, it just made sure I didn't stop. And then Mhairi and the girls—'

'Sorry. That was rude of me.'

'No, it was a fair question.' I stared at the scrubbed oak table top. 'So: what have you come here to say?'

'I'm here to reactivate you. Your unique talents are required. And I need someone I trust.'

'What if I say no?'

'That would be a problem. You're the best qualified for the job'.

I looked over to the alcove that held the fridge freezer, where blank-eyed Mhairi stood. I'd known what I would say from the moment the phone rang.

'Then you have a problem.'

In the piazza, humans couple and recouple without discrimination or control, moving from one partner to the next. Their incontinence disgusts me. Bread and wine are abandoned on the tables of osteria and trattoria. The band put down their instruments and join the throng around and in the fountain in front of the great door of the parish church, where, under the watchful eyes of the crucified Saviour and his blessed mother, the bacchanal is at its most intense.

My aunt is by my side.

'Have they no dignity?' she asked.

'We have stolen their future. If we must sit in judgement, it should not be on them.'

'Judgement? You wish for punishment?'

'No. Redemption.'

'You regret their sacrifice?'

'Our sacrifice. It's only their sacrifice if it is voluntary.'

'Sophistry. Don't let the Eldest hear you say that.'

Quite. Father wouldn't like to hear it. But Father missed things, dismisses them as unimportant. What do we do with our lives other than exist? We make no art, compose no music; we have no notion of purpose or meaning. We just are, without even the imagination to wonder why. Everything we have is made by humans, yet we think ourselves superior entitled to live while countless millions of them die at our hands. It would never have occurred to us to go to the Moon.

We live so long and breed so slowly, our gene pool is as stagnant as our society. Why do we persist in living except from fear of non-existence?

No, best not to say that to Father, who still mourned Ys, to whom he had dedicated the Gaia Cascade.

'Ming, we're in very deep shit. I'm trying not to get all formal about chains of command.'

'I know, and I appreciate it and I appreciate you coming here yourself. But it's not that simple anymore. Look at me, Jean: I'm sixty-four. I'm old.'

'Don't take this the wrong way, but I'm not here for your body.'

'Flatterer. What's the job, anyway?'

'We go to interesting places and meet interesting people. You assess and advise from your unique perspective without the usual bollocks of intelligence analysis. We keep you supplied with food and water and toilet paper while the country turns to crap, and make sure you're safe and warm when the real shit show starts.'

'You think that'll happen?'

'Yes.'

The knots and whirls of the wood of the table top formed random mandalas, bounded by the stains and rings of countless mugs. Marks and initials of the girls when they were children were scratched into it.

'Look at those. I got so cross with them for doing that. 'd give anything to have them here now.' And then 'I've never really been able to let Mumbai go, you know.'

'I hear you're sober.'

'One drink at a time.'

There was movement in the margins of the street where

morning hadn't reached. Indistinct forms, probably people, perhaps not, drifted by, eyeing up the personnel carrier.

'If you're worried enough to come all this way to speak to me, you must be pretty desperate. I need to find my girls.'

The words came out with the clarity of certainty. And dread. I remembered that odd feeling I'd had about the haemorrhagic fever in Africa forty years ago, and again when reports started coming out of Wuhan. This was the same, but this time I had a better idea of what it was, what it presaged.

'Coughs and sneezes spread diseases.'

'What?'

'Something my Gran used to say. This virus will be bad. I know it with every sense I possess. Even if I come with you, there's nothing I can do. I need to find Sarah and Marion, to warn them, if I can.'

'I'll do you a deal. I'll use my personal authority to assign resources to track your daughters down if you at least come and hear what we have to say.'

I looked around the kitchen, at the battered old farmhouse table, at the ornaments and utensils, the cookbooks unopened for fifteen years. At last I looked over to Mhairi, immobile in the alcove. She gave a barely perceptible, but definite, nod.

'Congratulations on your analysis, it corroborated what we suspected. You'll have to tell us how you did it, by the way. There are some embarrassed experts who missed it altogether.'

'Do you know what it is?'

'Not exactly: it's a variant of Ebolavirus we've never seen before. It spreads very rapidly and we're pretty sure it's airborne.'

'And it's everywhere, isn't it? That's what I picked up.'

'Yes. How did you do that?'

'I just asked the right questions and put two and two together when the answers came in. Nothing special.'

'It might not be special to you, but nobody else got it. There was no indication this outbreak was coming until people started dying. And it's worldwide so it probably has a long, asymptomatic gestation period that let it spread without us noticing.'

'So what's the scoop? Has Madagascar closed its ports yet? How long have we got?'

'Ebola's usually anything up to three weeks from infection to symptoms, but sometimes it's only days, and this is a mutation so we're left guessing. It isn't behaving how we expected: it's all numbers, but it isn't killing as many as the modelling predicted.'

'Are you sure it's a mutation, not engineered?'

'We're sure of nothing, and the people who'd normally be doing the sequencing and analysis have been dying too. I'd guess we have no more than 48 hours before word gets out, so there'll be an announcement today. The worst case is we'll be overwhelmed in days, and there's not a chance we'll cope.'

'So why haul me in?'

'To see if you can find anything we missed in the data, anything that might give us hope.'

She'd wasted her time: there wasn't anything to be found.

Sometimes I'm overcome by an overwhelming sense of isolation, of rootlessness, a feeling that I'm caught up in a dance with no beginning and no end and only death as my constant partner, stepping out the rhythms of the wayward tune of time. Time that compresses and contracts at the whim of our perception, of our consciousness, of the human awareness of moments gone and anticipation of moments to come. All meaningless: all times are one time, the past and future equally distant, equally present.

I once researched my family history. I hoped for some hint of an ancestor with my abilities, but only found the usual petty crooks and adulterers. I didn't get further than July 1834 and the birth of an illegitimate child to Barbara Menzies. I couldn't find any more about Barbara. I don't even know if Menzies was her real name or an alias. It seemed right, somehow, to adopt it when building my new identity.

On the rare occasions I met my cousins, who took great care to avoid me, there were no obvious hints of anything strange about them. All my known relatives were disappointingly normal. I could never decide whether Sarah and Marion inherited my oddness. Both suffered terrible nightmares when they were little, and talked about imaginary friends, but living with an alcoholic father with untreated PTSD will do that to you.

I missed them.

It's the paradox of parenthood: the joy of creating a child, of sharing their laughter and tears, tempered by the certain knowledge that one day they too will die and you won't be there to hold their hand and tell them that you love them.

Media vita in morte sumus.

I was in a country house in Berkshire. I had an official issue laptop/tablet hybrid that only hooked onto the secure official network. A splash screen reminded me that I was a commissioned officer and subject to disciplinary procedure at the Crown's discretion for any unspecified breaches of National Security I might contemplate.

Beyond the treeline in the extensive grounds, there was a restlessness in the shadows. I flashed back to the wood that once hosted Neil Heaton, where time tapped its rhythm to the beat of a different consciousness entirely. A stag broke cover, then was gone again, merging into bracken and myth

Jean kept her word. She had Sarah and Marion's addresses for me in less than two hours. Sarah was in Perth, Australia, Marion in San Francisco. I think I was meant to be impressed by her efficiency.

'Too soon.'

'Pardon?'

'You should have waited longer. How long have you had those addresses?'

She stuffed the paper with the contact details into my hand.

What could I say to Sarah and Marion that would get through the filters? What was there other than wishing them well? *By the way, I've seen your dead mum a few times recently, thought you might like to know.*

I told them I was thinking of them and would be happy to hear from them. If they didn't want to reply I would understand, but even a note from a mutual friend to let me know they how they were would be welcome.

'I would speak.'

The contralto voice has the gentle patina of aged wood. Long, finely manicured and painted fingernails tap the table top.

'None of you will be surprised by what I say. The situation is the direct result of strategies we adopted in the past. I do not repudiate them, I was party to them, but I said for a long time that we boxed ourselves in, and so it proved.

'The details are irrelevant. Were it not this crisis it would be some other. Four of us here remember when humans migrated from the east and gathered in ziggurats and temples and unified around worshipping us as Gods. We foresaw the dangers of hubris and put an end to it, scattering them, encouraging them to invent other gods to take the blame for the slaughter we unleashed. Was it a mistake to hide ourselves? Perhaps. I have been forgotten, except by scholars of ancient tablets, when once I was notorious amongst their calving females who thought I revelled in the foaming blood of their infants.'

'You did!'

'Even I was young once. We weren't gods then and we aren't gods now. We are stewards and we must respect those in our care, even as we do what is necessary. Farewell human.'

'Thank you. Is there another?'

'If I might, Eldest? I hope I cause no offence or breach the spirit of this occasion. I know some of us harbour doubts about what we do. I do not. Look out the window, go into any restaurant, see the humans defying their imminent deaths with their steaks and their racks of lamb. They will go to Mass and genuflect and chant their *Agnus Dei*, but are they concerned with the innocence of the lamb they eat? No: they hang it and butcher it and serve it with a mint sauce or berry *jus*. Their slaughterhouses are drenched in the blood of lambs.

'Shall I talk of their endless wars and skirmishes? Oh, they wring their hands and rend their clothes and wail to the heavens over the death of children, but still they bomb cities and towns, torture and massacre each other, release toxic chemicals and gases, all without a care. And when they're not doing that, mothers and fathers despatch their cast-off children to whither on the end of needles.

'Is it a crime we commit? Who will be our judge? By what criteria would we be measured? To whom could we appeal? The questions are meaningless: we are responsible only to ourselves.

'It would be hypocritical to mourn the death of so many but I follow the ancient rite and grieve for the death of the one before us, who died that we might live. Farewell human: thank you for the life you give us, though we didn't offer you a choice. May we make a better job of stewarding your descendants.'

I fell out with a bishop not long before he died. I'm not proud of it, but I don't regret it either.

I was short on sleep and we were under pressure. I hadn't had a reply from the girls. I'd already annoyed him over lunch.

'Organised religion is a poor substitute for direct experience of the sacred,' I said. 'The minute a priestly caste emerges, you're screwed.'

He made a remark about my past, about the 'inhuman' things I'd seen and done.

'Do you really want to know what I've seen, your reverence? Do you? Do you want to know the memories that never fade, drunk or sober? The children floating in their own filth, gently simmered by a disinterested sun reflecting off courtyard walls? The flies jumping and crawling on their parched flesh, in and out of nostrils and ears, laying their eggs in prolapsed arses dragging in the warm shit? All the kids standing there, patiently standing on their twig legs, their privates shaded by distended bellies, waiting to die?

'Do you want to know about the dysentery? The shit on the floor, the clots and swirls of blood all through it? Have you ever had sixty-three dying weans stare at you with blank eyes, your grace? Did they come to your cathedral and admire your hand-embroidered chasubles? Do they drop round to the Chapter House for tea and scones on a Wednesday afternoon? Have you been in the presence of walking corpses and felt their utter contempt for the gods in whose name they were massacred?

'And it happens again and again and again and again: always by humans to other humans, every single fucking time. And somewhere there is always a priest of some religion or another pronouncing the blessings of the divine on the weapons, finding reason to call the slaughter just. Don't lecture me about inhumanity: humanity is an aspiration at best.'

They let me come back to Edinburgh soon after that, the day before the Flu struck, about the time they figured out just how comprehensively the Ebola variant had been engineered.

It was a changed city. My house was intact, though some of my neighbours' properties had windows broken or smashed front doors.

I had boxes of rations and water purification tablets. The utilities still functioned, some of the time.

I hadn't had a reply from Sarah or Marion.

The death toll in Edinburgh, like everywhere else, was already pushing forty per cent, with more cases every day. The remains of the emergency services did their best, but we all knew it was futile. Someone on the radio said that if only Scotland were independent, we could have avoided the worst of the problem. Twenty-four-hour news channels had pivoted from the disaster-porn of the Pacific northwest wild fires to drone shots of bodies in the streets of cities and towns across the world, until the studios fell as silent as the politicians.

Mid-afternoon, I was surprised to see a steady stream of people walking into town. It reminded me of the heaving throngs of rugby fans leaving Murrayfield after even poorly-attended international match. It seemed natural to join them, to find out what was going on.

Shuffling of feet and the *caw*-ing of ravens on nearby roof-ridges echoed off empty buildings. On every street corner, a cluster of people huddled in prayer, sometimes solemn, sometimes with arms aloft in the throes of ecstatic experience. Sikhs, Christians and Moslems huddled together. Random passers-by sang along with Hare Krishna disciples. More than I expected communed with the three-fold Goddess, fingering esoteric jewellery as though rosaries. A half-glimpse of waxed-cotton jacket and jeans ahead reminded me of Mhairi.

In the city centre, young and old coalesced into transient groups. Some sang, some romanced, most just hung out. There was no form or organisation, but it did not feel random either. Perhaps deeper imperatives were at work, like in a murmuration of starlings, but I couldn't tell what they might be. It was as though we all needed human company but weren't sure what to do when we found it. We were all alone in a crowd.

I turned back at the Bridges and strolled westwards along Princes Street. I spoke to no-one, but there was unexpected exhilaration in the heightened atmosphere.

A fine sunset coloured the western sky, the warm glow shimmering through the evening air. Eyes glowed in the half-light, as if anticipating the Rapture. Scavenging seagulls wheeled and screeched, weaving aerial Celtic knots, undersides caught as if by anti-aircraft lights. The black spires of St Mary's Cathedral stood silhouetted against the deepening reds.

My exhilaration became a Zen-like sense of fulfilment, a moment when beauty and awareness point towards transcendence.

Shadows grew in Princes Street Gardens. Darkness warmed between the trees. Whatever gathered there forbade my eyes to focus on it, not yet ready to reveal itself.

But I sensed history coming together, lost memories trying to get home, finding uncertain substance in the thickening penumbra of the Castle Rock. Perhaps the stag standing quietly in St Cuthbert's graveyard, antlers proud in the gloaming, was just a trick of my confused eyes, but I don't think so.

When I got home, Mhairi stood in the alcove by the fridge freezer.

So did Sarah, her eyes as blank as her mother's.

The Gifted weren't difficult to find once I had a place to start. Most of the families did not manifest any ability at all. I kept a note of the incidence and variances. Father and his associates would be interested in the genetics of it. It made my work easier, in fact. Those with some degree of ability always recognised me and couldn't hide it. I suspect for most of them it was the first time their 'Gift' had awoken. They were easy to eliminate (not a single one chose to live and work for us). I gathered the infants and brought them to Father, but he could do nothing with them and had them put down.

Some individuals eluded me. Michael and David Menzies disappeared long ago. Hawking's files showed David was alive during the war of 1939-45 but disappeared. I was intrigued, but not concerned: David was born in 1898 and so was unlikely still to be alive. Of their sister Sarah's line only Mary could be found. She showed no significant abilities, and neither did her children. I euthanised them as a precaution. There was no trace of Charlie.

I couldn't let myself consider what I was doing as anything other than a clinical process. I might as well have worn a white lab. coat and carried a checklist on a clipboard.

ticking off the little humans as they died. I did what was necessary to complete my task without emotional engagement. I was, am, too complicit to do anything else.

Charlie had a distant cousin, Walter Pitcairn, who survived World War Two and worked incognito for Hawking until disappearing in 1972, just before Hawking was killed. Walter was born in 1917 and so was also unlikely still to be alive. He had been married briefly and there was a son, but his spouse remarried and moved to America.

That gave me pause: the dates were consistent with Joseph's disappearance. I remembered the story of a boy told by the woman whom Father dismissed as insane, the story of the ground swallowing them up. But Gaia would not do that, not when we were saving her, surely? The point was moot: I had no time to research American descendants.

Walter had two sisters, Jane and Mary. Both married and had children. All had disappeared. In fact, I concluded, too many had disappeared to be a coincidence. The implications of that were something I'd have to think about later.

And there were families that branched off further in the past, where the number of potential descendants was too large to identify. By the time the first virus struck, it was already too late for me to find most of those, who could be anywhere in the world.

There was one other I'd uncovered when reviewing records of one of the more obscure elements of the British Government. It wasn't clear how he was connected to the Mein cluster, or even if there was a connection. Perhaps he was the black swan that refuted Father's hypothesis.

He was born George Charles Berwick, but was discharged, or placed under-cover depending on how the file was to be interpreted, in 1987 under another name. His record had been cleansed of a lot of detail, but the early documents said he was recruited because of a reputed ability, later confirmed, to communicate with human dead. Older records associate him with a mysterious case of a disappearing child, though the relevance of that wasn't clear.

Unfortunately, I didn't have his current name, only an old photograph. I didn't get round to looking for Berwick until the first virus was already at work, and I got nowhere.

The Gaia Cascade seemed such a logical thing, such a sound academic proposal, when I wrote it. I gathered the premises and supporting analyses and martialled them into a rational case with an inescapable conclusion and recommendation. But I didn't anticipate the smell of death on this scale.

All around us, humans dropped in their hundreds of thousands. Father was proud his viruses and bacterium would be 'mercifully fast' to kill, but it didn't seem like mercy to the humans as they sickened and agonised.

At The Leyes, I took a bottle of cask-strength malt whisky and a glass to my private chamber in the basement, where I keep my sound system. I put Duruflé's *Requiem* on repeat, very loud, and drank myself into oblivion.

The Flu picked up where the haemorrhagic fever left off. I still got updates through security channels, with occasiona personal notes from Jean, but we only had power for two hours a day.

Jean died before the third wave, an engineered *pesti* variant, struck. I don't have proof it was engineered, but have no doubt of it – pneumonic transmission vector guessed, timed to run its course on an already fragil remainder of humanity. And it was a smart move: whil the focus was on anti-virals and rapid development mRN vaccines, the attack – it had to be an attack – switched t a bacterium. Jean's last message was cryptic: she hinted they knew who was responsible, that some had known all the time and concealed the truth.

By now they'd stopped calculating the mortality rate – there was no-one left to do the counting. When I got online or when the phone networks were up, the only messages I got were robo-calls about car accidents I'd never been in or pornbots. Soon they'd only be sending messages to themselves.

One morning, I woke to find that an email from Marion had somehow found its way to me.

Dad. I got your message. I'm sorry I didn't get back to you right away, but things are crazy here and I couldn't get online. I guess things are bad there too, but we don't get much news. I haven't heard from Sarah for ages, but my heart tells me she's gone.

I'm safe and have a message for you. Anyone else would think it was crazy, but I remember when we were wee and you said crazy things that didn't seem so crazy to me then, though I never dared tell you or Mum or anyone else, because Mum would have got upset.

I'm in a commune near the foot of the Cascades in California. I had to get out of the city, and just sort of ended up here. But they were waiting for me, John and Martha and Eliza and their children and grandchildren. It's like they knew all the time this was going to happen and prepared for it.

John is a healer. He has a real power and reminds me of you sometimes, the way his eyes go black. His kids are just the same. He wants me to tell you this: when you see my messenger, follow, then do what you think is right.

That's all he'll say. He assures me that this message will get through, but others might not. So in case they don't, I want to say I love you Dad. It's only now I'm older and have met John I'm starting to understand things about you, and about the Gift you passed to me (John calls it the Gift). The world is changing, and you have a part to play in how the future turns out. I can see that bit by myself.

There are too many things to say and no time to say them, but you can guess, I hope.

Love you Dad.

Marion xxx

I read the letter five times before the power died. I went to bed by candlelight, and shivered through my tears. The shivering was the onset of fever.

Father called. Even through my hangover I could tell he was disturbed, more flustered than I'd ever known him.

'Our calculations were wrong. A lot more are dying than planned. The humans worked out the diseases were designed of course, and are blaming each other, but sooner or later they'll retaliate if they can.'

'It will be too late by then, though?'

'I hope so. At least we neutralised their submarines. And there are no surveillance flights looking for us that we know of, but you must take care, find somewhere safe.'

'How many dead?'

'Too many. The effects are compounding, as designed but we underestimated the second and third order consequences. All the others with normal diseases who can

334

get treatment, who are starving, suffering all the other things they do when their society collapses. We'll have a breeding population, but might have to write off their infrastructure. We've taken them back to their stone age, and I'm concerned about their nuclear plants.'

'When will you be home?'

'Tomorrow, I think. There's nothing I need to be here for now. How's the search progressing?'

I told him what I'd done, and said there was only one other I might find, a seer of the dead. I didn't mention the Gifted who'd disappeared, or the worldwide diaspora and what that might mean.

'Good. Bring me up to date when I get back.'

I was in Edinburgh when the drone strike took out The Leyes.

Mhairi and Sarah were in the bedroom. They had a coyote with them. It looked magnificent in the morning half-light, its dusty shades merging into the faded brown of the furniture, white fur around its muzzle and around its eyes. It followed me to the kitchen where I managed a tea by reusing yesterday's leaves. It was a generic brand rather than the Ceylon broad leaf I prefer, but blessings are there to be counted, as Granny always said. Listen to me: the end of the world, and I was grumpy because I hadn't secured a supply of decent tea.

I went out to the old supermarket last night. There was nothing useable on the shelves. The power was still on, somehow, the speakers playing Kylie Minogue on permanent repeat. *Na Na Na, Na Na Na-Na Na* until the end of civilisation.

I alternated between hot and cold, shivering through

both. A headache threatened. The coyote waited at the front door. John's messenger, I assumed.

At the foot of the Royal Mile the crowds were large enough to impede progress. I hadn't thought there were so many people left alive. We'd all followed some gestalt impulse to congregate in a final 'fuck you' to fate. The coyote led me through the ancient complex of vennels, closes and wynds. Long-hidden water courses and wells had sprung forth from Craigwell, Abbey, Cowgate and the Pleasance, pooling around the smouldering remains of the Parliament, where window frames bobbed broken beneath the beams and dismasted sails of the collapsed roof.

On the margins of imagination and vision, *genii loci* splashed in the liberated waters. They gained solidity: I could no longer not see them, nor they me. A fine roan mare shook its mane and transformed into a nymph, fae and shimmering in the shallows of the pool, clad only in a too-tight replica Hibee shirt. She looked at me through deep green eyes.

We recognised each other straight away. She waved, a wave of complicity, just as she had when Colin came home. *Unseelie* I remembered, but the tenement walls whispered *ane seelie wycht*.

I passed through a vennel, out of its darkness, deep into the profane throng, following the coyote that found paths of least resistance up the High Street.

Fallen leaves accresced round clogged stanks in damp gutters. People clumped about unexpected stations and makeshift stages, where the ghosts of past pageants mingle with the still living and soon-to-be dead. At Canongate Kirk a wort of brewers distributed free beer to any and all who wanted it, for medicinal purposes they said, with frequent repeat prescriptions dispensed. Pop-up stands behind the impromptu bar bore stylised motifs from historic gravestones

336

grinning skulls nestled against femurs, hour-glasses and trees. Abstract stone angels stood guard over the gathered flesh, their human charges supping strong ales in the shadow of mortality.

Inevitably, a piper struck up a tune and a parade of drunks, legs as disarticulate as old bones in a plague pit, began a paralytic danse macabre to the infectious pull of a military march. A slow procession up towards the Castle got underway. I followed in its slipstream.

At the Netherbow, the ancient gate into the City, the congested road and pavements caused a bottleneck. An impromptu guild of storytellers and makars declaimed tales and poems, modern and ancient, dispensing tradition for the benefit of any inclined to listen and understand.

> *On to the ded goes all Estatis*
> *Princis, Prelotis and Potestatis,*
> *Baith riche and pur of all degree*
> *Timor mortis conturbat me.*

'The fuck's he oan about?'

'Christ knows. It's culture ya bam: you're supposed tae appreciate it, no' un'erstaun' it.'

The great dance reeled and span like a burn in spate when the piper blew up a storm with *The Black Bear* and *The Barren Rocks of Aden*. Cheers and *heuch*s echoed and decayed around the canyon walls of high buildings. Down closes, ardent strangers groped and fumbled in plain view, discarding clothes and inhibitions, fucking against barricades that barred access to where the dead lay rotting in their beds.

At the Tron the pipes yielded to a fresh stage where a Tommy in top hat and tails called the crowd closer with doggerel song.

Good people give ear to me story
It 'appens we've called 'ere by chance
Five heroes I've brought, blithe and bonnie
Intent for to give youse a dance

A Hohner melodeon, bellows taped and patched, farted and wheezed as five dancers clashed swords and walked in a circle on raised boards. Their tartan sashes flew from their waists, as they tappity-tapped their feet in 6/8 time, forming ever more complex and interlocking figures, swords dancing above their heads while they clung on for dear life below. A grotesque Betty, a bearded giant in a pastiche of washer-woman's clothing, wandered in and out of the set with precisely judged randomness.

I danced on, following the coyote. I had an insistent tingling, as though blood vessels in my skin were trying to burst. Was this it? Was this what death felt like? Not yet: it was something else. Rising from their resting places, the corpses interred in the Canongate, Calton and Greyfriars burial grounds ascended before my eyes, bones twitching like discarded blackthorn sticks caught in a culvert, beating time to the reedy sound of the melodeon, stepping out the changes with the dancers.

Spectres flitted in and out of the living, copying the sword-dancers' patterns, the shades of all those executed in the bloody history of the Auld Town, sporting their boot and thumbikins. Here were the mutilated, rack-broken, hanged, strangled, drowned and decollated; murderers, traitors, thieves, fornicators, sodomites and seditionaries, perjurers and papists; fire-raisers, house-breakers, adulterers, rebels and Covenanters; witches and warlocks; burgesses, baillies, blackmailers and bigamists; even heifers and mares burnt with their human consorts for abominations against the Natural Law.

Clothed and unclothed, quick and uncanny, all pushed ever uphill, past taverns with doors flung open by the thirsty, topping up with ale or whisky. Up past a dark suited Calvinist holding aloft his well-thumbed King James Bible, preaching his message of hellfire, judgement and damnation, smug in his certainty of salvation of the elect, amongst whom he counted himself.

Tarmac turned to cobbles. The ascent continued past jugglers and conjurers, mimes and musicians, between whom the coyote wove, to the Old Tolbooth where guisarts in outlandish costume performed for food:

> *The day will come when ye'll be deid*
> *Ye'll neither care for meal nor breid*
> *Rise up! Good folk and dinna spare*
> *Ye'll nae hae less and we'll hae mair.*

At last, the coyote led me into St Giles, where a service of sorts was in progress, with neither rubric nor liturgy to guide celebrants or worshippers. Makeshift altars had appeared as mysteriously as cairns on remote mountain paths, and gifts were offered there to mark the strange harvest of humankind: fruit and corn, bread and meat. Anamnetic echoes of sacrifice and resurrection.

She stood in the apse, tall, brunette, giving the impression of being in her mid-twenties. She was in a business suit beneath pierced and ornamented ears, but I saw through that. She was neither spirit nor spectre, nor one of the fae, but something other. It came to me with complete clarity, like I had been born with the knowledge encoded within me, that she was one of the race that brought death to humanity.

She looked surprised to see me.

'Hello George, what a coincidence. I've been looking for you everywhere. My name is Margaret. Would you like me to save your life?'

Something remarkable was happening in the centre of Edinburgh, like the bacchanal I witnessed in Italy, but shot through with Caledonian grandeur. It was Hogmanay, St Andrew's Night and Burns Night rolled into one, the final revels for the Lord of Misrule and the Abbot of Unreason. The pipes skirled, of course: they always did. And the drink, where would Edinburgh be without it? Not many remembered Edinburgh had once been the centre of the opium and heroin trade, except Father who was at the heart of it.

I was surprised by the nakedness and copulation on the streets: so very un-Scottish. I wandered through the crowds, trying to commit as much to memory as I could. Even if I couldn't remember faces, I wanted to remember the event, being here, part of the end. I had a responsibility to bear witness to the consequences of our actions – of *my* actions.

In the Gallery of Modern Art in Edinburgh are etchings from the humans' First World War, Percy Smith's *Dance of Death* series. The first time I saw them they had more impact on me than anything else on display. Later, I found similar works by Holbein, and Goya's *Disasters of War*. Jake and Dinos Chapman's reworkings of Goya had me laughing out loud, earning tutting opprobrium from stupid humans for whom art is too serious for humour. Meandering through Edinburgh was like walking through art.

There was a lot of movement around St Giles Cathedral and Parliament Square. I hadn't been in St. Giles for a long time, it was too austere for my Anglican tastes. I found it changed beyond recognition. Improvised altars and chapels sprang up at random at the hands of the worshippers.

340

recognised many of the figurines and rough icons as distinctly non-Christian, but no-one seemed to care. And why should they? Someone was trying to entice a tune out of the organ: it was crude but had a desperate authenticity that excused the player's shortcomings. A lone guitarist strummed along, half a beat behind the melody.

Many prone worshippers would never move anywhere again. Most didn't say much. I don't know whether it was the imminence of mortality or the immanence of the Lord that struck them dumb. Maybe they had just run out of things to say.

I tried to look at them all, to put faces to my victims, and I looked straight into the face of George Berwick.

Although I had met and exterminated many of his kind, he was the first of the truly Gifted I'd met. His eyes became deep wells of blackness.

I said something inane, but his eyes flickered to something behind me, he seemed to be listening to something I couldn't hear.

'What?' I said. 'What do you see? Who is it?'

'There's a dead girl behind you with a baby. She says you betrayed her. Her name is Eleanor.'

He reached forward and pressed my forehead with the tip of his index finger, and scored a new eye in my head.

It was like he'd touched me with the white tip of a hot poker. I was in a world that had been hidden from me, amongst all the creatures gathered in the High Kirk, living and dead, human and non-human, creatures that were legendary even amongst my own kind. A coyote cavorted in the aisle, leaping and twisting as if chasing bees, and a green-eyed creature watched us with satisfaction.

My left ankle was shackled, a bright thread running from a spectral binding to a matching clasp on the wrist of a wraith.

'Hello Margaret,' Eleanor said. 'Remember me?' She held her new-born in her arms, suckling it. 'I named her after you, remember? Would you like to hold her?'

I screamed, and fled, Eleanor at my side.

Father and I are by the paddock at the remains of The Leyes where rebuilding work has started, though Father's library can never be replaced. A rescued pony canters around its new home. A spider's web laces the spars and an upright of the fence: sunbeams and dewdrops struggle against the silken threads in vain. The garden is wrapped in thistledown and birdsong. No vapour trails criss-cross the clear sky.

'Have you named her?'

'Eleanor.'

'Again? Why always that name?'

'So I never forget.' I force myself to look straight ahead, to not look at the revenant mother and child, mocking me, taunting me, reminding me.

The pony trots over, hoping for carrots and ear-scratches

'We'll need a new process now. The survivors will take better care of their children.'

'No, they won't, they never have and never will. We managed well enough before: their poor will always be with us. It'll be just like the old days, picking the straggler off the road to Byzantium. What about the last of th Gifted?'

'I got as many as I could, but I can't guarantee som didn't survive. Are you sure they began with Allisoun?'

'That's when the trouble began. Why?'

'I was thinking of the Tales of the Elder Gods – th Dawn Stories.'

He didn't reply.

The spot where Berwick's finger touched burns. My new eye sees things I cannot name.

What have we done? What have I done?

We leave the whinnying pony and saunter to the ancient yew that survived the blast. Last night, under a thin crescent moon where humans once walked, I watched the bright light of the International Space Station transect the sky.

'I stayed out last night, in Edinburgh.'

'How was it?'

My forehead burns. Shadows in the woods seethe with myth and memory.

'Peaceful. Foxes everywhere, and lots of dogs. Owls too, picking off the rats and mice. I let the creatures in the zoo go free to take their chances. When it got dark, I went up to the old observatory on Blackford Hill and looked out over the city. All the street lights suddenly came on, shining across the void like stars in winter. It reminded me of Tacitus: *ubi solitudinem facet, pacem dicit.*'

'He had a way with words, didn't he? I prefer a different perspective.' He lifts a glass thimble to his lips.

'*Mortui sunt ut nos vivamus.*'

have a final look around, and check one more time there are rounds in the chamber, though one is enough. I'm surprised by a tentative touch on my shoulder. The fae girl with green eyes and the Hibee shirt stands behind me, diaphanous against the last of the sunlight. *Ane seelie wycht* whispers the river, woven through by golden flecks of light. She glances at the gun, which seems a foolish thing to have brought. I drop it and my empty whisky flask onto the grass.

'There is a place here if you want it.' She gestures behind her, where a sunlit grove hovers on the edges of the real, not quite convinced of its own existence. Her eyes are the deepest green I have ever seen.

'What is that?'

'It has many names.'

'I thought you were gone with the rest.'

'We're always here, and not here; somewhere, or somewhere else. We are impossible and yet are all possibilities. We are the anticipation of what has gone and the memory of what is to come.'

'Will I be part of that?'

'In a way. The molecules from which your awareness springs are older than life and will survive and be reborn, recombine in times to come, perhaps to spark life again, though your consciousness will fade. But I will be with you, to the end.'

'How long will that be?'

'Past and present, now and then, are not absolutes. You are now and so you will always have been and always will be.'

'Why me?'

'Because your love didn't twist into hate.'

'And the other survivors?'

'We've made provision.'

With a last look at the golden river, I go with her into the heart of the uncertain grove. Mhairi and Sarah are with me. We lie down together to watch the stars emerge in a suddenly clear sky, in the heart of a green wood of which we will soon be part.

CHANGELING

The voices did me in.

I was the youngest, the seventh. My dad could have been any one of dozens, Mam'd fuck anyone for a quarter of blow and a few quid. We took care of ourselves, mostly. The social work were always round making sure we got fed, but we never grassed Mam up.

Danny came to see me. He pulled a blade and told me to keep my mouth shut. I was pissed off at that, what made him think I would grass him up? I'm no' a grass.

They talk over me. They talk about their lunch, their children, their shift rotas. They sound funny through the masks. They don't know I'm here, listening and watching, they think I left ages ago. 'There's nothing left of her now,' they say. 'Elvis has left the building.'

No, silly: it's not *their* voices I'm talking about.

They're wrong: I'm talking to you now, aren't I? You're so patient, so accepting. Never judging. You just listen and hold my hand.

No! Don't interrupt. Can't you see I'm talking to someone here?

I know they care. They're clinical, and the gloves are cold sometimes, but gentle too: you can't fake it, not with some of the crap stuff they have to do. They only know a wee bit about me, only what's on my chart.

They don't know me at all.

They adjust my catheter and PEG tube, wipe away my shit, turn my useless body over and wait for me to die. 'Listen,' I say, 'I've got some stuff to tell you. I need to tell you what happened, what's going to happen.' But all they hear are noises and echoes of words without meaning.

Maybe if they could talk to my daughter she would tell them who I am, who I was, what I did. But that's—

Well, that's a problem, isn't it? Did I tell you about it? I can't remember.

She was so beautiful, and I never saw her again.

It's true, ken: there isn't much of me anymore. Just bones and patches of skin held together by sores. My brain's like snakes and ladders without ladders. 'Poor thing,' they say, behind their masks. 'It must be awful.'

They're wrong.

I mean, it's no' brilliant, but my mind wanders where it wants, leaving me in peace.

Me: the spark of whatever means I'm still alive.

I think my Da' might be Mam's Uncle Bill. He shagged pretty much everything that moved. He shagged me once too, though he waited until I was a bit older. He had kids everywhere. Half the scheme looked like him, but I'm the only one who hears the voices I think, so I didn't get them from him.

When he got killed, he wandered the stair wells for ages like he'd never been snuffed. I waived and said hello, but he was confused and kept looking for something he'd lost

Did I mention the voices? They're what did for me.

I can never remember what I've told you already.

They were always there: all the time, day and night. All the mouths talking, telling me what was happening, what was going to happen. Voices of dead people, voices of people who've never even existed.

I know she loved me. She took me to the country once, where the ducks and swans were, and painted boats with people on going past.

The worst were the ones who would never be born, who would never exist except in my ears and head. I could never get *them* to shut the fuck up.

I sometimes wonder where my mind is, but it walks in a different place. I don't understand it there. I can't find any paths in it. And I don't like some of the people.

No. I don't like them at all.

But you know that, don't you? I can see it in your face as you sit there, in your dress that never seems to be the same from minute to minute. Your face that stays still while your eyes dance. Your deep, deep, emerald eyes that are many, many things.

Except human.

can still smell it. Unwashed clothes. Everything damp, nothing ever dry. Black mould on the walls. All the mattresses stained and stinking of stale piss.

ook, I've told you once. Don't interrupt: can't you see I'm alking to someone?

I've forgotten what I was saying now. That's the trouble with the voices.

Have I told you about the voices yet? They never leave e alone.

We all fancied Danny. He left school after fourth year to work in the family business. He strutted around looking like the guy on *Knight Rider,* like that old guy was still cool. But Danny had slick hair and a black leather jacket and tight jeans, and a way of looking at you like you mattered.

He was rollin' in it, and we all kent where he got his money. His da' was Mam's dealer and he'd sometimes do her a cheap deal and eye me up. I was just a wee skinny thing with big bug eyes and plooks, but with a wee bit makeup I looked older. I practised my moves in the mirror, holding my hips just *so,* pouting and trying to look like the girls in Uncle Bill's porny videos, trying to look how guys wanted, 'cos that's what it's about, eh? What the guys want.

Sometimes, when they clean and change me, I'm lying on my side looking at the wall they think I can't see. I hate that. So I go for one of my wee trips: I see my wasted body down there on the bed; read my charts and stuff; float down the corridor, looking in on other patients. I check out the staff room to see who's about and what they're up to.

Don't look surprised: I guessed when you first came in. It's OK, I like having you here.

I like you.

I used to go to Danny's place to get Mam's 'prescription' as she called it. We got talking one day. I don't know why but I told him about the voices. Maybe I wanted to impress him or something. Anyway, he gave me a couple of jellies and said they'd help me sleep. Next time he gave me some more, but the third time it cost me a blow-job.

He hadn't washed, and he grabbed the back of my head and pulled until I gagged on his rubbery thing. It w nothing like the videos: the girls all enjoy it on them. He didn't tell me he was ready or pull out or anything and laughed when I gagged and swallowed and snorted.

'You'll like it better next time,' he said, and tossed me the bag, zipping himself up, like it was all I was good for, to empty himself into.

I was a toilet.

I didn't tell my pals, but they knew. Everyone. Danny told them all. They laughed behind their hands and looked at me like I was an animal in the zoo. *Suckin' Maggie* they called me.

But Danny was right: I didn't hear the voices while I slept, and he knew I'd come back.

Have I told you about the voices yet? I know I was going to.

I don't remember when first he said he had something extra to go with the jellies. I wasn't up for it. I'd seen junkies before and they gave me the creeps, and I only swallowed the jellies, but he kept on at me to try: *aw, c'mon Maggie, just a wee bit won't hurt, nothing heavy, just a wee score to see if it works.* He even had a clean needle. So I did, and it did.

But I had to earn it.

The routine was easy: I'd wear my school uniform and Danny would drive me to a flat in the New Town. A man in a suit would be there waiting. I was handed over to him and had to do whatever he wanted. Unprotected, of course, though I didn't know the word then. Mostly they were nice. Some weren't.

I never got any money – it all went to Danny, even when they asked for me again and paid extra.

loved jumping in puddles and kicking leaves when they ll in Autumn. I could do that my whole life.

I missed four periods before I figured out something was wrong and told the school nurse. She was checking for scabies and nits and stuff on one of the days I bothered to go. I got help after that. Mam was well out of the game, but the school helped and the social work too.

This place? Aye it's alright. It's a wee bit creepy sometimes with all the dead people an' that, but it's OK. I mean, I ken why I'm here, but it's OK.

And I hear voices all the time. I told you about the voices, right? Dead people, people who haven't been born, people who'll never be born. They keep me company when you're not here, and tell me things.

I like it best when you're here though.

I did Danny's pals too. They let me share their gear when we were jaggin'. Strange thing is, Danny never took anything. Ever.

My baby? Oh, she was the most brilliant thing. I just looked at her, at her scrunched-up eyes, her tight wee face and shock of hair, blonde like mine. She was beautiful: a baby of my own to look after. They took her away to get her clean while they stitched me up.

Danny was in the corridor outside the ward. He gave them some shite about being my big brother or something. He asked when I'd be able to work again and offered me a hit. God knows why I took it.

A nurse grassed me up.

I never saw my baby again. 'Emergency Place of Safety Order' they said.

Danny got away wi' it, of course, 'cos he's a jammy bastard and his family have too many polis and lawyers as clients, too many who'd done me in the flat.

I don't know why I'm telling you this.

I meant to tell you about the voices but don't think I have yet. Have I?

I don't even know who you are.

There isn't much to tell anyway. I was under sixteen so I got put in a place on the other side of the country. It was locked, but that was OK. A doctor listened and cared and got me clean. But they'd never tell me about my baby girl, my baby who I'd never even given a name. Never anything said to me, except she was adopted and doing fine.

She was all I ever wanted and we would have jumped in puddles and watched the ducks and painted boats and kicked leaves together all day long and they took her away from me and I never saw her again and Danny just laughed and the voices were back and I scored again.

I know, I know: I'll tell you about the voices in a minute. What was I saying?

It's great sometimes, floating down the corridor without having to drag my body with me. I feel free, like I'm starting again.

They called me *Suckin' Maggie*. Did I tell you that?
Suckin' Maggie, fuckin' slaggie
Suckin' cocks tae get her jaggie

It doesn't matter anymore. Doesn't hurt.
Not really.
Not.

read my charts when I'm floating up here, but I don't now what the letters mean. Well, HIV, everyone kens what at is. Septicaemia, that's blood poisoning, right? Pneumonia, ye. But what's ADC? And DNR?

The voices can't tell me. I was going to tell you about em, wasn't I?

Hey! Did I tell you about this really weird dream I had? There was this gigantic train flying to the stars with a boy on top and a big dog thing and a scary woman with red eyes and a big parade and all sorts of stuff. And do you know what the best part was? The very best pa ...

Oh!
Oh, would you look at that.

How pretty.

How lovely.

ACKNOWLEDGEMENTS

These stories have had a long development process, and have benefited immeasurably from comment, advice and encouragement by my first readers Rosemary Gretton and Rachel Connor, and from Mara Livingstone-McPhail (https://maraeditsblog.wordpress.com) who edited earlier drafts.

Grateful thanks also to other early readers who commented: Lindsay, Amy, Rebecca and Helen, Lizzie Bolton, and Adele Baree, who liked that I said nice things about libraries and librarians.

Book design and layout was by Heather Macpherson at Raspberry Creative Type in Edinburgh (https://www.raspberrycreativetype.com)

Author photograph by Tom Migot (https://tommigotphotography.com)

Special thanks, as always, to Kirstin, who has tolerated me for four decades.

SOURCES

The quote from Thomas Wolfe in the story Coyote In The Corner is from *The Names of The Nation*, published in Modern Monthly, December 1934. I have not been able to trace the current copyright holder.

Woody Guthrie described *The Wabash Cannonball* as 'the best train song I know' on BBC Children's Hour, 7 July 1944 (The Beast Astray)

Lament for the Makars (in To Dance the Dance Macabre) was composed by William Dunbar circa 1505

Tam O' The Lynn (in The Fearfull Aboundinge) is a traditional Scots song that I've adapted/rewritten to my needs.

Thomas The Rhymer (in The Fearfull Aboundinge) is a traditional Scots ballad (Child 37)

Good people give ear to me story— (in To Dance the Dance Macabre) is a traditional calling on song for Rapper dancers originating in the song of the Earsdon and Winlaton dancers notated by Cecil Sharp in 1910 and 1913 respectively.

The guisarts' rhyme *The day will come when ye'll be deid—* (in To Dance the Dance Macabre) is my own adaptatio of an old Scottish song, *Rise Up Gudewife,* collected a Roud 5887

Printed in Great Britain
by Amazon